A GRAY DOG AND A FLOCK OF SHEEP, TRAVELLING ALONG THE ROAD TOWARDS
THE DALESMAN'S DAUGHTER, MET THE MASTER (PAGE 341).

Bob Son of Battle

By ALFRED OLLIVANT

A. L. BURT COMPANY,   PUBLISHERS, NEW YORK

CONTENTS

PART I

THE COMING OF THE TAILLESS TYKE

PART II

THE LITTLE MAN

PART III

THE SHEPHERDS' TROPHY

Contents

PART IV

The Black Killer

PART V

Owd Bob o' Kenmuir

PART VI

The Black Killer

PART I

THE COMING OF THE TAILLESS TYKE

CHAPTER I

THE GRAY DOG

THE sun stared brazenly down on a gray farmhouse lying, long and low in the shadow of the Muir Pike; on the ruins of peel-tower and barmkyn, relics of the time of raids, it looked; on ranges of whitewashed outbuildings; on a goodly array of dark-thatched ricks.

In the stack-yard, behind the lengthy range of stables, two men were thatching. One lay sprawling on the crest of the rick, the other stood perched on a ladder at a lower level.

The latter, small, old, with shrewd nut-brown countenance, was Tammas Thornton, who had served the Moores of Kenmuir for more than half a century. The other, on top of the stack, wrapped apparently in gloomy meditation, was Sam'l Todd. A solid Dalesman, he, with huge hands and hairy arms; about his face an uncomely aureole of stiff, red hair; and on his features, deep-seated, an expression of resolute melancholy.

"Ay, the Gray Dogs, bless 'em!" the old man was saying. "Yo' canna beat 'em not nohow. Known 'em ony time this sixty year, I have, and niver knew a bad un yet. Not as

3

I say, mind ye, as any on 'em cooms up to Rex son o' Rally. Ah, he was a one, was Rex! We's never won Cup since his day."

"Nor niver shall agin, yo' may depend," said the other gloomily.

Tammas clucked irritably.

"G'long, Sam'l Todd!" he cried. "Yo' niver happy onless yo' making' yo'self miser-'ble. I niver see sich a chap. Niver win agin? Why, oor young Bob he'll mak' a right un, I tell yo', and I should know. Not as what he'll touch Rex son o' Rally, mark ye! I'm niver saying' so, Sam'l Todd. Ah, he was a one, was Rex! I could tell yo' a tale or two o' Rex. I mind me hoo——"

The big man interposed hurriedly.

"I've heard it afore, Tammas, I welly 'ave," he said.

Tammas paused and looked angrily up.

"Yo've heard it afore, have yo', Sam'l Todd?" he asked sharply. "And what have yo' heard afore?"

"Yo' stories, owd lad—yo' stories o' Rex son o' Rally."

"Which on' em

"All on 'em, Tammas, all on 'em—mony a time. I'm fair sick on 'em, Tammas, I welly am," he pleaded.

The old man gasped. He brought down his mallet with a vicious smack.

"I'll niver tell yo' a tale agin, Sam'l Todd, not if yo' was to go on yo' bended knees for't.

Nay; it bain't no manner o' use talkin'. Niver agin, says I."

"I niver askt yo'," declared honest Sam'l.

"Nor it wouldna ha' bin no manner o' use if yo' had," said the other viciously. "I'll niver tell yo' a tale agin if I was to live to be a hunderd."

"Yo'll not live to be a hunderd, Tammas Thornton, nor near it," said Sam'l brutally.

"I'll live as long as some, I warrant," the old man replied with spirit. "I'll live to see Cup back i' Kenmuir, as I said afore."

"If yo' do," the other declared with emphasis, "Sam'l Todd niver spake a true word. Nay, nay, lad; yo're owd, yo're wambly, your time's near run or I'm the more mistook."

"For mussy's sake hold yo' tongue, Sam'l Todd! It's clack-clack all day——" The old man broke off suddenly, and buckled to his work with suspicious vigor. "Mak' a show yo' bin workin', lad," he whispered. "Here's Master and oor Bob."

As he spoke, a tall gaitered man with weather-beaten face, strong, lean, austere, and the blue-gray eyes of the hill-country, came striding into the yard. And trotting soberly at his heels, with the gravest, saddest eyes ever you saw, a sheep-dog puppy.

A rare dark gray he was, his long coat, dashed here and there with lighter touches, like a stormy sea moonlit. Upon his chest an escutcheon of purest white, and the dome of his head showered, as it were, with a sprink-ling of snow. Perfectly compact, utterly lithe, inimitably graceful with his airy-fairy action; a gentleman every inch, you could not help but stare at him—Owd Bob o' Kenmuir.

At the foot of the ladder the two stopped. And the young dog, placing his forepaws on a lower rung, looked up, slowly waving his silvery brush.

"A proper Gray Dog!" mused Tammas, gazing down into the dark face beneath him. "Small, yet big; light to get about on backs o' his sheep, yet not too light. Wi' a coat hard a-top to keep oot Daleland weather, soft as sealskin beneath. And wi' them sorrerful eyes on him as niver goes but wi' a good un. Amaist he minds me o' Rex son o' Rally."

"Oh, dear! Oh, dear!" groaned Sam'l. But the old man heard him not.

"Did 'Enry Farewether tell yo' hoo he acted this mornin', Master?" he inquired, addressing the man at the foot of the ladder.

"Nay," said the other, his stern eyes lighting.

"Why, 'twas this way, it seems," Tammas continued. "Young bull gets 'isself loose somegate and marches oot into yard, o'erturns milkpail, and prods owd pigs i' ribs. And as he stands lookin' about un, thinking what he shall be up to next, oor Bob sees un. 'An' what yo' doin' here, Mr. Bull?' he seems to say, cockin' his ears and trottin' up gay-like. Wi' that bull bloats fit to bust 'isself, lashes wi's tail, waggles his head, and gets agate o' chargin' 'im. But Bob leaps oot o' way, quick as lightnin' yet cool as butter, and when he's done his foolin drives un back agin. "

"Who seed all this?" interposed Sam'l, sceptically.

" 'Enry Farewether from the loft. So there, Fat'ead!" Tammas replied, and continued his tale. "So they goes on; bull chargin' and Bob drivin' un back and back, hoppin' in and oot agin, quiet as a cowcumber, yet deter-mined. At last Mr. Bull sees it's no manner o' use that gate, so he turns, rares up, and tries to jump wall. Nary a bit. Young dog jumps in on un and nips him by tail. Wi' that, bull tumbles down in a hurry, turns wi' a kind o' groan, and marches back into stall, Bob after un. And then, dang me!"—the old man beat the ladder as he loosed off this last titbit,—"if he doesna sit' isself i' door like a sentrynel till 'Enry Farewether coom up. Hoo's that for a tyke not yet a year?"

Even Sam'l Todd was moved by the tale.

"Well done, oor Bob!" he cried.

"Good, lad!" said the Master, laying a hand on the dark head at his knee.

"Yo' may well say that," cried Tammas in a kind of ecstasy. "A proper Gray Dog, I tell yo'. Wi' the brains of a man and the way of

a woman. Ah, yo' canna beat 'em nohow, the
Gray Dogs o' Kenmuir!"

The patter of cheery feet rang out on the
plank-bridge over the stream below them.
Tammas glanced round.

"Here's David," he said. "Late this
mornin' he be."

A fair-haired boy came spurring up the
slope, his face all aglow with the speed of his
running. Straightway the young dog dashed
off to meet him with a fiery speed his sober
gait belied. The two raced back together into
the yard.

"Poor lad!" said Sam'l gloomily, regarding
the newcomer.

"Poor heart!" muttered Tammas. While
the Master's face softened visibly. Yet there
looked little to pity in this jolly, rocking lad
with the tousle of light hair and fresh, rosy
countenance.

"G'mornin', Mister Moore! Morn'n, Tammas! Morn'n, Sam'l!" he panted as he passed;
and ran on through the hay-carpeted yard, round
the corner of the stable, and into the house.

In the kitchen, a long room with red-tiled
floor and latticed windows, a woman, white-
aproned and frail-faced, was bustling about
her morning business. To her skirts clung a
sturdy, bare-legged boy; while at the oak
table in the centre of the room a girl with
brown eyes and straggling hair was seated before a basin of bread and milk.

"So yo've coom at last, David!" the woman cried, as the boy entered; and, bending, greeted him with a tender, motherly salutation, which he returned as affectionately. "I welly thowt yo'd forgot us this mornin'. Noo sit you' doon beside oor Maggie." And soon he, too, was engaged in a task twin to the girl's.

The two children munched away in silence, the little bare-legged boy watching them, the while, critically. Irritated by this prolonged stare, David at length turned on him.

"Weel, little Andrew," he said, speaking in that paternal fashion in which one small boy loves to address another. "Weel, ma little lad, yo'm coomin' along gradely." He leant back in his chair the better to criticise his subject. But Andrew, like all the Moores, slow of speech, preserved a stolid silence, sucking a chubby thumb, and regarding his patron a thought cynically.

David resented the expression on the boy's countenance, and half rose to his feet.

"Yo' put another face on yo', Andrew Moore," he cried threateningly, "or I'll put it for yo'."

Maggie, however, interposed opportunely.

"Did yo' feyther beat yo' last night?" she inquired in a low voice; and there was a shade of anxiety in the soft brown eyes.

"Nay," the boy answered; "he was a-goin' to, but he never did. Drunk," he added in explanation.

"What was he goin' to beat yo' for, David?" asked Mrs. Moore.

"What for? Why, for the fun o't—to see me squiggle," the boy replied, and laughed bitterly.

"Yo' shouldna speak so o' your dad, David," reproved the other as severely as was in her nature.

"Dad! a fine dad! I'd dad him an I'd the chance," the boy muttered beneath his breath. Then, to turn the conversation:

"Us should be startin', Maggie," he said, and going to the door. "Bob! Owd Bob, lad! Ar't coomin' along?" he called.

The gray dog came springing up like an antelope, and the three started off for school together.

Mrs. Moore stood in the doorway, holding Andrew by the hand, and watched the departing trio.

"'Tis a pretty pair, Master, surely," she said softly to her husband, who came up at the moment.

"Ay, he'll be a fine lad if his feyther'll let him," the tall man answered.

"'Tis a shame Mr. M'Adam should lead him such a life," the woman continued indignantly. She laid a hand on her husband's arm, and looked up at him coaxingly.

"Could yo' not say summat to un, Master, think 'ee? Happen he'd 'tend to you," she pleaded. For Mrs. Moore imagined that there could be no one but would gladly heed what

James Moore, Master of Kenmuir, might say to him. "He's not a bad un at bottom, I do believe," she continued. "He never took on so till his missus died. Eh, but he was main fond o' her."

Her husband shook his head

"Nay, mother," he said "'Twould nob' but mak' it worse for t' lad. M'Adam'd listen to no one, let alone me." And, indeed, he was right; for the tenant of the Grange made no secret of his animosity for his straight-going, straight-speaking neighbor.

. . . . .

Owd Bob, in the mean time, had escorted the children to the larch-copse bordering on the lane which leads to the village. Now he crept stealthily back to the yard, and established himself behind the water-butt.

How he played and how he laughed; how he teased old Whitecap till that gray gander all but expired of apoplexy and impotence; how he ran the roan bull-calf, and aroused the bitter wrath of a portly sow, mother of many, is of no account.

At last, in the midst of his merry mischief-making, a stern voice arrested him.

"Bob, lad, I see 'tis time we larned you yo' letters."

So the business of life began for that dog of whom the simple farmer-folk of the Daleland still love to talk,—Bob, son of Battle, last of the Gray Dogs of Kenmuir.

CHAPTER II

A SON OF HAGAR

It is a lonely country, that about the Wastrel-dale.

Parson Leggy Hornbut will tell you that his is the smallest church in the biggest parish north of the Derwent, and that his cure numbers more square miles than parishioners. Of fells and ghylls it consists, of becks and lakes; with here a scattered hamlet and there a solitary hill sheep-farm. It is a country in which sheep are paramount; and every other Dalesman is engaged in that profession which is as old as Abel. And the talk of the men of the land is of wethers and gimmers, of tup-hoggs, ewe tegs in wool, and other things which are but fearsome names to you and me; and always of the doings or misdoings, the intelligence or stupidity, of their adjutants, the sheep-dogs.

Of all the Daleland, the country from the Black Water to Grammoch Pike is the wildest. Above the tiny stone-built village of Wastreldale the Muir Pike nods its massive head. Westward, the desolate Mere Marches, from which the Sylvesters' great estate derives its name, reach away in mile on mile of sheep infested, wind-swept moorland. On the far side of the Marches is that twin dale where flows the gentle Silver Lea. And it is there in the paddocks at the back of the Dalesman's Daughter, that, in the late summer months, the famous sheep-dog Trials of the North are held. There that the battle for the Dale Cup, the world-known Shepherds' Trophy, is fought out.

Past the little inn leads the turnpike road to the market-centre of the district—Grammoch-town. At the bottom of the paddocks at the back of the inn winds the Silver Lea. Just there a plank bridge crosses the stream, and, beyond, the Murk Muir Pass crawls up the sheer side of the Scaur on to the Mere Marches.

At the head of the Pass, before it debouches on to those lonely sheep-walks which divide the two dales, is that hollow, shuddering with gloomy possibilities, aptly called the Devil's Bowl. In its centre the Lone Tarn, weirdly suggestive pool, lifts its still face to the sky. It was beside that black, frozen water, across whose cold surface the storm was swirling in white snow-wraiths, that, many, many years ago (not in this century), old Andrew Moore came upon the mother of the Gray Dogs of Kenmuir.

In the North, every one who has heard of the Muir Pike—and who has not?—has heard of the Gray Dogs of Kenmuir, every one who

has heard of the Shepherd's Trophy—and who
has not?—knows their fame. In that country
of good dogs and jealous masters the pride
of place has long been held unchallenged.
Whatever line may claim to follow the Gray
Dogs always lead the van. And there is a
saying in the land: "Faithfu' as the Moores
and their tykes."

.   .   .   .   .

On the top dresser to the right of the fireplace in the kitchen of Kenmuir lies the family
Bible. At the end you will find a loose sheet—
the pedigree of the Gray Dogs; at the beginning, pasted on the inside, an almost similar
sheet, long since yellow with age—the family
register of the Moores of Kenmuir.

Running your eye down the loose leaf, once,
twice, and again it will be caught by a small
red cross beneath a name, and under the cross
the one word "Cup." Lastly, opposite the
name of Rex son of Rally, are two of those
proud, tell-tale marks. The cup referred to
is the renowned Dale Cup—Champion Challenge Dale Cup, open to the world. Had Rex
won it but once again the Shepherds' Trophy,
which many men have lived to win, and died
still striving after, would have come to rest
forever in the little gray house below the Pike.

It was not to be, however. Comparing the
two sheets, you read beneath the dog's name
a date and a pathetic legend; and on the other
sheet, written in his son's boyish hand, beneath

the name of Andrew Moore the same date and
the same legend.

From that day James Moore, then but a boy,
was master of Kenmuir.

So past Grip and Rex and Rally, and a hundred others, until at the foot of the page you
come to that last name—Bob, son of Battle.

.   .   .   .   .

From the very first the young dog took to
his work in a manner to amaze even James
Moore. For a while he watched his mother,
Meg, at her business, and with that seemed to
have mastered the essentials of sheep tactics.
Rarely had such fiery élan been seen on the
sides of the Pike; and with it the young dog
combined a strange sobriety, an admirable
patience, that justified, indeed, the epithet
"Owd." Silent he worked, and resolute; and
even in those days had that famous trick of
coaxing the sheep to do his wishes;—blending,
in short, as Tammas put it, the brains of a
man with the way of a woman.

Parson Leggy, who was reckoned the best
judge of a sheep or sheep-dog 'twixt Tyne and
Tweed, summed him up in the one word
"Genius." And James Moore himself, cau-
tious man, was more than pleased.

In the village, the Dalesmen, who took a
personal pride in the Gray Dogs of Kenmuir,
began to nod sage heads when "oor" Bob was
mentioned. Jim Mason, the postman, whose
word went as far with the villagers as Parson

Leggy's with the gentry, reckoned he'd never seen a young un as so took his fancy.

That winter it grew quite the recognized thing, when they had gathered of a night round the fire in the Sylvester Arms, with Tammas in the centre, old Jonas Maddox on his right, Rob Saunderson of the Holt on the left, and the others radiating away toward the sides, for some one to begin with:

"Well, and what o' oor Bob, Mr. Thornton?"

To which Tammas would always make reply:

"Oh, yo' ask Sam'l there. He'll tell yo' better'n me,"—and would forthwith plunge, himself, into a yarn.

And the way in which, as the story proceeded, Tupper of Swinsthwaite winked at Ned Hoppin of Fellsgarth, and Long Kirby, the smith, poked Jem Burton, the publican, in the ribs, and Sexton Ross said, "Ma word, lad!" spoke more eloquently than many words.

One man only never joined in the chorus of admiration. Sitting always alone in the background, little M'Adam would listen with an incredulous grin on his sallow face.

"Oh, ma certes! The devil's in the dog! It's no cannie ava!" he would continually exclaim, as Tammas told his tale.

.   .   .   .   .

In the Daleland you rarely see a stranger's face. Wandering in the wild country about the twin dales at the time of this story, you might have met Parson Leggy, striding along with a couple of varmint terriers at his heels, and young Cyril Gilbraith, whom he was teaching to tie flies and fear God, beside him; or Jim Mason, postman by profession, poacher by predilection, honest man and sportsman by nature, hurrying along with the mail-bags on his shoulder, a rabbit in his pocket, and the faithful Betsy a yard behind. Besides these you might have hit upon a quiet shepherd and a wise-faced dog; Squire Sylvester, going his rounds upon a sturdy cob; or, had you been lucky, sweet Lady Eleanour bent upon some errand of mercy to one of the many tenants.

It was while the Squire's lady was driving through the village on a visit* to Tammas's slobbering grandson—it was shortly after Billy Thornton's advent into the world—that little M'Adam, standing in the door of the Sylvester Arms, with a twig in his mouth and a sneer fading from his lips, made his ever-memorable remark:

"Sall!" he said, speaking in low, earnest voice; " 'tis a muckle wumman."

---

*Note—It was this visit which figured in the Grammochtown *Argus* (local and radical) under the heading of "Alleged Wholesale Corruption by Tory Agents." And that is why, on the following market day, Herbert Trotter, journalist, erstwhile gentleman, and Secretary of the Dale Trials, found himself trying to swim in the public horse-trough.

"What? What be sayin', mon?" cried old
Jonas, startled out of his usual apathy.

M'Adam turned sharply on the old man.

"I said the wumman wears a muckle hat!"
he snapped.

Blotted out as it was, the observation still
remains—a tribute of honest admiration.
Doubtless the Recording Angel did not pass
it by. That one statement anent the gentle
lady of the manor is the only personal remark
ever credited to little M'Adam not born of
malice and all uncharitableness. And that is
why it is ever memorable.

The little Scotsman with the sardonic face
had been the tenant of the Grange these many
years; yet he had never grown acclimatized to
the land of the Southron. With his shrivelled
body and weakly legs he looked among the
sturdy, straight-limbed sons of the hill-country
like some brown, wrinkled leaf holding its
place midst a galaxy of green. And as he
differed from them physically, so he did morally.

He neither understood them nor attempted
to. The North-country character was an unsolved mystery to him, and that after ten
years' study. "One-half o' what ye say they
doot, and they let ye see it; t'ither half they
disbelieve, and they tell ye so," he once said.
And that explained his attitude toward them,
and consequently theirs toward him.

He stood entirely alone; a son of Hagar,

mocking. His sharp, ill tongue was rarely
still, and always bitter. There was hardly a
man in the land, from Langholm How to the
market-cross in Grammoch-town, but had at
one time known its sting, endured it in silence,—for they are slow of speech, these men
of the fells and meres,—and was nursing his
resentment till a day should bring that chance
which always comes. And when at the Sylvester Arms, on one of those rare occasions
when M'Adam was not present, Tammas
summed up the little man in that historic
phrase of his, "When he's drunk he's wi'lent,
and when he bain't he's wicious," there was an
applause to gratify the blasé heart of even
Tammas Thornton.

Yet it had not been till his wife's death
that the little man had allowed loose rein to
his ill-nature. With her firmly gentle hand
no longer on the tiller of his life, it burst into
fresh being. And alone in the world with
David, the whole venom of his vicious temperament was ever directed against the boy's
head. It was as though he saw in his fair-
haired son the unconscious cause of his ever-
living sorrow. All the more strange this,
seeing that, during her life, the boy had been
to poor Flora M'Adam as her heart's core.
And the lad was growing up the very antithesis of his father. Big and hearty, with
never an ache or ill in the whole of his sturdy
young body; of frank, open countenance; while

even his speech was slow and burring like any Dale-bred boy's. And the fact of it all, and that the lad was palpably more Englishman than Scot—ay, and gloried in it—exasperated the little man, a patriot before everything, to blows. While, on top of it, David evinced an amazing pertness fit to have tried a better man than Adam M'Adam.

On the death of his wife, kindly Elizabeth Moore had, more than once, offered such help to the lonely little man as a woman only can give in a house that knows no mistress. On the last of these occasions, after crossing the Stony Bottom, which divides the two farms, and toiling up the hill to the Grange, she had met M'Adam in the door.

" Yo' maun let me put yo' bit things straight for yo', mister," she had said shyly; for she feared the little man.

"Thank ye, Mrs. Moore," he had answered with the sour smile the Dalesmen knew so well, "but ye maun think I'm a waefu' cripple." And there he had stood, grinning sardonically, opposing his small bulk in the very centre of the door.

Mrs. Moore had turned down the hill, abashed and hurt at the reception of her offer; and her husband, proud to a fault, had forbidden her to repeat it. Nevertheless her motherly heart went out in a great tenderness for the little orphan David. She knew well the desolateness of his life; his father's

aversion from him, and its inevitable consequences.

It became an institution for the boy to call
every morning at Kenmuir, and trot off to the
village school with Maggie Moore. And soon
the lad came to look on Kenmuir as his true
home, and James and Elizabeth Moore as his
real parents. His greatest happiness was to be
away from the Grange. And the ferret-eyed
little man there noted the fact, bitterly resented it, and vented his ill-humor accordingly.

It was this, as he deemed it, uncalled-for
trespassing on his authority which was the
chief cause of his animosity against James
Moore. The Master of Kenmuir it was at
whom he was aiming when he remarked one
day at the Arms: "Masel', I aye prefaire the
good man who does no go to church, to the
bad man who does. But then, as ye say, Mr.
Burton, I'm peculiar."

The little man's treatment of David, exag-
gerated as it was by eager credulity, became
at length such a scandal to the Dale that Parson Leggy determined to bring him to task on
the matter.

Now M'Adam was the parson's pet antipathy. The bluff old minister, with his
brusque manner and big heart, would have no
truck with the man who never went to church,
was perpetually in liquor, and never spoke
good of his neighbors. Yet he entered upon
the interview fully resolved not to be betrayed

into an unworthy expression of feeling; rather
to appeal to the little man's better nature.

The conversation had not been in progress
two minutes, however, before he knew that,
where he had meant to be calmly persuasive,
he was fast become hotly abusive.

"You, Mr. Hornbut, wi' James Moore to
help ye, look after the lad's soul, I'll see to his
body," the little man was saying.

The parson's thick gray eyebrows lowered
threateningly over his eyes.

"You ought to be ashamed of yourself to
talk like that. Which d'you think the more
important, soul or body? Oughtn't you, his
father, to be the very first to care for the boy's
soul? If not, who should? Answer me, sir."

The little man stood smirking and sucking
his eternal twig, entirely unmoved by the
other's heat.

"Ye're right, Mr. Hornbut, as ye aye are.
But my argiment is this: that I get at his soul
best through his leetle carcase."

The honest parson brought down his stick
with an angry thud.

"M'Adam, you're a brute—a brute!" he
shouted. At which outburst the little man
was seized with a spasm of silent merriment.

"A fond dad first, a brute afterward, aiblins
—he! he! Ah, Mr. Hornbut! ye 'ford me
vast diversion, ye do indeed, 'my loved, my
honored, much-respected friend.'"

"If you paid as much heed to your **boy's**

welfare as you do to the bad poetry of that profligate ploughman——"

An angry gleam shot into the other's eyes. "D'ye ken what blasphemy is, Mr. Hornbut?" he asked, shouldering a pace forward.

For the first time in the dispute the parson thought he was about to score a point, and was calm accordingly.

"I should do; I fancy I've a specimen of the breed before me now. And d'you know what impertinence is?"

"I should do; I fancy I've—I awd say it's what gentlemen aften are unless their mammies whipped 'em as lads."

For a moment the parson looked as if about to seize his opponent and shake him.

"M'Adam," he roared, "I'll not stand your insolences!"

The little man turned, scuttled indoors, and came runnng back with a chair.

"Permit me!" he said blandly, holding it before him like a haircutter for a customer.

The parson turned away. At the gap in the hedge he paused.

"I'll only say one thing more," he called slowly. "When your wife, whom I think we all loved, lay dying in that room above you, she said to you in my presence——"

It was M'Adam's turn to be angry. He made a step forward with burning face.

"Aince and for a', Mr. Hornbut," he cried passionately, "onderstand I'll not ha' you and yer likes lay yer tongues on ma wife's memory whenever it suits ye. You can say what ye like aboot me—lies, sneers, snash—and I'll say nae-thin'. I dinna ask ye to respect me; I think ye might do sae muckle by her, puir lass. She never harmed ye. Gin ye canna let her bide in peace where she lies doon yonder"—he waved in the direction of the churchyard—"ye'll no come on ma land. Though she is dead she's mine."

Standing in front of his house, with flushed face and big eyes, the little man looked almost noble in his indignation. And the parson, striding away down the hill, was uneasily conscious that with him was not the victory.

CHAPTER III

THE winter came and went; the lambing season was over, and spring already shyly kissing the land. And the back of the year's work broken, and her master well started on a fresh season, M'Adam's old collie, Cuttie Sark, lay down one evening and passed quietly away.

The little black-and-tan lady, Parson Leggy used to say, had been the only thing on earth M'Adam cared for. Certainly the two had been wondrously devoted; and for many a market-day the Dalesmen missed the shrill, chuckling cry which heralded the pair's approach: "Weel done, Cuttie Sark!"

The little man felt his loss acutely, and, according to his wont, vented his ill-feeling on David and the Dalesmen. In return, Tammas, whose forte lay in invective and alliteration, called him behind his back, "A wenomous one!" and "A wiralent wiper!" to the applause of tinkling pewters.

A shepherd without his dog is like a ship without a rudder, and M'Adam felt his loss practically as well as otherwise. Especially did he experience this on a day when he had

to take a batch of draft-ewes over to Grammoch-town.   To help him Jem Burton had lent
the services of his herring-gutted, herring-
hearted, greyhound lurcher, Monkey.   But
before they had well topped Braithwaite Brow,
which leads from the village on to the marches,
M'Adam was standing in the track with a rock
in his hand, a smile on his face, and the ten-
derest blandishments in his voice as he coaxed
the dog to him.   But Master Monkey knew
too much for that.   However, after gambol-
ling a while longer in the middle of the flock,
a boulder, better aimed than its predecessors,
smote him on the hinder parts and sent him
back to the Sylvester Arms, with a sore tail
and a subdued heart.

For the rest, M'Adam would never have won
over the sheep-infested marches alone with his
convoy had it not been for the help of old
Saunderson and Shep, who caught him on the
way and aided him.

It was in a very wrathful mood that on his
way home he turned into the Dalesman's
Daughter in Silverdale.

The only occupants of the tap-room, as he
entered, were Teddy Bolstock, the publican,
Jim Mason, with the faithful Betsy beneath
his chair and the post-bags flung into the corner, and one long-limbed, drover-like man—a
stranger.

"And he coom up to Mr. Moore," Teddy was
saying, "and says he, 'I'll gie ye twal' pun for

yon gray dog o' yourn.' 'Ah,' says Moore, 'yo'
may gie me twal' hunner'd and yet you'll not
get ma Bob.'—Eh, Jim?"

"And he did thot," corroborated Jim.
" 'Twal' hunner'd,' says he."

"James Moore and his dog agin'" snapped
M'Adam. "There's ithers in the warld for
bye them twa."

"Ay, but none like 'em," quoth loyal Jim.

"Na, thanks be. Gin there were there'd be
no room for Adam M'Adam in this 'melancholy vale.' "

There was silence a moment, and then—:

"You're wantin' a tyke, bain't you, Mr.
M'Adam?" Jim asked.

The little man hopped round all in a
hurry.

"What!" he cried in well-affected eager-
ness, scanning the yellow mongrel beneath the
chair. "Betsy for sale! Guid life! Where's
ma check-book?" Whereat Jim, most easily
snubbed of men, collapsed.

M'Adam took off his dripping coat and
crossed the room to hang it on a chair-back.
The stranger drover followed the meagre,
shirt-clad figure with shifty eyes; then he
buried his face in his mug.

M'Adam reached out a hand for the chair;
and as he did so, a bomb in yellow leapt out
from beneath it, and, growling horribly, at
tacked his ankles.

"Curse ye!" cried M'Adam, starting back.

"Ye devil, let me alone!" Then turning fiercely on the drover, "Yours, mister?" he asked. The man nodded. "Then call him aff, can't ye? D—n ye!" At which Teddy Bolstock withdrew, sniggering; and Jim Mason slung the post-bags on to his shoulder and plunged out into the rain, the faithful Betsy following, disconsolate.

The cause of the squall, having beaten off the attacking force, had withdrawn again beneath its chair. M'Adam stooped down, still cursing, his wet coat on his arm, and beheld a tiny yellow puppy, crouching defiant in the dark, and glaring out with fiery light eyes. Seeing itself remarked, it bared its little teeth, raised its little bristles, and growled a hideous menace.

A sense of humor is many a man's salvation, and was M'Adam's one redeeming feature. The laughableness of the thing—this ferocious atomy defying him—struck home to the little man. Delighted at such a display of vice in so tender a plant, he fell to chuckling.

"Ye leetle devil!" he laughed. "He! he! ye leetle devil!" and flipped together finger and thumb in vain endeavor to coax the puppy to him.

But it growled, and glared more terribly.

"Stop it, ye little snake, or I'll flatten you!" cried the big drover, and shuffled his feet threateningly. Whereat the puppy, gurgling like hot water in a kettle, made a feint as though to advance and wipe them out, these two bad men.

M'Adam laughed again, and smote his leg. "Keep a ceevil tongue and yer distance," says he, "or I'll e'en ha' to mak' ye. Though he is but as big as a man's thumb, a dog's a dog for a' that—he! he! the leetle devil." And he fell to flipping finger and thumb afresh.

"Ye're maybe wantin' a dog?" inquired the stranger. "Yer friend said as much."

"Ma friend lied; it's his way," M'Adam replied.

"I'm willin' to part wi' him," the other pursued.

The little man yawned. "Weel, I'll tak' him to oblige ye," he said indifferently.

The drover rose to his feet.

"It's givin' 'im ye, fair givin' im ye, mind! But I'll do it!"—he smacked a great fist into a hollow palm. "Ye may have the dog for a pun'—I'll only ask *you* a pun'," and he walked away to the window.

M'Adam drew back, the better to scan his would-be benefactor; his lower jaw dropped, and he eyed the stranger with a drolly sarcastic air.

"A poun', man! A poun'—for yon noble dorg!" he pointed a crooked forefinger at the little creature, whose scowling mask peered from beneath the chair. "Man, I couldna do it. Na, na; ma conscience wadna permit me.

'Twad be fair robbin' ye.   Ah, ye Englishmen!"
he spoke half to himself, and sadly, as if deplor-
ing the unhappy accident of his nationality;
"it's yer grand, open-hairted generosity that
grips a puir Scotsman by the throat.   A poun'!
and for yon!"   He wagged his head mournfully,
cocking it sideways the better to scan his
subject.

"Take him or leave him," ordered the
drover truculently, still gazing out of the
window.

"Wi' yer permission I'll leave him," M'Adam
answered meekly.

"I'm short o' the ready," the big man pursued, "or I wouldna part with him.   Could I
bide me time there's many'd be glad to give
me a tenner for one o' that bree——" he
caught himself up hastily—"for a dog sic as
that."

"And yet ye offer him me for a poun'!
Noble indeed!"

Nevertheless the little man had pricked his
ears at the other's slip and quick correction.
Again he approached the puppy, dangling his
coat before him to protect his ankles; and
again that wee wild beast sprang out, seized
the coat in its small jaw, and worried it savagely.

M'Adam stooped quickly and picked up his
tiny assailant; and the puppy, suspended by
its neck, gurgled and slobbered; then, wrig-
gling desperately round, made its teeth meet

in its adversary's shirt. At which M'Adam
shook it gently and laughed. Then he set to
examining it.

Apparently some six weeks old; a tawny
coat, fiery eyes, a square head with small,
cropped ears, and a comparatively immense
jaw; the whole giving promise of great
strength, if little beauty. And this effect was
enhanced by the manner of its docking. For
the miserable relic of a tail, yet raw, looked
little more than a red button adhering to its
wearer's stern.

M'Adam's inspection was as minute as it
was apparently absorbing; he omitted nothing
from the square muzzle to the lozenge-like scut.
And every now and then he threw a quick glance
at the man at the window, who was watching
the careful scrutiny a thought uneasily.

"Ye've cut him short," he said at length,
swinging round on the drover.

"Ay; strengthens their backs," the big
man answered with averted gaze.

M'Adam's chin went up in the air; his
mouth partly opened and his eyelids partly
closed as he eyed his informant.

"Oh, ay," he said.

"Gie him back to me," ordered the drover
surlily. He took the puppy and set it on the
floor; whereupon it immediately resumed its
former fortified position. "Ye're no buyer;
I knoo that all along by that face on ye," he
said in insulting tones.

"Ye wad ha' bought him yerself', nae doot?"
M'Adam inquired blandly.

"In course; if you says so."

"Or airblins ye bred him?"

" 'Appen I did."

"Ye'll no be from these parts?"

"Will I no?" answered the other.

A smile of genuine pleasure stole over
M'Adam's face. He laid his hand on the
other's arm.

"Man," he said gently, "ye mind me o'
hame." Then almost in the same breath:
"Ye said ye found him?"

It was the stranger's turn to laugh.

"Ha! ha! Ye teeckle me, little mon.
Found 'im? Nay; I was give 'im by a friend.
But there's nowt amiss wi' his breedin', ye
may believe me."

The great fellow advanced to the chair under which the puppy lay. It leapt out like a
lion, and fastened on his huge boot.

"A rare bred un, look 'ee! a rare game un.
Ma word, he's a big-hearted un! Look at the
back on him; see the jaws to him; mark the
pluck of him!" He shook his booted foot fiercely, tossing his leg to and fro like a tree in a
wind. But the little creature, now raised ceiling-
ward, now dashed to the ground, held on with
incomparable doggedness, till its small jaw was
all bloody and muzzle wrinkled with the effort.

"Ay, ay, that'll do," M'Adam interposed,
irritably.

The drover ceased his efforts.

"Now, I'll mak' ye a last offer." He thrust his head down to a level with the other's, shooting out his neck. "It's throwin' him at ye, mind. 'Tain't buyin' him ye'll be— don't go for to deceive yourself. Ye may have him for fifteen shillin'. Why do I do it, ye ask? Why, 'cos I think ye'll be kind to him," as the puppy retreated to its chair, leaving a spotted track of red along its route.

"Ay, ye wadna be happy gin ye thocht he'd no a comfortable hame, conseederate man?" M'Adam answered, eyeing the dark track on the floor. Then he put on his coat.

"Na, na, he's no for me. Weel, I'll no detain ye. Good-nicht to ye, mister!" and he made for the door.

"A gran' worker he'll be," called the drover after him.

"Ay; muckle wark he'll mak' amang the sheep wi' sic a jaw and sic a temper. Weel, I maun be steppin'. Good-nicht to ye."

"Ye'll niver have sich anither chanst."

"Nor niver wush to. Na, na; he'll never mak' a sheep-dog"; and the little man turned up the collar of his coat.

"Will he not?" cried the other scornfully. "There niver yet was one o' that line——" he stopped abruptly.

The little man spun round.

"Iss?" he said, as innocent as any child; "ye were sayin'?"

The other turned to the window and watched the rain falling monotonously.

"Ye'll be wantin' wet," he said adroitly.

"Ay, we could do wi' a drappin'. And he'll never mak' a sheep-dog." He shoved his cap down on his head. "Weel, good-nicht to ye!" and he stepped out into the rain.

.　　.　　.　　.　　.

It was long after dark when the bargain was finally struck.

Adam M'Adam's Red Wull became that little man's property for the following realizable assets: ninepence in cash—three coppers and a doubtful sixpence; a plug of suspicious tobacco in a well-worn pouch; and an old watch.

"It's clean givin' 'im ye," said the stranger bitterly, at the end of the deal.

"It's mair the charity than aught else mak's me sae leeberal," the other answered gently. "I wad not like to see ye pinched."

"Thank ye kindly," the big man replied with some acerbity, and plunged out into the darkness and rain. Nor was that long-limbed drover-man ever again seen in the country-side. And the puppy's previous history—whether he was honestly come by or no, whether he was, indeed, of the famous Red McCulloch* strain, ever remained a mystery in the Daleland.

*N. B.—You may know a Red McCulloch anywhere by the ring of white upon his tail some two inches from the root.

CHAPTER IV

FIRST BLOOD

AFTER that first encounter in the Dalesman's Daughter, Red Wull, for so M'Adam
called him, resigned himself complacently to
his lot; recognizing, perhaps, his destiny.

Thenceforward the sour little man and the
vicious puppy grew, as it were, together. The
two were never apart. Where M'Adam was,
there was sure to be his tiny attendant, bristling defiance as he kept ludicrous guard over
his master.

The little man and his dog were inseparable.
M'Adam never left him even at the Grange.

"I couldna trust ma Wullie at hame alone
wi' the dear lad," was his explanation. "I ken
weel I'd come back to find a wee corpse on
the floor, and David singin':

'My heart is sair, I daur na tell,
My heart is sair for somebody.'

Ay, and he'd be sair elsewhere by the time
I'd done wi' him—he! he!"

The sneer at David's expense was as characteristic as it was unjust. For though the
puppy and the boy were already sworn enemies, yet the lad would have scorned to harm
so small a foe. And many a tale did David

tell at Kenmuir of Red Wull's viciousness, of
his hatred of him (David), and his devotion
to his master; how, whether immersed in the
pig-bucket or chasing the fleeting rabbit, he
would desist at once, and bundle, panting, up
at his master's call; how he routed the tom-
cat and drove him from the kitchen; and how
he clambered on to David's bed and pinned
him murderously by the nose.

Of late the relations between M'Adam and
James Moore had been unusually strained.
Though they were neighbors, communications
between the two were of the rarest; and it was
for the first time for many a long day that, on
an afternoon shortly after Red Wull had come
into his possession, M'Adam entered the yard
of Kenmuir, bent on girding at the master for
an alleged trespass at the Stony Bottom.

"Wi' yer permission, Mr. Moore," said the
little man, "I'll wheestle ma dog, " and, turning, he whistled a shrill, peculiar note like the
cry of a disturbed peewit.

Straightway there came scurrying desperately up, ears back, head down, tongue out,
as if the world depended on his speed, a little
tawny beetle of a thing, who placed his forepaws against his master's ankles and looked
up into his face; then, catching sight of the
strangers, hurriedly he took up his position
between them and M'Adam, assuming his
natural attitude of grisly defiance. Such a
laughable spectacle he made, that martial mite,

standing at bay with bristles up and teeth
bared, that even James Moore smiled.

"Ma word! Ha' yo' brought his muzzle,
man?" cried old Tammas, the humorist; and,
turning, climbed all in a heat on to an upturned bucket that stood by. Whereat the
puppy, emboldened by his foe's retreat, advanced savagely to the attack, buzzing round
the slippery pail like a wasp on a window-
pane, in vain attempt to reach the old man.

Tammas stood on the top, hitching his
trousers and looking down on his assailant,
the picture of mortal fear.

" 'Elp! Oh, 'elp!" he bawled. "Send for
the sogers! fetch the p'lice! For lawk-a-
mussy's sake call him off, man!" Even Sam'l
Todd, watching the scene from the cart-shed,
was tickled and burst into a loud guffaw,
heartily backed by 'Enry and oor Job. While
M'Adam remarked: "Ye're fitter for a stage
than a stable-bucket, Mr. Thornton."

"How didst coom by him?" asked Tammas, nodding at the puppy.

"Found him," the little man replied, sucking his twig. "Found him in ma stockin'
on ma birthday. A present from ma leetle
David for his auld dad, I doot."

"So do I," said Tammas, and was seized
with sudden spasm of seemingly causeless
merriment. For looking up as M'Adam was
speaking, he had caught a glimpse of a boy's
fair head, peering cautiously round the cow-

shed, and, behind, the flutter of short petticoats. They disappeared as silently as they
had come; and two small figures, just returned
from school, glided away and sought shelter
in the friendly darkness of a coal-hole.

"Coom awa', Maggie, coom awa'! 'Tis th'
owd un, 'isself," whispered a disrespectful voice.

M'Adam looked round suspiciously.

"What's that?" he asked sharply.

At the moment, however, Mrs. Moore put
her head out of the kitchen window.

"Coom thy ways in, Mister M'Adam, and
tak' a soop o' tea," she called hospitably.

"Thank ye kindly, Mrs. Moore, I will," he
answered, politely for him. And this one
good thing must be allowed of Adam M'Adam:
that, if there was only one woman of
whom he was ever known to speak well, there
was also only one, in the whole course of his
life, against whom he ever insinuated evil—and
that was years afterward, when men said his
brain was sapped. Flouts and jeers he had
for every man, but a woman, good or bad,
was sacred to him. For the sex that had
given him his mother and his wife he had
that sentiment of tender reverence which, if
a man still preserve, he cannot be altogether
bad. As he turned into the house he looked
back at Red Wull.

"Ay, we may leave him," he said. "That
is, gin ye're no afraid, Mr. Thornton?"

.   .   .   .

Of what happened while the men were within doors, it is enough to tell two things. First, that Owd Bob was no bully. Second, this: In the code of sheep-dog honor there is written a word in stark black letters; and opposite it another word, writ large in the color of blood. The first is "Sheep-murder"; the second, "Death." It is the one crime only to be wiped away in blood; and to accuse of the crime is to offer the one unpardonable insult. Every sheep-dog knows it, and every shepherd.

That afternoon, as the men still talked, the quiet echoes of the farm rung with a furious animal cry, twice repeated: "Shot for sheep-murder"—"Shot for sheep-murder"; followed by a hollow stillness.

.   .   .   .   .

The two men finished their colloquy. The matter was concluded peacefully, mainly owing to the pacifying influence of Mrs. Moore. Together the three went out into the yard; Mrs. Moore seizing the opportunity to shyly speak on David's behalf.

"He's such a good little lad, I do think," she was saying.

"Ye should ken, Mrs. Moore," the little man answered, a thought bitterly; "ye see enough of him."

"Yo' mun be main proud of un, mester," the woman continued, heedless of the sneer: "an' 'im growin' such a gradely lad."

M'Adam shrugged his shoulders.

"I barely ken the lad," he said. "By sight I know him, of course, but barely to speak to. He's but seldom at hame."

"An' hoo proud his mother'd be if she could see him," the woman continued, well aware of his one tender place. "Eh, but she was fond o' him, so she was."

An angry fiush stole over the little man's face. Well he understood the implied rebuke; and it hurt him like a knife.

"Ay, ay, Mrs. Moore," he began. Then breaking off, and looking about him— "Where's ma Wullie?" he cried excitedly. "James Moore!" whipping round on the Master, "ma Wullie's gone—gone, I say!"

Elizabeth Moore turned away indignantly.

"I do declar' he tak's more fash after yon little yaller beastie than iver he does after his own flesh," she muttered.

"Wullie, ma we doggie! Wullie, where are ye? James Moore, he's gone—ma Wullie's gone!" cried the little man, running about the yard, searching everywhere.

"Cannot 'a' gotten far," said the Master, reassuringly, looking about him.

"Niver no tellin'," said Sam'l, appearing on the scene, pig-bucket in hand. "I misdoot yo'll iver see your dog agin, mister." He turned sorrowfully to M'Adam.

That little man, all dishevelled, and with the perspiration standing on his face, came hurrying out of the cow-shed and danced up to the Master.

"It's robbed I am—robbed, I tell ye!" he cried recklessly. "Ma wee Wull's bin stolen while I was ben your hoose, James Moore!"

"Yo' munna say that, ma mon. No robbin' at Kenmuir," the Master answered sternly.

"Then where is he? It's for you to say."

"I've ma own idee, I 'ave," Sam'l announced opportunely, pig-bucket uplifted.

M'Adam turned on him.

"What, man? What is it?"

"I misdoot yo'll iver see your dog agin, mister," Sam'l repeated, as if he was supplying the key to the mystery.

"Noo, Sam'l, if yo' know owt tell it," ordered his master.

Sam'l grunted sulkily.

"Wheer's oor Bob, then?" he asked.

At that M'Adam turned on the Master.

" 'Tis that, nae doot. It's yer gray dog, James Moore, yer——dog. I might ha' kent it,"—and he loosed off a volley of foul words.

"Sweerin' will no find him," said the Master coldly. "Noo, Sam'l."

The big man shifted his feet, and looked mournfully at M'Adam.

" 'Twas 'appen 'alf an hour agone, when I sees oor Bob goin' oot o' yard wi' little yaller tyke in his mouth. In a minnit I looks agin— and theer! little yaller 'un was gone, and oor Bob a-sittin' a-lickin' his chops. Gone for-

iver, I do reck'n. Ah, yo' may well take on,
Tammas Thornton!" For the old man was
rolling about the yard, bent double with merriment.

M'Adam turned on the Master with the
resignation of despair.

"Man, Moore," he cried piteously, "it's yer
gray dog has murdered ma wee Wull! Ye
have it from yer ain man."

"Nonsense," said the Master encouragingly.
" 'Tis but yon girt oof."

Sam'l tossed his head and snorted.

"Coom, then, and I'll show yo'," he said,
and led the way out of the yard. And there
below them on the slope to the stream, sitting
like Justice at the Courts of Law, was Owd
Bob.

Straightway Sam'l whose humor was something of the calibre of old Ross's, the sexton,
burst into horse-merriment. "Why's he sittin' so still, think 'ee? Ho! Ho! See un lickin'
his chops—ha! ha!"—and he roared afresh.
While from afar you could hear the distant
rumbling of 'Enry and oor Job.

At the sight, M'Adam burst into a storm of
passionate invective, and would have rushed
on the dog had not James Moore forcibly restrained him.

"Bob, lad," called the Master, "coom here!"

But even as he spoke, the gray dog cocked
his ears, listened a moment, and then shot
down the slope. At the same moment Tam-

mas hallooed: "Theer he be! yon's yaller un
coomin' oot o' drain! La, Sam'l!" And there,
indeed, on the slope below them, a little angry,
smutty-faced figure was crawling out of a
rabbit-burrow.

"Ye murderin' devil, wad ye duar touch ma
Wullie?" yelled M'Adam, and, breaking
away, pursued hotly down the hill; for the
gray dog had picked up the puppy, like a
lancer a tent-peg, and was sweeping on, his
captive in his mouth, toward the stream.

Behind, hurried James Moore and Sam'l,
wondering what the issue of the comedy would
be. After them toddled old Tammas, chuckling. While over the yard-wall was now a
little cluster of heads: 'Enry, oor Job, Maggie
and David, and Vi'let Thornton, the dairy-
maid.

Straight on to the plank-bridge galloped
Owd Bob. In the middle he halted, leant
over, and dropped his prisoner; who fell with
a cool plop into the running water beneath.

Another moment and M'Adam had reached
the bank of the stream. In he plunged,
splashing and cursing, and seized the struggling puppy; then waded back, the waters
surging about his waist, and Red Wull, limp
as a wet rag, in his hand. The little man's
hair was dripping, for his cap was gone; his
clothes clung to him, exposing the miserable-
ness of his figure; and his eyes blazed like hot
ashes in his wet face.

He sprang on to the bank, and, beside himself with passion, rushed at Owd Bob.

"Curse ye for a——"

"Stan' back, or yo'll have him at your throat!" shouted the Master, thundering up. "Stan' back, I say, yo' fule!" And, as the little man still came madly on, he reached forth his hand and hurled him back; at the same moment, bending, he buried the other hand deep in Owd Bob's shaggy neck. It was but just in time; for if ever the fierce desire of battle gleamed in gray eyes, it did in the young dog's as M'Adam came down on him.

The little man staggered, tottered, and fell heavily. At the shock, the blood gushed from his nose, and, mixing with the water on his face, ran down in vague red streams, dripping off his chin; while Red Wull, jerked from his grasp, was thrown afar, and lay motionless.

"Curse ye!" M'Adam screamed, his face dead-white save for the running red about his jaw. "Curse ye for a cowardly Englishman!" and, struggling to his feet, he made at the Master.

But Sam'l interposed his great bulk between the two.

"Easy, little mon," he said leisurely, regarding the small fury before him with mournful interest. "Eh, but thee do be a little spit-cat, surely!"

James Moore stood, breathing deep, his hand still buried in Owd Bob's coat.

"If yo'd touched him," he explained, "I couldna ha' stopped him. He'd ha' mauled yo' afore iver I could ha' had him off. They're bad to hold, the Gray Dogs, when they're roosed."

"Ay, ma word, that they are!" corroborated Tammas, speaking from the experience of sixty years. "Once on, yo' canna get 'em off."

The little man turned away.

"Ye're all agin me," he said, and his voice shook. A pitiful figure he made, standing there with the water dripping from him. A red stream was running slowly from his chin; his head was bare, and face working.

James Moore stood eyeing him with some pity and some contempt. Behind was Tammas, enjoying the scene. While Sam'l regarded them all with an impassive melancholy.

M'Adam turned and bent over Red Wull, who still lay like a dead thing. As his master handled him, the button-tail quivered feebly; he opened his eyes, looked about him, snarled faintly, and glared with devilish hate at the gray dog and the group with him.

The little man picked him up, stroking him tenderly. Then he turned away and on to the bridge. Half-way across he stopped. It rattled feverishly beneath him, for he still trembled like a palsied man.

"Man, Moore!" he called, striving to quell the agitation in his voice—"I wad shoot yon dog."

Across the bridge he turned again.

"Man, Moore!" he called and paused. "Ye'll not forget this day." And with that the blood flared up a dull crimson into his white face.

PART II

THE LITTLE MAN

CHAPTER V

A MAN'S SON

THE storm, long threatened, having once
burst, M'Adam allowed loose rein to his bitter
animosity against James Moore.

The two often met. For the little man fre-
quently returned home from the village by the
footpath across Kenmuir. It was out of his
way, but he preferred it in order to annoy his
enemy and keep a watch upon his doings.

He haunted Kenmuir like its evil genius.
His sallow face was perpetually turning up
at inopportune moments. When Kenmuir
Queen, the prize short-horn heifer, calved un-
expectedly and unattended in the dip by the
lane, Tammas and the Master, summoned
hurriedly by Owd Bob, came running up to
find the little man leaning against the stile,
and shaking with silent merriment. Again,
poor old Staggy, daring still in his dotage,
took a fall while scrambling on the steep banks
of the Stony Bottom. There he lay for hours,
unnoticed and kicking, until James Moore and
Owd Bob came upon him at length, nearly
exhausted. But M'Adam was before them.
Standing on the far bank with Red Wull by
his side, he called across the gulf with appar-

ent concern: "He's bin so sin' yesternight."
Often James Moore, with all his great strength
of character, could barely control himself.

There were two attempts to patch up the
feud. Jim Mason, who went about the world
seeking to do good, tried in his shy way to set
things right. But M'Adam and his Red Wull
between them soon shut him and Betsy up.

"You mind yer letters and yer wires, Mr.
Poacher-Postman. Ay, I saw 'em baith: th'
ain doon by the Haughs, t'ither in the Bottom.
And there's Wullie, the humorsome chiel,
havin' a rare game wi' Betsy." There, indeed,
lay the faithful Betsy, suppliant on her back,
paws up, throat exposed, while Red Wull, now
a great-grown puppy, stood over her, his habit-
ually evil expression intensified into a fiendish
grin, as with wrinkled muzzle and savage
wheeze he waited for a movement as a pretext
to pin: "Wullie, let the leddy be—ye've had
yer dinner."

Parson Leggy was the other would-be medi-
ator; for he hated to see the two principal
parishioners of his tiny cure at enmity. First
he tackled James Moore on the subject; but
that laconic person cut him short with, "I've
nowt agin the little mon," and would say no
more. And, indeed, the quarrel was none of
his making.

Of the parson's interview with M'Adam, it
is enough to say here that, in the end, the
angry old minister would of a surety have as-

saulted his mocking adversary had not Cyril
Gilbraith forcibly withheld him.

And after that the vendetta must take its
course unchecked.

David was now the only link between the
two farms. Despite his father's angry commands, the boy clung to his intimacy with the
Moores with a doggedness that no thrashing
could overcome. Not a minute of the day
when out of school, holidays and Sundays in-
cluded, but was passed at Kenmuir. It was
not till late at night that he would sneak back
to the Grange, and creep quietly up to his tiny
bare room in the roof—not supperless, indeed,
motherly Mrs. Moore had seen to that. And
there he would lie awake and listen with a
fierce contempt as his father, hours later,
lurched into the kitchen below, lilting liquor-
ishly:

> "We are na fou, we're nae that fou,
>   But just a drappie in our e'e;
> The cock may craw, the day may daw',
>   And ay we'll taste the barley bree! "

And in the morning the boy would slip quietly
out of the house while his father still slept;
only Red Wull would thrust out his savage
head as the lad passed, and snarl hungrily.

Sometimes father and son would go thus
for weeks without sight of one another. And
that was David's aim—to escape attention.
It was only his cunning at this game of eva-
sion that saved him a thrashing.

The little man seemed devoid of all natural
affection for his son. He lavished the whole
fondness of which his small nature appeared
capable on the Tailless Tyke, for so the Dalesmen called Red Wull. And the dog he treated
with a careful tenderness that made David
smile bitterly.

The little man and his dog were as alike
morally as physically they were contrasted.
Each owed a grudge against the world and was
determined to pay it. Each was an Ishmael among his kind.

You saw them thus, standing apart, leper-
like, in the turmoil of life; and it came quite
as a revelation to happen upon them in some
quiet spot of nights, playing together, each
wrapped in the game, innocent, tender, forget-
ful of the hostile world.

The two were never separated except only
when M'Adam came home by the path across
Kenmuir. After that first misadventure he
never allowed his friend to accompany him on
the journey through the enemy's country; for
well he knew that sheep-dogs have long memories.

To the stile in the lane, then, Red Wull
would follow him. There he would stand, his
great head poked through the bars, watching
his master out of sight; and then would turn
and trot, self-reliant and defiant, sturdy and
surly, down the very centre of the road through
the village—no playing, no enticing away, and

woe to that man or dog who tried to stay him
in his course! And so on, past Mother Ross's
shop, past the Sylvester Arms, to the right by
Kirby's smithy, over the Wastrel by the
Haughs, to await his master at the edge of the
Stony Bottom.

The little man, when thus crossing Kenmuir, often met Owd Bob, who had the free
run of the farm. On these occasions he passed
discreetly by; for, though he was no coward,
yet it is bad, single-handed, to attack a Gray
Dog of Kenmuir; while the dog trotted soberly
on his way, only a steely glint in the big gray
eyes betraying his knowledge of the presence
of his foe. As surely, however, as the little
man, in his desire to spy out the nakedness of
the land, strayed off the public path, so surely
a gray figure, seeming to spring from out the
blue, would come fiercely, silently driving
down on him; and he would turn and run for
his life, amid the uproarious jeers of any of
the farm-hands who were witness to the encounter.

On these occasions David vied with Tammas in facetiousness at his father's expense.

"Good on yo', little un!" he roared from
behind a wall, on one such occurence.

"Bain't he a runner, neither?" yelled Tammas, not to be outdone. "See un skip it—
ho! ho!"

"Look to his knees a-wamblin'!" from the
undutiful son in ecstasy. "An' I'd knees like

yon, I'd wear petticoats." As he spoke, a swinging box on the ear nearly knocked the young reprobate down.

"D'yo' think God gave you a dad for you to jeer at? Y'ought to be ashamed o' yo'self. Serve yo' right if he does thrash yo' when yo' get home." And David, turning round, found James Moore close behind him, his heavy eyebrows lowering over his eyes.

Luckily, M'Adam had not distinguished his son's voice among the others. But David feared he had; for on the following morning the little man said to him:

"David, ye'll come hame immediately after school to-day."

"Will I?" said David pertly.

"Ye will."

"Why?"

"Because I tell ye to, ma lad"; and that was all the reason he would give. Had he told the simple fact that he wanted help to drench a "husking" ewe, things might have gone differently. As it was, David turned away defiantly down the hill.

The afternoon wore on. Schooltime was long over; still there was no David.

The little man waited at the door of the Grange, fuming, hopping from one leg to the other, talking to Red Wull, who lay at his feet, his head on his paws, like a tiger waiting for his prey.

At length he could restrain himself no longer;

and started running down the hill, his heart
burning with indignation.

"Wait till we lay hands on ye, ma lad," he
muttered as he ran. "We'll warm ye, we'll
teach ye."

At the edge of the Stony Bottom he, as
always, left Red Wull. Crossing it himself,
and rounding Langholm How, he espied James
Moore, David, and Owd Bob walking away
from him and in the direction of Kenmuir.
The gray dog and David were playing together.
wrestling, racing, and rolling. The boy had
never a thought for his father.

The little man ran up behind them, unseen
and unheard, his feet softly pattering on the
grass. His hand had fallen on David's shoulder before the boy had guessed his approach.

"Did I bid ye come hame after school,
David?" he asked, concealing his heat beneath
a suspicious suavity.

"Maybe. Did I say I would come?"

The pertness of tone and words, alike, fanned
his father's resentment into a blaze. In a burst
of passion he lunged forward at the boy with
his stick. But as he smote, a gray whirlwind
struck him fair on the chest, and he fell like a
snapped stake, and lay, half stunned, with a
dark muzzle an inch from his throat.

"Git back, Bob!" shouted James Moore,
hurrying up. "Git back, I tell yo'!" He
bent over the prostrate figure, propping it up
anxiously. "Are yo' hurt, M'Adam? Eh,

but I am sorry. He thought yo' were goin'
for to strike the lad."

David had now run up, and he, too, bent
over his father with a very scared face.

"Are yo' hurt, feyther?" he asked, his voice
trembling.

The little man rose unsteadily to his feet and
shook off his supporters. His face was twitching, and he stood, all dust-begrimed, looking
at his son.

"Ye're content, aiblins, noo ye've seen yer
father's gray head bowed in the dust," he
said.

" 'Twas an accident," pleaded James Moore.
"But I *am* sorry. He thought yo' were goin'
to beat the lad."

"So I was—so I will."

"If ony's beat it should be ma Bob here
tho' he nob'but thought he was doin' right.
An' yo' were aff the path."

The little man looked at his enemy, a sneer
on his face.

"Ye canna thrash him for doin' what ye bid
him. Set yer dog on me, if ye will, but dinna
beat him when he does yer biddin'!"

"I did not set him on yo', as you know,"
the Master replied warmly.

M'Adam shrugged his shoulders.

"I'll no argie wi' ye, James Moore," he said.
"I'll leave you and what ye call yer conscience
to settle that. My business is not wi' you.
—David!" turning to his son.

A stranger might well have mistaken the identity of the boy's father. For he stood now, holding the Master's arm; while a few paces above them was the little man, pale but determined, the expression on his face betraying his consciousness of the irony of the situation.

"Will ye come hame wi' me and have it noo, or stop wi' him and wait till ye get it?" he asked the boy.

"M'Adam, I'd like yo' to——"

"None o' that, James Moore.—David, what d'ye say?"

David looked up into his protector's face.

"Yo'd best go wi' your feyther, lad," said the Master at last, thickly. The boy hesitated, and clung tighter to the shielding arm; then he walked slowly over to his father.

A bitter smile spread over the little man's face as he marked this new test of the boy's obedience to the other.

"To obey his frien' he foregoes the pleasure o' disobeyin' his father," he muttered. "Noble!" Then he turned homeward, and the boy followed in his footsteps.

James Moore and the gray dog stood looking after them.

"I know yo'll not pay off yer spite agin me on the lad's head, M'Adam," he called, almost appealingly.

"I'll do ma duty, thank ye, James Moore, wi'oot respect o' persons," the little man cried back, never turning.

Father and son walked away, one behind
the other, like a man and his dog, and there
was no word said between them.   Across the
Stony Bottom, Red Wull, scowling with bared
teeth at David, joined them.   Together the
three went up the hill to the Grange.

In the kitchen M'Adam turned.

"Noo, I'm gaein' to gie ye the gran'est
thrashin' ye iver dreamed of.   Tak' aff yer
coat!"

The boy obeyed, and stood up in his thin
shirt, his face white and set as a statue's.
Red Wull seated himself on his haunches close
by, his ears pricked, licking his lips, all attention.

The little man suppled the great ash-plant
in his hands and raised it.   But the expression
on the boy's face arrested his arm.

"Say ye're sorry and I'll let yer aff easy."

"I'll not."

"One   mair   chance—yer   last!   Say   yer
'shamed o' yerself'!"

"I'm not."

The little man brandished his cruel, white
weapon, and Red Wull shifted a little to obtain a better view.

"Git on wi' it," ordered David angrily.

The little man raised the stick again and—
threw it into the farthest corner of the room.

It fell with a rattle on the floor, and M'Adam
turned away.

"Ye're the pitifulest son iver a man had,"

he cried brokenly. "Gin a man's son dinna haud to him, wha can he expect to?—no one. Ye're ondootiful, ye're disrespectfu', ye're maist ilka thing ye shouldna be; there's but ae thing I thocht ye were not—a coward. And as to that, ye've no the pluck to say ye're sorry when, God knows, ye might be. I car.na thrash ye this day. But ye shall gae nae mair to school. I send ye there to learn. Ye'll not learn—ye've learnt naethin' except disobedience to me—ye shall stop at hame and work."

His father's rare emotion, his broken voice and working face, moved David as all the stripes and jeers had failed to do. His conscience smote him. For the first time in his life it dimly dawned on him that, perhaps, his father, too, had some ground for complaint; that, perhaps, he was not a good son.

He half turned.

"Feyther——"

"Git oot o' ma sight!" M'Adam cried.

And the boy turned and went.

CHAPTER VI

A LICKING OR A LIE

THENCEFORWARD David buckled down to work at home, and in one point only father and son resembled—industry. A drunkard M'Adam was, but a drone, no.

The boy worked at the Grange with tireless, indomitable energy; yet he could never satisfy his father.

The little man would stand, a sneer on his face and his thin lips contemptuously curled, and flout the lad's brave labors.

' Is he no a gran' worker, Wullie? 'Tis a pleasure to watch him, his hands in his pockets, his eyes turned heavenward!" as the boy snatched a hard-earned moment's rest. "You and I, Wullie, we'll brak' oorsel's slavin' for him while he looks on and laffs. "

And so on, the whole day through, week in, week out; till he sickened with weariness of it all.

In his darkest hours David thought sometimes to run away. He was miserably alone on the cold bosom of the world. The very fact that he was the son of his father isolated him in the Daleland. Naturally of a reserved disposition, he had no single friend outside Kenmuir. And it was only the thought of his

friends there that witheld him. He could
not bring himself to part from them; they
were all he had in the world.

So he worked on at the Grange, miserably,
doggedly, taking blows and abuse alike in
burning silence. But every evening, when
work was ended, he stepped off to his other
home beyond the Stony Bottom. And on
Sundays and holidays—for of these latter he
took, unasking, what he knew to be his due—
all day long, from cock-crowing to the going
down of the sun, he would pass at Kenmuir.
In this one matter the boy was invincibly stub-
born. Nothing his father could say or do
sufficed to break him of the habit. He endured
everything with white-lipped, silent doggedness, and still held on his way.

Once past the Stony Bottom, he threw his
troubles behind him with a courage that did
him honor. Of all the people at Kenmuir two
only ever dreamed the whole depth of his unhappiness, and that not through David. James
Moore suspected something of it all, for he
knew more of M'Adam than did the others.
While Owd Bob knew it as did no one else.
He could tell it from the touch of the boy's
hand on his head; and the story was writ large
upon his face for a dog to read. And he would
follow the lad about with a compassion in his
sad gray eyes greater than words.

David might well compare his gray friend
at Kenmuir with that other at the Grange.

The Tailless Tyke had now grown into an immense dog, heavy of muscle and huge of bone. A great bull head; undershot jaw, square and lengthy and terrible; vicious, yellow-gleaming eyes; cropped ears; and an expression incomparably savage. His coat was a tawny, lion-like yellow, short, harsh, dense; and his back, running up from shoulder to loins, ended abruptly in the knob-like tail. He looked like the devil of a dogs' hell. And his reputation was as bad as his looks. He never attacked unprovoked; but a challenge was never ignored, and he was greedy of insults. Already he had nigh killed Rob Saunderson's collie, Shep; Jem Burton's Monkey fled incontinently at the sound of his approach; while he had even fought a round with that redoubtable trio, the Vexer, Venus, and Van Tromp.

Nor, in the matter of war, did he confine himself to his own kind. His huge strength and indomitable courage made him the match of almost anything that moved. Long Kirby once threatened him with a broomstick; the smith never did it again. While in the Border Ram he attacked Big Bell, the Squire's under-keeper, with such murderous fury that it took all the men in the room to pull him off.

More than once had he and Owd Bob essayed to wipe out mutual memories, Red Wull, in this case only, the aggressor. As yet, however, while they fenced a moment for that deadly throat-grip, the value of which each knew so well, James Moore had always seized the chance to intervene.

"That's right, hide him ahint yer petticoats," sneered M'Adam on one of these occasions.

"Hide? It'll not be him I'll hide, I warn you, M'Adam," the Master answered grimly, as he stood, twirling his good oak stick between the would-be duellists. Whereat there was a loud laugh at the little man's expense.

It seemed as if there were to be other points of rivalry between the two than memories. For, in the matter of his own business—the handling of sheep—Red Wull bid fair to be second only throughout the Daleland to the Gray Dog of Kenmuir. And M'Adam was patient and painstaking in the training of his Wullie in a manner to astonish David. It would have been touching, had it not been so unnatural in view of his treatment of his own blood, to watch the tender carefulness with which the little man moulded the dog beneath his hands. After a promising display he would stand, rubbing his palms together, as near content as ever he was.

"Weel done, Wullie! Weel done. Bide a wee and we'll show 'em a thing or two, you and I, Wullie.

> " 'The warld's wrack we share o't,
>   The warstle and the care o't.'

For it's you and I alane, lad." And the dog

would trot up to him, place his great forepaws on his shoulders, and stand thus with his
great head overtopping his master's, his ears
back, and stump tail vibrating.

You saw them at their best when thus together, displaying each his one soft side to the
other.

From the very first David and Red Wull
were open enemies: under the circumstances,
indeed, nothing else was possible. Sometimes
the great dog would follow on the lad's heels
with surly, greedy eyes, never leaving him
from sunrise to sundown, till David could
hardly hold his hands.

So matters went on for a never-ending year.
Then there came a climax.

One evening, on a day throughout which
Red Wull had dogged him thus hungrily,
David, his work finished, went to pick up his
coat, which he had left hard by. On it lay
Red Wull.

"Git off ma coat!" the boy ordered angrily.
marching up. But the great dog never stirred:
he lifted a lip to show a fence of white, even
teeth, and seemed to sink lower in the ground;
his head on his paws, his eyes in his forehead.

"Come and take it!" he seemed to say.

Now what, between master and dog, David
had endured almost more than he could bear
that day.

"Yo' won't, won't yo', girt brute!" he
shouted, and bending, snatched a corner of

the coat and attempted to jerk it away. At that, Red Wull rose, shivering, to his feet, and with a low gurgle sprang at the boy.

David, quick as a flash, dodged, bent, and picked up an ugly stake, lying at his feet. Swinging round, all in a moment, he dealt his antagonist a mighty buffet on the side of the head. Dazed with the blow, the great dog fell; then, recovering himself, with a terrible, deep roar he sprang again. Then it must have gone hard with the boy, fine-grown, muscular young giant though he was. For Red Wull was now in the first bloom of that great strength which earned him afterward an undying notoriety in the land.

As it chanced, however, M'Adam had watched the scene from the kitchen. And now he came hurrying out of the house, shrieking commands and curses at the combatants. As Red Wull sprang, he interposed between the two, head back and eyes flashing. His small person received the full shock of the charge. He staggered, but recovered, and in an imperative voice ordered the dog to heel.

Then he turned on David, seized the stake from his hand, and began furiously belaboring the boy.

"I'll teach ye to strike—a puir—dumb— harmless—creetur, ye—cruel—cruel—lad!" he cried. "Hoo daur ye strike—ma—Wullie? yer—father's—Wullie? Adam—M'Adam's— Red Wull?" He was panting from his exertions, and his eyes were blazing. "I pit up as best I can wi' all manner o' disrespect to masel'; but when it comes to takin' ma puir Wullie, I canna thole it. Ha' ye no heart?" he asked, unconscious of the irony of the question.

"As much as some, I reck'n," David muttered.

"Eh, what's that? What d'ye say?"

"Ye may thrash me till ye're blind; and it's nob'but yer duty; but if only one daurs so much as to look at yer Wullie ye're mad," the boy answered bitterly. And with that he turned away defiantly and openly in the direction of Kenmuir.

M'Adam made a step forward, and then stopped.

"I'll see ye agin, ma lad, this evenin'," he cried with cruel significance.

"I doot but yo'll be too drunk to see owt—except, 'appen, your bottle," the boy shouted back; and swaggered down the hill.

.   .   .   .   .

At Kenmuir that night the marked and particular kindness of Elizabeth Moore was too much for the overstrung lad. Overcome by the contrast of her sweet motherliness, he burst into a storm of invective against his father, his home, his life—everything.

"Don't 'ee, Davie, don't 'ee, dearie!" cried Mrs. Moore, much distressed. And taking him to her she talked to the great, sobbing boy as though he were a child. At length he lifted his face and looked up; and, seeing the white, wan countenance of his dear comforter, was struck with tender remorse that he had given way and pained her, who looked so frail and thin herself.

He mastered himself with an effort; and, for the rest of the evening, was his usual cheery self. He teased Maggie into tears; chaffed stolid little Andrew; and bantered Sam'l Todd until that generally impassive man threatened to bash his snout for him.

Yet it was with a great swallowing at his throat that, later, he turned down the slope for home.

James Moore and Parson Leggy accompanied him to the bridge over the Wastrel, and stood a while watching as he disappeared into the summer night.

"Yon's a good lad," said the Master half to himself.

"Yes," the parson replied ; "I always thought there was good in the boy, if only his father'd give him a chance. And look at the way Owd Bob there follows him. There's not another soul outside Kenmuir he'd do that for."

"Ay, sir," said the Master. "Bob knows a mon when he sees one."

"He does," acquiesced the other. "And by the by, James, the talk in the village is that you've settled not to run him for the Cup. Is that so?"

The Master nodded.

"It is, sir. They're all mad I should, but I mun cross 'em. They say he's reached his prime—and so he has o' his body, but not o' his brain. And a sheep-dog—unlike other dogs—is not at his best till his brain is at its best—and that takes a while developin', same as in a mon, I reck'n."

"Well, well," said the parson, pulling out a favorite phrase, "waiting's winning—waiting's winning."

.   .   .   .   .

David slipped up into his room and into bed unseen, he hoped. Alone with the darkness, he allowed himself the rare relief of tears; and at length fell asleep. He awoke to find his father standing at his bedside. The little man held a feeble dip-candle in his hand, which lit his sallow face in crude black and white. In the doorway, dimly outlined, was the great figure of Red Wull.

"Whaur ha' ye been the day?" the little man asked. Then, looking down on the white stained face beneath him, he added hurriedly: "If ye like to lie, I'll believe ye."

David was out of bed and standing up in his night-shirt. He looked at his father contemptuously.

"I ha' bin at Kenmuir. I'll not lie for yo' or your likes," he said proudly.

The little man shrugged his shoulders.

" 'Tell a lee and stick to it,' is my rule, and

a good one, too, in honest England. I for one
'll no think ony the worse o' ye if yer memory
plays yer false."

"D'yo' think I care a kick what yo' think o'
me?" the boy asked brutally. "Nay; there's
'nough liars in this fam'ly wi'oot me."

The candle trembled and was still again.

"A lickin' or a lie—tak' yer choice!"

The boy looked scornfully down on his
father. Standing on his naked feet, he already towered half a head above the other and
was twice the man.

"D'yo' think I'm fear'd o' a thrashin' fra
yo'? Goo' gracious me!" he sneered. "Why,
I'd as lief let owd Grammer Maddox lick me,
for all I care."

A reference to his physical insufficiencies
fired the little man as surely as a lighted match
powder.

"Ye maun be cauld, standin' there so.
Rin ye doon and fetch oor little frien'"—a
reference to a certain strap hanging in the
kitchen. "I'll see if I can warm ye."

David turned and stumbled down the unlit,
narrow stairs. The hard, cold boards struck
like death against his naked feet. At his heels
followed Red Wull, his hot breath fanning the
boy's bare legs.

So into the kitchen and back up the stairs,
and Red Wull always following.

"I'll no despair yet o' teachin' ye the fifth
commandment, though I kill masel' in doin'

it!'' cried the little man, seizing the strap from
the boy's numb grasp.

.　　.　　.　　　　.

When it was over, M'Adam turned, breathless, away. At the threshold of the room he
stopped and looked round: a little, dim-lit,
devilish figure, framed in the door; while from
the blackness behind, Red Wull's eyes gleamed
yellow.

Glancing back, the little man caught such an
expression on David's face that for once he
was fairly afraid. He banged the door and
hobbled actively down the stairs.

CHAPTER VII

THE WHITE WINTER

M'ADAM—in his sober moments at least—
never touched David again; instead, he devoted
himself to the more congenial exercise of the
whiplash of his tongue. And he was wise;
for David, who was already nigh a head the
taller of the two, and comely and strong in
proportion, could, if he would, have taken
his father in the hollow of his hand and crumpled him like a dry leaf. Moreover, with his
tongue, at least, the little man enjoyed the
noble pleasure of making the boy wince. And
so the war was carried on none the less vin-
dictively.

Meanwhile another summer was passing
away, and every day brought fresh proofs of
the prowess of Owd Bob. Tammas, whose
stock of yarns anent Rex son of Rally had
after forty years' hard wear begun to pall on
the loyal ears of even old Jonas, found no lack
of new material now. In the Dalesman's
Daughter in Silverdale and in the Border Ram
at Grammoch-town, each succeeding market
day brought some fresh tale. Men told how
the gray dog had outdone Gypsy Jack, the
sheep-sneak; how he had cut out a Kenmuir

shearling from the very centre of Londesley's pack; and a thousand like stories.

The Gray Dogs of Kenmuir have always been equally heroes and favorites in the Daleland. And the confidence of the Dalesmen in Owd Bob was now invincible. Sometimes on market days he would execute some unaccountable maneuvre, and a strange shepherd would ask: "What's the gray dog at?" To which the nearest Dalesman would reply: "Nay, I canno tell ye! But he's reet enough. Yon's Owd Bob o' Kenmuir."

Whereon the stranger would prick his ears and watch with close attention.

"Yon's Owd Bob o' Kenmuir, is he?" he would say; for already among the faculty the name was becoming known. And never in such a case did the young dog fail to justify the faith of his supporters.

It came, therefore, as a keen disappointment to every Dalesman, from Herbert Trotter, Secretary of the Trials, to little Billy Thornton, when the Master persisted in his decision not to run the dog for the Cup in the approaching Dale Trials; and that though parson, squire, and even Lady Eleanour essayed to shake his purpose. It was nigh fifty years since Rex son o' Rally had won back the Trophy for the land that gave it birth; it was time, they thought, for a Daleland dog, a Gray Dog of Kenmuir—the terms are practically synonymous—to bring it home again. And Tammas, that polished phrase-maker, was only expressing the feelings of every Dalesman in the room when, one night at the Arms, he declared of Owd Bob that "to ha' run was to ha' won." At which M'Adam sniggered audibly and winked at Red Wull. "To ha' run was to ha' one—lickin'; to rin next year'll be to——"

"Win next year." Tammas interposed dogmatically. "Onless"—with shivering sarcasm—"you and yer Wullie are thinkin' o' winnin'."

The little man rose from his solitary seat at the back of the room and pattered across.

"Wullie and I are thinkin' o' t," he whispered loudly in the old man's ear. "And mair: what Adam M'Adam and his Red Wull think o' doin', that, ye may remairk, Mr. Thornton, they do. Next year we rin, and next year— we win. Come, Wullie, we'll leave 'em to chew that"; and he marched out of the room amid the jeers of the assembled topers. When quiet was restored, it was Jim Mason who declared: "One thing certain, win or no, they'll not be far off."

.   .   .   .

Meanwhile the summer ended abruptly. Hard on the heels of a sweltering autumn the winter came down. In that year the Daleland assumed very early its white cloak. The Silver Mere was soon ice-veiled; the Wastrel rolled sullenly down below Kenmuir, its creeks and quiet places tented with jagged sheets of ice; while the Scaur and Muir Pike raised hoary heads against the frosty blue. It was the season still remembered in the North as the White Winter—the worst, they say, since the famous 1808.

For days together Jim Mason was stuck with his bags in the Dalesman's Daughter, and there was no communication between the two Dales. On the Mere Marches the snow massed deep and impassable in thick, billowy drifts. In the Devil's Bowl men said it lay piled some score feet deep. And sheep, seeking shelter in the ghylls and protected spots, were buried and lost in their hundreds.

That is the time to test the hearts of shepherds and sheep-dogs, when the wind runs ice-cold across the waste of white, and the low woods on the upland walks shiver black through a veil of snow, and sheep must be found and folded or lost: a trial of head as well as heart, of resource as well as resolution.

In that winter more than one man and many a dog lost his life in the quiet performance of his duty, gliding to death over the slippery snow-shelves, or overwhelmed beneath an avalanche of the warm, suffocating white: "smoored," as they call it. Many a deed was done, many a death died, recorded only in that Book which holds the names of those—men or animals, souls or no souls—who Tried.

They found old Wrottesley, the squire's head shepherd, lying one morning at Gill's foot, like a statue in its white bed, the snow

gently blowing about the venerable face, calm
and beautiful in death. And stretched upon
his bosom, her master's hands blue, and stiff,
still clasped about her neck, his old dog Jess.
She had huddled there, as a last hope, to keep
the dear, dead master warm, her great heart
riven, hoping where there was no hope.

That night she followed him to herd sheep
in a better land. Death from exposure, Dingley, the vet., gave it; but as little M'Adam,
his eyes dimmer than their wont, declared
huskily; "We ken better, Wullie."

Cyril Gilbraith, a young man not over-
burdened with emotions, told with a sob in his
voice how, at the terrible Rowan Rock, Jim
Mason had stood, impotent, dumb, big-eyed,
watching Betsy—Betsy, the friend and partner
of the last ten years—slipping over the ice-cold
surface, silently appealing to the hand that
had never failed her before—sliding to Eternity.

In the Daleland that winter the endurance
of many a shepherd and his dog was strained
past breaking-point. From the frozen Black
Water to the white-peaked Grammoch Pike
two men only, each always with his shaggy
adjutant, never owned defeat; never turned
back; never failed in a thing attempted.

In the following spring, Mr. Tinkerton, the
squire's agent, declared that James Moore and
Adam M'Adam—Owd Bob, rather, and Red
Wull—had lost between them fewer sheep

than any single farmer on the whole March
Mere Estate—a proud record.

Of the two, many a tale was told that winter.
They were invincible, incomparable; worthy
antagonists.

It was Owd Bob who, when he could not
drive the band of Black Faces over the narrow
Razorback which led to safety, induced them
to *follow* him across that ten-inch death-track,
one by one, like children behind their mistress. It was Red Wull who was seen coming down the precipitous Saddler's How,
shouldering up that grand old gentleman,
King o' the Dale, whose leg was broken.

The gray dog it was who found Cyril Gilbraith
by the White Stones, with a cigarette and a
sprained ankle, on the night the whole village
was out with lanterns searching for the well-
loved young scapegrace. It was the Tailless
Tyke and his master who one bitter evening
came upon little Mrs. Burton, lying in a huddle
beneath the lea of the fast-whitening Druid's
Pillar with her latest baby on her breast. It
was little M'Adam who took off his coat and
wrapped the child in it; little M'Adam who
unwound his plaid, threw it like a breastband
across the dog's great chest, and tied the ends
round the weary woman's waist. Red Wull
it was who dragged her back to the Sylvester
Arms and life, straining like a giant through
the snow, while his master staggered behind
with the babe in his arms. When they reached

the inn it was M'Adam who, with a smile on
his face, told the landlord what he thought
of him for sending his wife across the Marches
on such a day and on *his* errand. To which:
"I'd a cauld," pleaded honest Jem.

For days together David could not cross the
Stony Bottom to Kenmuir. His enforced con-
finement to the Grange led, however, to no
more frequent collisions than usual with his
father. For M'Adam and Red Wull were out
at all hours, in all weathers, night and day,
toiling at their work of salvation.

At last, one afternoon, David managed to
cross the Bottom at a point where a fallen
thorn-tree gave him a bridge over the soft
snow. He stayed but a little while at Kenmuir,
yet when he started for home it was snowing
again.

By the time he had crossed the ice-draped
bridge over the Wastrel, a blizzard was raging.
The wind roared past him, smiting him so that
he could barely stand; and the snow leaped
at him so that he could not see. But he held
on doggedly; slipping, sliding, tripping, down
and up again, with one arm shielding his face.
On, on, into the white darkness, blindly on
sobbing, stumbling, dazed.

At length, nigh dead, he reached the brink
of the Stony Bottom. He looked up and he
looked down, but nowhere in that blinding
mist could he see the fallen thorn-tree. He
took a step forward into the white morass, and

sank up to his thigh. He struggled feebly to free himself, and sank deeper. The snow wreathed, twisting, round him like a white flame, and he collapsed, softly crying, on that soft bed.

"I canna—I canna!" he moaned.

.   .   .   .   .

Little Mrs. Moore, her face whiter and frailer than ever, stood at the window, looking out into the storm.

"I canna rest for thinkin' o' th' lad," she said. Then, turning, she saw her husband, his fur cap down over his ears, buttoning his pilot-coat about his throat, while Owd Bob stood at his feet, waiting.

"Ye're no goin', James?" she asked, anxiously.

"But I am, lass," he answered; and she knew him too well to say more.

So those two went quietly out to save life or lose it, nor counted the cost.

Down a wind-shattered slope—over a spar of ice—up an eternal hill—a forlorn hope.

In a whirlwind chaos of snow, the tempest storming at them, the white earth lashing them, they fought a good fight. In front, Owd Bob, the snow clogging his shaggy coat, his hair cutting like lashes of steel across eyes, his head lowered as he followed the finger of God; and close behind, James Moore, his back stern against the storm, stalwart still, yet swaying like a tree before the wind.

So they battled through to the brink of the Stony Bottom—only to arrive too late.

For, just as the Master peering about him, had caught sight of a shapeless lump lying motionless in front, there loomed across the snow-choked gulf through the white riot of the storm a gigantic figure forging, doggedly forward, his great head down to meet the hurricane. And close behind, buffeted and bruised, stiff and staggering, a little dauntless figure holding stubbornly on, clutching with one hand at the gale; and a shrill voice, whirled away on the trumpet tones of the wind, crying:

"Noo, Wullie, wi' me!

> "'Scots wha' hae wi' Wallace bled !
> Scots wham Bruce has often led !
> Welcome to——!'

Here he is, Wullie!

> "'—or to victorie !'"

The brave little voice died away.   The quest was over; the lost sheep found.   And the last James Moore saw of them was the same small, gallant form, half carrying, half dragging the rescued boy out of the Valley of the Shadow and away.

David was none the worse for his adventure, for on reaching home M'Adam produced a familiar bottle.

"Here's something to warm yer inside, and" —making a feint at the strap on the wall—

"here's something to do the same by yer——
But, Wullie, oot again!"

And out they went—unreckoned heroes.

.   .   .   .   .

It was but a week later, in the very heart of
the bitter time, that there came a day when,
from gray dawn to grayer eve, neither James
Moore nor Owd Bob stirred out into the
wintry white. And the Master's face was
hard and set as it always was in time of trouble.

Outside, the wind screamed down the Dale;
while the snow fell relentlessly; softly finger-
ing the windows, blocking the doors, and pil-
ing deep against the walls. Inside the house
there was a strange quiet; no sound save for
hushed voices, and upstairs the shuffling of
muffled feet.

Below, all day long, Owd Bob patrolled the
passage like some silent, gray spectre.

Once there came a low knocking at the door;
and David, his face and hair and cap smothered in the all-pervading white, came in with
an eddy of snow. He patted Owd Bob, and
moved on tiptoe into the kitchen. To him
came Maggie softly, shoes in hand, with white,
frightened face. The two whispered anxiously
awhile like brother and sister as they were;
then the boy crept quietly away; only a little
pool of water on the floor and wet, treacherous
foot-dabs toward the door testifying to the
visitor.

Toward evening the wind died down, but the mourning flakes still fell.

With the darkening of night Owd Bob retreated to the porch and lay down on his blanket. The light from the lamp at the head of the stairs shone through the crack of open door on his dark head and the eyes that never slept.

The hours passed, and the gray knight still kept his vigil. Alone in the darkness—alone, it almost seemed, in the house—he watched. His head lay motionless along his paws, but the steady gray eyes never flinched or drooped.

Time tramped on on leaden foot, and still he waited; and ever the pain of hovering anxiety was stamped deeper in the gray eyes.

At length it grew past bearing; the hollow stillness of the house overcame him. He rose, pushed open the door, and softly pattered across the passage.

At the foot of the stairs he halted, his forepaws on the first step, his grave face and pleading eyes uplifted, as though he were praying. The dim light fell on the raised head; and the white escutcheon on his breast shone out like the snow on Salmon.

At length, with a sound like a sob, he dropped to the ground, and stood listening, his tail dropping and head raised. Then he turned and began softly pacing up and down, like some velvet-footed sentinel at the gate of death.

Up and down, up and down, softly as the falling snow, for a weary, weary while.

Again he stopped and stood, listening intently, at the foot of the stairs; and his gray coat quivered as though there were a draught.

Of a sudden, the deathly stillness of the house was broken. Upstairs, feet were running hurriedly. There was a cry, and again silence.

A life was coming in; a life was going out.

The minutes passed; hours passed; and, at the sunless dawn, a life passed.

And all through that night of age-long agony the gray figure stood, still as a statue, at the foot of the stairs. Only, when, with the first chill breath of the morning, a dry, quick-quenched sob of a strong man sorrowing for the helpmeet of a score of years, and a tiny cry of a new-born child wailing because its mother was not, came down to his ears, the Gray Watchman dropped his head upon his bosom, and, with a little whimpering note, crept back to his blanket.

A little later the door above opened, and James Moore tramped down the stairs. He looked taller and gaunter than his wont, but there was no trace of emotion on his face.

At the foot of the stairs Owd Bob stole out to meet him. He came crouching up, head and tail down, in a manner no man ever saw before or since. At his master's feet he stopped and whined pitifully.

Then, for one short moment, James Moore's whole face quivered.

"Well, lad," he said, quite low, and his voice broke; "she's awa'!"

That was all; for they were an undemonstrative couple.

Then they turned and went out together into the bleak morning.

CHAPTER VIII

M'ADAM AND HIS COAT

To David M'Adam the loss of gentle Elizabeth Moore was as real a grief as to her children. Yet he manfully smothered his own
aching heart and devoted himself to comforting the mourners at Kenmuir.

In the days succeeding Mrs. Moore's death
the boy recklessly neglected his duties at the
Grange. But little M'Adam forbore to rebuke
him. At times, indeed, he essayed to be pas-
sively kind. David, however, was too deeply
sunk in his great sorrow to note the change.

The day of the funeral came. The earth
was throwing off its ice-fetters; and the Dale
was lost in a mourning mist.

In the afternoon M'Adam was standing at
the window of the kitchen, contemplating the
infinite weariness of the scene, when the door
of the house opened and shut noiselessly. Red
Wull raised himself on to the sill and growled,
and David hurried past the window making for
Kenmuir. M'Adam watched the passing figure
indifferently; then with an angry oath sprang
to the window.

"Bring me back that coat, ye thief!" he

cried, tapping fiercely on the pane. "Tak' it aff at onst, ye muckle gowk, or I'll come and tear it aff ye. D'ye see him, Wullie? the great coof has ma coat—me black coat, new last Michaelmas, and it rainin' 'nough to melt it."

He threw the window up with a bang and leaned out.

"Bring it back, I tell ye, ondootiful, or I'll summons ye. Though ye've no respect for me, ye might have for ma claithes. Ye're too big for yer ain boots, let alane ma coat. D'ye think I had it cut for a elephant? It's burst-in', I tell ye. Tak' it aff! Fetch it here, or I'll e'en send Wullie to bring it!"

David paid no heed except to begin running heavily down the hill. The coat was stretched in wrinkled agony across his back; his big, red wrists protruded like shank-bones from the sleeves; and the little tails flapped wearily in vain attempts to reach the wearer's legs.

M'Adam, bubbling over with indignation, scrambled half through the open window. Then, tickled at the amazing impudence of the thing, he paused, smiled, dropped to the ground again, and watched the uncouth, re-treating figure with chuckling amusement.

"Did ye ever see the like o' that, Wullie?" he muttered. "Ma puir coat—puir wee coatie! it gars me greet to see her in her pain. A man's coat, Wullie, is aften unco sma' for his son's back; and David there is strainin' and

stretchin' her nigh to brakin', for a' the world
as he does ma forbearance. And what's he
care aboot the one or t'ither?—not a finger-
flip."

As he stood watching the disappearing figure
there began the slow tolling of the minute-
bell in the little Dale church. Now near, now
far, now loud, now low, its dull chant rang out
through the mist like the slow-dropping tears of
a mourning world.

M'Adam listened, almost reverently, as the
bell tolled on, the only sound in the quiet Dale.
Outside, a drizzling rain was falling; the snow
dribbled down the hill in muddy tricklets;
and trees and roofs and windows dripped.

And still the bell tolled on, calling up relentlessly sad memories of the long ago.

It was on just such another dreary day, in
just such another December, and not so many
years gone by, that the light had gone forever
out of his life.

The whole picture rose as instant to his eyes
as if it had been but yesterday. That insistent
bell brought the scene surging back to him:
the dismal day; the drizzle; the few mourners; little David decked out in black, his fair
hair contrasting with his gloomy clothes, his
face swollen with weeping; the Dale hushed,
it seemed in death, save for the tolling of the
bell; and his love had left him and gone to the
happy land the hymn-books talk of.

Red Wull, who had been watching him un-

easily, now came up and shoved his muzzle
into his master's hand. The cold touch brought
the little man back to earth. He shook
himself, turned wearily away from the window,
and went to the door of the house.

He stood there looking out; and all round
him was the eternal drip, drip of the thaw.
The wind lulled, and again the minute-bell
tolled out clear and inexorable, resolute to
recall what was and what had been.

With a choking gasp the little man turned
into the house, and ran up the stairs and into
his room. He dropped on his knees beside
the great chest in the corner, and unlocked the
bottom drawer, the key turning noisily in its
socket.

In the drawer he searched with feverish
fingers, and produced at length a little paper
packet wrapped about with a stained yellow
ribbon. It was the ribbon she had used to
weave on Sundays into her soft hair.

Inside the packet was a cheap, heart-shaped
frame, and in it a photograph.

Up there it was too dark to see. The little
man ran down the stairs, Red Wull jostling
him as he went, and hurried to the window in
the kitchen.

It was a sweet, laughing face that looked up
at him from the frame, demure yet arch, shy
yet roguish—a face to look at and a face to love.

As he looked a wintry smile, wholly tender,
half tearful, stole over the little man's face.

"Lassie," he whispered, and his voice was infinitely soft, "it's lang sin' I've daured look at ye. But it's no that ye're forgotten, dearie."

Then he covered his eyes with his hand as though he were blinded.

"Dinna look at me sae, lass!" he cried, and fell on his knees, kissing the picture, hugging it to him and sobbing passionately.

Red Wull came up and pushed his face compassionately into his master's; but the little man shoved him roughly away, and the dog retreated into a corner, abashed and reproachful.

Memories swarmed back on the little man.

It was more than a decade ago now, and yet he dared barely think of that last evening when she had lain so white and still in the little room above.

"Pit the bairn on the bed, Adam man," she had said in low tones. "I'll be gaein' in a wee while noo. It's the lang good-by to you—and him."

He had done her bidding and lifted David up. The tiny boy lay still a moment, looking at this white-faced mother whom he hardly recognized.

"Minnie!" he called piteously. Then, thrusting a small, dirty hand into his pocket, he pulled out a grubby sweet.

"Minnie, ha' a sweetie—ain o' Davie's sweeties!" and he held it out anxiously in his

warm plump palm, thinking it a certain cure
for any ill.

"Eat it for mither," she said, smiling tenderly; and then: "Davie, ma heart, I'm leavin'
ye."

The boy ceased sucking the sweet, and looked
at her, the corners of his mouth drooping
pitifully.

"Ye're no gaein' awa', mither?" he asked,
his face all working. "Ye'll no leave yer wee
laddie?"

"Ay, laddie, awa'—reet awa'. HE's callin'
me." She tried to smile; but her mother's
heart was near to bursting.

"Ye'll tak' yer wee Davie wi' ye mither!"
the child pleaded, crawling up toward her face.

The great tears rolled, unrestrained, down
her wan cheeks, and M'Adam, at the head of
the bed, was sobbing openly.

"Eh, ma bairn, ma bairn, I'm sair to leave
ye!" she cried brokenly. "Lift him for me,
Adam."

He placed the child in her arms; but she
was too weak to hold him. So he laid him
upon his mother's pillows; and the boy
wreathed his soft arms about her neck and
sobbed tempestuously.

And the two lay thus together.

Just before she died, Flora turned her head
and whispered:

"Adam, ma man, ye'll ha' to be mither and
father baith to the lad noo"; and she looked

at him with tender confidence in her dying eyes.

"I wull! afore God as I stan' here I wull!" he declared passionately. Then she died, and there was a look of ineffable peace upon her face.

.　　　.　　　.　　　.

"Mither and father baith!"

The little man rose to his feet and flung the photograph from him. Red Wull pounced upon it; but M'Adam leapt at him as he mouthed it.

"Git awa', ye devil!" he screamed; and, picking it up, stroked it lovingly with trembling fingers.

"Maither and father baith!"

How had he fulfilled his love's last wish? How!

"Oh God!"—and he fell upon his knees at the table-side, hugging the picture, sobbing and praying.

Red Wull cowered in the far corner of the room, and then crept whining up to where his master knelt. But M'Adam heeded him not, and the great dog slunk away again.

There the little man knelt in the gloom of the winter's afternoon, a miserable penitent. His gray-flecked head was bowed upon his arms; his hands clutched the picture; and he prayed aloud in gasping, halting tones.

"Gie me grace, O God! 'Father and mither baith,' ye said, Flora—and I ha'na done it.

But 'tis no too late—say it's no, lass. **Tell**
me there's time yet, and say ye forgie me.
I've tried to bear wi' him mony and mony a
time. But he's vexed me, and set himself
agin me, and stiffened my back, and ye ken
hoo I was aye quick to tak' offence. But I'll
mak' it up to him—mak' it up to him, and
mair. I'll humble masel' afore him, and that'll
be bitter enough. And I'll be father and
mither baith to him. But there's bin none to
help me; and it's bin sair wi'oot ye. And—
but, eh, lassie, I'm wearyin' for ye!"

    .   .   .   .   .

It was a dreary little procession that wound
in the drizzle from Kenmuir to the little Dale
Church. At the head stalked James Moore,
and close behind David in his meagre coat.
While last of all, as if to guide the stragglers
in the weary road, come Owd Bob.

There was a full congregation in the tiny
church now. In the squire's pew were Cyril
Gilbraith, Muriel Sylvester, and, most conspicuous, Lady Eleanour. Her slender figure
was simply draped in gray, with gray fur
about the neck and gray fur edging sleeves and
jacket; her veil was lifted, and you could see
the soft hair about her temples, like waves
breaking on white cliffs, and her eyes big with
tender sympathy as she glanced toward the
pew upon her right.

For there were the mourners from Kenmuir:
the Master, tall, grim, and gaunt; and beside

him Maggie, striving to be calm, and little
Andrew, the miniature of his father.

Alone, in the pew behind, David M'Adam
in his father's coat.

The back of the church was packed with
farmers from the whole March Mere Estate;
friends from Silverdale and Grammoch-town;
and nearly every soul in Wastrel-dale, come
to show their sympathy for the living and
reverence for the dead.

.   .   .   .   .

At last the end came in the wet dreariness
of the little churchyard, and slowly the mourners departed, until at length were left only the
parson, the Master, and Owd Bob.

The parson was speaking in rough, short
accents, digging nervously at the wet ground.
The other, tall and gaunt, his face drawn and
half-averted, stood listening. By his side was
Owd Bob, scanning his master's countenance,
a wistful compassion deep in the sad gray eyes;
while close by, one of the parson's terriers was
nosing inquisitively in the wet grass.

Of a sudden, James Moore, his face still
turned away, stretched out a hand. The parson, broke off abruptly and grasped it. Then
the two men strode away in opposite directions,
the terrier hopping on three legs and shaking
the rain off his hard coat.

.   .   .   .   .

David's steps sounded outside.   M'Adam
rose from his knees. The door of the house

opened, and the boy's feet shuffled in the passage.

"David!" the little man called in a tremulous voice.

He stood in the half-light, one hand on the table, the other clasping the picture. His eyes were bleared, his thin hair all tossed, and he was shaking.

"David," he called again; "I've somethin' I wush to say to ye!"

The boy burst into the room. His face was stained with tears and rain; and the new black coat was wet and slimy all down the front, and on the elbows were green-brown, muddy blots. For, on his way home, he had flung himself down in the Stony Bottom just as he was, heedless of the wet earth and his father's coat, and, lying on his face thinking of that second mother lost to him, had wept his heart out in a storm of passionate grief.

Now he stood defiantly, his hand upon the door.

"What d'yo' want?"

The little man looked from him to the picture in his hand.

"Help me, Flora—he'll no," he prayed. Then raising his eyes, he began: "I'd like to say—I've bin thinkin'—I think I should tell ye—it's no an easy thing for a man to say——"

He broke off short. The self-imposed task was almost more than he could accomplish.

He looked appealingly at David. But there

was no glimmer of understanding in that white, set countenance.

"O God, it's maist mair than I can do!" the little man muttered; and the perspiration stood upon his forehead. Again he began: "David, after I saw ye this afternoon steppin' doon the hill——"

Again he paused. His glance rested unconsciously upon the coat. David mistook the look; mistook the dimness in his father's eyes; mistook the tremor in his voice.

"Here 'tis! tak' yo' coat!" he cried passionately; and, tearing it off, flung it down at his father's feet. "Tak' it—and—and—curse yo'."

He banged out of the room and ran upstairs; and, locking himself in, threw himself on to his bed and sobbed.

Red Wull made a movement to fly at the retreating figure; then turned to his master, his stump-tail vibrating with pleasure.

But little M'Adam was looking at the wet coat now lying in a wet bundle at his feet.

"Curse ye," he repeated softly. "Curse ye —ye heard him, Wullie?"

A bitter smile crept across his face. He looked again at the picture now lying crushed in his hand.

"Ye canna say I didna try; ye canna ask me to agin," he muttered, and slipped it into his pocket. "Niver agin, Wullie; not if the Queen were to ask it."

Then he went out into the gloom and drizzle, still smiling the same bitter smile.

.   .   .   .   .

That night, when it came to closing-time at the Sylvester Arms, Jem Burton found a little gray-haired figure lying on the floor in the tap-room. At the little man's head lay a great dog.

"Yo' beast!" said the righteous publican, regarding the figure of his best customer with fine scorn. Then catching sight of a photograph in the little man's hand:

"Oh, yo're that sort, are yo', foxy?" he leered. "Gie us a look at 'er," and he tried to disengage the picture from the other's grasp. But at the attempt the great dog rose, bared his teeth, and assumed such a diabolical expression that the big landlord retreated hurriedly behind the bar.

"Two on ye!" he shouted viciously, rattling his heels; "beasts baith!"

PART III

———

THE SHEPHERDS' TROPHY

CHAPTER IX

RIVALS

M'ADAM never forgave his son. After the
scene on the evening of the funeral there could
be no alternative but war for all time. The
little man had attempted to humble himself,
and been rejected; and the bitterness of defeat, when he had deserved victory, rankled
like a poisoned barb in his bosom.

Yet the heat of his indignation was directed
not against David, but against the Master of
Kenmuir. To the influence and agency of
James Moore he attributed his discomfiture,
and bore himself accordingly. In public or in
private, in tap-room or market, he never
wearied of abusing his enemy.

"Feel the loss o' his wife, d'ye say?" he
would cry. "Ay, as muckle as I feel the loss
o' my hair. James Moore can feel naethin',
I tell ye, except, aiblins, a mischance to his
meeserable dog."

When the two met, as they often must, it
was always M'Adam's endeavor to betray his
enemy into an unworthy expression of feeling.
But James Moore, sorely tried as he often
was, never gave way. He met the little man's
sneers with a quelling silence, looking down

on his asp-tongued antagonist with such a contempt flashing from his blue-gray eyes as hurt
his adversary more than words.

Only once was he spurred into reply. It
was in the tap-room of the Dalesman's Daughter on the occasion of the big spring fair in
Grammoch-town, when there was a goodly
gathering of farmers and their dogs in the
room.

M'Adam was standing at the fireplace with
Red Wull at his side.

"It's a noble pairt ye play, James Moore,"
he cried loudly across the room, "settin' son
against father, and dividin' hoose against hoose.
It's worthy o' ye we' yer churchgoin', and
yer psalm-singin', and yer godliness."

The Master looked up from the far end of
the room.

"Happen yo're not aware, M'Adam," he
said sternly, "that, an' it had not bin for me,
David'd ha' left you years agone—and 'twould
nob'but ha' served yo' right, I'm thinkin'."

The little man was beaten on his own ground,
so he changed front.

"Dinna shout so, man—I have ears to hear.
Forbye ye irritate Wullie."

The Tailless Tyke, indeed, had advanced
from the fireplace, and now stood, huge and
hideous, in the very centre of the room.
There was distant thunder in his throat, a
threat upon his face, a challenge in every
wrinkle. And the Gray Dog stole gladly out

from behind his master to take up the gage of battle.

Straightway there was silence; tongues ceased to wag, tankards to clink. Every man and every dog was quietly gathering about those two central figures. Not one of them all but had his score to wipe off against the Tailless Tyke; not one of them but was burning to join in, the battle once begun. And the two gladiators stood looking past one another, muzzle to muzzle, each with a tiny flash of teeth glinting between his lips.

But the fight was not to be; for the twentieth time the Master intervened.

"Bob, lad, coom in!" he called, and, bending, grasped his favorite by the neck.

M'Adam laughed softly.

"Wullie, Wullie, to me!" he cried. "The look o' you's enough for that gentleman."

"If they get fightin' it'll no be Bob here I'll hit, I warn yo', M'Adam," said the Master grimly.

"Gin ye sae muckle as touched Wullie d'ye ken what I'd do, James Moore?" asked the little man very smoothly.

"Yes—sweer," the other replied, and strode out of the room amid a roar of derisive laughter at M'Adam's expense.

Owd Bob had now attained wellnigh the perfection of his art. Parson Leggy declared roundly that his like had not been seen since the days of Rex son of Rally. Among the

Dalesmen he was a heroic favorite, his prowess
and gentle ways winning him friends on every
hand. But the point that told most heavily
for him was that in all things he was the very
antithesis of Red Wull.

Barely a man in the country-side but owed
that ferocious savage a grudge; not a man of
them all who dared pay it.   Once Long Kirby,
full of beer and valor, tried to settle his account.   Coming on M'Adam and Red Wull as
he was driving into Grammoch-town, he lent
over and with his thong dealt the dog a terrible
sword-like slash that raised an angry ridge of
red from hip to shoulder; and was twenty
yards down the road before the little man's
shrill curse reached his ear, drowned in a hideous bellow.

He stood up and lashed the colt, who, quick
on his legs for a young un, soon settled to
his gallop. But, glancing over his shoulder,
he saw a hounding form behind, catching him
as though he were walking. His face turned
sickly white; he screamed; he flogged; he
looked back. Right beneath the tail-board
was the red devil in the dust; while racing a
furlong behind on the turnpike road was the
mad figure of M'Adam.

The smith struck back and flogged forward.
It was of no avail. With a tiger-like bound
the murderous brute leapt on the flying trap.
At the shock of the great body the colt was
thrown violently on his side ; Kirby was tossed

over the hedge; and Red Wull pinned beneath the débris.

M'Adam had time to rush up and save a tragedy.

"I've a mind to knife ye, Kirby," he panted, as he bandaged the smith's broken head.

After that you may be sure the Dalesmen preferred to swallow insults rather than to risk their lives; and their impotence only served to fan their hatred to white heat.

The working methods of the antagonists were as contrasted as their appearances. In a word, the one compelled where the other coaxed.

His enemies said the Tailless Tyke was rough; not even Tammas denied he was ready. His brain was as big as his body, and he used them both to some purpose. "As quick as a cat, with the heart of a lion and the temper of Nick's self," was Parson Leggy's description.

What determination could effect, that could Red Wull; but achievement by inaction—supremest of all strategies—was not for him. In matters of the subtlest handling, where to act anything except indifference was to lose, with sheep restless, fearful forebodings hymned to them by the wind, panic hovering unseen above them, when an ill-considered movement spelt catastrophe—then was Owd Bob o' Kenmuir incomparable.

Men still tell how, when the squire's new

thrashing-machine ran amuck in Grammoch-town, and for some minutes the market square was a turbulent sea of blaspheming men, yelp-ing dogs, and stampeding sheep, only one flock stood calm as a mill-pond by the bull-ring, watching the riot with almost indifference. And in front, sitting between them and the storm, was a quiet gray dog, his mouth stretched in a capacious yawn: to yawn was to win, and he won.

When the worst of the uproar was over, many a glance of triumph was shot first at that one still pack, and then at M'Adam, as he waded through the disorder of huddling sheep.

"And wheer's your Wullie noo?" asked Tupper scornfully.

"Weel," the little man answered with a quiet smile, "at this minute he's killin' your Rasper doon by the pump." Which was in-deed the case; for big blue Rasper had inter-fered with the great dog in the performance of his duty, and suffered accordingly.

.   .   .   .   .

Spring passed into summer; and the excite-ment as to the event of the approaching Trials, when at length the rivals would be pitted against one another, reached such a height as old Jonas Maddox, the octogenarian, could hardly recall.

Down in the Sylvester Arms there was al-most nightly a conflict between M'Adam and Tammas Thornton, spokesman of the Dales-

men. Many a long-drawn bout of words had
the two anent the respective merits and Cup
chances of red and gray. In these duels Tammas was usually worsted. His temper would
get the better of his discretion; and the cynical
debater would be lost in the hot-tongued
partisan.

During these encounters the others would,
as a rule, maintain a rigid silence. Only when
their champion was being beaten, and it was
time for strength of voice to vanquish strength
of argument, they joined in right lustily and
.oared the little man down, for all the world
like the gentlemen who rule the Empire at
Westminster.

Tammas was an easy subject for M'Adam to
draw, but David was an easier. Insults directed at himself the boy bore with a stolidity
born of long use. But a poisonous dart shot
against his friends at Kenmuir never failed to
achieve its object. And the little man evinced
an amazing talent for the concoction of deft
lies respecting James Moore.

"I'm hearin'," said he, one evening, sitting
in the kitchen, sucking his twig; "I'm hearin'
James Moore is gaein' to git married agin."

"Yo're hearin' lies — or mair-like tellin'
'em," David answered shortly. For he treated
his father now with contemptuous indifference.

"Seven months sin' his wife died," the little
man continued meditatively. "Weel, I'm on'y

'stonished he's waited sae lang. Ain buried, anither come on—that's James Moore."

David burst angrily out of the room.

"Gaein' to ask him if it's true?" called his father after him. "Gude luck to ye—and him."

David had now a new interest at Kenmuir. In Maggie he found an endless source of study. On the death of her mother the girl had taken up the reins of government at Kenmuir; and gallantly she played her part, whether in tenderly mothering the baby, wee Anne, or in the sterner matters of household work. She did her duty, young though she was, with a surprising, old-fashioned womanliness that won many a smile of approval from her father, and caused David's eyes to open with astonishment.

And he soon discovered that Maggie, mistress of Kenmuir, was another person from his erstwhile playfellow and servant.

The happy days when might ruled right were gone, never to be recalled. David often regretted them, especially when in a conflict of tongues, Maggie, with her quick answers and teasing eyes, was driving him sulky and vanquished from the field. The two were perpetually squabbling now. In the good old days, he remembered bitterly, squabbles between them were unknown. He had never permitted them; any attempt at independent thought or action was as sternly quelled as in the Middle Ages. She must follow where he led on—"Ma word!"

Now she was mistress where he had been master; hers was to command, his to obey. In consequence they were perpetually at war. And yet he would sit for hours in the kitchen and watch her, as she went about her business, with solemn, interested eyes, half of admiration, half of amusement. In the end Maggie always turned on him with a little laugh touched with irritation.

"Han't yo' got nothin' better'n that to do, nor lookin' at me?" she asked one Saturday about a month before Cup Day.

"No, I han't," the pert fellow rejoined.

"Then I wish yo' had. It mak's me fair jumpety yo' watchin' me so like ony cat a mouse."

"Niver yo' fash yo'sel' account o' me, ma wench," he answered calmly.

"Yo' wench, indeed!" she cried, tossing her head.

"Ay, or will be," he muttered.

"What's that?" she cried, springing round, a flush of color on her face.

"Nowt, my dear. Yo'll know so soon as I want yo' to, yo' may be sure, and no sooner."

The girl resumed her baking, half angry, half suspicious.

"I dunno' what yo' mean, Mr. M'Adam," she said.

"Don't yo', Mrs. M'A——"

The rest was lost in the crash of a falling plate; whereat David laughed quietly, and asked if he should help pick up the bits.

.   .   .   .   .

On the same evening at the Sylvester Arms an announcement was made that knocked the breath out of its hearers.

In the debate that night on the fast-approaching Dale Trials and the relative abilities of red and gray, M'Adam on the one side, and Tammas, backed by Long Kirby and the rest, on the other, had cudgelled each other with more than usual vigor. The controversy rose to fever-heat; abuse succeeded argument; and the little man again and again was hooted into silence.

"It's easy laffin'," he cried at last, "but ye'll laff t'ither side o' yer ugly faces on Cup Day."

"Will us, indeed? Us'll see," came the derisive chorus.

"We'll whip ye till ye're deaf, dumb, and blind, Wullie and I."

"Yo'll not!"

"We will!"

The voices were rising like the east wind in March.

"Yo'll not, and for a very good reason too," asseverated Tammas loudly.

"Gie us yer reason, ye muckle liar," cried the little man, turning on him.

"Becos——" began Jim Mason and stopped to rub his nose.

"Yo' 'old yo ' noise, Jim," recommended Rob Saunderson.

"Becos——" it was Tammas this time who paused.

"Git on wi' it, ye stammerin' stirk!" cried M'Adam. "Why?"

"Becos—Owd Bob'll not rin."

Tammas sat back in his chair.

"What!" screamed the little man, thrusting forward.

"What's that!" yelled Long Kirby, leaping to his feet.

"Mon, say it agin!" shouted Rob.

"What's owd addled egg tellin'?" cried Liz Burton.

"Dang his 'ead for him!" shouts Tupper.

"Fill his eye!" says Ned Hoppin.

They jostled round the old man's chair: M'Adam in front; Jem Burton and Long Kirby leaning over his shoulder; Liz behind her father; Saunderson and Tupper tackling him on either side; while the rest peered and elbowed in the rear.

The announcement had fallen like a thunderbolt among them.

Tammas looked slowly up at the little mob of eager faces above him.   Pride at the sensation caused by his news struggled in his countenance with genuine sorrow for the matter of it.

"Ay, yo' may well 'earken all on yo'.   Tis enough to mak' the deadies listen.   I says

agin: We's'll no rin oor Bob fot' Cup.   And
yo' may guess why.   Bain't every mon, Mr.
M'Adam, as'd pit aside his chanst o' the Cup,
and that 'maist a gift for him"—M'Adam's
tongue was in his cheek—"and it a certainty,"
the old man continued warmly, "oot o' respect
for his wife's memory."

The news was received in utter silence.
The shock of the surprise, coupled with the
bitterness of the disappointment, froze the
slow tongues of his listeners.

Only one small voice broke the stillness.

"Oh, the feelin' man! He should git a re-
duction o' rent for sic a display o' proper
speerit.   I'll mind Mr. Hornbut to let auld
Sylvester ken o't."

Which he did, and would have got a thrashing for his pains had not Cyril Gilbraith thrown
him out of the parsonage before the angry
cleric could lay hands upon him.

CHAPTER X

TAMMAS had but told the melancholy truth.
Owd Bob was not to run for the cup. And
this self-denying ordinance speaks more for
James Moore's love of his lost wife than many
a lordly cenotaph.

To the people of the Daleland, from the
Black Water to the market-cross in Grammoch-
town, the news came with the shock of a sudden blow. They had set their hearts on the
Gray Dog's success; and had felt serenely
confident of his victory. But the sting of
the matter lay in this: that now the Tailless
Tyke might well win.

M'Adam, on the other hand, was plunged
into a fervor of delight at the news. For to
win the Shepherds' Trophy was the goal of his
ambition. David was now less than nothing
to the lonely little man, Red Wull everything
to him. And to have that name handed down
to posterity, gallantly holding its place among
those of the most famous sheep-dogs of all
time, was his heart's desire.

As Cup Day drew near, the little man, his
fine-drawn temperament strung to the highest
pitch of nervousness, was tossed on a sea of

apprehension. His hopes and fears ebbed and
flowed on the tide of the moment. His moods
were as uncertain as the winds in March; and
there was no dependence on his humor for a
unit of time. At one minute he paced up and
down the kitchen, his face already flushed with
the glow of victory, chanting:

"Scots wha hae wi' Wallace bled!"

At the next he was down at the table, his
head buried in his hands, his whole figure
shaking, as he cried in choking voice: "Eh,
Wullie, Wullie, they're all agin us."

David found that life with his father now was
life with an unamiable hornet. Careless as he
affected to be of his father's vagaries, he was
tried almost to madness, and fled away at every
moment to Kenmuir; for, as he told Maggie,
"I'd sooner put up wi' your h'airs and h'im-
perences, miss, than wi' him, the wemon that
he be!"

.   .   .   .   .

At length the great day came. Fears,
hopes, doubts, dismays, all dispersed in the
presence of the reality.

Cup Day is always a general holiday in the
Daleland, and every soul crowds over to Silverdale. Shops were shut; special trains ran in
to Grammoch-town; and the road from the
little town was dazed with char-a-bancs, brakes,
wagonettes, carriages, carts, foot-passengers,
wending toward the Dalesman's Daughter.

And soon the paddock below that little inn
was humming with the crowd of sportsmen
and spectators come to see the battle for the
Shepherd's Trophy.

There, very noticeable with its red body and
yellow wheels, was the great Kenmuir wagon.
Many an eye was directed on the handsome
young pair who stood in it, conspicuous and
unconscious, above the crowd: Maggie, looking in her simple print frock as sweet and
fresh as any mountain flower; while David's fair face was all gloomy and his brows
knit.

In front of the wagon was a black cluster of
Dalesmen, discussing M'Adam's chances. In
the centre was Tammas holding forth. Had
you passed close to the group you might have
heard: "A man, d'yo say, Mr. Maddox? A
h'ape, I call him"; or: "A dog? more like an
'og, I tell yo'." Round the old orator were
Jonas, 'Enry, and oor Job, Jem Burton, Rob
Saunderson, Tupper, Jim Mason, Hoppin, and
others; while on the outskirts stood Sam'l
Todd prophesying rain and M'Adam's victory.
Close at hand Bessie Bolstock, who was reputed
to have designs on David, was giggling spite-
fully at the pair in the Kenmuir wagon, and
singing:

> "Let a lad aloan, lass,
> Let a lad a-be."

While her father, Teddy, dodged in and out
among the crowd with tray and glasses: for

Cup Day was the great day of the year for
him.

Past the group of Dalesmen and on all sides
was a mass of bobbing heads—Scots, Northerners, Yorkshiremen, Taffies. To right and
left a long array of carriages and carts, rang-
ing from the squire's quiet landau and Viscount Birdsaye's gorgeous barouche to Liz
Burton's three-legged moke-cart with little
Mrs. Burton, the twins, young Jake (who
should have walked), and Monkey (ditto)
packed away inside. Beyond the Silver Lea
the gaunt Scaur raised its craggy peak, and
the Pass, trending along its side, shone white
in the sunshine.

At the back of the carriages were booths,
cocoanut-shies, Aunt Sallies, shows, bookmakers' stools, and all the panoply of such a
meeting. Here Master Launcelot Bilks and
Jacky Sylvester were fighting; Cyril Gilbraith
was offering to take on the boxing man; Long
Kirby was snapping up the odds against Red
Wull; and Liz Burton and young Ned Hoppin were being photographed together, while
Melia Ross in the background was pretending
she didn't care.

On the far bank of the stream was a little
bevy of men and dogs, observed of all.

The Juvenile Stakes had been run and won;
Londesley's Lassie had carried off the Locals;
and the fight for the Shepherds' Trophy was
about to begin.

"Yo're not lookin' at me noo," whispered Maggie to the silent boy by her side.

"Nay; nor niver don't wush to agin." David answered roughly. His gaze was directed over the array of heads in front to where, beyond the Silver Lea, a group of shepherds and their dogs was clustered. While standing apart from the rest, in characteristic isolation, was the bent figure of his father, and beside him the Tailless Tyke.

"Doest'o not want yo' feyther to win?" asked Maggie softly, following his gaze.

"I'm prayin' he'll be beat," the boy answered moodily.

"Eh, Davie, hoo can ye?" cried the girl, shocked.

"It's easy to say, 'Eh, David,' " he snapped. "But if yo' lived along o' them two "—he nodded toward the stream—"'appen yo'd understand a bit. . . . . 'Eh, David,' indeed! I never did!"

"I know it, lad," she said tenderly; and he was appeased.

"He'd give his right hand for his bless'd Wullie to win; I'd give me right arm to see him beat. . . . And oor Bob there all the while,—he nodded to the far left of the line, where stood James Moore and Owd Bob, with Parson Leggy and the Squire.

When at length Red Wull came out to run his course, he worked with the savage dash that always characterized him. His method was his own; but the work was admirably done.

"Keeps right on the back of his sheep," said the parson, watching intently. "Strange thing they don't break!" But they didn't. There was no waiting, no coaxing; it was drive and devilry all through. He brought his sheep along at a terrific rate, never missing a turn, never faltering, never running out. And the crowd applauded, for the crowd loves a dashing display. While little M'Adam, hopping agilely about, his face ablaze with excitement, handled dog and sheep with a masterly precision that compelled the admiration even of his enemies.

"M'Adam wins!" roared a bookmaker. "Twelve to one agin the field!"

"He wins, dang him!" said David, low.

"Wull wins!" said the parson, shutting his lips.

"And deserves too!" said James Moore.

"Wull wins!" softly cried the crowd.

"We don't!" said Sam'l gloomily.

And in the end Red Wull did win; and there were none save Tammas, the bigot, and Long Kirby, who had lost a good deal of his wife's money and a little of his own, to challenge the justice of the verdict.

The win had but a chilling reception. At first there was faint cheering; but it sounded like the echo of an echo, and soon died of inanition. To get up an ovation, there must be

money at the back, or a few roaring fanatics
to lead the dance. Here there was neither;
ugly stories, disparaging remarks, on every
hand. And the hundreds who did not know
took their tone, as always, from those who
said they did.

M'Adam could but remark the absence of
enthusiasm as he pushed up through the
throng toward the committee tent. No single
voice hailed him victor; no friendly hand
smote its congratulations. Broad backs were
turned; contemptuous glances levelled; spite-
ful remarks shot. Only the foreign element
looked curiously at the little bent figure with
the glowing face, and shrank back at the size
and savage aspect of the great dog at his
heels.

But what cared he? His Wullie was acknowledged champion, the best sheep-dog of
the year; and the little man was happy. They
could turn their backs on him; but they could
not alter that; and he could afford to be indifferent. "They dinna like it, lad—he! he!
But they'll e'en ha' to thole it. Ye've won it,
Wullie—won it fair."

He elbowed through the press, making for
the rope-guarded inclosure in front of the committee tent, round which the people were now
packing. In the door of the tent stood the
secretary, various stewards, and members of
the committee. In front, alone in the roped-
off space, was Lady Eleanour, fragile, dainty,

graceful, waiting with a smile upon her face
to receive the winner. And on a table beside her, naked and dignified, the Shepherd's
Trophy.

There it stood, kingly and impressive; its
fair white sides inscribed with many names;
cradled in three shepherds' crooks; and on
the top, as if to guard the Cup's contents, an
exquisitely carved collie's head. The Shepherds' Trophy, the goal of his life's race, and
many another man's.

He climbed over the rope, followed by Red
Wull, and took off his hat with almost courtly
deference to the fair lady before him.

As he walked up to the table on which the
Cup stood, a shrill voice, easily recognizable,
broke the silence.

"You'd like it better if 'twas full and yo'
could swim in it, you and yer Wullie," it
called. Whereat the crowd giggled, and Lady
Eleanour looked indignant.

The little man turned.

"I'll mind drink yer health, Mr. Thornton,
never fear, though I ken ye'd prefaire to drink
yer ain," he said. At which the crowd giggled
afresh; and a gray head at the back, which had
hoped itself unrecognized, disappeared suddenly.

The little man stood there in the stillness,
sourly smiling, his face still wet from his exertions; while the Tailless Tyke at his side
fronted defiantly the serried ring of onlookers,

a white fence of teeth faintly visible between
his lips.

Lady Eleanour looked uneasy. Usually the
lucky winner was unable to hear her little
speech, as she gave the Cup away, so deafening was the applause. Now there was utter
silence. She glanced up at the crowd, but
there was no response to her unspoken appeal
in that forest of hostile faces. And her gentle
heart bled for the forlorn little man before
her. To make it up she smiled on him so
sweetly as to more than compensate him.

"I'm sure you deserve your success, Mr.
M'Adam," she said. "You and Red Wull
there worked splendidly—everybody says so."

"I've heard naethin' o't," the little man answered dryly. At which some one in the crowd
sniggered.

"And we all know what a grand dog he is;
though"—with a reproving smile as she
glanced at Red Wull's square, truncated stern
—"he's not very polite."

"His heart is good, your Leddyship, if his
manners are not," M'Adam answered, smiling.

"Liar!" came a loud voice in the silence.
Lady Eleanour looked up, hot with indignation, and half rose from her seat. But M'Adam
merely smiled.

"Wullie, turn and mak' yer bow to the
leddy," he said. "They'll no hurt us noo
we're up; it's when we're doon they'll flock
like corbies to the carrion."

At that Red Wull walked up to Lady Eleanour, faintly wagging his tail; and she put her
hand on his huge bull head and said, "Dear
old Ugly!" at which the crowd cheered in
earnest.

After that, for some moments, the only
sound was the gentle ripple of the good lady's
voice and the little man's caustic replies.

"Why, last winter the country was full of
Red Wull's doings and yours. It was always
M'Adam and his Red Wull have done this and
that and the other. I declare I got quite tired
of you both, I heard such a lot about you."

The little man, cap in hand, smiled, blushed
and looked genuinely pleased.

"And when it wasn't you it was Mr. Moore
and Owd Bob."

"Owd Bob, bless him!" called a stentorian
voice.   "There cheers for oor Bob!"

" 'Ip! 'ip! 'ooray!" It was taken up gallantly, and cast from mouth to mouth; and
strangers, though they did not understand,
caught the contagion and cheered too; and
the uproar continued for some minutes.

When it was ended Lady Eleanour was
standing up, a faint flush on her cheeks and
her eyes flashing dangerously, like a queen
at bay.

"Yes," she cried, and her clear voice thrilled
through the air like a trumpet. "Yes; and
now three cheers for Mr. M'Adam and his
Red Wull! Hip! hip——"

"Hooray!" A little knowt of stalwarts at the back—James Moore, Parson Leggy, Jim Mason, and you may be sure in heart, at least, Owd Bob—responded to the call right lustily. The crowd joined in; and, once off, cheered and cheered again.

"Three cheers more for Mr. M'Adam!"

But the little man waved to them.

"Dinna be bigger heepocrites than ye can help," he said. "Ye've done enough for one day, and thank ye for it."

Then Lady Eleanour handed him the Cup.

"Mr. M'Adam, I present you with the Champion Challenge Dale Cup, open to all comers. Keep it, guard it, love it as your own, and win it again if you can. Twice more and it's yours, you know, and it will stop forever beneath the shadow of the Pike. And the right place for it, say I—the Dale Cup for Dalesmen."

The little man took the Cup tenderly.

"It shall no leave the Estate or ma hoose, yer Leddyship, gin Wullie and I can help it," he said emphatically.

Lady Eleanour retreated into the tent, and the crowd swarmed over the ropes and round the little man, who held the Cup beneath his arm.

Long Kirby laid irreverent hands upon it.

"Dinna finger it!" ordered M'Adam.

"Shall!"

"Shan't! Wullie, keep him aff." Which

the great dog proceeded to do amid the laughter of the onlookers.

Among the last, James Moore was borne past the little man. At sight of him, M'Adam's face assumed an expression of intense concern.

"Man, Moore!" he cried, peering forward as though in alarm; "man, Moore, ye're green—positeevely verdant. Are ye in pain?" Then, catching sight of Owd Bob, he started back in affected horror.

"And, ma certes! so's yer dog! Yer dog as was gray is green. Oh, guid life!"—and he made as though about to fall fainting to the ground.

Then, in bantering tones: "Ah, but ye shouldna covet——"

"He'll ha' no need to covet it long, I can tell yo'," interposed Tammas's shrill accents.

"And why for no?"

"Becos next year he'll win it fra yo'. Oor Bob'll win it, little mon. Why? thot's why."

The retort was greeted with a yell of applause from the sprinkling of Dalesmen in the crowd.

But M'Adam swaggered away into the tent, his head up, the Cup beneath his arm, and Red Wull guarding his rear.

"First of a' ye'll ha' to beat Adam M'Adam and his Red Wull!" he cried back proudly.

CHAPTER XI

M'ADAM's pride in the great Cup that now graced his kitchen was supreme. It stood alone in the very centre of the mantelpiece, just below the old bell-mouthed blunderbuss that hung upon the wall. The only ornament in the bare room, it shone out in its silvery chastity like the moon in a gloomy sky.

For once the little man was content. Since his mother's death David had never known such peace. It was not that his father became actively kind; rather that he forgot to be actively unkind.

"Not as I care a brazen button one way or t'ither," the boy informed Maggie.

"Then yo' should," that proper little person replied.

M'Adam was, indeed, a changed being. He forgot to curse James Moore; he forgot to sneer at Owd Bob; he rarely visited the Sylvester Arms, to the detriment of Jem Burton's pocket and temper; and he was never drunk.

"Soaks 'isself at home, instead," suggested Tammas, the prejudiced. But the accusation was untrue.

"Too drunk to git so far," said Long Kirby, kindly man.

"I reck'n the Cup is kind o' company to him," said Jim Mason. "Happen it's lonesomeness as drives him here so much." And happen you were right, charitable Jim.

"Best mak' maist on it while he has it, 'cos he'll not have it for long," Tammas remarked amid applause.

Even Parson Leggy allowed—rather reluctantly, indeed, for he was but human—that the little man was changed wonderfully for the better.

"But I am afraid it may not last," he said. "We shall see what happens when Owd Bob beats him for the Cup, as he certainly will. That'll be the critical moment."

As things were, the little man spent all his spare moments with the Cup between his knees, burnishing it and crooning to Wullie:

> "I never saw a fairer,
>   I never lo'ed a dearer,
>   And neist my heart I'll wear her,
>   For fear my jewel tine."

There, Wullie! look at her! is she no bonnie? She shines like a twinkle—twinkle in the sky." And he would hold it out at arm's length, his head cocked sideways the better to scan its bright beauties.

The little man was very jealous for his treasure. David might not touch it; might not smoke in the kitchen lest the fumes should

tarnish its glory; while if he approached too
closely he was ordered abruptly away.

"As if I wanted to touch his nasty Cup!"
he complained to Maggie. "I'd sooner ony
day——"

"Hands aff, Mr. David, immediate!" she
cried indignantly. "'Pertinence, indeed!" as
she tossed her head clear of the big fingers
that were fondling her pretty hair.

So it was that M'Adam, on coming quietly
into the kitchen one day, was consumed with
angry resentment to find David actually handling the object of his reverence; and the manner of his doing it added a thousandfold to the
offence.

The boy was lolling indolently against the
mantelpiece, his fair head shoved right into
the Cup, his breath dimming its lustre, and
his two hands, big and dirty, slowly revolving
it before his eyes.

Bursting with indignation, the little man
crept up behind the boy. David was reading
through the long list of winners.

"Theer's the first on 'em," he muttered,
shooting out his tongue to indicate the local-
ity: "'Andrew Moore's Rough, 178-.' And
theer agin—'James Moore's Pinch, 179-.'
And agin—'Beck, 182-.' Ah, and theer's 'im
Tammas tells on! 'Rex, 183-,' and 'Rex,
183-.' Ay, but he was a rare un by all tellin's! If he'd nob'but won but onst agin!
Ah, and theer's none like the Gray Dogs—they

all says that, and I say so masel'; none like
the Gray Dogs o' Kenmuir, bless 'em! And
we'll win agin too——" he broke off short;
his eye had travelled down to the last name on
the list.

"'M'Adam's Wull'!" he read with unspeak-
able contempt, and put his great thumb across
the name as though to wipe it out. "'M'-
Adam's Wull'! Goo' gracious sakes! P-h-
g-h-r-r!"—and he made a motion as though to
spit upon the ground.

But a little shoulder was into his side, two
small fists were beating at his chest, and a
shrill voice was yelling: "Devil! devil! stan'
awa'!"—and he was tumbled precipitately
away from the mantelpiece, and brought up
abruptly against the side-wall.

The precious Cup swayed on its ebony stand,
the boy's hands, rudely withdrawn, almost
overthrowing it.   But the little man's first im-
pulse, cursing and screaming though he was,
was to steady it.

"'M'Adam's Wull'! I wish he was here to
teach ye, ye snod-faced, ox-limbed profleegit!"
he cried, standing in front of the Cup, his
eyes blazing.

"Ay, 'M'Adam's Wull'!   And why not
'M'Adam's Wull'? Ha' ye any objection to
the name?"

"I didn't know yo' was theer," said David,
a thought sheepishly.

"Na; or ye'd not ha' said it."

"I'd ha' thought it, though," muttered the boy.

Luckily, however, his father did not hear. He stretched his hands up tenderly for the Cup, lifted it down, and began reverently to polish the dimmed sides with his handkerchief.

"Ye're thinkin', nae doot," he cried, casting up a vicious glance at David, "that Wullie's no gude enough to ha' his name alangside o' they cursed Gray Dogs. Are ye no? Let's ha' the truth for aince—for a diversion."

"Reck'n he's good enough if there's none better," David replied dispassionately.

"And wha should there be better? Tell me that, ye muckle gowk."

David smiled.

"Eh, but that'd be long tellin', he said.

"And what wad ye mean by that?" his father cried.

"Nay; I was but thinkin' that Mr. Moore's Bob'll look gradely writ under yon." He pointed to the vacant space below Red Wull's name.

The little man put the Cup back on its pedestal with hurried hands. The handkerchief dropped unconsidered to the floor; he turned and sprang furiously at the boy, who stood against the wall, still smiling; and, seizing him by the collar of his coat, shook him to and fro with fiery energy.

"So ye're hopin', prayin', nae doot, that

James Moore—curse him!—will win ma Cup awa' from me, yer ain dad. I wonder ye're no 'shamed to crass ma door! Ye live on me; ye suck ma blood, ye foul-mouthed leech. Wullie and me brak' oorsel's to keep ye in hoose and hame—and what's yer gratitude? Ye plot to rob us of oor rights."

He dropped the boy's coat and stood back.

"No rights about it," said David, still keeping his temper.

"If I win is it no ma right as muckle as ony Englishman's?"

Red Wull, who had heard the rising voices, came trotting in, scowled at David, and took his stand beside his master.

"Ay, *if* yo' win it," said David, with significant emphasis on the conjunction.

"And wha's to beat us?"

David looked at his father in well-affected surprise.

"I tell yo' Owd Bob's rinin'," he answered.

"And what if he is?" the other cried.

"Why, even yo' should know so much," the boy sneered.

The little man could not fail to understand.

"So that's it!" he said. Then, in a scream, with one finger pointing to the great dog:

"And what o' him? What'll ma Wullie be doin' the while? Tell me that, and ha' a care! Mind ye, he stan's here hearkenin'!" And, indeed, the Tailless Tyke was bristling for battle.

David did not like the look of things; and
edged away toward the door.

"What'll Wullie be doin', ye chicken-hearted
brock?" his father cried.

" 'Im?" said the boy, now close on the door!
" 'Im?" he said, with a slow contempt that
made the red bristles [quiver on the dog's
neck. "Lookin' on, I should think—lookin'
on. What else is he fit for?   I tell yo' oor
Bob——"

"— 'Oor Bob'!" screamed the little man
darting forward.   " 'Oor Bob'!   Hark to him,
I'll 'oor——'   At him, Wullie! at him!"

But the Tailless Tyke needed no encourage-
ment.   With a harsh roar he sprang through
the air, only to crash against the closing door!

The outer door banged, and in another second a mocking finger tapped on the window-
pane.

"Better luck to the two on yo' next time!"
laughed a scornful voice; and David ran down
the hill toward Kenmuir.

CHAPTER XII

HOW RED WULL HELD THE BRIDGE

FROM that hour the fire of M'Adam's jealousy blazed into a mighty flame. The winning of the Dale Cup had become a mania with him. He had won it once, and would again despite all the Moores, all the Gray Dogs, all the undutiful sons in existence; on that point he was resolved. The fact of his having tasted the joys of victory served to whet his desire. And now he felt he could never be happy till the Cup was his own—won outright.

At home David might barely enter the room There the trophy stood.

"I'll not ha' ye touch ma Cup, ye dirty-fingered, ill-begotten wastrel. Wullie and me won it—you'd naught to do wi' it. Go you to James Moore and James Moore's dog."

"Ay, and shall I tak' Cup wi' me? or will ye bide till it's took from ye?"

So the two went on; and every day the tension approached nearer breaking-point.

In the Dale the little man met with no sympathy. The hearts of the Dalesmen were to a man with Owd Bob and his master.

Whereas once at the Sylvester Arms his shrill, ill tongue had been rarely still, now he maintained a sullen silence; Jem Burton, at least, had no cause of complaint. Crouched away in a corner, with Red Wull beside him, the little man would sit watching and listening as the Dalesmen talked of Owd Bob's doings, his staunchness, sagacity, and coming victory.

Sometimes he could restrain himself no longer. Then he would spring to his feet, and stand, a little swaying figure, and denounce them passionately in almost pathetic eloquence. These orations always concluded in set fashion.

"Ye're all agin us!" the little man would cry in quivering voice.

"We are that," Tammas would answer complacently.

"Fair means or foul, ye're content sae lang as Wullie and me are beat. I wonder ye dinna poison him—a little arsenic, and the way's clear for your Bob."

"The way is clear enough wi'oot that," from Tammas caustically. Then a lengthy silence, only broken by that exceeding bitter cry: "Eh, Wullie, Wullie, they're all agin us!"

.   .   .   .   .

And always the rivals—red and gray—went about seeking their opportunity. But the Master, with his commanding presence and stern eyes, was ever ready for them. Toward the end, M'Adam, silent and sneering, would secretly urge on Red Wull to the attack; until, one day in Grammoch-town, James Moore

turned on him, his blue eyes glittering. "D'yo'
think, yo' little fule," he cried in that hard
voice of his, "that onst they got set we should
iver git either of them off alive?" It seemed
to strike the little man as a novel idea; for,
from that moment, he was ever the first in
his feverish endeavors to oppose his small
form, buffer-like, between the would-be combatants.

.   .   .   .

Curse as M'Adam might, threaten as he
might, when the time came Owd Bob won.

The styles of the rivals were well contrasted :
the patience, the insinuating eloquence, combined with the splendid dash, of the one; and
the fierce, driving fury of the other.

The issue was never in doubt. It may have
been that the temper of the Tailless Tyke gave
in the time of trial; it may have been that his
sheep were wild, as M'Adam declared; certainly not, as the little man alleged in choking
voice, that they had been chosen and pur-
posely set aside to ruin his chance. Certain
it is that his tactics scared them hopelessly:
and he never had them in hand.

As for Owd Bob, his dropping, his driving,
his penning, aroused the loud-tongued admiration of crowd and competitors alike. He was
patient yet persistent, quiet yet firm, and
seemed to coax his charges in the right way
in that inimitable manner of his own.

When, at length, the verdict was given, and

it was known that, after an interval of half a
century, the Shepherds' Trophy was won again
by a Gray Dog of Kenmuir, there was such a
scene as has been rarely witnessed on the slope
behind the Dalesman's Daughter.

Great fists were slapped on mighty backs;
great feet were stamped on the sun-dried banks
of the Silver Lea; stalwart lungs were strained
to their uttermost capacity; and roars of
"Moore!" "Owd Bob o' Kenmuir!" "The
Gray Dogs!" thundered up the hillside, and
were flung, thundering, back.

Even James Moore was visibly moved as he
worked his way through the cheering mob;
and Owd Bob, trotting alongside him in quiet
dignity, seemed to wave his silvery brush in
acknowledgement.

Master Jacky Sylvester alternately turned
cart-wheels and felled the Hon. Launcelot
Bilks to the ground. Lady Eleanour, her
cheeks flushed with pleasure, waved her para-
sol, and attempted to restrain her son's exu-
berance. Parson Leggy danced an unclerical
jig, and shook hands with the squire till both
those fine old gentlemen were purple in the
face. Long Kirby selected a small man in the
crowd, and bashed his hat down over his eyes.
While Tammas, Rob Saunderson, Tupper,
Hoppin, Londesley, and the rest joined hands
and went raving round like so many giddy
girls.

Of them all, however, none was so uproarious in the mad heat of his enthusiasm as David M'Adam. He stood in the Kenmuir wagon beside Maggie, a conspicuous figure above the crowd, as he roared in hoarse ecstasy:

"Weel done, oor Bob! Weel done, Mr. Moore! Yo've knocked him! Knock him agin! Owd Bob o' Kenmuir! Moore! Moore o' Kenmuir! Hip! Hip!" until the noisy young giant attracted such attention in his boisterous delight that Maggie had to lay a hand upon his arm to restrain his violence.

Alone, on the far bank of the stream, stood the vanquished pair.

The little man was trembling slightly; his face was still hot from his exertions; and as he listened to the ovation accorded to his conqueror, there was a piteous set grin upon his face. In front stood the defeated dog, his lips wrinkling and hackles rising, as he, too, saw and heard and understood.

"It's a gran' thing to ha' a dutiful son. Wullie," the little man whispered, watching David's waving figure. "He's happy—and so are they a'—not sae much that James Moore has won, as that you and I are beat."

Then, breaking down for a moment:

"Eh, Wullie, Wullie! they're all agin us. It's you and I alane, lad."

Again, seeing the squire followed by Parson Leggy, Viscount Birdsaye, and others of the gentry, forcing their way through the press to shake hands with the victor, he continued:

"It's good to be in wi' the quality, Wullie.
Niver mak' a friend of a man beneath ye in
rank, nor an enemy of a man aboon ye: that's
a soond principle, Wullie, if ye'd get on in
honest England."

He stood there, alone with his dog, watching
the crowd on the far slope as it surged upward
in the direction of the committee tent. Only
when the black mass had packed itself in solid
phalanges about that ring, inside which, just
a year ago, he had stood in very different circumstances, and was at length still, a wintry
smile played for a moment about his lips. He
laughed a mirthless laugh.

"Bide a wee, Wullie — he! he! Bide a
wee.

> 'The best-laid schemes o' mice and men
>   Gang aft agley.' "

As he spoke, there came down to him, above
the tumult, a faint cry of mingled surprise and
anger. The cheering ceased abruptly. There
was silence; then there burst on the stillness
a hurricane of indignation.

The crowd surged forward, then turned.
Every eye was directed across the stream.
A hundred damning fingers pointed at the
solitary figure there. There were hoarse yells
of: "There he be! Yon's him! What's he done
wi' it? Thief! Throttle him!"

The mob came lumbering down the slope
like one man, thundering their imprecations
on a thousand throats. They looked danger-

ous, and their wrath was stimulated by the
knot of angry Dalesmen who led the van.
There was more than one white face among
the women at the top of the slope as they
watched the crowd blundering blindly down
the hill. There were more men than Parson
Leggy, the squire, James Moore, and the local
constables in the thick of it all, striving fran-
tically with voice and gesture, ay, and stick
too, to stem the advance.

It was useless; on the dark wave rolled, irre-
sistible.

On the far bank stood the little man, motionless, awaiting them with a grin upon his face.
And a little farther in front was the Tailless
Tyke, his back and neck like a new-shorn
wheat-field, as he rumbled a vast challenge.

"Come on, gentlemen!" the little man cried.
"Come on! I'll bide for ye, never fear. Ye're
a thousand to one and a dog. It's the odds
ye like, Englishmen a'."

And the mob, with murder in its throat, ac-
cepted the invitation and came on.

At the moment, however, from the slope
above, clear above the tramp of the mulitude,
a great voice bellowed: "Way! Way! Way
for Mr. Trotter!" The advancing host checked
and opened out; and the secretary of the
meeting bundled through.

He was a small, fat man, fussy at any time,
and perpetually perspiring. Now his face was
crimson with rage and running; he gesticu-

lated wildly; vague words bubbled forth, as
his short legs twinkled down the slope.

The crowd paused to admire. Some one
shouted a witticism, and the crowd laughed.
For the moment the situation was saved.

The fat secretary hurried on down the slope,
unheeding of any insult but the one. He
bounced over the plank-bridge: and as he
came closer, M'Adam saw that in each hand
brandished a brick.

"Hoots, man! dinna throw!" he cried,
making a feint as though to turn in sudden
terror.

"What's this? What's this?" gasped the
secretary, waving his arms.

"Bricks, 'twad seem," the other answered,
staying his flight.

The secretary puffed up like a pudding in a
hurry.

"Where's the Cup? Champion, Challenge,
etc.," he jerked out. "Mind, sir, you're responsible! wholly responsible! Dents, dam-
ages, delays! What's it all mean, sir? These
—these monstrous creations"—he brandished
the bricks, and M'Adam started back—
"wrapped, as I live, in straw, sir, in the Cup
case, sir! the Cup case! No Cup! Infamous!
Disgraceful! Insult me—meeting—committee—every one! What's it mean, sir?" He
paused to pant, his body filling and emptying
like a bladder.

M'Adam approached him with one eye on

the crowd, which was heaving forward again,
threatening still, but sullen and silent.

"I pit 'em there," he whispered; and drew
back to watch the effect of his disclosure.

The secretary gasped.

"You—you not only do this—amazing thing
—these monstrosities"—he hurled the bricks
furiously on the unoffending ground—"but
you dare to tell me so!"

The little man smiled.

"'Do wrang and conceal it, do right and
confess it,' that's Englishmen's motto, and
mine, as a rule; but this time I had ma reasons."

"Reasons, sir! No reasons can justify such
an extraordinary breach of all the—the decen-
cies. Reasons? the reasons of a maniac. Not
to say more, sir. Fraudulent detention—fraudulent, I say, sir! What were your precious
reasons?"

The mob with Tammas and Long Kirby at
their head had now wellnigh reached the
plank-bridge. They still looked dangerous,
and there were isolated cries of:

"Duck him!"

"Chuck him in!"

"An' the dog!"

"Wi' one o' they bricks about their necks!"

"There are my reasons!" said M'Adam,
pointing to the forest of menacing faces. "Ye
see I'm no beloved amang yonder gentlemen,
and"—in a stage whisper in the other's ear

—"I thocht maybe I'd be 'tacked on the road."

Tammas foremost of the crowd, had now his foot upon the first plank.

"Ye robber! ye thief! Wait till we set hands on ye, you and yer gorilla!" he called.

M'Adam half turned.

"Wullie," he said quietly, "keep the bridge."

At the order the Tailless Tyke shot gladly forward, and the leaders on the bridge as hastily back. The dog galloped on to the rattling plank, took his post fair and square in the centre of the narrow way, and stood facing the hostile crew like Cerberus guarding the gates of hell: his bull-head was thrust forward, hackles up, teeth glinting, and a distant rumbling in his throat, as though daring them to come on.

"Yo' first, ole lad!" said Tammas, hopping agilely behind Long Kirby.

"Nay; the old uns lead!" cried the big smith, his face gray-white. He wrenched round, pinned the old man by the arms, and held him forcibly before him as a covering shield. There ensued an unseemly struggle betwixt the two valiants, Tammas bellowing and kicking in the throes of mortal fear.

"Jim Mason'll show us," he suggested at last.

"Nay," said honest Jim; "I'm fear'd." He could say it with impunity; for the pluck of Postie Jim was a matter long past dispute.

Then Jem Burton'd go first?

Nay; Jem had a lovin' wife and dear little
kids at 'ome.

Then Big Bell?

Big Bell'd see 'isself further first.

A tall figure came forcing through the
crowd, his face a little paler than its wont, and
a formidable knob-kerry in his hand.

"I'm goin'!" said David.

"But yo're not," answered burly Sam'l,
gripping the boy from behind with arms like
the roots of an oak. "Your time'll coom soon
enough by the look on yo' wi' niver no hurry."
And the sense of the Dalesmen was with the
big man; for, as old Rob Saunderson said:

"I reck'n he'd liefer claw on to your throat,
lad, nor ony o' oors."

As there was no one forthcoming to claim
the honor of the lead, Tammas came forward
with cunning counsel.

"Tell yo' what, lads, we'd best let 'em as
don't know nowt at all aboot him go first.
And onst they're on, mind, we winna let 'em
off; but keep a-shovin' and a-bovin 'on 'em
forra'd. *Then* us'll foller."

By this time there was a little naked space
of green round the bridge-head, like a fairy
circle, into which the uninitiated might not
penetrate. Round this the mob hedged: the
Dalesmen in front, striving knavishly back
and bawling to those behind to leggo that
shovin'; and these latter urging valorously

forward, yelling jeers and contumely at the
front rank. "Come on! 'O's afraid? Lerrus
through to 'em, then, ye Royal Stan'-backs!"
—for well they knew the impossibility of their
demand.

And as they wedged and jostled thus, there
stole out from their midst as gallant a champion as ever trod the grass. He trotted out
into the ring, the observed of all, and paused
to gaze at the gaunt figure on the bridge.
The sun lit the sprinkling of snow on the dome
of his head; one forepaw was off the ground;
and he stood there, royally alert, scanning his
antagonist.

"Th' Owd Un!" went up in a roar fit to
split the air as the hero of the day was recognized. And the Dalesmen gave a pace forward
spontaneously as the gray knight-errant stole
across the green.

"Oor Bob'll fetch him!" they roared, their
blood leaping to fever heat, and gripped their
sticks, determined in stern reality to follow
now.

The gray champion trotted up on to the
bridge, and paused again, the long hair about
his neck rising like a ruff, and a strange glint
in his eyes; and the holder of the bridge never
moved. Red and Gray stood thus, face to
face: the one gay yet resolute, the other motionless, his great head slowly sinking between
his forelegs, seemingly petrified.

There was no shouting now: it was time for

deeds, not words.   Only, above the stillness,
came a sound from the bridge like the snore of
a giant in his sleep, and blending, with it, a
low, deep, purring thunder like some monster
cat well pleased.

"Wullie," came a solitary voice from the far
side, "keep the bridge!"

One ear went back, one ear was still forward; the great head was low and lower between his forelegs and the glowing eyes rolled
upward so that the watchers could see the
murderous white.

Forward the gray dog stepped.

Then, for the second time that afternoon, a
voice, stern and hard, came ringing down
from the slope above over the heads of the
many.

"Bob, lad, coom back!"

"He! he! I thocht that was comin'," sneered
the small voice over the stream.

The gray dog heard, and checked.

"Bob, lad, coom in, I say!"

At that he swung round and marched slowly
back, gallant as he had come, dignified still in
his mortification.

And Red Wull threw back his head and bellowed a pæan of victory—challenge, triumph,
scorn, all blended in that bull-like, blood-
chilling blare.

.   .   .   .   .

In the mean time, M'Adam and the secretary
had concluded their business. It had been

settled that the Cup was to be delivered over
to James Moore not later than the following
Saturday.

"Saturday, see! at the latest!" the secretary
cried as he turned and trotted off.

"Mr. Trotter," M'Adam called after him,
"I'm sorry, but ye maun bide this side the Lea
till I've reached the foot o' the Pass. Gin
they gentlemen"—nodding toward the crowd
—"should set hands on me, why——" and he
shrugged his shoulders significantly. "Forbye, Wullie's keepin' the bridge."

With that the little man strolled off leisurely; now dallying to pick a flower, now to
wave a mocking hand at the furious mob, and
so slowly on to the foot of the Muirk Muir Pass.

There he turned and whistled that shrill,
peculiar note.

"Wullie, Wullie, to me!" he called.

At that, with one last threat thrown at the
thousand souls he had held at bay for thirty
minutes, the Tailless Tyke swung about and
galloped after his lord.

CHAPTER XIII

THE FACE IN THE FRAME

ALL Friday M'Adam never left the kitchen. He sat opposite the Cup, in a coma, as it were; and Red Wull lay motionless at his feet.

Saturday came, and still the two never budged. Toward the evening the little man rose, all in a tremble, and took the Cup down from the mantelpiece; then he sat down again with it in his arms.

"Eh, Wullie, Wullie, is it a dream? Ha' they took her fra us? Eh, but it's you and I alane, lad."

He hugged it to him, crying silently, and rocking to and fro like a mother with a dying child. And Red Wull sat up on his haunches, and weaved from side to side in sympathy.

As the dark was falling, David looked in.

At the sound of the opening door the little man swung round noiselessly, the Cup nursed in his arms, and glared, sullen and suspicious, at the boy; yet seemed not to recognize him. In the half-light David could see the tears coursing down the little wizened face.

" 'Pon ma life, he's gaein' daft!" was his comment as he turned away to Kenmuir. And again the mourners were left alone.

"A few hours noo, Wullie," the little man wailed, "and she'll be gane. We won her, Wullie, you and I, won her fair: she's lit the hoose for us; she's softened a' for us—and God kens we needed it; she was the ae thing we had to look to and love. And noo they're takin' her awa', and 'twill be night agin. We've cherished her, we've garnished her, we've loved her like oor ain; and noo she maun gang to strangers who know her not."

He rose to his feet, and the great dog rose with him. His voice heightened to a scream, and he swayed with the Cup in his arms till it seemed he must fall.

"Did they win her fair, Wullie? Na; they plotted, they conspired, they worked ilka ain o' them agin us, and they beat us. Ay, and noo they're robbin' us—robbin' us! But they shallna ha' her. Oor's or naebody's, Wullie! We'll finish her sooner nor that."

He banged the Cup down on the table and rushed madly out of the room, Red Wull at his heels. In a moment he came running back, brandishing a great axe about his head.

"Come on, Wullie!" he cried. "'Scots wha hae'! Noo's the day and noo's the hour! Come on!"

On the table before him, serene and beautiful, stood the target of his madness. The little man ran at it, swinging his murderous weapon like a flail.

"Oor's or naebody's Wullie! Come on!

'Lay the proud usurpers low'!'' He aimed a
mighty buffet; and the Shepherds' Trophy—
the Shepherds' Trophy which had won through
the hardships of a hundred years—was almost
gone. It seemed to quiver as the blow fell.
But the cruel steel missed, and the axe-head
sank into the wood, clean and deep, like a
spade in snow.

Red Wull had leapt on to the table, and in
his cavernous voice was grumbling a chorus to
his master's yells. The little man danced up
and down, tugging and straining at the axe-
handle.

"You and I, Wullie!

> 'Tyrants fall in every foe!
> Liberty's in every blow!' ''

The axe-head was as immoveable as the Muir
Pike.

> " 'Let us do or die!' ''

The shaft snapped, and the little man tottered back. Red Wull jumped down from the
table, and, in doing so, brushed against the
Cup. It toppled* over on to the floor, and
rolled tinkling away in the dust. And the
little man fled madly out of the house, still
screaming his war-song.

    .   .   .   .

When, late that night, M'Adam returned
home, the Cup was gone. Down on his hands

*N. B.—You may see the dent in the Cup's white sides
to this day.

and knees he traced out its path, plain to see, where it had rolled along the dusty floor. Beyond that there was no sign.

At first he was too much overcome to speak. Then he raved round the room like a derelict ship, Red Wull following uneasily behind. He cursed; he blasphemed; he screamed and beat the walls with feverish hands. A stranger, passing, might well have thought this was a private Bedlam. At last, exhausted, he sat down and cried.

"It's David, Wullie, ye may depend; David that's robbed his father's hoose. Oh, it's a grand thing to ha' a dutiful son!"—and he bowed his gray head in his hands.

David, indeed, it was. He had come back to the Grange during his father's absence, and, taking the Cup from its grimy bed, had marched it away to its rightful home. For that evening at Kenmuir, James Moore had said to him:

"David, your father's not sent the Cup. I shall come and fetch it to-morrow." And David knew he meant it. Therefore, in order to save a collision between his father and his friend—a collision the issue of which he dared hardly contemplate, knowing, as he did, the unalterable determination of the one and the lunatic passion of the other—the boy had resolved to fetch the Cup himself, then and there, in the teeth, if needs be, of his father and the Tailless Tyke. And he had done it.

When he reached home that night he
marched, contrary to his wont, straight into
the kitchen.

There sat his father facing the door, awaiting him, his hands upon his knees. For once
the little man was alone; and David, brave
though he was, thanked heaven devoutly that
Red Wull was elsewhere.

For a while father and son kept silence,
watching one another like two fencers.

" 'Twas you as took ma Cup?" asked the
little man at last, leaning forward in his chair.

" 'Twas me as took Mr. Moore's Cup," the
boy replied. "I thowt yo' mun ha' done wi'
it—I found it all bashed upon the floor."

"You took it—pit up to it, nae doot, by
James Moore."

David made a gesture of dissent.

"Ay, by James Moore," his father continued.
"He dursena come hissel' for his ill-gotten
spoils, so he sent the son to rob the father.
The coward!"—his whole frame shook with
passion. "I'd ha' thocht James Moore'd ha'
bin man enough to come himself for what he
wanted. I see noo I did him a wrang—I mis-
judged him. I kent him a heepocrite; ain o'
yer unco gudes; a man as looks one thing,
says anither, and does a third; and noo I ken
he's a coward. He's fear'd o' me, sic as I am,
five foot twa in ma stockin's." He rose from
his chair and drew himself up to his full
height.

"Mr. Moore had nowt to do wi' it," David persisted.

"Ye're lyin'. James Moore pit ye to it."

"I tell yo' he did not."

"Ye'd ha' bin willin' enough wi'oot him, if ye'd thocht o't, I grant ye. But ye've no the wits. All there is o' ye has gane to mak' yer muckle body. Hooiver, that's no matter. I'll settle wi' James Moore anither time. I'll settle wi' you noo, David M'Adam."

He paused, and looked the boy over from head to foot.

"So, ye're not only an idler! a wastrel! a liar!"—he spat the words out. "Ye're—God help ye—a thief!"

"I'm no thief!" the boy returned hotly. "I did but give to a mon what ma feyther— shame on him!—wrongfully kept from him."

"Wrangfully?" cried the little man, advancing with burning face.

" 'Twas honorably done, keepin' what wasna your'n to keep! Holdin' back his rights from a man! Ay, if ony one's the thief, it's not me: it's you, I say, you!"—and he looked his father in the face with flashing eyes.

"I'm the thief, am I?" cried the other, incoherent with passion. "Though ye're three times ma size, I'll teach ma son to speak so to me."

The old strap, now long disused, hung in the chimney corner. As he spoke the little man sprang back, ripped it from the wall, and,

almost before David realized what he was at,
had brought it down with a savage slash across
his son's shoulders; and as he smote he whistled
a shrill, imperative note:

"Wullie, Wullie, to me!"

David felt the blow through his coat like a
bar of hot iron laid across his back. His passion seethed within him; every vein throbbed;
every nerve quivered. In a minute he would
wipe out, once and for all, the score of years;
for the moment, however, there was urgent
business on hand. For outside he could hear
the quick patter of feet hard-galloping, and
the scurry of a huge creature racing madly
to a call.

With a bound he sprang at the open door;
and again the strap came lashing down, and a
wild voice:

"Quick, Wullie! For God's sake, quick!"

David slammed the door to. It shut with a
rasping snap; and at the same moment a great
body from without thundered against it with
terrific violence, and a deep voice roared like
the sea when thwarted of its prey.

"Too late, agin!" said David, breathing
hard; and shot the bolt home with a clang.
Then he turned on his father.

"Noo," said he, "man to man!"

"Ay," cried the other, "father to son!"

The little man half turned and leapt at the
old musketoon hanging on the wall. He
missed it, turned again, and struck with the

strap full at the other's face. David caught the falling arm at the wrist, hitting it aside with such tremendous force that the bone all but snapped. Then he smote his father a terrible blow on the chest, and the little man staggered back, gasping, into the corner; while the strap dropped from his numbed fingers.

Outside Red Wull whined and scratched; but the two men paid no heed.

David strode forward; there was murder in his face. The little man saw it: his time was come; but his bitterest foe never impugned Adam M'Adam's courage.

He stood huddled in the corner, all dishevelled, nursing one arm with the other, entirely unafraid.

"Mind, David," he said, quite calm, "murder 'twill be, not manslaughter."

"Murder 'twill be," the boy answered, in thick, low voice, and was across the room.

Outside Red Wull banged and clawed high up on the door with impotent pats.

The little man suddenly slipped his hand in his pocket, pulled out something, and flung it. The missile pattered on his son's face like a rain-drop on a charging bull, and David smiled as he came on. It dropped softly on the table at his side; he looked down and—it was the face of his mother which gazed up at him!

"Mither!" he sobbed, stopping short. "Mither! Ma God, ye saved him—and me!"

He stood there, utterly unhinged, shaking and whimpering.

It was some minutes before he pulled himself together; then he walked to the wall, took down a pair of shears, and seated himself at the table, still trembling. Near him lay the miniature, all torn and crumpled, and beside it the deep-buried axe-head.

He picked up the strap and began cutting it into little pieces.

"There! and there! and there!" he said with each snip. "An' ye hit me agin there may be no mither to save ye."

M'Adam stood huddling in the corner. He shook like an aspen leaf; his eyes blazed in his white face; and he still nursed one arm with the other.

"Honor yer father," he quoted in small, low voice.

PART IV

THE BLACK KILLER

CHAPTER XIV

A MAD MAN

TAMMAS is on his feet in the tap-room of the Arms, brandishing a pewter mug.

"Gen'lemen!" he cries, his old face flushed; "I gie you a toast. Stan' oop!"

The knot of Dalesmen round the fire rises like one. The old man waves his mug before him, reckless of the good ale that drips on to the floor.

"The best sheep-dog i' th' North—Owd Bob o' Kenmuir!" he cries. In an instant there is uproar: the merry applause of clinking pewters; the stamping of feet; the rattle of sticks. Rob Saunderson and old Jonas are cheering with the best; Tupper and Ned Hoppin are bellowing in one another's ears; Long Kirby and Jem Burton are thumping each other on the back; even Sam'l Todd and Sexton Ross are roused from their habitual melancholy.

"Here's to Th' Owd Un! Here's to oor Bob!" yell stentorian voices; while Rob Saunderson has jumped on to a chair.

"Wi' the best sheep-dog i' th' North I gie yo' the Shepherd's Trophy!—won outreet as will be!" he cries.   Instantly the clamor re-doubles.

"The Dale Cup and Th' Owd Un!   The Trophy and oor Bob!   'Ip, 'ip, for the gray dogs!   'Ip, 'ip, for the best sheep-dog as ever was or will be!   'Ooray, 'ooray!"

It is some minutes before the noise sub-sides; and slowly the enthusiasts resume their seats with hoarse throats and red faces.

"Gentlemen a'!"

A little unconsidered man is standing up at the back of the room.   His face is aflame, and his hands twitch spasmodically; and, in front, with hackles up and eyes gleaming, is a huge, bull-like dog.

"Noo," cries the little man, "I daur ye to repeat that lie!"

"Lie!" screams Tammas; "lie!   I'll gie 'im lie!   Lemme at im', I say!"

The old man in his fury is half over the sur-rounding ring of chairs before Jim Mason on the one hand and Jonas Maddox on the other can pull him back.

"Coom, Mr. Thornton," soothes the octo-genarian, "let un be.   Yo' surely bain't anger-ed by the likes o' 'im!"—and he jerks con-temptuously toward the solitary figure at his back.

Tammas resumes his seat unwillingly.

The little man in the far corner of the room remains silent, waiting for his challenge to be taken up.   It is in vain.   And as he looks at the range of broad, impassive backs turned on him, he smiles bitterly.

"They dursen't Wullie, not a man of them a'!" he cries. "They're one—two—three—four—eleven to one, Wullie, and yet they dursen't. Eleven of them, and every man a coward! Long Kirby—Thornton—Tupper—Todd—Hoppin—Ross—Burton—and the rest, and not one but's a bigger man nor me, and yet——Weel, we might ha' kent it. We should ha' kent Englishmen by noo. They're aye the same and aye have bin. They tell lies, black lies——"

Tammas is again half out his chair and, only forcibly restrained by the men on either hand.

"——and then they ha' na the courage to stan' by 'em. Ye're English, ivery man o' ye, to yer marrow."

The little man's voice rises as he speaks. He seizes the tankard from the table at his side.

"Englishmen!" he cries, waving it before him. "Here's a health! The best sheep-dog as iver penned a flock—Adam M'Adam's Red Wull!"

He pauses, the pewter at his lips, and looks at his audience with flashing eyes. There is no response from them.

"Wullie, here's to you!" he cries. "Luck and life to ye, ma trusty fier! Death and defeat to yer enemies!

> " 'The warld's wrack we share o't,
>   The warstle and the care o't;' "

He raises the tankard and drains it to its
uttermost dreg.

Then drawing himself up, he addresses his
audience once more:

"An' noo I'll warn ye aince and for a', and
ye may tell James Moore I said it: He may
plot agin us, Wullie and me; he may threaten
us; he may win the Cup outright for his muckle
favorite; but there was niver a man or dog
yet as did Adam M'Adam and his Red Wull a
hurt but in the end he wush't his mither hadna
borne him."

A little later, and he walks out of the inn,
the Tailless Tyke at his heels.

After he is gone it is Rob Saunderson who
says: "The little mon's mad; he'll stop at
nothin'"; and Tammas who answers:

"Nay; not even murder."

. . . . .

The little man had aged much of late. His
hair was quite white, his eyes unnaturally
bright, and his hands were never still, as though
he were in everlasting pain. He looked the
picture of disease.

After Owd Bob's second victory he had become morose and untalkative. At home he
often sat silent for hours together, drinking
and glaring at the place where the Cup had
been. Sometimes he talked in low, eerie voice
to Red Wull; and on two occasions, David,
turning, suddenly, had caught his father glowering stealthily at him with such an expression

on his face as chilled the boy's blood. The
two never spoke now; and David held this
silent, deadly enmity far worse than the old-
time perpetual warfare.

It was the same at the Sylvester Arms. The
little man sat alone with Red Wull, exchanging
words with no man, drinking steadily, brooding over his wrongs, only now and again galvan-
ized into sudden action.

Other people than Tammas Thornton came
to the conclusion that M'Adam would stop at
nothing in the undoing of James Moore or the
gray dog. They said drink and disappointment had turned his head; that he was mad
and dangerous. And on New Year's day
matters seemed coming to a crisis; for it was
reported that in the gloom of a snowy evening
he had drawn a knife on the Master in the
High Street, but slipped before he could accomplish his fell purpose.

Most of them all, David was haunted with
an ever-present anxiety as to the little man's
intentions. The boy even went so far as to
warn his friend against his father. But the
Master only smiled grimly.

"Thank ye, lad," he said. "But I reck'n
we can 'fend for oorsel's, Bob and I. Eh,
Owd Un?"

Anxious as David might be, he was not so
anxious as to be above taking a mean advan-
tage of this state of strained apprehension to
work on Maggie's fears.

One evening he was escorting her home from church, when, just before they reached the larch copse:

"Goo' sakes!   What's that?" he ejaculated in horror-laden accents, starting back.

"What, Davie?" cried the girl, shrinking up to him all in a tremble.

"Couldna say for sure.   It mought be owt, or agin it mought be nowt.   But yo' grip my arm, I'll grip yo' waist."

Maggie demurred.

"Canst see onythin'?" she asked, still in a flutter.

" Be'ind the 'edge. "

"Wheer?"

"Theer!"—pointing vaguely.

" I canna see nowt. "

"Why, theer, lass.   Can yo' not see?   Then yo' pit your head along o' mine—so—closer—closer."   Then, in aggrieved tones: "What-iver is the matter wi' yo', wench?   I might be a leprosy."

But the girl was walking away with her head high as the snow-capped Pike.

"So long as I live, David M'Adam," she cried, "I'll niver go to church wi' you agin!"

"Iss, but you will though—onst," he an-swered low.

Maggie whisked round in a flash, superbly indignant.

"What d'yo' mean, sir-r-r?"

"Yo' know what I mean, lass," he replied

sheepish and shuffling before her queenly
anger.

She looked him up and down, and down and
up again.

"I'll niver speak to you agin, Mr. M'Adam,"
she cried; "not if it was ever so——Nay,
I'll walk home by myself, thank you. I'll ha'
nowt to do wi' you."

So the two must return to Kenmuir, one
behind the other, like a lady and her footman.

David's audacity had more than once already
all but caused a rupture between the pair. And
the occurrence behind the hedge set the cap
on his impertinences. That was past enduring and Maggie by her bearing let him
know it.

David tolerated the girl's new attitude for
exactly twelve minutes by the kitchen clock.
Then: "Sulk wi' me, indeed! I'll teach her!"
and he marched out of the door, "Niver to
cross it agin, ma word!"

Afterward, however, he relented so far as
to continue his visits as before; but he made
it clear that he only came to see the Master
and hear of Owd Bob's doings. On these occasions he loved best to sit on the window-sill
outside the kitchen, and talk and chaff with
Tammas and the men in the yard, feigning
an uneasy bashfulness was reference made
to Bessie Bolstock. And after sitting thus for
some time, he would half turn, look over his
shoulder, and remark in indifferent tones to

the girl within: "Oh, good-evenin'! I forgot
yo'," —and then resume his conversation.
While the girl within, her face a little pinker,
her lips a little tighter, and her chin a little
higher, would go about her business, pretending neither to hear nor care.

The suspicions that M'Adam nourished dark
designs against James Moore were somewhat
confirmed in that, on several occasions in the
bitter dusks of January afternoons, a little insidious figure was reported to have been seen
lurking among the farm-buildings of Kenmuir.

Once Sam'l Todd caught the little man
fairly, skulking away in the woodshed. Sam'l
took him up bodily and carried him down the
slope to the Wastrel, shaking him gently as
he went.

Across the stream he put him on his feet.

"If I catches yo' cadgerin' aroun' the farm
agin, little mon," he admonished, holding up
a warning finger; "I'll tak' yo' and drap yo'
in t' Sheep-wash, I warn yo' fair. I'd ha'
done it noo an' yo'd bin a bigger and a younger
mon. But theer! yo'm sic a scrappety bit.
Noo, rin whoam." And the little man slunk
silently away.

For a time he appeared there no more.
Then, one evening when it was almost dark,
James Moore, going the round of the outbuildings, felt Owd Bob stiffen against his
side.

"What's oop, lad?" he whispered, halting;

and, dropping his hand on the old dog's neck felt a ruff of rising hair beneath it.

"Steady, lad, steady," he whispered; "what is 't?" He peered forward into the gloom; and at length discerned a little familiar figure huddled away in the crevice between two stacks.

"It's yo, is it, M'Adam?" he said, and, bending, seized a wisp of Owd Bob's coat in a grip like a vice.

Then, in a great voice, moved to rare anger: "Oot o' this afore I do ye a hurt, ye meeserable spyin' creetur!" he roared. "Yo' mun wait till dark cooms to hide yo', yo' coward, afore yo daur coom crawlin' aboot ma hoose, frightenin' the women-folk and up to yer devilments. If yo've owt to say to me, coom like a mon in the open day. Noo git aff wi' yo', afore I lay hands to yo'!"

He stood there in the dusk, tall and mighty, a terrible figure, one hand pointing to the gate, the other still grasping the gray dog.

The little man scuttled away in the half-light, and out of the yard.

On the plank-bridge he turned and shook his fist at the darkening house.

"Curse ye, James Moore!" he sobbed, "I'll be even wi' ye yet."

CHAPTER XV

DEATH ON THE MARCHES

On the top of this there followed an attempt to poison Th' Owd Un. At least there was no other accounting for the affair.

In the dead of a long-remembered night James Moore was waked by a low moaning beneath his room. He leapt out of bed and ran to the window to see his favorite dragging about the moonlit yard, the dark head down, the proud tail for once lowered, the lithe limbs wooden, heavy, unnatural—altogether pitiful.

In a moment he was downstairs and out to his friend's assistance. "Whativer is't, Owd Un?" he cried in anguish.

At the sound of that dear voice the old dog tried to struggle to him, could not, and fell, whimpering.

In a second the Master was with him, examining him tenderly, and crying for Sam'l, who slept above the stables.

There was every symptom of foul play: the tongue was swollen and almost black; the breathing labored; the body twiched horribly; and the soft gray eyes all bloodshot and straining in agony.

With the aid of Sam'l and Maggie, drenching first and stimulants after, the Master pulled him around for the moment. And soon Jim Mason and Parson Leggy, hurriedly summoned, came running hot-foot to the rescue.

Prompt and stringent measures saved the victim—but only just. For a time the best sheep-dog in the North was pawing at the Gate of Death. In the end, as the gray dawn broke, the danger passed.

The attempt to get at him, if attempt it was, aroused passionate indignation in the countryside. It seemed the culminating-point of the excitement long bubbling.

There were no traces of the culprit; not a vestige to lead to incrimination, so cunningly had the criminal accomplished his foul task. But as to the perpetrator, if there where no proofs there were yet fewer doubts.

At the Sylvester Arms Long Kirby asked M'Adam point-blank for his explanation of the matter.

"Hoo do I 'count for it?" the little man cried. "I dinna 'count for it ava."

"Then hoo did it happen?" asked Tammas with asperity.

"I dinna believe it did happen," the little man replied. "It's a lee o' James Moore's— a charactereestic lee." Whereon they chucked him out incontinently; for the Terror for once was elsewhere.

Now that afternoon is to be remembered for threefold causes. Firstly, because, as has

been said, M'Adam was alone. Secondly, because, a few minutes after his ejectment, the
window of the tap-room was thrown open from
without, and the little man looked in. He
spoke no word, but those dim, smouldering
eyes of his wandered from face to face, resting
for a second on each, as if to burn them on his
memory. "I'll remember ye, gentlemen," he
said at length quietly, shut the window, and
was gone.

Thirdly, for a reason now to be told.

Though ten days had elapsed since the attempt on him, the gray dog had never been
his old self since. He had attacks of shivering; his vitality seemed sapped; he tired easily,
and, great heart, would never own it. At
length on this day, James Moore, leaving the
old dog behind him, had gone over to
Grammoch-town to consult Dingley, the vet.
On his way home he met Jim Mason with
Gyp, the faithful Betsy's unworthy successor,
at the Dalesman's Daughter. Together they
started for the long tramp home over the
Marches. And that journey is marked with a
red stone in this story.

All day long the hills had been bathed in
inpenetrable fog. Throughout there had been
an accompanying drizzle; and in the distance
the wind had moaned a storm-menace. To the
darkness of the day was added the sombreness
of falling night as the three began the ascent
of the Murk Muir Pass. By the time they

emerged into the Devil's Bowl it was altogether black and blind. But the threat of
wind had passed, leaving utter stillness; and
they could hear the splash of an otter on the
far side of the Lone Tarn as they skirted that
gloomy water's edge. When at length the
last steep rise on to the Marches had been
topped, a breath of soft air smote them lightly,
and the curtain of fog began drifting away.

The two men swung steadily through the
heather with that reaching stride the birth-
right of moor-men and highlanders. They
talked but little, for such was their nature: a
word or two on sheep and the approaching
lambing-time; thence on to the coming Trials;
the Shepherds' Trophy; Owd Bob and the
attempt on him; and from that to M'Adam
and the Tailless Tyke.

"D'yo' reck'n M'Adam had a hand in't?"
the postman was asking.

"Nay; there's no proof."

"'Ceptin' he's mad to get shut o' Th' Owd
Un afore Cup Day."

"'Im or me—it mak's no differ." For a
dog is disqualified from competing for the
Trophy who has changed hands during the
six months prior to the meeting. And this
holds good though the change be only from
father to son on the decease of the former.

Jim looked up inquiringly at his companion.

"D'yo' think it'll coom to that?" he asked.

"What?"

"Why—murder "

"Not if I can help it," the other answered
grimly.

The fog had cleared away by now, and the
moon was up. To their right, on the crest of
a rise some two hundred yards away, a low
wood stood out black against the sky. As they
passed it, a blackbird rose up screaming, and
a brace of wood-pigeons winged noisily away.

"Hullo! hark to the yammerin'!" muttered Jim, stopping; "and at this time o' night
too!"

Some rabbits, playing in the moonlight on
the outskirts of the wood, sat up, listened, and
hopped back into security. At the same moment a big hill-fox slunk out of the covert.
He stole a pace forward and halted, listening
with one ear back and one pad raised; then
cantered silently away in the gloom, passing
close to the two men and yet not observing
them.

"What's up, I wonder?" mused the postman.

"The fox set 'em clackerin', I reck'n," said
the Master.

"Not he; he was scared 'maist oot o' his
skin," the other answered. Then in tones of
suppressed excitement, with his hands on James
Moore's arm: "And, look'ee, theer's ma Gyp
a-beckonin' on us!"

There, indeed, on the crest of the rise beside the wood, was the little lurcher, now

looking back at his master, now creeping stealthily forward.

"Ma word! theer's summat wrong yonder!" cried Jim, and jerked the post-bags off his shoulder. "Coom on, Master!"—and he set off running toward the dog; while James Moore, himself excited now, followed with an agility that belied his years.

Some score yards from the lower edge of the spinney, upon the farther side of the ridge, a tiny beck babbled through its bed of peat. The two men, as they topped the rise, noticed a flock of black-faced mountain-sheep clustered in the dip 'twixt wood and stream. They stood martialled in close array, facing half toward the wood, half toward the newcomers, heads up, eyes glaring, handsome as sheep only look when scared.

On the crest of the ridge the two men halted beside Gyp. The postman stood with his head a little forward, listening intently. Then he dropped in the heather like a dead man, pulling the other with him.

"Doon, mon!" he whispered, clutching at Gyp with his spare hand.

"What is't, Jim?" asked the Master, now thoroughly roused.

"Summat movin' i' th' wood," the other whispered, listening weasel-eared.

So they lay motionless for a while; but there came no sound from the copse.

"'Appen 'twas nowt," the postman at length

allowed, peering cautiously about. "And yet
I thowt—I dunno reetly what I thowt."

Then, starting to his knees with a hoarse cry
of terror: "Save us! what's yon theer?"

Then for the first time the Master raised his
head and noticed, lying in the gloom between
them and the array of sheep, a still, white heap.

James Moore was a man of deeds, not words.
"It's past waitin'!" he said, and sprang forward, his heart in his mouth.

The sheep stamped and shuffled as he came,
and yet did not break.

"Ah, thanks be!" he cried, dropping beside
the motionless body; "it's nob'but a sheep."
As he spoke his hands wandered deftly over
the carcase. "But what's this?" he called.
"Stout¹ she was as me. Look at her fleece—
crisp, close, strong; feel the flesh—firm as a
rock. And ne'er a bone broke, ne're a scrat
on her body a pin could mak'. As healthy as
a mon—and yet dead as mutton!"

Jim, still trembling from the horror of his
fear, came up, and knelt beside his friend.
"Ah, but there's bin devilry in this!" he said;
'I reck'ned they sheep had bin badly skeared,
and not so long agone."

"Sheep-murder, sure enough!" the other
answered. "No fox's doin'—a girt-grown two-
shear as could 'maist knock a h'ox."

Jim's hands travelled from the body to the
dead creature's throat. He screamed.

¹Stout—hearty.

"By gob, Master! look 'ee theer!" He held his hand up in the moonlight, and it dripped red. "And warm yet! warm!"

"Tear some bracken, Jim!" ordered the other, "and set a-light. We mun see to this."

The postman did as bid. For a moment the fern smouldered and smoked, then the flame ran crackling along and shot up in the darkness, weirdly lighting the scene: to the right the low wood, a block of solid blackness against the sky; in front the wall of sheep, staring out of the gloom with bright eyes; and as centre-piece that still, white body, with the kneeling men and lurcher sniffing tentatively round.

The victim was subjected to a critical examination. The throat, and that only, had been hideously mauled; from the raw wounds the flesh hung in horrid shreds; on the ground all about were little pitiful dabs of wool, wrenched off apparently in a struggle; and, crawling among the fern-roots, a snake-like track of red led down to the stream.

"A dog's doin', and no mistakin' thot," said Jim at length, after a minute inspection.

"Ay," declared the Master with slow emphasis, "and a sheep-dog's too, and an old un's, or I'm no shepherd."

The postman looked up.

"Why thot?" he asked, puzzled.

"Becos," the Master answered, "'im as did this killed for blood—and for blood only.   If had bin ony other dog—greyhound, bull, tarrier, or even a young sheep-dog—d'yo' think he'd ha' stopped wi' the one? Not he; he'd ha' gone through 'em, and be runnin' 'em as like as not yet, nippin' 'em, pullin' 'em down, till he'd maybe killed the half. But 'im as did this killed for blood, I say. He got it—killed just the one, and nary touched the others, d'yo' 'see, Jim?''

The postman whistled, long and low.

"It's just what owd Wrottesley'd tell on," he said. "I never nob'but half believed him then—I do now though. D'yo' mind what th' owd lad'd tell, Master?"

James Moore nodded.

"Thot's it. I've never seen the like afore myself, but I've heard ma grandad speak o't mony's the time. An owd dog'll git the cravin' for sheep's blood on him, just the same as a mon does for the drink; he creeps oot o' nights, gallops afar, hunts his sheep, downs 'er, and satisfies the cravin'. And he nary kills but the one, they say, for he knows the vallie o' sheep same as you and me. He has his gallop, quenches the thirst, and then he's for home, maybe a score mile away, and no one the wiser i' th' mornin'. And so on, till he cooms to a bloody death, the murderin' traitor."

"If he does!" said Jim.

"And he does, they say, nigh always. For he gets bolder and bolder wi' not bein' caught, until one fine night a bullet lets light into him. And some mon gets knocked nigh endways when they bring his best tyke home i' th' mornin', dead, wi' the sheep's wool yet stickin' in his mouth."

The postman whistled again.

"It's what owd Wrottesley'd tell on to a tick. And he'd say, if ye mind, Master, as hoo the dog'd niver kill his master's sheep—kind o' conscience-like."

"Ay, I've heard that," said the Master. "Queer too, and 'im bein' such a bad un!"

Jim Mason rose slowly from his knees.

"Ma word," he said, "I wish Th' Owd Un was here. He'd 'appen show us summat!"

"I nob'but wish he was, pore owd lad!" said the Master.

As he spoke there was a crash in the wood above them; a sound as of some big body bursting furiously through brushwood.

The two men rushed to the top of the rise. In the darkness they could see nothing; only, standing still and holding their breaths, they could hear the faint sound, ever growing fainter, of some creature splashing in a hasty gallop over the wet moors.

"Yon's him! Yon's no fox, I'll tak' oath. And a main big un, too, hark to him!" cried Jim. Then to Gyp, who had rushed off in hot pursuit: "Coom back, chunk-'ead. What's use o' you agin a gallopin' 'potamus?"

Gradually the sounds died away and away, and were no more.

"Thot's 'im, the devil!" said the Master at length.

"Nay; the devil has a tail, they do say," replied Jim thoughtfully. For already the light of suspicion was focusing its red glare.

"Noo I reck'n we're in for bloody times amang the sheep for a while," said the Master, as Jim picked up his bags.

"Better a sheep nor a mon," answered the postman, still harping on the old theme.

CHAPTER XVI

THE BLACK KILLER

THAT, as James Moore had predicted, was the first only of a long succession of such solitary crimes.

Those who have not lived in a desolate country like that about the Muir Pike, where sheep are paramount and every other man engaged in the profession pastoral, can barely imagine the sensation aroused. In market-place, tavern, or cottage, the subject of conversation was always the latest sheep-murder and the yet-undetected criminal.

Sometimes there would be a lull, and the shepherds would begin to breath more freely. Then there would come a stormy night, when the heavens were veiled in the cloak of crime, and the wind moaned fitfully over meres and marches, and another victim would be added to the lengthening list.

It was always such black nights, nights of wind and weather, when no man would be abroad, that the murderer chose for his bloody work; and that was how he became known from the Red Screes to the Muir Pike as the Black Killer. In the Daleland they still call a wild, wet night "A Black Killer's night;"

for they say: "His ghaist'll be oot the night."

There was hardly a farm in the country-side but was marked with the seal of blood. Kenmuir escaped, and the Grange; Rob Saunderson at the Holt, and Tupper at Swinsthwaite; and they were about the only lucky ones.

As for Kenmuir, Tammas declared with a certain grim pride: "He knows better'n to coom wheer Th' Owd Un be." Whereat M'Adam was taken with a fit of internal spasms, rubbing his knees and cackling insanely for a half-hour afterward. And as for the luck of the Grange—well, there was a reason for that too, so the Dalesmen said.

Though the area of crime stretched from the Black Water to Grammoch-town, twenty odd miles, there was never a sign of the perpetrator. The Killer did his bloody work with a thoroughness and a devilish cunning that defied detection.

It was plain that each murder might be set down to the same agency. Each was stamped with the same unmistakable sign-manual: one sheep killed, its throat torn into red ribands, and the others untouched.

It was at the instigation of Parson Leggy that the squire imported a bloodhound to track the Killer to his doom. Set on at a fresh-killed carcase at the One Tree Knowe, he carried the line a distance in the direction of the Muir Pike; then was thrown out by a

little bustling beck, and never acknowledged
the scent again. Afterward he became un-
manageable, and could be no further utilized.
Then there was talk of inducing Tommy Dob-
son and his pack to come over from Eskdale,
but that came to nothing. The Master of the
Border Hunt lent a couple of foxhounds, who
effected nothing; and there were a hundred
other attempts and as many failures. Jim
Mason set a cunning trap or two and caught
his own bob-tailed tortoise-shell and a terrible
wigging from his missus; Ned Hoppin sat up
with a gun two nights over a new slain victim
and Londesley of the Home Farm poisoned a
carcase. But the Killer never returned to the
kill, and went about in the midst of them all,
carrying on his infamous traffic and laughing up
his sleeve.

In the mean while the Dalesmen raged and
swore vengeance; their impotence, their unsuccess, and their losses heating their wrath to
madness. And the bitterest sting of it all lay
in this; that though they could not detect him,
they were nigh to positive as to the culprit.

Many a time was the Black Killer named in
low-voiced conclave; many a time did Long
Kirby, as he stood in the Border Ram and
watched M'Adam and the Terror walking
down the High, nudge Jim Mason and whisper:

"Theer's the Killer—oneasy be his grave!"
To which practical Jim always made the same
retort:

"Ay, theer's the Killer; but wheer's the proof?"

And therein lay the crux. There was scarcely a man in the country-side who doubted the guilt of the Tailless Tyke; but, as Jim said, where was the proof? They could but point to his well-won nickname; his evil notoriety; say that, magnificent sheep-dog as he was, he was known even in his work as a rough handler of stock; and lastly remark significantly that the Grange was one of the few farms that had so far escaped unscathed. For with the belief that the Black Killer was a sheep-dog they held it as an article of faith that he would in honor spare his master's flock.

There may, indeed, have been prejudice in their judgment. For each had his private grudge against the Terror; and nigh every man bore on his own person, or his clothes, or on the body of his dog, the mark of that huge savage.

Proof?

"Why, he near killed ma Lassie!" cries Londesley.

"And he did kill the Wexer!"

"And Wan Tromp!"

"And see pore old Wenus!" says John Swan, and pulls out that fair Amazon, battered almost past recognition, but a warrioress still.

"That's Red Wull—bloody be his end!"

"And he laid ma Rasper by for nigh three weeks!" continues Tupper, pointing to the yet-unhealed scars on the neck of the big bobtail. "See thisey—his work."

"And look here!" cries Saunderson, exposing a ragged wound on Shep's throat; "thot's the Terror—black be his fa'!"

"Ay," says Long Kirby with an oath; "the tykes love him nigh as much as we do."

"Yes," says Tammas. "Yo' jest watch!"

The old man slips out of the tap-room; and in another moment from the road without comes a heavy, regular pat-pat-pat, as of some big creature approaching, and, blending with the sound, little shuffling footsteps.

In an instant every dog in the room has risen to his feet and stands staring at the door with sullen, glowing eyes; lips wrinkling, bristles rising, throats rumbling.

An unsteady hand fumbles at the door; a reedy voice calls, "Wullie, come here!" and the dogs move away, surly, to either side the fireplace, tails down, ears back, grumbling still; the picture of cowed passion.

Then the door opens; Tammas enters, grinning; and each, after a moment's scrutiny, resumes his former position before the fire.

    .   .   '   .   .

Meanwhile over M'Adam, seemingly all unsuspicious of these suspicions, a change had come. Whether it was that for the time he heard less of the best sheep-dog in the North, or for some more occult reason, certain it is that he became his old self. His tongue

wagged as gayly and bitterly as ever; and
hardly a night passed but he infuriated Tammas almost to blows with his innuendoes and
insidious sarcasms.

Old Jonas Maddox, one evening at the Sylvester Arms, inquired of him what his notion
was as to identity of the Killer.

"I hae ma suspicions, Mr. Maddox; I hae
ma suspicions," the little man replied, cunningly wagging his head and giggling. But
more than that they could not elicit from him.
A week later, however, to the question:

"And what are yo' thinkin' o' this black
Killer, Mr. M'Adam?"

"Why _black?_" the little man asked ear-
nestly; "why _black_ mair than white—or _gray_,
we'll say?" Luckily for him, however, the
Dalesmen are slow of wit as of speech.

David, too, marked the difference in his
father, who nagged at him now with all the
old spirit. At first he rejoiced in the change,
preferring this outward and open warfare to
that aforetime stealthy enmity. But soon he
almost wished the other back; for the older he
grew the more difficult did he find it to endure
calmly these everlasting bickerings.

For one reason he was truly glad of the altered condition of affairs; he believed that,
for the nonce at least, his father had abandoned
any ill designs he might have cherished against
James Moore; those sneaking night-visits to
Kenmuir were, he hoped, discontinued.

Yet Maggie Moore, had she been on speaking terms with him, could have undeceived him.   For, one night, when alone in the kitchen, on suddenly looking up, she had seen to her horror a dim, moonlike face glued against the window-pane.   In the first mad panic of the moment she almost screamed, and dropped her work; then—a true Moore—controlled herself and sat feigning to work, yet watching all the while.

It was M'Adam, she recognized that: the face pale in its framework of black; the hair lying dank and dark on his forehead; and the white eyelids blinking, slow, regular, horrible. She thought of the stories she had heard of his sworn vengeance on her father, and her heart stood still, though she never moved.   At length with a gasp of relief she discerned that the eyes were not directed on her.   Stealthily following their gaze, she saw they rested on the Shepherds' Trophy; and on the Cup they remained fixed immovable, while she sat motionless and watched.

An hour, it seemed to her, elapsed before they shifted their direction, and wandered round the room.   For a second they dwelt upon her; then the face withdrew into the night.

Maggie told no one what she had seen. Knowing well how terrible her father was in anger, she deemed it wiser to keep silence. While as for David M'Adam, she should never speak to him again!

And not for a moment did that young man
surmise whence his father came when, on the
night in question, M'Adam returned to the
Grange, chuckling to himself. David was growing of late accustomed to these fits of silent,
unprovoked merriment; and when his father
began giggling and muttering to Red Wull,
at first he paid no heed.

"He! he! Wullie. Aiblins we'll beat him
yet. There's many a slip twixt Cup and lip—
eh, Wullie, he! he!" And he made allusion
to the flourishing of the wicked and their fall;
ending always with the same refrain: "He!
he! Wullie. Aiblins we'll beat him yet."

In this strain he continued until David, his
patience exhausted, asked roughly:

"What is't yo' mumblin' aboot? Wha is it
yo'll beat, you and yer Wullie?"

The lad's tone was as contemptuous as his
words. Long ago he had cast aside any sem-
blance of respect for his father.

M'Adam only rubbed his knees and giggled.

"Hark to the dear lad, Wullie! Listen hoo
pleasantly he addresses his auld dad!" Then
turning on his son, and leering at him: "Wha
is it, ye ask? Wha should it be but the Black
Killer? Wha else is there I'd be wushin' to
hurt?"

"The Black Killer!" echoed the boy, and
looked at his father in amazement.

Now David was almost the only man in

Wastrel-dale who denied Red Wull's identity with the Killer. "Nay," he said once; "he'd kill me, given half a chance, but a sheep—no." Yet, though himself of this opinion, he knew well what the talk was, and was astonished accordingly at his father's remark.

"The Black Killer, is it? What d'you know o' the Killer?" he inquired.

"Why *black*, I wad ken? Why *black?*" the little man asked, leaning forward in his chair.

Now David, though repudiating in the village Red Wull's complicity with the crimes, at home was never so happy as when casting cunning innuendoes to that effect.

"What would you have him then?" he asked. "Red, yaller, muck-dirt color?"—and he stared significantly at the Tailless Tyke, who was lying at his master's feet. The little man ceased rubbing his knees and eyed the boy. David shifted uneasily beneath that dim, persistent stare.

"Well?" he said at length gruffly.

The little man giggled, and his two thin hands took up their task again.

"Aiblins his puir auld doited fool of a dad kens mair than the dear lad thinks for, ay, or wushes—eh, Wullie, he! he!"

"Then what is it you do know, or think yo' know?" David asked irritably.

The little man nodded and chuckled.

"Naethin' ava, laddie, naethin' worth the

mention. Only aiblins the Killer'll be caught afore sae lang."

David smiled incredulously, wagging his head in offensive scepticism.

"Yo'll catch him yo'self, I s'pose, you and yer Wullie? Tak' a chair on to the Marches, whistle a while, and when the Killer comes, why! pit a pinch o' salt upon his tail—if he has one."

At the last words, heavily punctuated by the speaker, the little man stopped his rubbing as though shot.

"What wad ye mean by that?" he asked softly.

"What wad I?" the boy replied.

"I dinna ken for sure," the little man answered; "and it's aiblins just as well for you, dear lad"—in fawning accents—"that I dinna." He began rubbing and giggling afresh. "It's a gran' thing, Wullie, to ha' a dutiful son; a shairp lad wha has no silly sense o' shame aboot sharpenin' his wits at his auld dad's expense. And yet, despite oor facetious lad there, aiblins we will ha' a hand in the Killer's catchin', you and I, Wullie—he! he!" And the great dog at his feet wagged his stump tail in reply.

David rose from his chair and walked across the room to where his father sat.

"If yo' know sic a mighty heap," he shouted, "happen yo'll just tell me what yo' do know!"

M'Adam stopped stroking Red Wull's massive head, and looked up.

"Tell ye? Ay, wha should I tell if not ma dear David? Tell? Ay, I'll tell ye this"— with a sudden snarl of bitterness—"that you'd be the vairy last person I wad tell."

CHAPTER XVII

A MAD DOG

DAVID and Maggie, meanwhile, were drifting further and further apart. He now thought the girl took too much upon herself; that this assumption of the woman and the mother was overdone. Once, on a Sunday, he caught her hearing Andrew his catechism. He watched the performance through a crack in the door, and listened, giggling, to her simple teaching. At length his merriment grew so boisterous that she looked up, saw him, and, straightway rising to her feet, crossed the room and shut the door; tendering her unspoken rebuke with such a sweet dignity that he slunk away for once decently ashamed. And the incident served to add point to his hostility.

Consequently he was seldom at Kenmuir, and more often at home, quarrelling with his father.

Since that day, two years before, when the boy had been an instrument in the taking of the Cup from him, father and son had been like two vessels charged with electricity, contact between which might result at any moment in a shock and a flash. This was the outcome not of a moment, but of years.

Of late the contest had raged markedly fierce; for M'Adam noticed his son's more frequent presence at home, and commented on the fact in his usual spirit of playful raillery.

"What's come to ye, David?" he asked one day. "Yer auld dad's head is nigh turned wi' yer condescension. Is James Moore feared ye'll steal the Cup fra him, as ye stole it from me, that he'll not ha' ye at Kenmuir? or what is it?"

"I thought I could maybe keep an eye on the Killer gin I stayed here," David answered, leering at Red Wull.

"Ye'd do better at Kenmuir—eh, Wullie!" the little man replied.

"Nay," the other answered, "he'll not go to Kenmuir. There's Th' Owd Un to see to him there o' nights."

The little man whipped round.

"Are ye so sure he is there o' nights, ma lad?" he asked with slow significance.

"He was there when some one—I dinna say who, though I have ma thoughts—tried to poison him," sneered the boy, mimicking his father's manner.

M'Adam shook his head.

"If he was poisoned, and noo I think aiblins he was, he didna pick it up at Kenmuir, I tell ye that," he said, and marched out of the room.

In the mean time the Black Killer pursued

his bloody trade unchecked. The public, always greedy of a new sensation, took up the matter. In several of the great dailies, articles on the "Agrarian Outrages" appeared, followed by lengthy correspondence. Controversy raged high; each correspondent had his own theory and his own solution of the problem; and each waxed indignant as his were discarded for another's.

The Terror had reigned already two months when, with the advent of the lambing-time, matters took a yet more serious aspect.

It was bad enough to lose one sheep, often the finest in the pack; but the hunting of a flock at a critical moment, which was incidental to the slaughter of the one, the scaring of these woolly mothers-about-to-be almost out of their fleeces, spelt for the small farmers something akin to ruin, for the bigger ones a loss hardly bearable.

Such a woful season had never been known; loud were the curses, deep the vows of revenge. Many a shepherd at that time patrolled all night through with his dogs, only to find in the morning that the Killer had slipped him and havocked in some secluded portion of his beat.

It was heartrending work; and all the more so in that, though his incrimination seemed as far off as ever, there was still the same positiveness as to the culprit's identity.

Long Kirby, indeed, greatly daring, went

so far on one occasion as to say to the little man: "And d'yo' reck'n the Killer is a sheep-dog, M'Adam?"

"I do," the little man replied with conviction.

"And that he'll spare his own sheep?"

"Niver a doubt of it."

"Then," said the smith with a nervous cackle, "it must lie between you and Tupper and Saunderson."

The little man leant forward and tapped the other on the arm.

"Or Kenmuir, ma friend," he said. "Ye've forgot Kenmuir."

"So I have," laughed the smith, "so I have."

"Then I'd not anither time," the other continued, still tapping. "I'd mind Kenmuir, d'ye see, Kirby?"

.   .   .   .   .

It was about the middle of the lambing-time, when the Killer was working his worst, that the Dalesmen had a lurid glimpse of Adam M'Adam as he might be were he wounded through his Wullie.

Thus it came about: It was market-day in Grammoch-town, and in the Border Ram old Rob Saunderson was the centre of interest. For on the previous night Rob, who till then had escaped unscathed, had lost a sheep to the Killer: and—far worse—his flock of Herd-wicks, heavy in lamb, had been galloped with disastrous consequences.

The old man, with tears in his eyes, was telling how on four nights that week he had been up with Shep to guard against mishap; and on the fifth, worn out with his double labor, had fallen asleep at his post. But a very little while he slumbered; yet when, in the dawn, he woke and hurried on his rounds, he quickly came upon a mangled sheep and the pitiful relic of his flock. A relic, indeed! For all about were cold wee lambkins and their mothers, dead and dying of exhaustion and their unripe travail—a slaughter of the innocents.

The Dalesmen were clustered round the old shepherd, listening with lowering countenances, when a dark gray head peered in at the door and two wistful eyes dwelt for a moment on the speaker.

"Talk o' the devil!" muttered M'Adam, but no man heard him. For Red Wull, too, had seen that sad face, and, rising from his master's feet, had leapt with a roar at his enemy, toppling Jim Mason like a ninepin in the fury of his charge.

In a second every dog in the room, from the battered Venus to Tupper's big Rasper, was on his feet, bristling to have at the tyrant and wipe out past injuries, if the gray dog would but lead the dance.

It was not to be, however. For Long Kirby was standing at the door with a cup of hot coffee in his hand. Barely had he greeted the gray dog with—

" 'Ullo, Owd Un!" when hoarse yells of
" 'Ware, lad! The Terror!" mingled with Red
Wull's roar.

Half turning, he saw the great dog bounding to the attack. Straightway he flung the
boiling contents of his cup full in that rage-
wracked countenance. The burning liquid
swished against the huge bull-head. Blinding, bubbling, scalding, it did its fell work
well; nothing escaped that merciless torrent.
With a cry of agony, half bellow, half howl,
Red Wull checked in his charge. From
without the door was banged to; and
again the duel was postponed. While within
the tap-room a huddle of men and dogs
were left alone with a mad man and a madder
brute.

Blind, demented, agonized, the Tailless
Tyke thundered about the little room gnash-
ing, snapping, oversetting; men, tables, chairs
swirled off their legs as though they had
been dolls. He spun round like a monstrous
teetotum; he banged his tortured head against
the wall; he burrowed into the unyielding
floor. And all the while M'Adam pattered
after him, laying hands upon him only to be
flung aside as a terrier flings a rat. Now up,
now down again, now tossed into a corner,
now dragged upon the floor, yet always following on and crying in supplicating tones, "Wullie, Wullie, let me to ye! let yer man ease ye!"
and then, with a scream and a murderous

glance, "By——, Kirby, I'll deal wi' you later!"

The uproar was like hell let loose. You could hear the noise of oaths and blows, as the men fought for the door, a half-mile away. And above it the horrid bellowing and the screaming of that shrill voice.

Long Kirby was the first man out of that murder-hole; and after him the others toppled one by one—men and dogs jostling one another in the frenzy of their fear. Big Bell, Londesley, Tupper, Hoppin, Teddy Bolstock, white-faced and trembling; and old Saunderson they pulled out by his heels. Then the door was shut with a clang, and the little man and mad dog were left alone.

In the street was already a big-eyed crowd, attracted by the uproar; while at the door was James Moore, seeking entrance. "Happen I could lend the little mon a hand," said he; but they withheld him forcibly.

Inside was pandemonium: bangings like the doors of hell; the bellowing of that great voice; the patter of little feet; the slithering of a body on the floor; and always that shrill, beseeching prayer, "Wullie, Wullie, let me to ye!" and, in a scream, "By——, Kirby, I'll be wi' ye soon!"

Jim Mason it was who turned, at length, to the smith and whispered, "Kirby, lad, yo'd best skip it."

The big man obeyed and ran. The stamp,

stamp of his feet on the hard road rang above the turmoil. As the long legs vanished round the corner and the sound of the fugitive died away, a panic seized the listening crowd.

A woman shrieked; a girl fainted; and in two minutes the street was as naked of men as the steppes of Russia in winter: here a white face at a window; there a door ajar; and peering round a far corner a frightened boy. One man only scorned to run. Alone, James Moore stalked down the centre of the road, slow and calm, Owd Bob trotting at his heels.

It was a long half-hour before the door of the inn burst open, and M'Adam came out with a run, flinging the door behind him.

He rushed into the middle of the road; his sleeves were rolled at the wrist like a surgeon's; and in his right hand was a black-handled jack-knife.

"Noo, by——!" he cried in a terrible voice, "where is he?"

He looked up and down the road, darting his fiery glances everywhere; and his face was whiter than his hair.

Then he turned and hunted madly down the whole length of the High, nosing like a weasel in every cranny, stabbing at the air as he went, and screaming, "By——, Kirby, wait till I get ye!"

CHAPTER XVIII

HOW THE KILLER WAS SINGED

No further harm came of the incident; but it served as a healthy object-lesson for the Dalesmen.

A coincidence it may have been, but, as a fact, for the fortnight succeeding Kirby's exploit there was a lull in the crimes. There followed, as though to make amends, the seven days still remembered in the Daleland as the Bloody Week.

On the Sunday the Squire lost a Cheviot ewe, killed not a hundred yards from the Manor wall. On the Monday a farm on the Black Water was marked with the red cross. On Tuesday—a black night—Tupper at Swinsthwaite came upon the murderer at his work; he fired into the darkness without effect; and the Killer escaped with a scaring. On the following night Viscount Birdsaye lost a shearling ram, for which he was reported to have paid a fabulous sum. Thursday was the one blank night of the week. On Friday Tupper was again visited and punished heavily, as though in revenge for that shot.

On the Saturday afternoon a big meeting

was held at the Manor to discuss measures.
The Squire presided; gentlemen and magis-
trates were there in numbers, and every farmer
in the country-side.

To start the proceedings the Special Commissioner read a futile letter from the Board
of Agriculture. After him Viscount Birdsaye
rose and proposed that a reward more suitable
to the seriousness of the case than the paltry
£5 of the Police should be offered, and backed
his proposal with a £25 cheque. Several others spoke, and, last of all, Parson Leggy rose.

He briefly summarized the history of the
crimes; reiterated his belief that a sheep-dog
was the criminal; declared that nothing had
occurred to shake his conviction; and concluded by offering a remedy for their consideration. Simple it was, so he said, to laughableness; yet, if their surmise was correct, it
would serve as an effectual preventive if not
cure, and would at least give them time to
turn round. He paused.

"My suggestion is: That every man-jack of
you who owns a sheep-dog ties him up at
night."

The farmers were given half an hour to consider the proposal, and clustered in knots talking it over. Many an eye was directed on
M'Adam; but that little man appeared all
unconscious.

"Weel, Mr. Saunderson," he was saying in
shrill accents, "and shall ye tie Shep?"

"What d'yo' think?" asked Rob, eying the man at whom the measure was aimed.

"Why, it's this way, I'm thinkin'," the little man replied. "Gin ye haud Shep's the guilty one I *wad*, by all manner o' means—or shootin'd be ailbins better. If not, why"—he shrugged his shoulders significantly; and having shown his hand and driven the nail well home, the little man left the meeting.

James Moore stayed to see the Parson's resolution negatived by a large majority, and then he too quitted the hall. He had foreseen the result, and, previous to the meeting, had warned the Parson how it would be.

"Tie up!" he cried almost indignantly, as Owd Bob came galloping up to his whistle; "I think I see myself chainin' yo', owd lad, like ony murderer. Why, it's yo' has kept the Killer off Kenmuir so far, I'll lay."

At the lodge-gate was M'Adam, for once without his familiar spirit, playing with the lodge-keeper's child; for the little man loved all children but his own, and was beloved of them. As the Master approached he looked up.

"Weel, Moore," he called, "and are you gaein' to tie yer dog?"

"I will if you will yours," the Master answered grimly.

"Na," the little man replied, "it's Wullie as frichts the Killer aff the Grange. That's why I've left him there noo."

"It's the same wi' me," the Master said. "He's not come to Kenmuir yet, nor he'll not so long as Th' Owd Un's loose, I reck'n."

"Loose or tied, for the matter o' that," the little man rejoined, "Kenmuir'll escape." He made the statement dogmatically, snapping his lips.

The Master frowned.

"Why that?" he asked.

"Ha' ye no heard what they're sayin'?" the little man inquired with raised eyebrows.

"Nay; what?"

"Why, that the mere repitation o' th' best sheep-dog in the North' should keep him aff. An' I guess they're reet," and he laughed shrilly as he spoke.

The Master passed on, puzzled.

"Which road are ye gaein' hame?" M'Adam called after him. "Because," with a polite smile, "I'll tak' t'ither."

"I'm off by the Windy Brae," the Master answered, striding on. "Squire asked me to leave a note wi' his shepherd t'other side o' the Chair." So he headed away to the left, making for home by the route along the Silver Mere.

It is a long sweep of almost unbroken moorland, the well-called Windy Brae; sloping gently down in mile on mile of heather from the Mere Marches on the top to the fringe of the Silver Mere below. In all that waste of moor the only break is the quaint-shaped

Giant's Chair, puzzle of geologists, looking as
though plumped down by accident in the
heathery wild. The ground rises suddenly
from the uniform grade of the Brae; up it
goes, ever growing steeper, until at length it
runs abruptly into a sheer curtain of rock—the
Fall—which rises perpendicular some forty
feet, on the top of which rests that tiny grassy
bowl—not twenty yards across—they call the
Scoop.

The Scoop forms the seat of the Chair and
reposes on its collar of rock, cool and green
and out of the world, like wine in a metal cup;
in front is the forty-foot Fall; behind, rising
sheer again, the wall of rock which makes the
back of the Chair. Inaccessible from above,
the only means of entrance to that little dell
are two narrow sheep-tracks, which crawl dangerously up between the sheer wall on the one
hand and the sheer Fall on the other, entering
it at opposite sides.

It stands out clear-cut from the gradual in-
cline, that peculiar eminence; yet as the Master and Owd Bob debouched on to the Brae it
was already invisible in the darkening night.

Through the heather the two swung, the
Master thinking now with a smile of David
and Maggie; wondering what M'Adam had
meant; musing with a frown on the Killer;
pondering on his identity—for he was half of
David's opinion as to Red Wull's innocence;
and thanking his stars that so far Kenmuir

had escaped, a piece of luck he attributed entirely to the vigilance of Th' Owd Un, who, sleeping in the porch, slipped out at all hours and went his rounds, warding off danger. And at the thought he looked down for the dark head which should be travelling at his knee; yet could not see it, so thick hung the pall of night.

So he brushed his way along, and ever the night grew blacker; until, from the swell of the ground beneath his feet, he knew himself skirting the Giant's Chair.

Now as he sped along the foot of the rise, of a sudden there burst on his ear the myriad patter of galloping feet. He turned, and at the second a swirl of sheep almost bore him down. It was velvet-black, and they fled furiously by, yet he dimly discovered, driving at their trails, a vague hound-like form.

"The Killer, by thunder!" he ejaculated, and, startled though he was, struck down at that last pursuing shape, to miss and almost fall.

"Bob, lad!" he cried, "follow on!" and swung round; but in the darkness could not see if the gray dog had obeyed.

The chase swept on into the night, and, far above him on the hill-side, he could now hear the rattle of the flying feet. He started hotly in pursuit, and then, recognizing the futility of following where he could not see his hand, desisted. So he stood motionless, listening

and peering into the blackness, hoping Th'
Owd Un was on the villain's heels.

He prayed for the moon; and, as though in
answer, the lantern of the night shone out and
lit the dour face of the Chair above him.   He
shot a glance at his feet; and thanked heaven
on finding the gray dog was not beside
him.

Then he looked up.   The sheep had broken,
and were scattered over the steep hill-side, still
galloping madly.   In the rout one pair of
darting figures caught and held his gaze: the
foremost dodging, twisting, speeding upward,
the hinder hard on the leader's heels, swift,
remorseless, never changing.   He looked for
a third pursuing form; but none could he discern.

"He mun ha' missed him in the dark," the
Master muttered, the sweat standing on his
brow, as he strained his eyes upward.

Higher and higher sped those two dark
specks, far out-topping the scattered remnant
of the flock.   Up and up, until of a sudden
the sheer Fall dropped its relentless barrier in
the path of the fugitive.   Away, scudding
along the foot of the rock-wall struck the
familiar track leading to the Scoop, and up it,
bleating pitifully, nigh spent, the Killer hard
on her now.

"He'll doon her in the Scoop!" cried the
Master hoarsely, following with fascinated
eyes.   "Owd Un! Owd Un! wheer iver are

yo' gotten to?" he called in agony; but no Owd Un made reply.

As they reached the summit, just as he had prophesied, the two black dots were one; and down they rolled together into the hollow of the Scoop, out of the Master's ken. At the same instant the moon, as though loth to watch the last act of the bloody play, veiled her face.

It was his chance. "Noo!"—and up the hillside he sped like a young man, girding his loins for the struggle. The slope grew steep and steeper; but on and on he held in the darkness, gasping painfully, yet running still, until the face of the Fall blocked his way too.

There he paused a moment, and whistled a low call. Could he but dispatch the old dog up the one path to the Scoop, while he took the other, the murderer's one road to safety would be blocked.

He waited, all expectant; but no cold muzzle was shoved into his hand. Again he whistled. A pebble from above almost dropped on him, as if the criminal up there had moved to the brink of the Fall to listen; and he dared no more.

He waited till all was still again, then crept, cat-like, along the rock-foot, and hit, at length, the track up which a while before had fled Killer and victim. Up that ragged way he crawled on hands and knees. The perspiration rolled off his face; one elbow brushed the

rock perpetually; one hand plunged ever and
anon into that naked emptiness on the other
side.

He prayed that the moon might keep in but
a little longer; that his feet might be saved
from falling, where a slip might well mean
death, certain destruction to any chance of
success. He cursed his luck that Th' Owd Un
had somehow missed him in the dark; for now
he must trust to chance, his own great
strength, and his good oak stick. And he as
climbed, he laid his plan: to rush in on the
Killer as he still gorged and grapple with
him. If in the darkness he missed—and in
that narrow arena the contingency was im-
probable—the murderer might still, in the
panic of the moment, forget the one path to
safety and leap over the Fall to his destruction.

At length he reached the summit and paused
to draw breath. The black void before him
was the Scoop, and in its bosom—not ten
yards away—must be lying the Killer and the
killed.

He crouched against the wet rock-face and
listened. In that dark silence, poised 'twixt
heaven and earth, he seemed a million miles
apart from living soul.

No sound, and yet the murderer must
be there. Ay, there was the tinkle of a dis-
lodged stone; and again, the tread of stealthy
feet.

The Killer was moving; alarmed; was off. Quick!

He rose to his full height; gathered himself, and leapt.

Something collided with him as he sprang; something wrestled madly with him; something wrenched from beneath him; and in a clap he heard the thud of a body striking ground far below, and the slithering and splattering of some creature speeding furiously down the hill-side and away.

"Who the blazes?" roared he.

"What the devil?" screamed a little voice.

The moon shone out.

"Moore!"

"M'Adam!"

And there they were still struggling over the body of a dead sheep.

In a second they had disengaged and rushed to the edge of the Fall. In the quiet they could still hear the scrambling hurry of the fugitive far below them. Nothing was to be seen, however, save an array of startled sheep on the hill-side, mute witnesses of the murderer's escape.

The two men turned and eyed each other; the one grim, the other sardonic: both dishevelled and suspicious.

"Well?"

"Weel?"

A pause and, careful scrutiny.

"There's blood on your coat."

"And on yours."

Together they walked back into the little
moon-lit hollow. There lay the murdered
sheep in a pool of blood. Plain it was to see
whence the marks on their coats came.
M'Adam touched the victim's head with his
foot. The movement exposed its throat,
With a shudder he replaced it as it was.

The two men stood back and eyed one another.

"What are yo' doin' here?"

"After the Killer. What are you?"

"After the Killer?"

"Hoo did you come?"

"Up this path," pointing to the one behind
him. "Hoo did you?"

"Up this."

Silence; then again:

"I'd ha' had him but for yo'."

"I did have him, but ye tore me aff,"

A pause again.

"Where's yer gray dog?" This time the
challenge was unmistakable.

"I sent him after the Killer. Wheer's your
Red Wull?"

"At hame, as I tell't ye before."

"Yo' mean yo' left him there?"

M'Adams' fingers twitched.

"He's where I left him."

James Moore shrugged his shoulders. And
the other began:

"When did yer dog leave ye?"

"When the Killer came past."

"Ye wad say ye missed him then?"

"I say what I mean."

"Ye say he went after the Killer. Noo the Killer was here," pointing to the dead sheep. "Was your dog here, too?"

"If he had been he'd been here still."

"Onless he went over the Fall!"

"That was the Killer, yo' fule."

"Or your dog."

"There was only *one* beneath me. I felt him."

"Just so," said M'Adam, and laughed. The other's brow contracted.

"An' that was a big un," he said slowly. The little man stopped his cackling.

"There ye lie," he said, smoothly. "He was small."

They looked one another full in the eyes.

"That's a matter of opinion," said the Master.

"It's a matter of fact," said the other.

The two stared at one another, silent and stern, each trying to fathom the other's soul; then they turned again to the brink of the Fall. Beneath them, plain to see, was the splash and furrow in the shingle marking the Killer's line of retreat. They looked at one another again, and then each departed the way he had come to give his version of the story.

"We mucked it atween us," said the Master.

'If Th' Owd Un had kept wi' me, I should
ha' had him.''

And—

"I tell ye I did have him, but James Moore
pulled me aff.   Strange, too, his dog not bein'
wi' him!''

CHAPTER XIX

LAD AND LASS

AN immense sensation this affair of the Scoop created in the Daleland. It spurred the Dalesmen into fresh endeavors. James Moore and M'Adam were examined and re-examined as to the minutest details of the matter. The whole country-side was placarded with huge bills, offering £100 reward for the capture of the criminal dead or alive. While the vigilance of the watchers was such that in a single week they bagged a donkey, an old woman, and two amateur detectives.

In Wastrel-dale the near escape of the Killer, the collision between James Moore and Adam, and Owd Bob's unsuccess, who was not wont to fail, aroused intense excitement, with which was mingled a certain anxiety as to their favorite.

For when the Master had reached home that night, he had found the old dog already there, and he must have wrenched his foot in the pursuit or run a thorn into it, for he was very lame. Whereat, when it was reported at the Sylvester Arms, M'Adam winked at Red Wull and muttered, "Ah, forty foot is an ugly tumble."

A week later the little man called at Kenmuir. As he entered the yard, David was standing outside the kitchen window, looking very glum and miserable. On seeing his father, however, the boy started forward, all alert.

"What d'yo' want here?" he cried roughly.

"Same as you, dear lad," the little man giggled, advancing. "I come on a visit."

"Your visits to Kenmuir are usually paid by night, so I've heard," David sneered.

The little man affected not to hear.

"So they dinna allow ye indoors wi' the Cup," he laughed. "They know yer little ways then, David,"

"Nay, I'm not wanted in there," David answered bitterly, but not so loud that his father could hear. Maggie within the kitchen heard, however, but paid no heed; for her heart was hard against the boy, who of late, though he never addressed her, had made himself as unpleasant in a thousand little ways as only David M'Adam could.

At that moment the Master came stalking into the yard, Owd Bob preceding him; and as the old dog recognized his visitor he bristled involuntarily.

At the sight of the Master M'Adam hurried forward.

"I did but come to ask after the tyke," he said. "Is he gettin' over his lameness?"

James Moore looked surprised; then his

stern face relaxed into a cordial smile. Such
generous anxiety as to the welfare of Red
Wull's rival was a wholly new characteristic
in the little man.

"I tak' it kind in yo', M'Adam," he said,
"to come and inquire."

"Is the thorn oot?" asked the little man
with eager interest, shooting his head forward
to stare closely at the other.

"It came oot last night wi' the poulticin',"
the Master answered, returning the other's
gaze, calm and steady.

"I'm glad o' that," said the little man, still
staring. But his yellow, grinning face said as
plain as words, "What a liar ye are, James
Moore."

The days passed on. His father's taunts
and gibes, always becoming more bitter, drove
David almost to distraction.

He longed to make it up with Maggie; he
longed for that tender sympathy which the
girl had always extended to him when his
troubles with his father were heavy on him.
The quarrel had lasted for months now, and
he was well weary of it, and utterly ashamed.
For, at least, he had the good grace to acknowledge that no one was to blame but himself; and that it had been fostered solely by
his ugly pride.

At length he could endure it no longer, and
determined to go to the girl and ask forgive-

ness.   It would be a bitter ordeal to him; always unwilling to acknowledge a fault, even to
himself, how much harder would it be to confess it to this strip of a girl.   For a time he
thought it was almost more than he could do.
Yet, like his father, once set upon a course,
nothing could divert him.   So, after a week
of doubts and determinations, of cowardice
and courage, he pulled himself together and
off he set.

An hour it took him from the Grange to the
bridge over the Wastrel—an hour which had
wont to be a quarter.   Now, as he walked
on up the slope from the stream, very slowly,
heartening himself for his penance, he was
aware of a strange disturbance in the yard
above him: the noisy cackling of hens, the
snorting of pigs disturbed, and above the rest
the cry of a little child ringing out in shrill
distress.

He set to running, and sped up the slope as
fast as his long legs would carry him.   As he
took the gate in his stride, he saw the white-
clad figure of Wee Anne fleeing with unsteady,
toddling steps, her fair hair streaming out behind, and one bare arm striking wildly back at
a great pursuing sow.

David shouted as he cleared the gate, but
the brute paid no heed, and was almost touching the fugitive when Owd Bob came galloping
round the corner, and in a second had flashed
between pursuer and pursued.   So close were

the two that as he swung round on the startled
sow, his tail brushed the baby to the ground;
and there she lay kicking fat legs to heaven
and calling on all her gods.

David, leaving the old dog to secure the
warrior pig, ran round to her; but he was anticipated. The whole matter had barely occu-
pied a minute's time; and Maggie, rushing
from the kitchen, now had the child in her
arms and was hurrying back with her to the
house.

"Eh, ma pet, are yo' hurted, dearie?" David
could hear her asking tearfully, as he crossed
the yard and established himself in the door.

"Well," said he, in bantering tones, "yo'm
a nice wench to ha' charge o' oor Annie!"

It was a sore subject with the girl, and well
he knew it. Wee Anne, that golden-haired
imp of mischief, was forever evading her
sister-mother's eye and attempting to immo-
late herself. More than once she had only
been saved from serious hurt by the watchful
devotion of Owd Bob, who always found time,
despite his many labors, to keep a guardian
eye on his well-loved lassie. In the previous
winter she had been lost on a bitter night on
the Muir Pike; once she had climbed into a
field with the Highland bull, and barely escaped with her life, while the gray dog held
the brute in check; but a little while before
she had been rescued from drowning by the
Tailless Tyke; there had been numerous other

mischances; and now the present mishap.
But the girl paid no heed to her tormentor in
her joy at finding the child all unhurt.

"Theer! yo' bain't so much as scratted, ma
precious, is yo'?" she cried. "Rin oot agin,
then," and the baby toddled joyfully away.

Maggie rose to her feet and stood with face
averted. David's eyes dwelt lovingly upon
her, admiring the pose of the neat head with
its thatch of pretty brown hair; the slim figure,
and slender ankles, peeping modestly from
beneath her print frock.

"Ma word! if yo' dad should hear tell o'
hoo his Anne——" he broke off into a long-
drawn whistle.

Maggie kept silence; but her lips quivered,
and the flush deepened on her cheek.

"I'm fear'd I'll ha' to tell him," the boy
continued, "'Tis but ma duty."

"Yo' may tell wham yo' like what yo' like,"
the girl replied coldly; yet there was a tremor
in her voice.

"First yo' throws her in the stream," David
went on remorselessly; "then yo' chucks her
to the pig, and if it had not bin for me——"

"Yo', indeed!" she broke in contemptuously. "Yo'! 'twas Owd Bob reskied her.
Yo'd nowt' to do wi' it, 'cept lookin' on—'bout
what yo're fit for."

"I tell yo'," David pursued stubbornly,
"an' it had not bin for me yo' wouldn't have
no sister by noo. She'd be lying', she would,

pore little lass, cold as ice, pore mite, wi' no
breath in her.   An' when yo' dad coom home
there'd be no Wee Anne to rin to him, and
climb on his knee, and yammer to him, and
beat his face.   An he'd say, 'What's gotten
to oor Annie, as I left wi' yo'?'   And then
yo'd have to tell him, 'I never took no manner
o' fash after her, dad; d'reckly yo' back was
turned, I——'"

The girl sat down, buried her face in her
apron, and indulged in the rare luxury of tears.

"Yo're the cruellest mon as iver was, David
M'Adam," she sobbed, rocking to and fro.

He was at her side in a moment, tenderly
bending over her.

"Eh, Maggie, but I am sorry, lass——"

She wrenched away from beneath his hands.

"I hate yo'," she cried passionately.

He gently removed her hands from before
her tear-stained face.

"I was nob'but laffin', Maggie," he pleaded;
"say yo' forgie me."

"I don't," she cried, struggling.   "I think
yo're the hatefullest lad as iver lived."

The moment was critical; it was a time for
heroic measures.

"No, yo' don't, lass," he remonstrated;
and, releasing her wrists, lifted the little
drooping face, wet as it was, like the earth
after a spring shower, and, holding it between
his two big hands, kissed it twice.

"Yo' coward!" she cried, a flood of warm

red crimsoning her cheeks; and she struggled vainly to be free.

"Yo' used to let me," he reminded her in aggrieved tones.

"I niver did!" she cried, more indignant than truthful.

"Yes, yo' did, when we was little uns; that is, yo' was allus for kissin' and I was allus agin it. And noo," with whole-souled bitterness, "I mayn't so much as keek at yo' over a stone wall."

However that might be, he was keeking at her from closer range now; and in that position—for he held her firmly still—she could not help but keek back. He looked so handsome —humble for once; penitent yet reproachful; his own eyes a little moist; and, withal, his old audacious self,—that, despite herself, her anger grew less hot.

"Say yo' forgie me and I'll let yo' go."

"I don't, nor niver shall," she answered firmly; but there was less conviction in her heart than voice.

"Iss yo' do, lass," he coaxed, and kissed her again.

She struggled faintly.

"Hoo daur yo'?" she cried through her tears. But he was not to be moved.

"Will yo' noo?" he asked.

She remained dumb, and he kissed her again.

"Impidence!" she cried.

"Ay," said he, closing her mouth.

"I wonder at ye, Davie!" she said, surrendering.

After that Maggie must needs give in; and it was well understood, though nothing definite had been said, that the boy and girl were courting. And in the Dale the unanimous opinion was that the young couple would make "a gradely pair, surely."

M'Adam was the last person to hear the news, long after it had been common knowledge in the village. It was in the Sylvester Arms he first heard it, and straightway fell into one of those foaming frenzies characteristic of him.

"The dochter o' Moore o' Kenmuir, d'ye say? sic a dochter o' sic a man! The dochter o' th' one man in the warld that's harmed me aboon the rest! I'd no ha' believed it gin ye'd no tell't me. Oh, David, David! I'd no ha' thocht it even o' you, ill son as ye've aye bin to me. I think he might ha' waited till his auld dad was gone, and he'd no had to wait lang the noo." Then the little man sat down and burst into tears. Gradually, however, he resigned himself, and the more readily when he realized that David by his act had exposed a fresh wound into which he might plunge his barbed shafts. And he availed himself to the full of his new opportunities. Often and often David was sore pressed to restrain himself.

"Is't true what they're sayin' that Maggie Moore's nae better than she should be?" the little man asked one evening with anxious interest.

"They're not sayin' so, and if they were 'twad be a lie," the boy answered angrily.

M'Adam leant back in his chair and nodded his head.

"Ay, they tell't me that gin ony man knew 'twad be David M'Adam."

David strode across the room.

"No, no mair o' that," he shouted. "Y'ought to be 'shamed, an owd mon like you, to speak so o' a lass." The little man edged close up to his son, and looked up into the fair flushed face towering above him.

"David," he said in smooth soft tones, "I'm 'stonished ye dinna strike yer auld dad." He stood with his hands clasped behind his back as if daring the young giant to raise a finger against him. "Ye maist might noo," he continued suavely. "Ye maun be sax inches taller, and a good four stane heavier. Hooiver, aiblins ye're wise to wait. Anither year twa I'll be an auld man, as ye say, and feebler, and Wullie here'll be gettin' on, while you'll be in the prime o' yer strength. Then I think ye might hit me wi' safety to your person, and honor to yourself."

He took a pace back, smiling.

"Feyther," said David, huskily, "one day yo'll drive me too far."

CHAPTER XX

THE SNAPPING OF THE STRING

THE spring was passing, marked throughout with the bloody trail of the Killer. The
adventure in the Scoop scared him for a while
into innocuousness; then he resumed his game
again with redoubled zest. It seemed likely
he would harry the district till some lucky
accident carried him off, for all chance there
was of arresting him.

You could still hear nightly in the Sylvester
Arms and elsewhere the assertion, delivered
with the same dogmatic certainty as of old,
"It's the Terror, I tell yo'!" and that irrita-
ting, inevitable reply: "Ay; but wheer's the
proof?" While often, at the same moment,
in a house not far away, a little lonely man
was sitting before a low-burnt fire, rocking to
and fro, biting his nails, and muttering to the
great dog whose head lay between his knees:
"If we had but the proof, Wullie! if we had
but the proof! I'd give ma right hand aff my
arm gin we had the proof to-morrow."

Long Kirby, who was always for war when
some one else was to do the fighting, suggested
that David should be requested, in the name
of the Dalesmen, to tell M'Adam that he must

make an end to Red Wull. But Jim Mason
quashed the proposal, remarking truly enough
that there was too much bad blood as it was
between father and son; while Tammas proposed with a sneer that the smith should be
his own agent in the matter.

Whether it was this remark of Tammas's
which stung the big man into action, or
whether it was that the intensity of his hate
gave him unusual courage, anyhow, a few days
later, M'Adam caught him lurking in the
granary of the Grange.

The little man may not have guessed his
murderous intent; yet the blacksmith's white-
faced terror, as he crouched away in the darkest corner, could hardly have escaped remark;
though—and Kirby may thank his stars for it
—the treacherous gleam of a gun-barrel, ill-
concealed behind him, did.

"Hullo, Kirby!" said M'Adam cordially,
"ye'll stay the night wi' me?" And the next
thing the big man heard was a giggle on the far
side the door, lost in the clank of padlock and
rattle of chain. Then—through a crack—
"Good-night to ye. Hope ye'll be comfie."
And there he stayed that night, the following
day and next night—thirty-six hours in all,
with swedes for his hunger and the dew off
the thatch for his thirst.

Meanwhile the struggle between David and
his father seemed coming to a head. The
little man's tongue wagged more bitterly than

ever; now it was never at rest—searching out
sores, stinging, piercing.

Worst of all, he was continually dropping
innuendoes, seemingly innocent enough, yet
with a world of subtile meaning at their back,
respecting Maggie. The leer and wink with
which, when David came home from Kenmuir
at nights, he would ask the simple question,
"And was she kind, David—eh, eh?" made
the boy's blood boil within him.

And the more effective the little man saw
his shots to be, the more persistently he plied
them. And David retaliated in kind. It was
a war of reprisals. There was no peace; there
were no truces in which to bury the dead before the opponents set to slaying others. And
every day brought the combatants nearer to
that final struggle, the issue of which neither
cared to contemplate.

There came a Saturday, toward the end of
the spring, long to be remembered by more
than David in the Dale.

For that young man the day started sensa-
tionally. Rising before cock-crow, and going
to the window, the first thing he saw in the
misty dawn was the gaunt, gigantic figure of
Red Wull, hounding up the hill from the
Stony Bottom; and in an instant his faith was
shaken to its foundation.

The dog was travelling up at a long, slouch-
ing trot; and as he rapidly approached the

house, David saw that his flanks were all splashed with red mud, his tongue out, and the foam dripping from his jaws, as though he had come far and fast.

He slunk up to the house, leapt on to the sill of the unused back-kitchen, some five feet from the ground, pushed with his paw at the cranky old hatchment, which was its only covering; and, in a second, the boy, straining out of the window the better to see, heard the rattle of the boards as the dog dropped within the house.

For the moment, excited as he was, David held his peace. Even the Black Killer took only second place in his thoughts that morning. For this was to be a momentous day for him.

That afternoon James Moore and Andrew would, he knew, be over at Grammoch-town, and, his work finished for the day, he was resolved to tackle Maggie and decide his fate. If she would have him—well, he would go next morning and thank God for it, kneeling beside her in the tiny village church; if not, he would leave the Grange and all its unhappiness behind, and straightway plunge out into the world.

All through a week of stern work he had looked forward to this hard-won half-holiday. Therefore, when, as he was breaking off at noon, his father turned to him and said abruptly:

"David, ye're to tak' the Cheviot lot o'er to Grammoch-town at once," he answered shortly:

"Yo' mun tak' 'em yo'sel', if yo' wish 'em to go to-day."

"Na," the little man answered; "Wullie and me, we're busy. Ye're to tak' 'em, I tell ye."

"I'll not," David replied. "If they wait for me, they wait till Monday," and with that he left the room.

"I see what 'tis," his father called after him; "she's give ye a tryst at Kenmuir. Oh, ye randy David!"

"Yo' tend yo' business; I'll tend mine," the boy answered hotly.

Now it happened that on the previous day Maggie had given him a photograph of herself, or, rather, David had taken it and Maggie had demurred. As he left the room it dropped from his pocket. He failed to notice his loss, but directly he was gone M'Adam pounced on it.

"He! he! Wullie, what's this?" he giggled, holding the photograph into his face. "He! he! it's the jade hersel', I war'nt; it's Jezebel!"

He peered into the picture.

"She kens what's what, I'll tak' oath, Wullie. See her eyes—sae saft and languishin'; and her lips—such lips, Wullie!" He held the picture down for the great dog to see: then walked out of the room, still sniggering, and chucking the face insanely beneath its card-board chin.

Outside the house he collided against David. The boy had missed his treasure and was hurrying back for it.

"What yo' got theer?" he asked suspiciously.

"Only the pictur' o' some randy quean," his father answered, chucking away at the inanimate chin.

"Gie it me!" David ordered fiercely. "It's mine."

"Na, na," the little man replied. "It's no for sic douce lads as dear David to ha' ony touch wi' leddies sic as this."

"Gie it me, I tell ye, or I'll tak' it!" the boy shouted.

"Na, na; it's ma duty as yer dad to keep ye from sic limmers." He turned, still smiling, to Red Wull.

"There ye are, Wullie!" He threw the photograph to the dog. "Tear her, Wullie, the Jezebel!"

The Tailless Tyke sprang on the picture, placed one big paw in the very centre of the face, forcing it into the muck, and tore a corner off; then he chewed the scrap with unctious, slobbering gluttony, dropped it, and tore a fresh piece.

David dashed forward.

"Touch it, if ye daur, ye brute!" he yelled; but his father seized him and held him back.

" 'And the dogs o' the street,' " he quoted.
David turned furiously on him.

"I've half a mind to brak' ivery bone in yer
body!" he shouted, "robbin' me o' what's
mine and throwin' it to yon black brute!"

"Whist, David, whist!" soothed the little
man. "Twas but for yer ain good yer auld
dad did it. 'Twas that he had at heart as he
aye has. Rin aff wi' ye noo to Kenmuir.
She'll mak' it up to ye, I war'nt. She's leeberal wi' her favors, I hear. Ye've but to
whistle and she'll come."

David seized his father by the shoulder.

"An' yo' gie me much more o' your sauce,"
he roared.

"Sauce, Wullie," the little man echoed in
gentle voice.

"I'll twist yer neck for yo'!"

"He'll twist my neck for me."

"I'll gang reet awa', I warn yo', and leave
you and yer Wullie to yer lone."

The little man began to whimper.

"It'll brak' yer auld dad's heart, lad," he
said.

"Nay; yo've got none. But 'twill ruin yo',
please God. For yo' and yer Wullie'll get
ne'er a soul to work for yo'—yo' cheeseparin',
dirty-tongued Jew."

The little man burst into an agony of affected tears, rocking to and fro, his face in his
hands.

"Waesucks, Wullie! d'ye hear him? He's

gaein' to leave us—the son o' my bosom! my Benjamin! my little Davie! he's gaein' awa'!"

David turned away down the hill; and M'Adam lifted his stricken face and waved a hand at him.

" 'Adieu, dear amiable youth!' " he cried in broken voice; and straightway set to sobbing again.

Half-way down to the Stony Bottom David turned.

"I'll gie yo' a word o' warnin'," he shouted back. "I'd advise yo' to keep a closer eye to yer Wullie's goings on, 'specially o' nights, or happen yo'll wake to a surprise one mornin'."

In an instant the little man ceased his fooling.

"And why that?" he asked, following down the hill.

"I'll tell yo'. When I wak' this mornin' I walked to the window, and what d'yo' think I see? Why, your Wullie gollopin' like a good un up from the Bottom, all foamin', too, and red-splashed, as if he'd coom from the Screes. What had he bin up to, I'd like to know?"

"What should he be doin'," the little man replied, "but havin' an eye to the stock? and that when the Killer might be oot."

David laughed harshly.

"Ay, the Killer was oot, I'll go bail, and yo' may hear o't afore the evenin', ma man," and with that he turned away again.

As he had foreseen, David found Maggie

"Maggie sat in her father's chair by the fire, knitting; while he
lounged on the kitchen table."

alone. But in the heat of his indignation against his father he seemed to have forgotten his original intent, and instead poured his latest troubles into the girl's sympathetic ear.

"There's but one mon in the world he wishes worse nor me," he was saying. It was late in the afternoon, and he was still inveighing against his father and his fate. Maggie sat in her father's chair by the fire, knitting; while he lounged on the kitchen table, swinging his long legs.

"And who may that be?" the girl asked.

"Why, Mr. Moore, to be sure, and Th' Owd Un, too. He'd do either o' them a mischief if he could."

"But why, David?" she asked anxiously. "I'm sure dad niver hurt him, or ony ither mon for the matter o' that."

David nodded toward the Dale Cup which rested on the mantelpiece in silvery majesty.

"It's yon done it," he said. "And if Th' Owd Un wins agin, as win he will, bless him! why, look out for 'me and ma Wullie'; that's all."

Maggie shuddered, and thought of the face at the window.

" 'Me and ma Wullie,' " David continued; "I've had about as much of them as I can swaller. It's aye the same—'Me and ma Wullie,' and 'Wullie and me,' as if I never put ma hand to a stroke! Ugh!"—he made a gesture of passionate disgust—"the two on 'em fair

madden me. I could strike the one and throttle t'other," and he rattled his heels angrily
together.

"Hush, David," interposed the girl; "yo'
munna speak so o' your dad; it's agin the
commandments."

" 'Tain't agin human nature," he snapped in
answer. "Why, 'twas nob'but yester' morn'
he says in his nasty way, 'David, ma gran'
fellow, hoo ye work! ye 'stonish me!' And on
ma word, Maggie"—there were tears in the
great boy's eyes—"ma back was nigh broke
wi' toilin'. And the Terror, he stands by and
shows his teeth, and looks at me as much as
to say, 'Some day, by the grace o' goodness,
I'll ha' my teeth in your throat, young mon.' "

Maggie's knitting dropped into her lap and
she looked up, her soft eyes for once flashing.

"It's cruel, David; so 'tis!" she cried. "I
wonder yo' bide wi' him. If he treated me so,
I'd no stay anither minute. If it meant the
House for me I'd go," and she looked as if she
meant it.

David jumped off the table.

"Han' yo' niver guessed why I stop, lass,
and me so happy at home?" he asked eagerly.

Maggie's eyes dropped again.

"Hoo should I know?" she asked innocently.

"Nor care, neither, I s'pose," he said in reproachful accents. "Yo' want me me to go and
leave yo', and go reet awa'; I see hoo 'tis. Yo'
wouldna mind, not yo', if yo' was niver to see

pore David agin. I niver thowt yo' welly
like me, Maggie; and noo I know it."

"Yo' silly lad," the girl murmured, knitting
steadfastly.

"Then yo' do," he cried, triumphant, "I
knew yo' did." He approached close to her
chair, his face clouded with eager anxiety.

"But d'yo' like me more'n just *likin'*, Maggie? dy'yo'," he bent and whispered in the little ear.

The girl cuddled over her work so that he
could not see her face.

"If yo' won't tell me yo' can show me," he
coaxed. "There's other things besides words,"

He stood before her, one hand on the chair-
back on either side. She sat thus, caged
between his arms, with drooping eyes and
heightened color.

"Not so close, David, please," she begged,
fidgeting uneasily; but the request was unheeded.

"Do'ee move away a wee," she implored.

"Not till yo've showed me," he said, relentless.

"I canna, Davie," she cried with laughing
petulance.

"Yes, yo' can, lass."

"Tak' your hands away, then."

"Nay; not till yo've showed me."

A pause.

"Do'ee, Davie," she supplicated.

And—

"Do'ee," he pleaded.

She tilted her face provokingly, but her eyes were still down.

"It's no manner o' use, Davie."

"Iss, 'tis," he coaxed.

"Niver."

"Please."

A lengthy pause.

"Well, then——" She looked up, at last, shy, trustful, happy; and the sweet lips were tilted further to meet his.

And thus they were situated, lover-like, when a low, rapt voice broke in on them,—

> "'A dear-lov'd lad, convenience snug,
>   A treacherous inclination.'

Oh, Wullie, I wush you were here!"

It was little M'Adam. He was leaning in at the open window, leering at the young couple, his eyes puckered, an evil expression on his face.

"The creetical moment! and I interfere! David, ye'll never forgie me."

The boy jumped round with an oath; and Maggie, her face flaming, started to her feet. The tone, the words, the look of the little man at the window were alike insufferable.

"By thunder! I'll teach yo' to come spyin' on me!" roared David. Above him on the mantel-piece blazed the Shepherds' Trophy. Searching any missile in his fury, he reached up a hand for it.

"Ay, gie it me back. Ye robbed me o't,"
the little man cried, holding out his arms as if
to receive it.

"Dinna, David," pleaded Maggie, with restraining hand on her lover's arm.

"By the Lord! I'll give him something!"
yelled the boy. Close by there stood a pail of
soapy water. He seized it, swung it, and
slashed its contents at the leering face in the
window.

The little man started back, but the dirty
torrent caught him and soused him through.
The bucket followed, struck him full on the
chest, and rolled him over in the mud. After
it with a rush came David.

"I'll let yo' know, spyin' on me!" he yelled.
"I'll——" Maggie, whose face was as white
now as it had been crimson, clung to him,
hampering him.

"Dinna, David, dinna!" she implored. "He's
yer ain dad."

"I'll dad him! I'll learn him!" roared
David half through the window.

At the moment Sam'l Todd came flounder-
ing furiously round the corner, closely followed by 'Enry and oor Job.

"Is he dead?" shouted Sam'l seeing the
prostrate form.

"Ho! ho!" went the other two.

They picked up the draggled little man and
hustled him out of the yard like a thief, a man
on either side and a man behind.

As they forced him through the gate, he struggled round.

"By Him that made ye! ye shall pay for this, David M'Adam, you and yer——"

But Sam'l's big hand descended on his mouth, and he was borne away before that last ill word had flitted into being.

CHAPTER XXI

HORROR OF DARKNESS

It was long past dark that night when M'Adam staggered home.

All that evening at the Sylvester Arms his imprecations against David had made even the hardest shudder. James Moore, Owd Bob, and the Dale Cup were for once forgotten as, in his passion, he cursed his son.

The Dalesmen gathered fearfully away from the little dripping madman. For once these men, whom, as a rule, no such geyser outbursts could quell, were dumb before him; only now and then shooting furtive glances in his direction, as though on the brink of some daring enterprise of which he was the objective. But M'Adam noticed nothing, suspected nothing.

When, at length, he lurched into the kitchen of the Grange, there was no light and the fire burnt low. So dark was the room that a white riband of paper pinned on to the table escaped his remark.

The little man sat down heavily, his clothes still sodden, and resumed his tireless anathema.

"I've tholed mair fra him, Wullie, than Adam M'Adam ever thocht to thole from ony man. And noo it's gane past bearin'. He

struck me, Wullie! struck his ain father. Ye
see it yersel', Wullie. Na, ye werena there.
Oh, gin ye had but bin, Wullie! Him and his
madam! But I'll gar him ken Adam M'Adam.
I'll stan' nae mair!"

He sprang to his feet and, reaching up with
trembling hands, pulled down the old bell-
mouthed blunderbuss that hung above the
mantel-piece.

"We'll mak' an end to't, Wullie, so we will,
aince and for a'!" And he banged the weapon
down upon the table. It lay right athwart that
slip of still condemning paper, yet the little
man saw it not.

Resuming his seat, he prepared to wait.
His hand sought the pocket of his coat, and
fingered tenderly a small stone bottle, the fond
companion of his widowhood. He pulled it
out, uncorked it, and took a long pull; then
placed it on the table by his side.

Gradually the gray head lolled; the shrivelled hand dropped and hung limply down, the
finger-tips brushing the floor; and he dozed off
into a heavy sleep, while Red Wull watched at
his feet.

It was not till an hour later that David returned home.

As he approached the lightless house, standing in the darkness like a body with the spirit
fled, he could but contrast this dreary home of
his with the bright kitchen and cheery faces
he had left.

Entering the house, he groped to the kitchen door and opened it; then struck a match and stood in the doorway peering in.

"Not home, bain't he?" he muttered, the tiny light above his head. "Wet inside as well as oot by noo, I'll lay. By gum! but 'twas a lucky thing for him I didna get ma hand on him this evenin'. I could ha' killed him." He held the match above his head.

Two yellow eyes, glowing in the darkness like cairngorms, and a small dim figure bunched up in a chair, told him his surmise was wrong. Many a time had he seen his father in such case before, and now he muttered contemptuously:

"Drunk; the leetle swab! Sleepin' it off, I reck'n."

Then he saw his mistake. The hand that hung above the floor twitched and was still again.

There was a clammy silence. A mouse, emboldened by the quiet, scuttled across the hearth. One mighty paw lightly moved; a lightning tap, and the tiny beast lay dead.

Again that hollow stillness: no sound, no movement; only those two unwinking eyes fixed on him immovable.

At length a small voice from the fireside broke the quiet.

"Drunk—the—leetle—swab!"

Again a clammy silence, and a life-long pause.

"I thowt yo' was sleepin'," said David, at length, lamely.

"Ay, so ye said. 'Sleepin' it aff'; I heard ye." Then, still in the same small voice, now quivering imperceptibly, "Wad ye obleege me, sir, by leetin' the lamp? Or, d'ye think, Wullie, 'twad be soilin' his dainty fingers? They're mair used, I'm told, to danderin' wi' the bonnie brown hair o' his——"

"I'll not ha' ye talk o' ma Maggie so," interposed the boy passionately.

"*His* Maggie, mark ye, Wullie—*his!* I thocht 'twad soon get that far."

"Tak' care, dad! I'll stan' but little more," the boy warned him in choking voice; and began to trim the lamp with trembling fingers.

M'Adam forthwith addressed himself to Red Wull.

"I suppose no man iver had sic a son as him, Wullie. Ye ken what I've done for him, an' ye ken hoo he's repaid it. He's set himsel' agin me; he's misca'd me; he's robbed me o' ma Cup; last of all, he struck me—struck me afore them a'. We've toiled for him, you and I, Wullie; we've slaved to keep him in hoose an' hame, an' he's passed his time, the while, in riotous leevin', carousin' at Kenmuir, amusin' himself' wi' his——" He broke off short. The lamp was lit, and the strip of paper, pinned on to the table, naked and glaring, caught his eye.

"What's this?" he muttered; and unloosed the nail that clamped it down.

This is what he read:

"Adam Mackadam yer warned to mak' an end to yer Red Wull will be best for him and the Sheep. This is the first yoll have two more the third will be the last →"

It was written in pencil, and the only sig‑ nature was a dagger, rudely limned in red.

M'Adam read the paper once, twice, thrice. As he slowly assimilated its meaning, the blood faded from his face. He stared at it and still stared, with whitening face and pursed lips. Then he stole a glance at David's broad back.

"What d'ye ken o' this, David?" he asked, at length, in a dry thin voice, reaching for‑ ward in his chair.

"O' what?"

"O' this," holding up the slip. "And ye'd obleege me by the truth for once."

David turned, took up the paper, read it, and laughed harshly.

"It's coom to this, has it?" he said, still laughing, and yet with blanching face.

"Ye ken what it means. I daresay ye pit it there; aiblins writ it. Ye'll explain it." The little man spoke in the same small, even voice, and his eyes never moved off his son's face.

"It's plain as day. Ha' ye no heard?"

"Ive heard naethin'. . . . I'd like the truth, David, if ye can tell it."

The boy smiled a forced, unnatural smile, looking from his father to the paper in his hand.

"Yo' shall have it, but yo'll not like it. It's this: Tupper lost a sheep to the Killer last night."

"And what if he did?" The little man rose smoothly to his feet. Each noticed the others' face—dead-white.

"Why, he—lost—it—on—— Wheer d'yo' think?" He drawled the words out, dwelling almost lovingly on each.

"Where?"

"On—the—Red—Screes."

The crash was coming—inevitable now. David knew it, knew that nothing could avert it, and braced himself to meet it. The smile had fled from his face, and his breath fluttered in his throat like the wind before a thunderstorm.

"What of it?" The little man's voice was calm as a summer sea.

"Why, your Wullie—as I told yo'—was on the Screes last night."

"Go on, David."

"And this," holding up the paper, "tells you that they ken as I ken noo, as maist o' them ha' kent this mony a day, that your Wullie, Red Wull—the Terror——"

"Go on."

"Is——"

"Yes."

"The Black Killer."

It was spoken.

The frayed string was snapped at last. The little man's hand flashed to the bottle that stood before him.

"Ye—liar!" he shrieked, and threw it with all his strength at the boy's head. David dodged and ducked, and the bottle hurtled over his shoulder.

Crash! it whizzed into the lamp behind, and broke on the wall beyond, its contents trickling down the wall to the floor.

For a moment, darkness. Then the spirits met the lamp's smouldering wick and blazed into flame.

By the sudden light David saw his father on the far side the table, pointing with crooked forefinger. By his side Red Wull was standing alert, hackles up, yellow fangs bared, eyes lurid; and, at his feet, the wee brown mouse lay still and lifeless.

"Oot o' ma hoose! Back to Kenmuir! Back to yer——" The unpardonable word, unmistakable, hovered for a second on his lips like some foul bubble, and never burst.

"No mither this time!" panted David, racing round the table.

"Wullie!"

The Terror leapt to the attack; but David overturned the table as he ran, the blunderbuss crashing to the floor; it fell, opposing a momentary barrier in the dog's path.

"Stan' off, ye——!" screeched the little man, seizing a chair in both hands; "stan' off, or I'll brain ye!"

But David was on him.

"Wullie, Wullie, to me!"

Again the Terror came with a roar like the sea. But David, with a mighty kick catching him full on the jaw, repelled the attack.

Then he gripped his father round the waist and lifted him from the ground. The little man, struggling in those iron arms, screamed, cursed, and battered at the face above him, kicking and biting in his frenzy.

"The Killer! wad ye ken wha's the Killer? Go and ask 'em at Kenmuir! Ask yer——"

David swayed slightly, crushing the body in his arms till it seemed every rib must break; then hurled it from him with all the might of passion. The little man fell with a crash and a groan.

The blaze in the corner flared, flickered, and died. There was hell-black darkness, and silence of the dead.

David stood against the wall, panting, every nerve tightstrung as the hawser of a straining ship.

In the corner lay the body of his father, limp and still; and in the room one other living thing was moving.

He clung close to the wall, pressing it with

wet hands. The horror of it all, the darkness, the man in the corner, that moving something, petrified him.

"Feyther!" he whispered.

There was no reply. A chair creaked at an invisible touch. Something was creeping, stealing, crawlng closer.

David was afraid.

"Feyther!" he whispered in hoarse agony, "are yo' hurt?"

The words were stifled in his throat. A chair overturned with a crash; a great body struck him on the chest; a hot, pestilent breath volleyed in his face, and wolfish teeth were reaching for his throat.

"Come on, Killer!" he screamed.

The horror of suspense was past. It had come, and with it he was himself again.

Back, back, back, along the wall he was borne. His hands entwined themselves around a hairy throat; he forced the great head with its horrid lightsome eyes from him; he braced himself for the effort, lifted the huge body at his breast, and heaved it from him. It struck the wall and fell with a soft thud.

As he recoiled a hand clutched his ankle and sought to trip him. David kicked back and down with all his strength. There was one awful groan, and he staggered against the door and out.

There he paused, leaning against the wall to breathe.

He struck a match and lifted his foot to see where the hand had clutched him.

God! there was blood on his heel.

Then a great fear laid hold on him. A cry was suffocated in his breast by the panting of his heart.

He crept back to the kitchen door and listened.

Not a sound.

Fearfully he opened it a crack.

Silence of the tomb.

He banged it to. It opened behind him, and the fact lent wings to his feet.

He turned and plunged out into the night, and ran through the blackness for his life. And a great owl swooped softly by and hooted mockingly:

"For your life! for your life! for your life!"

PART V

OWD BOB O' KENMUIR

CHAPTER XXII

A MAN AND A MAID

In the village even the Black Killer and the
murder on the Screes were forgotten in this
new sensation. The mystery in which the
affair was wrapped, and the ignorance as to all
its details, served to whet the general interest.
There had been a fight; M'Adam and the Terror had been mauled; and David had disappeared—those were the facts. But what was
the origin of the affray no one could say.

One or two of the Dalesmen had, indeed,
a shrewd suspicion. Tupper looked guilty;
Jem Burton muttered, "I knoo hoo 'twould
be"; while as for Long Kirby, he vanished
entirely, not to reappear till three months had
sped.

Injured as he had been, M'Adam was yet
sufficiently recovered to appear in the Sylvester Arms on the Saturday following the battle.
He entered the tap-room silently with never a
word to a soul; one arm was in a sling and
his head bandaged. He eyed every man present critically; and all, except Tammas, who
was brazen, and Jim Mason, who was innocent, fidgeted beneath the stare. Maybe it
was well for Long Kirby he was not there.

"Onythin' the matter?" asked Jem, at

length, rather lamely, in view of the plain evidences of battle.

"Na, na; naethin' oot o' the ordinar'," the little man replied, giggling. "Only David set on me, and me sleepin'. And," with a shrug, "here I am noo." He sat down, wagging his bandaged head and grinning. "Ye see he's sae playfu', is Davie. He wangs ye o'er the head wi' a chair, kicks ye in the jaw, stamps on yer wame, and all as merry as May." And nothing further could they get from him, except that if David reappeared it was his [M'Adam's] firm resolve to hand him over to the police for attempted parricide.

" 'Brutal assault on an auld man by his son!' 'Twill look well in the *Argus;* he! he! They couldna let him aff under two years, I'm thinkin'."

M'Adam's version of the affair was received with quiet incredulity. The general verdict was that he had brought his punishment entirely on his own head. Tammas, indeed, who was always rude when he was not witty, and, in fact, the difference between the two things is only one of degree, told him straight: "It served yo' well reet. An' I nob'but wish he'd made an end to yo'."

"He did his best, puir lad," M'Adam reminded him gently.

"We've had enough o' yo'," continued the uncompromising old man. "I'm fair grieved he didna slice yer throat while he was at it."

At that M'Adam raised his eyebrows, stared, and then broke into a low whistle.

"That's it, is it?" he muttered, as though a new light was dawning on him. "Ah, noo I see."

The days passed on. There was still no news of the missing one, and Maggie's face became pitifully white and haggard.

Of course she did not believe that David had attempted to murder his father, desperately tried as she knew he had been. Still, it was a terrible thought to her that he might at any moment be arrested; and her girlish imagination was perpetually conjuring up horrid pictures of a trial, conviction, and the things that followed.

Then Sam'l started a wild theory that the little man had murdered his son, and thrown the mangled body down the dry well at the Grange. The story was, of course, preposterous, and, coming from such a source, might well have been discarded with the ridicule it deserved. Yet it served to set the cap on the girl's fears; and she resolved, at whatever cost, to visit the Grange, beard M'Adam, and discover whether he could not or would not allay her gnawing apprehension.

Her intent she concealed from her father, knowing well that were she to reveal it to him, he would gently but firmly forbid the attempt; and on an afternoon some fortnight after

David's disappearance, choosing her opportunity, she picked up a shawl, threw it over her head, and fled with palpitating heart out of the farm and down the slope to the Wastrel.

The little plank-bridge rattled as she tripped across it; and she fled faster lest any one should have heard and come to look. And, indeed, at the moment it rattled again behind her, and she started guiltily round. It proved, however, to be only Owd Bob, sweeping after, and she was glad.

"Comin' wi' me, lad?" she asked as the old dog cantered up, thankful to have that gray protector with her.

Round Langholm now fled the two conspirators; over the summer-clad lower slopes of the Pike, until, at length, they reached the Stony Bottom. Down the bramble-covered bank of the ravine the girl slid; picked her way from stone to stone across the streamlet tinkling in that rocky bed; and scrambled up the opposite bank.

At the top she halted and looked back. The smoke from Kenmuir was winding slowly up against the sky; to her right the low gray cottages of the village cuddled in the bosom of the Dale; far away over the Marches towered the gaunt Scaur; before her rolled the swelling slopes of the Muir Pike; while behind—she glanced timidly over her shoulder—was the hill, at the top of which squatted the Grange, lifeless, cold, scowling.

Her heart failed her. In her whole life she had never spoken to M'Adam. Yet she knew him well enough from all David's accounts—ay, and hated him for David's sake. She hated him and feared him, too; feared him mortally—this terrible little man. And, with a shudder, she recalled the dim face at the window, and thought of his notorious hatred of her father. But even M'Adam could hardly harm a girl coming, broken-hearted, to seek her lover. Besides, was not Owd Bob with her?

And, turning, she saw the old dog standing a little way up the hill, looking back at her as though he wondered why she waited. "Am I not enough?" the faithful gray eyes seemed to say.

"Lad, I'm fear'd," was her answer to the unspoken question.

Yet that look determined her. She clenched her little teeth, drew the shawl about her, and set off running up the hill.

Soon the run dwindled to a walk, the walk to a crawl, and the crawl to a halt. Her breath was coming painfully, and her heart pattered against her side like the beatings of an imprisoned bird. Again her gray guardian looked up, encouraging her forward.

"Keep close, lad," she whispered, starting forward afresh. And the old dog ranged up beside her, shoving into her skirt, as though to let her feel his presence.

So they reached the top of the hill; and the house stood before them, grim, unfriendly.

The girl's face was now quite white, yet set; the resemblance to her father was plain to see. With lips compressed and breath quick-coming, she crossed the threshold, treading softly as though in a house of the dead. There she paused and lifted a warning finger at her companion, bidding him halt without; then she turned to the door on the left of the entrance and tapped.

She listened, her head buried in the shawl, close to the wood panelling. There was no answer; she could only hear the drumming of her heart.

She knocked again. From within came the scraping of a chair cautiously shoved back, followed by a deep-mouthed cavernous growl.

Her heart stood still, but she turned the handle and entered, leaving a crack open behind.

On the far side the room a little man was sitting. His head was swathed in dirty bandages, and a bottle was on the table beside him. He was leaning forward; his face was gray, and there was a stare of naked horror in his eyes. One hand grasped the great dog who stood at his side, with yellow teeth glinting, and muzzle hideously wrinkled; with the other he pointed a palsied finger at her.

"Ma God! wha are ye?" he cried hoarsely.

The girl stood hard against the door, her

fingers still on the handle; trembling like an aspen at the sight of that uncannie pair.

That look in the little man's eyes petrified her: the swollen pupils; lashless lids, yawning wide; the broken range of teeth in that gaping mouth, froze her very soul. Rumors of the man's insanity tided back on her memory.

"I'm—I——" the words came in trembling gasps.

At the first utterance, however, the little man's hand dropped; he leant back in his chair and gave a soul-bursting sigh of relief.

No woman had crossed that threshold since his wife died; and, for a moment, when first the girl had entered silent-footed, aroused from dreaming of the long ago, he had thought this shawl-clad figure with the pale face and peeping hair no earthly visitor; the spirit, rather, of one he had loved long since and lost, come to reproach him with a broken troth.

"Speak up, I canna hear," he said, in tones mild compared with those last wild words.

"I—I'm Maggie Moore," the girl quavered.

"Moore! Maggie Moore, d'ye say?" he cried, half rising from his chair, a flush of color sweeping across his face, "the dochter o' James Moore?" He paused for an answer, glowering at her; and she shrank, trembling, against the door.

The little man leant back in his chair. Gradually a grim smile crept across his countenance.

"Weel, Maggie Moore," he said, half-amused, "ony gate ye're a good plucked un." And his wizened countenance looked at her almost kindly from beneath its dirty crown of bandages.

At that the girl's courage returned with a rush. After all this little man was not so very terrible. Perhaps he would be kind. And in the relief of the moment, the blood swept back into her face.

There was not to be peace yet, however. The blush was still hot upon her cheeks, when she caught the patter of soft steps in the passage without. A dark muzzle flecked with gray pushed in at the crack of the door; two anxious gray eyes followed.

Before she could wave him back, Red Wull had marked the intruder. With a roar he tore himself from his master's restraining hand, and dashed across the room.

"Back, Bob!" screamed Maggie, and the dark head withdrew. The door slammed with a crash as the great dog flung himself against it, and Maggie was hurled, breathless and white-faced, into a corner.

M'Adam was on his feet, pointing with a shrivelled finger, his face diabolical.

"Did you bring him? did you bring *that* to ma door?"

Maggie huddled in the corner in a palsy of trepidation. Her eyes gleamed big and black in the white face peering from the shawl.

Red Wull was now beside her snarling horribly. With nose to the bottom of the door and
busy paws he was trying to get out; while,
on the other side, Owd Bob, snuffling also at
the crack, scratched and pleaded to get in.
Only two miserable wooden inches separated
the pair.

"I brought him to protect me. I—I was
afraid."

M'Adam sat down and laughed abruptly.

"Afraid! I wonder ye were na afraid to
bring him here. It's the first time iver he's
set foot on ma land, and 't had best be the
last." He turned to the great dog. "Wullie,
Wullie, wad ye?" he called. "Come here.
Lay ye doon—so—under ma chair—good lad.
Noo's no the time to settle wi' him"—nodding
toward the door. "We can wait for that,
Wullie; we can wait." Then, turning to Maggie, "Gin ye want him to mak' a show at the
Trials two months hence, he'd best not come
here agin. Gin he does, he'll no leave ma
land alive; Wullie'll see to that. Noo, what is
't ye want o' me?"

The girl in the corner, scared almost out of
her senses by this last occurrence, remained
dumb.

M'Adam marked her hesitation, and grinned
sardonically.

"I see hoo 'tis," said he; "yer dad's sent
ye. Aince before he wanted somethin' o' me,
and did he come to fetch it himself like a man?

Not he. He sent the son to rob the father."
Then, leaning forward in his chair and glaring
at the girl, "Ay, and mair than that! The
night the lad set on me he cam' "—with hiss-
ing emphasis—"straight from Kenmuir!" He
paused and stared at her intently ,and she was
still dumb before him. "Gin I'd ben killed,
Wullie'd ha' bin disqualified from competin'
for the Cup. With Adam M'Adam's Red
Wull oot o' the way—noo d'ye see? Noo d'ye
onderstan'? "

She did not, and he saw it and was satisfied.
What he had been saying she neither knew
nor cared. She only remembered the object of
her mission; she only saw before her the father
of the man she loved; and a wave of emotion
surged up in her breast.

She advanced timidly toward him, holding
out her hands.

"Eh, Mr. M'Adam," she pleaded, "I come
to ask ye after David." The shawl had slipped
from her head, and lay loose upon her shoulders; and she stood before him with her sad
face, her pretty hair all tossed, and her eyes
big with unshed tears—a touching suppliant.

"Will ye no tell me wheer he is? I'd not
ask it, I'd not trouble yo', but I've bin waitin'
a waefu' while, it seems, and I'm wearyin' for
news o' him."

The little man looked at her curiously. "Ah,
noo I mind me,"—this to himself. "You're
the lass as is thinkin' o' marryin' him?"

"We're promised," the girl answered simply.

"Weel," the other remarked, "as I said afore, ye're a good plucked un." Then, in a tone in which, despite the cynicism, a certain indefinable sadness was blended, "Gin he mak's you as good husband as he mad' son to me, ye'll ha' made a maist remairkable match, my dear."

Maggie fired in a moment.

"A good feyther makes a good son," she answered almost pertly; and then, with infinite tenderness, "and I'm prayin' a good wife'll make a good husband."

He smiled scoffingly.

"I'm feared that'll no help ye much," he said.

But the girl never heeded this last sneer, so set was she on her purpose. She had heard of the one tender place in the heart of this little man with the tired face and mocking tongue, and she resolved to attain her end by appealing to it.

"Yo' loved a lass yo'sel' aince, Mr. M'Adam," she said. "Hoo would yo' ha' felt had she gone away and left yo'? Yo'd ha' bin mad; yo' know yo' would. And, Mr. M'Adam, I love the lad yer wife loved." She was kneeling at his feet now with both hands on his knees, looking up at him. Her sad face and quivering lips pleaded for her more eloquently than any words

The little man was visibly touched.

"Ay, ay, lass, that's enough," he said, trying to avoid those big beseeching eyes which would not be avoided.

"Will ye no tell me?" she pleaded.

"I canna tell ye, lass, for why, I dinna ken," he answered querulously. In truth, he was moved to the heart by her misery.

The girl's last hopes were dashed. She had played her last card and failed. She had clung with the fervor of despair to this last resource, and now it was torn from her. She had hoped, and now there was no hope. In the anguish of her disappointment she remembered that this was the man who, by his persistent cruelty, had driven her love into exile.

She rose to her feet and stood back.

"Nor ken, nor care!" she cried bitterly.

At the words all the softness fled from the little man's face.

"Ye do me a wrang, lass; ye do indeed," he said, looking up at her with an assumed ingenuousness which, had she known him better, would have warned her to beware. "Gin I kent where the lad was I'd be the vairy first to let you, and the p'lice, ken it too; eh, Wullie! he! he!" He chuckled at his wit and rubbed his knees, regardless of the contempt blazing in the girl's face.

"I canna tell ye where he is now, but ye'd aiblins care to hear o' when I saw him last." He turned his chair the better to address her.

"Twas like so: I was sittin' in this vairy chair it was, asleep, when he crep' up behind an' lep' on ma back. I knew naethin' o't till I found masel' on the floor an' him kneelin' on me. I saw by the look on him he was set on finishin' me, so I said——"

The girl waved her hand at him, superbly disdainful.

"Yo' ken yo're lyin', ivery word o't," she cried.

The little man hitched his trousers, crossed his legs, and yawned.

"An honest lee for an honest purpose is a matter ony man may be proud of, as you'll ken by the time you're my years, ma lass."

The girl slowly crossed the room. At the door she turned.

"Then ye'll no tell me wheer he is?" she asked with a heart-breaking trill in her voice.

"On ma word, lass, I dinna ken," he cried, half passionately.

"On your word, Mr. M'Adam!" she said with a quiet scorn in her voice that might have stung Iscariot.

The little man spun round in his chair, an angry red dyeing his cheeks. In another moment he was suave and smiling again.

"I canna tell ye where he is noo," he said, unctuously; "but aiblins, I could let ye know where he's gaein' to."

"Can yo'? will yo'?" cried the simple girl

all unsuspecting. In a moment she was across
the room and at his knees.

"Closer, and I'll whisper." The little ear,
peeping from its nest of brown, was trem-
blingly approached to his lips. The little man
lent forward and whispered one short, sharp
word, then sat back, grinning, to watch the
effect of his disclosure.

He had his revenge, an unworthy revenge
on such a victim. And, watching the girl's
face, the cruel disappointment merging in the
heat of her indignation, he had yet enough
nobility to regret his triumph.

She sprang from him as though he were un-
clean.

"An' yo' his father!" she cried, in burning
tones.

She crossed the room, and at the door
paused. Her face was white again and she
was quite composed.

"If David did strike you, you drove him to
it," she said, speaking in calm, gentle accents.
"Yo' know, none so well, whether yo've bin a
good feyther to him, and him no mither, poor
laddie! whether yo've bin to him what she'd
ha' had yo' be. Ask yer conscience, Mr.
M'Adam. An' if he was a wee aggravatin' at
times, had he no reason? He'd a heavy cross
to bear, had David, and yo' know best if yo'
helped to ease it for him."

The little man pointed to the door; but the
girl paid no heed.

"D'yo' think when yo' were cruel to him, jeerin' and fleerin', he never felt it, because he was too proud to show ye? He'd a big saft heart, had David, beneath the varnish. Mony's the time when mither was alive, I've seen him throw himsel' into her arms, sobbin', and cry, 'Eh, if I had but mither! 'Twas different when mither was alive; he was kinder to me then. An' noo I've no one; I'm alone.' An' he'd sob and sob in mither's arms, and she, weepin' hersel', would comfort him, while he, wee laddie, would no be comforted, cryin' broken-like, 'There's none to care for me noo; I'm alone. Mither's left me and eh! I'm prayin' to be wi' her!'"

The clear, girlish voice shook. M'Adam, sitting with face averted, waved to her, mutely ordering her to be gone. But she held on, gentle, sorrowful, relentless.

"An' what'll yo' say to his mither when yo' meet her, as yo' must soon noo, and she asks yo', 'An what o' David? What o' th' lad I left wi' yo', Adam, to guard and keep for me, faithful and true, till this Day?' And then yo'll ha' to speak the truth, God's truth; and yo'll ha' to answer, 'Sin' the day yo' left me I niver said a kind word to the lad. I niver bore wi' him, and niver tried to. And in the end I drove him by persecution to try and murder me.' Then maybe she'll look at yo' —yo' best ken hoo—and she'll say, 'Adam, Adam! is this what I deserved fra yo'?'"

The gentle, implacable voice ceased. The girl turned and slipped softly out of the room; and M'Adam was left alone to his thoughts and his dead wife's memory.

"Mither and father, baith! Mither and father, baith!" rang remorselessly in his ears.

CHAPTER XXIII

TH' OWD UN

THE Black Killer still cursed the land.
Sometimes there would be a cessation in the
crimes; then a shepherd, going his rounds,
would notice his sheep herding together, packing in unaccustomed squares; a raven, gorged
to the crop, would rise before him and flap
wearily away, and he would come upon the
murderer's latest victim.

The Dalesmen were in despair, so utterly
futile had their efforts been. There was no
proof; no hope, no apparent probability that
the end was near. As for the Tailless Tyke,
the only piece of evidence against him had
flown with David, who, as it chanced, had di-
vulged what he had seen to no man.

The £100 reward offered had brought no
issue. The police had done nothing. The
Special Commissioner had been equally successful. After the affair in the Scoop the
Killer never ran a risk, yet never missed a
chance.

Then, as a last resource, Jim Mason made
his attempt. He took a holiday from his
duties and disappeared into the wilderness.
Three days and three nights no man saw him.

On the morning of the fourth he reappeared, haggard, unkempt, a furtive look haunting his eyes, sullen for once, irritable, who had never been irritable before—to confess his failure. Cross-examined further, he answered with unaccustomed fierceness: "I seed nowt, I tell ye. Who's the liar as said I did?"

But that night his missus heard him in his sleep conning over something to himself in slow, fearful whisper, "Two on 'em; one ahint t'other. The first big—bull-like; t'ither——" At which point Mrs. Mason smote him a smashing blow in the ribs, and he woke in a sweat, crying terribly, "Who said I seed——"

.   .   .   .   .

The days were slipping away; the summer was hot upon the land, and with it the Black Killer was forgotten; David was forgotten; everything sank into oblivion before the all-absorbing interest of the coming Dale trials.

The long-anticipated battle for the Shepherds' Trophy was looming close; soon everything that hung upon the issue of that struggle would be decided finally. For ever the justice of Th' Owd Un' claim to his proud title would be settled. If he won, he won outright —a thing unprecedented in the annals of the Cup; if he won, the place of Owd Bob o' Kenmuir as first in his profession was assured for all time. Above all, it was the last event in the six years' struggle 'twixt Red and Gray It was the last time those two great rivals

would meet in battle. The supremacy of one
would be decided once and for all. For win or
lose, it was the last public appearance of the
Gray Dog of Kenmuir.

And as every hour brought the great day
nearer, nothing else was talked of in the
country-side. The heat of the Dalesmen's
enthusiasm was only intensified by the fever
of their apprehension. Many a man would
lose more than he cared to contemplate were
Th' Owd Un beat. But he'd not be! Nay;
owd, indeed, he was—two years older than his
great rival; there were a hundred risks, a
hundred chances; still: "What's the odds
agin Owd Bob o' Kenmuir? I'm takin' 'em.
Who'll lay agin Th' Owd Un?"

And with the air saturated with this perpetual talk of the old dog, these everlasting refer-
ences to his certain victory; his ears drumming
with the often boast that the gray dog was the
best in the North, M'Adam became the silent,
ill-designing man of six months since—morose,
brooding, suspicious, muttering of conspiracy,
plotting revenge.

The scenes at the Sylvester Arms were rep-
licas of those of previous years. Usually the
little man sat isolated in a far corner, silent
and glowering, with Red Wull at his feet.
Now and then he burst into a paroxysm of
insane giggling, slapping his thigh, and muttering, "Ay, it's likely they'll beat us, Wullie.
Yet aiblins there's a wee somethin'—a some-

thin' we ken and they dinna, Wullie,—eh! Wullie, he! he!'' And sometimes he would leap
to his feet and address his pot-house audience,
appealing to them passionately, satirically,
tearfully, as the mood might be on him; and
his theme was always the same: James Moore,
Owd Bob, the Cup, and the plots agin him and
his Wullie; and always he concluded with that
hint of the surprise to come.

Meantime, there was no news of David; he
had gone as utterly as a ship foundered in
mid-Atlantic. Some said he'd 'listed; some,
that he'd gone to sea. And "So he 'as," corroborated Sam'l, "floatin', 'eels uppards."

With no gleam of consolation, Maggie's misery was such as to rouse compassion in all
hearts. She went no longer blithely singing
about her work; and all the springiness had
fled from her gait. The people of Kenmuir
vied with one another in their attempts to con-
sole their young mistress.

.   .   .   .   .

Maggie was not the only one in whose life
David's absence had created a void. Last as
he would have been to own it, M' Adam felt
acutely the boy's loss. It may have been he
missed the ever-present butt; it may have
been a nobler feeling. Alone with Red Wull,
too late he felt his loneliness. Sometimes,
sitting in the kitchen by himself, thinking of
the past, he experienced sharp pangs of remorse; and this was all the more the case after

Maggie's visit. Subsequent to that day the little man, to do him justice, was never known to hint by word or look an ill thing of his enemy's daughter. Once, indeed, when Melia Ross was drawing on a dirty imagination with Maggie for subject, M'Adam shut her up with: "Ye're a maist amazin' big liar, Melia Ross."

Yet, though for the daughter he had now no evil thought, his hatred for the father had never been so uncompromising.

He grew reckless in his assertions. His life was one long threat against James Moore's. Now he openly stated his conviction that, on the evenful night of the fight, James Moore, with object easily discernible, had egged David on to murder him.

"Then why don't yo' go and tell him so, yo' muckle liar?" roared Tammas at last, enraged to madness.

"I will!" said M'Adam. And he did.

   .   .   .   .   .

It was on the day preceding the great summer sheep fair at Grammoch-town that he fulfilled his vow.

That is always a big field-day at Kenmuir; and on this occasion James Moore and Owd Bob had been up and working on the Pike from the rising of the sun. Throughout the straggling lands of Kenmuir the Master went with his untiring adjutant, rounding up, cutting out, drafting. It was already noon when the flock started from the yard.

On the gate by the stile, as the party came up, sat M'Adam.

"I've a word to say to you, James Moore," he announced, as the Master approached.

"Say it then, and quick. I've no time to stand gossipin' here, if yo' have," said the Master.

M'Adam strained forward till he nearly toppled off the gate.

"Queer thing, James Moore, you should be the only one to escape this Killer."

"Yo' forget yoursel', M'Adam."

"Ay, there's me," acquiesced the little man. "But you—hoo d'yo' 'count for *your* luck?"

James Moore swung round and pointed proudly at the gray dog, now patrolling round the flock.

"There's my luck!" he said.

M'Adam laughed unpleasantly.

"So I thought," he said, "so I thought! And I s'pose ye're thinkin' that yer luck," nodding at the gray dog, "will win you the Cup for certain a month hence,"

"I hope so!" said the Master.

"Strange if he should not after all," mused the little man.

James Moore eyed him suspiciously.

"What d'yo' mean?" he asked sternly.

M'Adam shrugged his shoulders.

"There's mony a slip 'twixt Cup and lip, that's a'. I was thinkin' some mischance might come to him."

" 'That 'll do, M'Adam,' he said. 'Noo git off this gate,
yo're trespassin' as 'tis.' "

The Master's eyes flashed dangerously. He recalled the many rumors he had heard, and the attempt on the old dog early in the year.

"I canna think ony one would be coward enough to murder him," he said, drawing himself up.

M'Adam lent forward. There was a nasty glitter in his eye, and his face was all a-tremble.

"Ye'd no think ony one 'd be cooard enough to set the son to murder the father. Yet some one did,—set the lad on to 'sassinate me. He failed at me, and next, I suppose, he'll try at Wullie!" There was a flush on the sallow face, and a vindictive ring in the thin voice. "One way or t'ither, fair or foul, Wullie or me, ain or baith, has got to go afore Cup Day, eh, James Moore! eh?"

The Master put his hand on the latch of the gate, "That'll do, M'Adam," he said. "I'll stop to hear no more, else I might get angry we' yo'. Noo git off this gate, yo're trespassin' as 'tis."

He shook the gate. M'Adam tumbled off, and went sprawling into the sheep clustered below. Picking himself up, he dashed on through the flock, waving his arms, kicking fantastically, and scattering confusion everywhere.

"Just wait till I'm thro' wi' 'em, will yo'?" shouted the Master, seeing the danger.

It was a request which, according to the

etiquette of shepherding, one man was bound to grant another. But M'Adam rushed on regardless, dancing and gesticulating. Save for the lightning vigilance of Owd Bob, the flock must have broken.

"I think yo' might ha' waited!" remonstrated the Master, as the little man burst his way through.

"Noo, I've forgot somethin'!" the other cried, and back he started as he had gone.

It was more than human nature could tolerate.

"Bob, keep him off!"

A flash of teeth; a blaze of gray eyes; and the old dog had leapt forward to oppose the little man's advance.

"Shift oot o' ma light!" cried he, striving to dash past.

"Hold him, lad!"

And hold him the old dog did, while his master opened the gate and put the flock through, the opponents dodging in front of one another like opposing three-quarter-backs at the Rugby game.

"Oot o' ma path, or I'll strike!" shouted the little man in a fury, as the last sheep passed through the gate.

"I'd not," warned the Master.

"But I will!" yelled M'Adam; and, darting forward as the gate swung to, struck furiously at his opponent.

He missed, and the gray dog charged at him like a mail-train.

"Hi! James Moore——" but over he went
like a toppled wheelbarrow, while the old dog
turned again, raced at the gate, took it mag-
nificently in his stride, and galloped up the
lane after his master.

At M'Adam's yell, James Moore had turned.
"Served yo' properly!" he called back.
"He'll larn ye yet it's not wise to tamper wi'
a gray dog or his sheep. Not the first time
he's downed ye, I'm thinkin'!"

The little man raised himself painfully to
his elbow and crawled toward the gate. The
Master, up the lane, could hear him cursing
as he dragged himself. Another moment, and
a head was poked through the bars of the
gate, and a devilish little face looked after
him.

"Downed me, by——, he did!" the little
man cried passionately. "I owed ye baith
somethin' before this, and noo, by——, I owe
ye somethin' more. An' mind ye, Adam
M'Adam pays his debts!"

"I've heard the contrary," the Master replied drily, and turned away up the lane
toward the Marches.

CHAPTER XXIV

A SHOT IN THE NIGHT

It was only three short weeks before Cup Day that one afternoon Jim Mason brought a letter to Kenmuir. James Moore opened it as the postman still stood in the door.

It was from Long Kirby—still in retirement —begging him for mercy's sake to keep Owd Bob safe within doors at nights; at all events till after the great event was over. For Kirby knew, as did every Dalesman, that the old dog slept in the porch, between the two doors of the house, of which the outer was only loosely closed by a chain, so that the ever-watchful guardian might slip in and out and go his rounds at any moment of the night.

This was how the smith concluded his ill-spelt note: "Look out for M'Adam i tell you i *know* hel tri at thowd un afore cup day—failin im you. if the ole dog's bete i'm a ruined man i say so for the luv o God keep yer eyes wide."

The Master read the letter, and handed it to the postman, who perused it carefully.

"I tell yo' what," said Jim at length, speaking with an earnestness that made the other stare, "I wish yo'd do what he asks yo': keep

Th' Owd Un in o' nights, I mean, just for the present."

The Master shook his head and laughed, tearing the letter to pieces.

"Nay," said he; "M'Adam or no M'Adam, Cup or no Cup, Th' Owd Un has the run o' ma land same as he's had since a puppy. Why, Jim, the first night I shut him up that night the Killer comes, I'll lay."

The postman turned wearily away, and the Master stood looking after him, wondering what had come of late to his former cheery friend.

Those two were not the only warnings James Moore received. During the weeks immediately preceding the Trials, the danger signal was perpetually flaunted beneath his nose.

Twice did Watch, the black cross-bred chained in the straw-yard, hurl a brazen challenge on the night air. Twice did the Master, with lantern, Sam'l and Owd Bob, sally forth and search every hole and corner on the premises—to find nothing. One of the dairy-maids gave notice, avowing that the farm was haunted; that, on several occasions in the early morning, she had seen a bogie flitting down the slope to the Wastrel—a sure portent, Sam'l declared, of an approaching death in the house. While once a shearer, coming up from the village, reported having seen, in the twilight of dawn, a little ghostly figure, haggard and startled, stealing silently from tree

to tree in the larch-copse by the lane. The
Master, however, irritated by these constant
alarms, dismissed the story summarily.

"One thing I'm sartin o'," said he. "There's
not a critter moves on Kenmuir at nights but
Th' Owd Un knows it."

Yet, even as he said it, a little man, draggled, weary-eyed, smeared with dew and dust,
was limping in at the door of a house barely a
mile away. "Nae luck, Wullie, curse it!" he
cried, throwing himself into a chair, and addressing some one who was not there—"nae
luck. An' yet I'm sure o't as I am that there's
a God in heaven."

.   .   .   .   .

M'Adam had become an old man of late.
But little more than fifty, yet he looked to have
reached man's allotted years. His sparse hair
was quite white; his body shrunk and bowed;
and his thin hand shook like an aspen as it
groped to the familiar bottle.

In another matter, too, he was altogether
changed. Formerly, whatever his faults, there
had been no harder-working man in the
country-side. At all hours, in all weathers,
you might have seen him with his gigantic
attendant going his rounds. Now all that was
different: he never put his hand to the plough,
and with none to help him the land was left
wholly untended; so that men said that, of a
surety, there would be a farm to let on the
March Mere Estate come Michaelmas.

Instead of working, the little man sat all day in the kitchen at home, brooding over his wrongs, and brewing vengeance. Even the Sylvester Arms knew him no more; for he stayed where he was with his dog and his bottle. Only, when the shroud of night had come down to cover him, he slipped out and away on some errand on which not even Red Wull accompanied him.

.　　.　　.　　.　　.

So the time glided on, till the Sunday before the Trials came round.

All that day M'Adam sat in his kitchen, drinking, muttering, hatching revenge.

"Curse it, Wullie! curse it! The time's slippin'—slippin'—slippin'! Thursday next—but three days mair! and I haena the proof—I haena the proof!"—and he rocked to and fro, biting his nails in the agony of his impotence.

All day long he never moved. Long after sunset he sat on; long after dark had eliminated the features of the room.

"They're all agin us, Wullie. It's you and I alane, lad. M'Adam's to be beat somehow, onyhow; and Moore's to win. So they've settled it, and so 'twill be—onless, Wullie, onless—but curse it! I've no the proof!"—and he hammered the table before him and stamped on the floor.

At midnight he arose, a mad, desperate plan looming through his fuddled brain.

"I swore I'd pay him, Wullie, and I will. If I hang for it I'll be even wi' him. I haena the proof, but I *know*—I *know!*" He groped his way to the mantel piece wth blind eyes and swirling brain. Reaching up with fumbling hands, he took down the old blunderbuss from above the fireplace.

"Wullie," he whispered, chuckling hideously, "Wullie, come on! You and I—he! he!" But the Tailless Tyke was not there. At nightfall he had slouched silently out of the house on business he best wot of. So his master crept out of the room alone—on tiptoe, still chuckling.

The cool night air refreshed him, and he stepped stealthily along, his quaint weapon over his shoulder: down the hill; across the Bottom; skirting the Pike; till he reached the plank-bridge over the Wastrel.

He crossed it safely, that Providence whose care is drunkards placing his footsteps. Then he stole up the slope like a hunter stalking his prey.

Arrived at the gate, he raised himself cautiously, and peered over into the moonlit yard. There was no sign or sound of living creature. The little gray house slept peacefully in the shadow of the Pike, all unaware of the man with murder in his heart laboriously climbing the yard-gate.

The door of the porch was wide, the chain hanging limply down, unused; and the little man could see within, the moon shining on the iron studs of the inner door, and the blanket of him who should have slept there, *and did not.*

"He's no there, Wullie! He's no there!"

He jumped down from the gate. Throwing all caution to the winds, he reeled recklessly across the yard. The drunken delirium of battle was on him. The fever of anticipated victory flushed his veins. At length he would take toll for the injuries of years.

Another moment, and he was in front of the good oak door, battering at it madly with clubbed weapon, yelling, dancing, screaming vengeance.

"Where is he? What's he at? Come and tell me that, James Moore! Come doon, I say, ye coward! Come and meet me like a man!"

> " 'Scots wha hae wi' Wallace bled,
>   Scots wham Bruce has aften led—
>   Welcome to your gory bed
>   Or to victorie !' "

The soft moonlight streamed down on the white-haired madman thundering at the door, screaming his war-song.

The quiet farmyard, startled from its sleep, awoke in an uproar. Cattle shifted in their stalls; horses whinnied; fowls chattered, aroused by the din and dull thudding of the blows: and above the rest, loud and piercing, the shrill cry of a terrified child.

Maggie, wakened from a vivid dream of
David chasing the police, hurried a shawl
around her, and in a minute had the baby in
her arms and was comforting her—vaguely
fearing the while that the police were after
David.

James Moore flung open a window, and,
leaning out, looked down on the dishevelled
figure below him.

M'Adam heard the noise, glanced up, and
saw his enemy. Straightway he ceased his
attack on the door, and, running beneath the
window, shook his weapon up at his foe.

"There ye are, are ye? Curse ye for a
coward! curse ye for a liar! Come doon, I
say, James Moore! come doon—I daur ye to
it! Aince and for a' let's settle oor account."

The Master, looking down from above,
thought that at length the little man's brain
had gone.

"What is't yo' want?" he asked, as calmly
as he could, hoping to gain time.

"What is't I want?" screamed the madman. "Hark to him! He crosses mi in ilka
thing; he plots agin me; he robs me o' ma
Cup; he sets ma son agin me and pits him on
to murder me! And in the end he——"

"Coom, then, coom! I'll——"

"Gie me back the Cup ye stole, James
Moore! Gie me back ma son ye've took from
me! And there's anither thing. What's yer
gray dog doin'? Where's yer——"

The Master interposed again:

"I'll coom doon and talk things over wi' yo'." he said soothingly. But before he could withdraw, M'Adam had jerked his weapon to his shoulder and aimed it full at his enemy's head.

The threatened man looked down the gun's great quivering mouth, wholly unmoved.

"Yo' mon hold it steadier, little mon, if yo'd hit!" he said grimly. "There, I'll coom help yo'!" He withdrew slowly; and all the time was wondering where the gray dog was.

In another moment he was downstairs, undoing the bolts and bars of the door. On the other side stood M'Adam, his blunderbuss at his shoulder, his finger trembling on the trigger, waiting.

"Hi, Master! Stop, or yo're dead!" roared a voice from the loft on the other side the yard.

"Feyther! feyther! git yo' back!" screamed Maggie, who saw it all from the window above the door.

Their cries were too late! The blunderbuss went off with a roar, belching out a storm of sparks and smoke. The shot peppered the door like hail, and the whole yard seemed for a moment wrapped in flame.

"Aw! oh! ma gummy! A'm waounded! A'm a goner! A'm shot! 'Elp! Murder! Eh! Oh!" bellowed a lusty voice—and it was not James Moore's.

The little man, the cause of the uproar, lay

quite still upon the ground, with another figure standing over him. As he had stood, finger on trigger, waiting for that last bolt to be
drawn, a gray form, shooting whence no one
knew, had suddenly and silently attacked him
from behind, and jerked him backward to the
ground. With the shock of the fall the blunderbuss had gone off.

The last bolt was thrown back with a clat-
ter, and the Master emerged. In a glance he
took in the whole scene: the fallen man; the
gray dog; the still-smoking weapon.

"Yo', was't Bob lad?" he said. "I was
wonderin' wheer yo' were. Yo' came just
at the reet moment, as yo' aye do!" Then, in
a loud voice, addressing the darkness: "Yo're
not hurt, Sam'l Todd—I can tell that by yer
noise; it was nob'but the shot off the door
warmed yo'. Coom away doon and gie me a
hand."

He walked up to M'Adam, who still lay
gasping on the ground. The shock of the
fall and recoil of the weapon had knocked the
breath out of the little man's body; beyond
that he was barely hurt.

The Master stood over his fallen enemy and
looked sternly down at him.

"I've put up wi' more from you, M'Adam,
than I would from ony other man," he said.
"But this is too much—comin' here at night
wi' loaded arms, scarin' the wimmen and chil-
der oot o' their lives, and I can but think

meanin' worse. If yo' were half a man I'd
gie yo' the finest thrashin' iver yo' had in yer
life. But, as yo' know well, I could no more
hit yo' than I could a woman. Why yo've
got this down on me yo' ken best. I niver
did yo' or ony ither mon a harm. As to the
Cup, I've got it and I'm goin' to do ma best
to keep it—it's for yo' to win it from me if yo'
can o' Thursday. As for what yo' say o' David, yo' know it's a lie. And as for what yo're
drivin' at wi' yer hints and mysteries, I've no
more idee than a babe unborn. Noo I'm goin'
to lock yo' up, yo're not safe abroad. I'm
thinkin' I'll ha' to hand ye o'er to the p'lice."

With the help of Sam'l he half dragged,
half supported the stunned little man across
the yard; and shoved him into a tiny semi-
subterraneous room, used for the storage of
coal, at the end of the farm-buildings.

"Yo' think it over that side, ma lad," called
the Master grimly, as he turned the key, "and
I will this." And with that he retired to bed.

.   .   .   .   .

Early in the morning he went to release his
prisoner. But he was a minute too late. For
scuttling down the slope and away was a little black-begrimed, tottering figure with white
hair blowing in the wind. The little man had
broken away a wooden hatchment which covered a manhole in the wall of his prison-house,
squeezed his small body through, and so escaped.

"Happen it's as well," thought the Master, watching the flying figure. Then, "Hi, Bob, lad!" he called; for the gray dog, ears back, tail streaming, was hurling down the slope after the fugitive.

On the bridge M'Adam turned, and, seeing his pursuer hot upon him, screamed, missed his footing, and fell with a loud splash into the stream—almost in that identical spot into which, years before, he had plunged voluntarily to save Red Wull.

On the bridge Owd Bob halted and looked down at the man struggling in the water below. He made a half move as though to leap in to the rescue of his enemy; then, seeing it was unnecessary, turned and trotted back to his master.

" Yo' nob'but served him right, I'm thinkin'," said the Master. "Like as not he came here wi' the intent to mak' an end to yo.' Well, after Thursday, I pray God we'll ha' peace. It's gettin' above a joke." The two turned back into the yard.

But down below them, along the edge of the stream, for the second time in this story, a little dripping figure was tottering homeward. The little man was crying—the hot tears mingling on his cheeks with the undried waters of the Wastrel—crying with rage, mortification, weariness.

CHAPTER XXV

THE SHEPHERDS' TROPHY

Cup Day.

It broke calm and beautiful, no cloud on the horizon, no threat of storm in the air; a fitting day on which the Shepherds' Trophy must be won outright.

And well it was so. For never since the founding of the Dale Trials had such a concourse been gathered together on the North bank of the Silver Lea. From the Highlands they came; from the far Campbell country; from the Peak; from the county of many acres; from all along the silver fringes of the Solway; assembling in that quiet corner of the earth to see the famous Gray Dog of Kenmuir fight his last great battle for the Shepherds' Trophy.

By noon the gaunt Scaur looked down on such a gathering as it had never seen. The paddock at the back of the Dalesman's Daughter was packed with a clammering, chattering multitude: animated groups of farmers; bevies of solid rustics; sharp-faced townsmen; loud-voiced bookmakers; giggling girls; amorous boys,—thrown together like toys in a sawdust bath; whilst here and there, on the outskirts of the crowd, a lonely man and wise-faced dog, come from afar to wrest his proud title from the best sheep-dog in the North.

At the back of the enclosure was drawn up a formidale array of carts and carriages, varying as much in quality and character as did their owners. There was the squire's landau rubbing axle-boxes with Jem Burton's modest moke-cart; and there Viscount Birdsaye's flaring barouche side by side with the red-wheeled wagon of Kenmuir.

In the latter, Maggie, sad and sweet in her simple summer garb, leant over to talk to Lady Eleanour; while golden-haired wee Anne, delighted with the surging crowd around, trotted about the wagon, waving to her friends, and shouting from very joyousness.

Thick as flies clustered that motley assembly on the north bank of the Silver Lea. While on the other side the stream was a little group of judges, inspecting the course.

The line laid out ran thus: the sheep must first be found in the big enclosure to the right of the starting flag; then up the slope and away from the spectators; around a flag and obliquely down the hill again; through a gap in the wall; along the hillside, parrallel to the Silver Lea; abruptly to the left through a pair of flags—the trickiest turn of them all; then down the slope to the pen, which was set up close to the bridge over the stream.

The proceedings began with the Local Stakes, won by Rob Saunderson's veteran, Shep. There followed the Open Juveniles, carried off by Ned Hoppin's young dog. It was late in the afternoon when, at length, the great event of the meeting was reached.

In the enclosure behind the Dalesman's Daughter the clamor of the crowd increased tenfold, and the yells of the bookmakers were redoubled.

"Walk up, gen'lemen, walk up! the ole firm! Rasper? Yessir—twenty to one bar two! Twenty to one bar two! Bob? What price Bob? Even money, sir—no, not a penny longer, couldn't do it! Red Wull? 'oo says Red Wull?"

On the far side the stream is clustered about the starting flag the finest array of sheep-dogs ever seen together.

"I've never seen such a field, and I've seen fifty," is Parson Leggy's verdict.

There, beside the tall form of his master, stands Owd Bob o' Kenmuir, the observed of all. His silvery brush fans the air, and he holds his dark head high as he scans his challengers, proudly conscious that to-day will make or mar his fame. Below him, the mean-looking, smooth-coated black dog is the unbeaten Pip, winner of the renowned Cambrian Stakes at Llangollen—as many think the best of all the good dogs that have come from sheep-dotted Wales. Beside him that handsome sable collie, with the tremendous coat and slash of white on throat and face, is the famous MacCallum More, fresh from his victory at the Highland meeting. The cobby, brown dog, seeming of many breeds, is from the land o' the Tykes—Merry, on whom the Yorkshiremen are laying as though they loved him. And Jess, the wiry black-and-tan, is the favorite of the men of of the Derwent and Dove. Tupper's big blue Rasper is there; Londesley's Lassie; and many more—too many to mention: big and small, grand and mean, smooth and rough—and not a bad dog there.

And alone, his back to the others, stands a little bowed, conspicuous figure—Adam M'Adam; while the great dog beside him, a hideous incarnation of scowling defiance, is Red Wull, the Terror o' the Border.

The Tailless Tyke had already run up his fighting colors. For MacCallum More, going up to examine this forlorn great adversary, had conceived for him a violent antipathy, and, straightway, had spun at him with all the fury of the Highland cateran, who attacks first and explains afterward. Red Wull, forthwith, had turned on him with savage, silent gluttony; bob-tailed Rasper was racing up to join in the attack; and in another second the three would have been locked inseparably —but just in time M'Adam intervened.

One of the judges came hurrying up.

"Mr. M'Adam," he cried angrily, "if that

brute of yours gets fighting again, hang me
if I don't disqualify him! Only last year at
the Trials he killed the young Cossack dog."

A dull flash of passion swept across M'Adam's face. "Come here, Wullie!" he called.
"Gin yon Hielant tyke attacks ye agin, ye're
to be disqualified."

He was unheeded. The battle for the Cup
had begun—little Pip leading the dance.

On the opposite slope the babel had subsided
now. Hucksters left their wares, and bookmakers their stools, to watch the struggle.
Every eye was intent on the moving figures of
man and dog and three sheep over the stream.

One after one the competitors ran their
course and penned their sheep—there was no
single failure. And all received their just
meed of applause, save only Adam M'Adam's
Red Wull.

Last of all, when Owd Bob trotted out to
uphold his title, there went up such a shout as
made Maggie's wan cheeks to blush with pleasure, and wee Anne to scream right lustily.

His was an incomparable exhibition. Sheep
should be humored rather than hurried;
coaxed, rather than coerced. And that sheep-
dog has attained the summit of his art who
subdues his own personality and leads his
sheep in pretending to be led. Well might
the bosoms of the Dalesmen swell with pride
as they watched their favorite at his work;
well might Tammas pull out that hackneyed

phrase, "The brains of a mon and the way of a woman"; well might the crowd bawl their enthusiasm, and Long Kirby puff his cheeks and rattle the money in his trouser pockets.

But of this part it is enough to say that Pip, Owd Bob, and Red Wull were selected to fight out the struggle afresh.

.   .   .   .   .

The course was altered and stiffened. On the far side the stream it remained as before; up the slope; round a flag; down the hill again; through the gap in the wall; along the hillside; down through the two flags; turn; and to the stream again. But the pen was removed from its former position, carried over the bridge, up the near slope, and the hurdles put together at the very foot of the spectators.

The sheep had to be driven over the plank bridge, and the penning done beneath the very nose of the crowd. A stiff course, if ever there was one; and the time allowed, ten short minutes.

.   .   .   .   .

The spectators hustled and elbowed in their endeavors to obtain a good position. And well they might; for about to begin was the finest exhibition of sheep-handling any man there was ever to behold.

.   .   .   .   .

Evan Jones and little Pip led off.

Those two, who had won on many a hard-fought field, worked together as they had never worked before.   Smooth and swift, like a yacht in Southampton Water; round the flag, through the gap, they brought their sheep.   Down between the two flags—accomplishing right well that awkward turn; and back to the bridge.

There they stopped: the sheep would not face that narrow way.   Once, twice, and again, they broke; and each time the gallant little Pip, his tongue out and tail quivering, brought them back to the bridge-head.

At length one faced it; then another, and—it was too late.   Time was up.   The judges signalled; and the Welshman called off his dog and withdrew.

Out of sight of mortal eye, in a dip of the ground, Evan Jones sat down and took the small dark head between his knees—and you may be sure the dog's heart was heavy as the man's.   "We did our pest, Pip," he cried brokenly, "but we're peat—the first time ever we've been!"

.   .   .   .   .   .

No time to dally.

James Moore and Owd Bob were off on their last run.

No applause this time; not a voice was raised; anxious faces; twitching fingers; the whole crowd tense as a stretched wire.   A false turn, a wilful sheep, a cantankerous judge, and the gray dog would he beat. And not a man there but knew it.

Yet over the stream master and dog went about their business never so quiet, never so collected; for all the world as though they were rounding up a flock on the Muir Pike.

The old dog found his sheep in a twinkling and a wild, scared trio they proved. Rounding the first flag, one bright-eyed wether made a dash for the open. He was quick; but the gray dog was quicker: a splendid recover, and a sound like a sob from the watchers on the hill.

Down the slope they came for the gap in the wall. A little below the opening, James Moore took his stand to stop and turn them; while a distance behind his sheep loitered Owd Bob, seeming to follow rather than drive, yet watchful of every movement and anticipating it. On he came, one eye on his master, the other on his sheep; never hurrying them, never flurrying them, yet bringing them rapidly along.

No word was spoken; barely a gesture made; yet they worked, master and dog, like one divided.

Through the gap, along the hill parallel to the spectators, playing into one another's hands like men at polo.

A wide sweep for the turn at the flags, and the sheep wheeled as though at the word of command, dropped through them, and travelled rapidly for the bridge.

"Steady!" whispered the crowd.

"Steady, man!" muttered Parson Leggy.

"Hold 'em, for God's sake!" croaked Kirby huskily. "D——n! I knew it! I saw it coming!"

The pace down the hill had grown quicker —too quick. Close on the bridge the three sheep made an effort to break. A dash—and two were checked; but the third went away like the wind, and after him Owd Bob, a gray streak against the green.

Tammas was cursing silently; Kirby was white to the lips; and in the stillness you could plainly hear the Dalesmen's sobbing breath, as it fluttered in their throats.

"Gallop! they say he's old and slow!" muttered the Parson. "Dash! Look at that!" For the gray dog, racing like the Nor'easter over the sea, had already retrieved the fugitive.

Man and dog were coaxing the three a step at a time toward the bridge.

One ventured—the others followed.

In the middle the leader stopped and tried to turn—and time was flying, flying, and the penning alone must take minutes. Many a man's hand was at his watch, but no one could take his eyes off the group below him to look.

"We're beat! I've won bet, Tammas!" groaned Sam'l. (The two had a long-standing

wager on the matter.) "I allus knoo hoo
'twould be. I allus told yo' th' owd tyke——"
Then breaking into a bellow, his honest face
crimson with enthusiasm: "Coom on, Master!
Good for yo', Owd Un! Yon's the style!"

For the gray dog had leapt on the back of
the hindmost sheep; it had surged forward
against the next, and they were over, and
making up the slope amidst a thunder of applause.

At the pen it was a sight to see shepherd
and dog working together. The Master, his
face stern and a little whiter than its wont,
casting forward with both hands, herding the
sheep in; the gray dog, his eyes big and
bright, dropping to hand; crawling and creeping, closer and closer.

"They're in!—Nay—Ay—dang me! Stop
'er! Good, Owd Un! Ah-h-h, they're in!"
And the last sheep reluctantly passed through
—on the stroke of time.

A roar went up from the crowd; Maggie's
white face turned pink; and the Dalesmen
mopped their wet brows. The mob surged
forward, but the stewards held them back.

"Back, please! Don't encroach! M'Adam's
to come!"

From the far bank the little man watched
the scene. His coat and cap were off, and his
hair gleamed white in the sun; his sleeves
were rolled up; and his face was twitching
but set as he stood—ready.

The hubbub over the stream at length subsided. One of the judges nodded to him.

"Noo, Wullie—noo or niver!—'Scots wha hae'!"—and they were off.

"Back, gentlemen! back! He's off—he's coming! 'M'Adam's coming!"

They might well shout and push; for the great dog was on to his sheep before they knew it; and they went away with a rush, with him right on their backs. Up the slope they swept and round the first flag, already galloping. Down the hill for the gap, and M'Adam was flying ahead to turn them. But they passed him like a hurricane, and Red Wull was in front with a rush and turned them alone.

"M'Adam wins! Five to four M'Adam! I lay agin Owd Bob!" rang out a clear voice in the silence.

Through the gap they rattled, ears back, feet twinkling like the wings of driven grouse.

"He's lost 'em! They'll break! They're away!" was the cry.

Sam'l was half up the wheel of the Kenmuir wagon; every man was on his toes; ladies were standing in their carriages; even Jim Mason's face flushed with momentary excitement.

The sheep were tearing along the hillside, all together, like a white scud. After them,, galloping like a Waterloo winner, raced Red Wull. And last of all, leaping over the ground like a demoniac, making not for the two flags, but the plank-bridge, the white-haired figure of M'Adam.

"He's beat! The Killer's beat!" roared a strident voice.

"M'Adam wins! Five to four M'Adam! I lay agin Owd Bob!" rang out the clear reply.

Red Wull was now racing parallel to the fugitives and above them. All four were travelling at a terrific rate; while the two flags were barely twenty yards in front, below the line of flight and almost parallel to it. To effect the turn a change of direction must be made almost through a right angle.

"He's beat! he's beat! M'Adam's beat! Can't make it nohow!" was the roar.

From over the stream a yell—

"Turn 'em, Wullie!"

At the word the great dog swerved down on the flying three. They turned, still at the gallop, like a troop of cavalry, and dropped, clean and neat, between the flags; and down to the stream they rattled, passing M'Adam on the way as though he was standing.

"Weel done, Wullie!" came the scream from the far bank; and from the crowd went up an involuntary burst of applause.

"Ma word! "

"Did yo' see that?"

"By gob!"

It was a turn, indeed, of which the smartest team in the galloping horse-gunners might well have been proud. A shade later, and they must have overshot the mark; a shade sooner, and a miss.

"He's not been two minutes so far. We're beaten—don't you think so, Uncle Leggy?" asked Muriel Sylvester, looking up piteously into the parson's face.

"It's not what I think, my dear; it's what the judges think," the parson replied; and what he thought their verdict would be was plainly writ on his face for all to read.

Right on to the centre of the bridge the leading sheep galloped and—stopped abruptly.

Up above in the crowd there was utter silence; staring eyes; rigid fingers. The sweat was dripping off Long Kirby's face; and, at the back, a green-coated bookmaker slipped his note-book in his pocket, and glanced behind him. James Moore, standing in front of them all, was the calmest there.

Red Wull was not to be denied. Like his forerunner he leapt on the back of the hindmost sheep. But the red dog was heavy where the gray was light. The sheep staggered, slipped, and fell.

Almost before it had touched the water, M'Adam, his face afire and eyes flaming, was in the stream. In a second he had hold of the struggling creature, and, with an almost superhuman effort, had half thrown, half shoved it on to the bank.

Again a tribute of admiration, led by James Moore.

The little man scrambled, panting, on to the bank and raced after sheep and dog. His face was white beneath the perspiration; his breath came in quavering gasps; his trousers were wet and clinging to his legs; he was trembling in every limb, and yet indomitable.

They were up to the pen, and the last wrestle began. The crowd, silent and motionless, craned forward to watch the uncanny, white-haired little man and the huge dog, working so close below them. M'Adam's face was white; his eyes staring, unnaturally bright; his bent body projected forward; and he tapped with his stick on the ground like a blind man, coaxing the sheep in. And the Tailless Tyke, his tongue out and flanks heaving, crept and crawled and worked up to the opening, patient as he had never been before.

They were in at last.

There was a lukewarm, half-hearted cheer; then silence.

Exhausted and trembling, the little man leant against the pen, one hand on it; while Red Wull, his flanks still heaving, gently licked the other. Quite close stood James Moore and the gray dog; above was the black wall of people, utterly still; below, the judges comparing notes. In the silence you could almost hear the panting of the crowd.

Then one of the judges went up to James Moore and shook him by the hand.

The gray dog had won. Owd Bob o' Kenmuir had won the Shepherds' Trophy outright.

A second's palpitating silence; a woman's hysterical laugh,—and a deep-mouthed bellow rent the expectant air: shouts, screams, hat-tossings, back-clappings blending in a din that made the many-winding waters of the Silver Lea quiver and quiver again.

Owd Bob o' Kenmuir had won the Shepherds' Trophy outright.

Maggie's face flushed a scarlet hue. Wee Anne flung fat arms toward her triumphant Bob, and screamed with the best. Squire and parson, each red-cheeked, were boisterously shaking hands. Long Kirby, who had not prayed for thirty years, ejaculated with heartfelt earnestness, "Thank God!" Sam'l Todd bellowed in Tammas's ear, and almost slew him with his mighty buffets. Among the Dalesmen some laughed like drunken men; some cried like children; all joined in that roaring song of victory.

To little M'Adam, standing with his back to the crowd, that storm of cheering came as the first announcement of defeat.

A wintry smile, like the sun over a March sea, crept across his face.

"We might a kent it, Wullie," he muttered, soft and low. The tension loosed, the battle lost, the little man almost broke down. There were red dabs of color in his face; his eyes

were big; his lips pitifully quivering; he was
near to sobbing.

An old man—utterly alone—he had staked
his all on a throw—and lost.

Lady Eleanour marked the forlorn little figure, standing solitary on the fringe of the uproarious mob. She noticed the expression on
his face; and her tender heart went out to the
lone man in his defeat.

She went up to him and laid a hand upon
his arm.

"Mr. M'Adam," she said timidly, "won't
you come and sit down in the tent? You look
so tired! I can find you a corner where no one
shall disturb you."

The little man wrenched roughly away.
The unexpected kindness, coming at that moment, was almost too much for him. A few
paces off he turned again.

"It's reel kind o' yer ladyship," he said
huskily; and tottered away to be alone with
Red Wull.

.   .   .   .   .

Meanwhile the victors stood like rocks in
the tideway. About them surged a continually changing throng, shaking the man's hand,
patting the dog.

Maggie had carried wee Anne to tender
her congratulations; Long Kirby had come;
Tammas, Saunderson, Hoppin, Tupper, Londesley—all but Jim Mason; and now, elbow-
ing through the press, came squire and parson.

"Well done, James! well done, indeed!
Knew you'd win! told you so—eh, eh!"
Then facetiously to Owd Bob: "Knew you
would, Robert, old man! Ought to—Robert
the Dev—musn't be a naughty boy—eh, eh!"

"The first time ever the Dale Cup's been
won outright!" said the Parson, "and I daresay it never will again. And I think Kenmuir's the very fittest place for its final home,
and a Gray Dog of Kenmuir for its winner."

"Oh, by the by!" burst in the squire.
"I've fixed the Manor dinner for to-day fortnight, James. Tell Saunderson and Tupper,
will you? Want all the tenants there." He
disappeared into the crowd, but in a minute
had fought his way back. "I'd forgotten
something!" he shouted. "Tell your Maggie
perhaps you'll have news for her after it—eh!
eh!"—and he was gone again.

Last of all, James Moore was aware of a
white, blotchy, grinning face at his elbow.

"I maun congratulate ye, Mr. Moore. Ye've
beat us—you and the gentlemen—judges."

"'Twas a close thing, M'Adam," the other
answered. "An' yo' made a gran' fight. In
ma life I niver saw a finer turn than yours by
the two flags yonder. I hope yo' bear no
malice."

"Malice! Me? Is it likely? Na, na. 'Do
onto ivery man as he does onto you—and
somethin' over,' that's my motter. I owe ye
mony a good turn, which I'll pay ye yet. Na,

na; there's nae good fechtin' again fate—
and the judges. Weel, I wush you well o'
yer victory. Aiblins' twill be oor turn next."

Then a rush, headed by Sam'l, roughly
hustled the one away and bore the other off
on its shoulders in boisterous triumph.

.   .   .   .   .

In giving the Cup away, Lady Eleanour made
a prettier speech than ever. Yet all the while
she was haunted by a white, miserable face;
and all the while she was conscious of two
black moving dots in the Murk Muir Pass opposite her—solitary, desolate, a contrast to the
huzzaing crowd around.

.   .   .   .   .

That is how the champion challenge Dale
Cup, the world-known Shepherds' Trophy,
came to wander no more; won outright by the
last of the Gray Dogs of Kenmuir—Owd Bob.

Why he was the last of the Gray Dogs is
now to be told.

PART VI

THE BLACK KILLER

CHAPTER XXVI

RED-HANDED

THE sun was hiding behind the Pike. Over the lowlands the feathery breath of night hovered still. And the hillside was shivering in the chillness of dawn.

Down on the silvery sward beside the Stony Bottom there lay the ruffled body of a dead sheep. All about the victim the dewy ground was dark and patchy like dishevelled velvet; bracken trampled down; stones displaced as though by striving feet; and the whole spotted with the all-pervading red.

A score yards up the hill, in a writhing confusion of red and gray, two dogs at death-grips. While yet higher, a pack of wild-eyed hill-sheep watched, fascinated, the bloody drama.

The fight raged. Red and gray, blood-spattered, murderous-eyed; the crimson froth dripping from their jaws; now rearing high with arching crests and wrestling paws; now rolling over in tumbling, tossing, worrying disorder—the two fought out their blood-feud.

Above, the close-packed flock huddled and stamped, ever edging nearer to watch the issue. Just so must the women of Rome have craned round the arenas to see two men striving in death-struggle.

The first cold flicker of dawn stole across the green. The red eye of the morning peered aghast over the shoulder of the Pike. And from the sleeping dale there arose the yodling of a man driving his cattle home.

Day was upon them.

.   .   .   .   .

James Moore was waked by a little whimpering cry beneath his window. He leapt out of bed and rushed to look; for well he knew 'twas not for nothing that the old dog was calling.

"Lord o' mercy! whativer's come to yo', Owd Un?" he cried in anguish. And, indeed, his favorite, war-daubed almost past recognition, presented a pitiful spectacle.

In a moment the Master was downstairs and out, examining him.

"Poor old lad, yo' have caught it this time!" he cried. There was a ragged tear on the dog's cheek; a deep gash in his throat from which the blood still welled, staining the white escutcheon on his chest; while head and neck were clotted with the red.

Hastily the Master summoned Maggie. After her, Andrew came hurrying down. And a little later a tiny, night-clad, naked-footed figure appeared in the door, wide-eyed, and then fled, screaming.

They doctored the old warrior on the table

in the kitchen. Maggie tenderly washed his wounds, and dressed them with gentle, pitying fingers; and he stood all the while grateful yet fidgeting, looking up into his master's face as if imploring to be gone.

"He mun a had a rare tussle wi' some one— eh, dad?" said the girl, as she worked.

"Ay; and wi' whom? 'Twasn't for nowt he got fightin', I war'nt. Nay; he's a tale to tell, has The Owd Un, and——Ah-h-h! I thowt as much. Look 'ee!" For bathing the bloody jaws, he had come upon a cluster of tawny red hair, hiding in the corners of the lips.

The secret was out. Those few hairs told their own accusing tale. To but one creature in the Daleland could they belong—"Th' Tailless Tyke."

"He mun a bin trespassin'!" cried Andrew.

"Ay, and up to some o' his bloody work, I'll lay my life," the Master answered. "But Th' Owd Un shall show us."

The old dog's hurts proved less severe than had at first seemed possible. His good gray coat, forest-thick about his throat, had never served him in such good stead. And at length, the wounds washed and sewn up, he jumped down all in a hurry from the table and made for the door.

"Noo, owd lad, yo' may show us," said the Master, and, with Andrew, hurried after him down the hill, along the stream, and over

Langholm How. And as they neared the Stony Bottom, the sheep, herding in groups, raised frightened heads to stare.

Of a sudden a cloud of poisonous flies rose, buzzing, up before them; and there in a dimple of the ground lay a murdered sheep. Deserted by its comrades, the glazed eyes staring helplessly upward, the throat horribly worried, it slept its last sleep.

The matter was plain to see. At last the Black Killer had visited Kenmuir.

"I guessed as much," said the Master, standing over the mangled body. "Well, it's the worst night's work ever the Killer done. I reck'n Th' Owd Un come on him while he was at it; and then they fought. And, ma word! *it* munn ha' bin a fight too." For all around were traces of that terrible struggle: the earth torn up and tossed, bracken uprooted, and throughout little dabs of wool and tufts of tawny hair, mingling with dark-stained iron-gray wisps.

James Moore walked slowly over the battle-field, stooping down as though he were gleaning. And gleaning he was.

A long time he bent so, and at length raised himself.

"The Killer has killed his last," he muttered; "Red Wull has run his course." Then, turning to Andrew: "Run yo' home, lad, and fetch the men to carry yon away," pointing to the carcass, "And Bob, lad, yo've

done your work for to-day, and right well too;
go yo' home wi' him. I'm off to see to this!"

He turned and crossed the Stony Bottom.
His face was set like a rock. At length the
proof was in his hand. Once and for all the
hill-country should be rid of its scourge.

As he stalked up the hill, a dark head appeared at his knee. Two big grey eyes, half
doubting, half penitent, wholly wistful, looked
up at him, and a silvery brush signalled a mute
request.

"Eh, Owd Un, but yo' should ha' gone wi'
Andrew," the Master said. "Hooiver, as yo'
are here, come along." And he strode away
up the hill, gaunt and menacing, with the
gray dog at his heels.

As they approached the house, M'Adam was
standing in the door, sucking his eternal twig.
James Moore eyed him closely as he came, but
the sour face framed in the door betrayed nothing. Sarcasm, surprise, challenge, were all
writ there, plain to read; but no guilty consciousness of the other's errand, no storm of
passion to hide a failing heart. If it was act-
ing it was splendidly done.

As man and dog passed through the gap
in the hedge, the expression on the little
man's face changed again. He started forward.

"James Moore, as I live!" he cried, and advanced with both hands extended, as though
welcoming a long-lost brother. "'Deed and

it's a weary while sin' ye've honored ma
puir hoose." And, in fact, it was nigh twenty
years. "I tak' it gey kind in ye to look in on
a lonely auld man. Come ben and let's ha' a
crack. James Moore kens weel hoo welcome
he aye is in ma bit biggin'."

The Master ignored the greeting.

"One o' ma sheep been killed back o' t'
Dyke," he announced shortly, jerking his
thumb over his shoulder.

"The Killer?"

"The Killer."

The cordiality beaming in every wrinkle of
the little man's face was absorbed in a wondering interest; and that again gave place to
sorrowful sympathy.

"Dear, dear! it's come to that, has it—at
last?" he said gently, and his eyes wandered
to the gray dog and dwelt mournfully upon
him. "Man, I'm sorry—I canna tell ye I'm
surprised. Masel', I kent it all alang. But
gin Adam M'Adam had tell't ye, no ha'
believed him. Weel, weel, he's lived his life,
gin ony dog iver did; and noo he maun gang
where he's sent a many before him. Puir
mon! puir tyke!" He heaved a sigh, pro-
foundly melancholy, tenderly sympathetic.
Then, brightening up a little: "Ye'll ha'
come for the gun?"

James Moore listened to this harangue at
first puzzled. Then he caught the other's
meaning, and his eyes flashed.

"Ye fool, M'Adam! did ye hear iver tell o' a sheep-dog worryin' his master's sheep?"

The little man was smiling and suave again now, rubbing his hands softly together.

"Ye're right, I never did. But your dog is not as ither dogs—'There's none like him— none,' I've heard ye say so yersel, mony a time. An' I'm wi' ye. There's none like him—for devilment." His voice began to quiver and his face to blaze. "It's his cursed cunning that's deceived ivery one but me— whelp o' Satan that he is!" He shouldered up to his tall adversary. "If not him, wha else had done it?" he asked, looking, up into the other's face as if daring him to speak.

The Master's shaggy eyebrows lowered. He towered above the other like the Muir Pike above its surrounding hills.

"Wha, ye ask?" he replied coldly, "and I answer you. Your Red Wull, M'Adam, your Red Wull. It's your Wull's the Black Killer! It's your Wull's bin the plague o' the land these months past! It's your Wull's killed ma sheep back o' yon!"

At that all the little man's affected good-humor fled.

"Ye lee, mon! ye lee!" he cried in a dreadful scream, dancing up to his antagonist. "I knoo hoo 'twad be. I said so. I see what ye're at. Ye've found at last—blind that ye've been!—that it's yer ain hell's tyke that's the Killer; and noo ye think by yer leein' impita-

tions to throw the blame on ma Wullie. Ye
rob me o' ma Cup, ye rob me o' ma son, ye
wrang me in ilka thing; there's but ae thing
left me—Wullie. And noo ye're set on takin'
him awa'. But ye shall not—I'll kill ye first!"

He was all a-shake, bobbing up and down
like a stopper in a soda-water bottle, and almost sobbing.

"Ha' ye no wranged me enough wi' oo
that? Ye lang-leggit liar, wi' yer skulkin
murderin' tyke!" he cried. "Ye say it's Wullie. Where's yer proof?"—and he snapped
his fingers in the other's face.

The Master was now as calm as his foe was
passionate. "Where?" he replied sternly;
"why, there!" holding out his right hand.
"Yon's proof enough to hang a hunner'd."
For lying in his broad palm was a little bundle of that damning red hair.

"Where?"

"There!"

"Let's see it!" The little man bent to look
closer.

"There's for yer proof!" he cried, and spat
deliberately down into the other's naked palm.
Then he stood back, facing his enemy in a
manner to have done credit to a nobler deed.

James Moore strode forward. It looked as
if he was about to make an end of his miserable adversary, so strongly was he moved.
His chest heaved, and the blue eyes blazed.
But just as one had thought to see him take

his foe in the hollow of his hand and crush
him, who should come stalking round the corner of the house but the Tailless Tyke?

A droll spectacle he made, laughable even
at that moment. He limped sorely, his head
and neck were swathed in bandages, and
beneath their ragged fringe the little eyes
gleamed out fiery and bloodshot.

Round the corner he came, unaware of
strangers; then straightway recognizing his
visitors, halted abruptly. His hackles ran up,
each individual hair stood on end till his whole
body resembled a new-shorn wheat-field; and
a snarl, like a rusty brake shoved hard down,
escaped from between his teeth. Then he
trotted heavily forward, his head sinking low
and lower as he came.

And Owd Bob, eager to take up the gage of
battle, advanced, glad and gallant, to meet
him. Daintily he picked his way across the
yard, head and tail erect, perfectly self-
contained. Only the long gray hair about his
neck stood up like the ruff of a lady of the
court of Queen Elizabeth.

But the war-worn warriors were not to be
allowed their will.

"Wullie, Wullie, wad ye!" cried the little
man.

"Bob, lad, coom in!" called the other. Then
he turned and looked down at the man beside
him, contempt flaunting in every feature.

"Well?" he said shortly.

M'Adam's hands were opening and shut-ing; his face was quite white beneath the tan; but he spoke calmly.

"I'll tell ye the whole story, and it's the truth," he said slowly. "I was up there the morn"—pointing to the window above—"and I see Wullie crouchin' down alangside the Stony Bottom. (Ye ken he has the run o' ma land o' neets, the same as your dog.) In a minnit I see anither dog squatterin' alang on your side the Bottom. He creeps up to the sheep on th' hillside, chases 'em, and doons one. The sun was risen by then, and I see the dog clear as I see you noo. It was that dog there—I swear it!" His voice rose as he spoke, and he pointed an accusing finger at Owd Bob.

"Noo, Wullie! thinks I. And afore ye could clap yer hands, Wullie was over the Bottom and on to him as he gorged—the bloody-minded murderer! They fought and fought —I could hear the roarin' a't where I stood. I watched till I could watch nae langer, and, all in a sweat, I rin doon the stairs and oot. When I got there, there was yer tyke makin' fu' split for Kenmuir, and Wullie comin' up the hill to me. It's God's truth, I'm tellin' ye. Tak' him hame, James Moore, and let his dinner be an ounce o' lead. 'Twill be the best day's work iver ye done."

The little man must be lying—lying palpa-bly. Yet he spoke with an earnestness, a seeming belief in his own story, that might have convinced one who knew him less well. But the Master only looked down on him with a great scorn.

"It's Monday to-day," he said coldly. "I gie yo' till Saturday. If yo've not done your duty by then—and well you know what 'tis—I shall come do it for ye. Ony gate, I shall come and see. I'll remind ye agin o' Thursday—yo'll be at the Manor dinner, I suppose. Noo I've warned yo', and you know best whether I'm in earnest or no. Bob, lad!"

He turned away, but turned again.

"I'm sorry for ye, but I've ma duty to do—so've you. Till Saturday I shall breathe no word to ony soul o' this business, so that if you see good to put him oot o' the way wi'oot bother, no one need iver know as hoo Adam M'Adam's Red Wull was the Black Killer."

He turned away for the second time. But the little man sprang after him, and clutched him by the arm.

"Look ye here, James Moore!" he cried in thick, shaky, horrible voice. "Ye're big, I'm sma'; ye're strang, I'm weak; ye've ivery one to your back, I've niver a one; you tell your story, and they'll believe ye—for you gae to church; I'll tell mine, and they'll think I lie —for I dinna. But a word in your ear! If iver agin I catch ye on ma land, by—!"—he swore a great oath—"I'll no spare ye. You ken best if I'm in earnest or no." And his face was dreadful to see in its hideous determinedness.

CHAPTER XXVII

FOR THE DEFENCE

THAT night a vague story was whispered in
the Sylvester Arms. But Tammas, on being
interrogated, pursed his lips and said: "Nay,
I'm sworn to say nowt." Which was the old
man's way of putting that he knew nowt.

. . . . .

On Thursday morning, James Moore and
Andrew came down arrayed in all their best.
It was the day of the squire's annual dinner to
his tenants.

The two, however, were not allowed to start
upon their way until they had undergone a
critical inspection by Maggie; for the girl
liked her mankind to do honor to Kenmuir
on these occasions. So she brushed up Andrew, tied his scarf, saw his boots and hands
were clean, and titivated him generally till she
had converted the ungainly hobbledehoy into
a thoroughly "likely young mon."

And all the while she was thinking of that
other boy for whom on such gala days she had
been wont to perform like offices. And her
father, marking the tears in her eyes, and
mindful of the squire's mysterious hint, said
gently:

"Cheer up, lass. Happen I'll ha' news for you the night!"

The girl nodded, and smiled wanly.

"Happen so, dad," she said. But in her heart she doubted.

Nevertheless it was with a cheerful countenance that, a little later, she stood in the door with wee Anne and Owd Bob and waved the travellers Godspeed; while the golden-haired lassie, fiercely gripping the old dog's tail with one hand and her sister with the other, screamed them a wordless farewell.

.   .   .   .   .

The sun had reached its highest when the two wayfarers passed through the gray portals of the Manor.

In the stately entrance hall, imposing with all the evidences of a long and honorable line, were gathered now the many tenants throughout the wide March Mere Estate. Weather-beaten, rent-paying sons of the soil; most of them native-born, many of them like James Moore, whose fathers had for generations owned and farmed the land they now leased at the hands of the Sylvesters—there in the old hall they were assembled, a mighty host. And apart from the others, standing as though in irony beneath the frown of one of those steel-clad warriors who held the door, was little M'Adam, puny always, paltry now, mocking his manhood.

The door at the far end of the hall opened,

and the squire entered, beaming on every
one.

"Here you are—eh, eh! How are you all?
Glad to see ye! Good-day, James! Good-day,
Saunderson! Good-day to you all! Bringin' a
friend with me—eh, eh!" and he stood aside
to let by his agent, Parson Leggy, and last of
all, shy and blushing, a fair-haired young
giant.

"If it bain't David!" was the cry. "Eh,
lad, we's fain to see yo'! And yo'm lookin'
stout, surely!" And they thronged about the
boy, shaking him by the hand, and asking him
his story.

'Twas but a simple tale. After his flight on
the eventful night he had gone south, drover-
ing. He had written to Maggie, and been surprised and hurt to receive no reply. In vain
he had waited, and too proud to write again,
had remained ignorant of his father's recovery,
neither caring nor daring to return. Then
by mere chance, he had met the squire at the
York cattle-show; and that kind man, who
knew his story, had eased his fears and ob-
tained from him a promise to return as soon as
the term of his engagement had expired. And
there he was.

The Dalesmen gathered round the boy, listening to his tale, and in return telling him the
home news, and chaffing him about Maggie.

Of all the people present, only one seemed
unmoved, and that was M'Adam. When first

David had entered he had started forward, a
flush of color warming his thin cheeks; but
no one had noticed his emotion; and now,
back again beneath his armor, he watched
the scene, a sour smile playing about his lips.

"I think the lad might ha' the grace to come
and say he's sorry for 'temptin' to murder me.
Hooiver"—with a characteristic shrug—"I
suppose I'm onraisonable."

Then the gong rang out its summons, and
the squire led the way into the great dining-
hall. At the one end of the long table, heavy
with all the solid delicacies of such a feast, he
took his seat with the Master of Kenmuir upon
his right. At the other end was Parson Leggy.
While down the sides the stalwart Dalesmen
were arrayed, with M'Adam a little lost figure
in the centre.

At first they talked but little, awed like children: knives plied, glasses tinkled, the carvers
had all their work, only the tongues were at
rest. But the squire's ringing laugh and the
parson's cheery tones soon put them at their
ease; and a babel of voices rose and waxed.

Of them all, only M'Adam sat silent. He
talked to no man, and you may be sure no one
talked to him. His hand crept oftener to his
glass than plate, till the sallow face began to
flush, and the dim eyes to grow unnaturally
bright.

Toward the end of the meal there was loud
tapping on the table, calls for silence, and men

pushed back their chairs. The squire was on his feet to make his annual speech.

He started by telling them how glad he was to see them there. He made an allusion to Owd Bob and the Shepherds' Trophy which was heartily applauded. He touched on the Black Killer, and said he had a remedy to propose: that Th' Owd Un should be set upon the criminal's track—a suggestion which was received with enthusiasm, while M'Adam's cackling laugh could be heard high above the rest.

From that he dwelt upon the existing condition of agriculture, the depression in which he attributed to the late Radical Government. He said that now with the Conservatives in office, and a ministry composed of "honorable men and gentlemen," he felt convinced that things would brighten. The Radicals' one ambition was to set class against class, landlord against tenant. Well, during the last five hundred years, the Sylvesters had rarely been—he was sorry to have to confess it—good men (laughter and dissent); but he never yet heard of the Sylvester—though he shouldn't say it—who was a bad landlord (loud applause).

This was a free country, and any tenant of his who was not content (a voice, "'Oo says we bain't?")—"thank you, thank you!"—well, there was room for him outside. (Cheers.) He thanked God from the bottom of his heart that, during the forty years he had been responsible for the March Mere Estate, there

had never been any friction between him and
his people (cheers), and he didn't think there
ever would be. (Loud cheers.)

"Thank you, thank you!" And his motto
was, "Shun a Radical as you do the devil!"—
and he was very glad to see them all there—
very glad; and he wished to give them a toast,
"The Queen! God bless her!" and—wait a
minute!—with her Majesty's name to couple
—he was sure that gracious lady would wish
it—that of "Owd Bob o' Kenmuir!" Then he
sat down abruptly amid thundering applause.

The toasts duly honoured, James Moore, by
prescriptive right as Master of Kenmuir, rose
to answer.

He began by saying that he spoke "as rep-
resenting all the tenants,"—but he was interrupted.

"Na," came a shrill voice from half-way
down the table. "Ye'll except me, James
Moore. I'd as lief be represented by Judas!"

There were cries of "Hold ye gab, little
mon!" and the squire's voice, "That'll do, Mr.
M'Adam!"

The little man restrained his tongue, but his
eyes gleamed like a ferret's; and the Master
continued his speech.

He spoke briefly and to the point, in short
phrases. And all the while M'Adam kept up
a low-voiced, running commentary. At length
he could control himself no longer. Half rising from his chair, he leant forward with hot

face and burning eyes, and cried: "Sit doon, James Moore! Hoo daur ye stan' there like an honest man, ye whitewashed sepulchre? Sit doon, I say, or"—threateningly—"wad ye hae me come to ye?"

At that the Dalesmen laughed uproariously, and even the Master's grim face relaxed. But the squire's voice rang out sharp and stern.

"Keep silence and sit down, Mr. M'Adam! D'you hear me, sir? If I have to speak to you again it will be to order you to leave the room."

The little man obeyed, sullen and vengeful, like a beaten cat.

The Master concluded his speech by calling on all present to give three cheers for the squire, her ladyship, and the young ladies.

The call was responded to enthusiastically, every man standing. Just as the noise was at its zenith, Lady Eleanour herself, with her two fair daughters, glided into the gallery at the end of the hall; whereat the cheering became deafening.

Slowly the clamor subsided. One by one the tenants sat down. At length there was left standing only one solitary figure— M'Adam.

His face was set, and he gripped the chair in front of him with thin, nervous hands.

"Mr. Sylvester," he began in low yet clear voice, "ye said this is a free country and we're a' free men. And that bein' so, I'll tak' the liberty, wi' yer permission, to say a word. It's maybe the last time I'll be wi' ye, so I hope ye'll listen to me."

The Dalesmen looked surprised, and the squire uneasy. Nevertheless he nodded assent.

The little man straightened himself. His face was tense as though strung up to a high resolve. All the passion had fled from it, all the bitterness was gone; and left behind was a strange, enobling earnestness. Standing there in the silence of that great hall, with every eye upon him, he looked like some prisoner at the bar about to plead for his life.

"Gentlemen," he began, "I've bin amang ye noo a score years, and I can truly say there's not a man in this room I can ca' 'Friend.'" He looked along the ranks of upturned faces. "Ay, David, I see ye, and you, Mr. Hornbut, and you, Mr. Sylvester—ilka one o' you, and not one as'd back me like a comrade gin a trouble came upon me." There was no rebuke in the grave little voice—it merely stated a hard fact.

"There's I doot no one amang ye but has some one—friend or blood—wham he can turn to when things are sair wi' him. I've no one.

' I bear alane my lade o' care'—

alane wi' Wullie, who stands to me, blaw or snaw, rain or shine. And whiles I'm feared he'll be took from me." He spoke this last

half to himself, a grieved, puzzled expression
on his face, as though lately he had dreamed
some ill dream.

"Forbye Wullie, I've no friend on God's
earth. And, mind ye, a bad man aften mak's
a good friend—but ye've never given me the
chance. It's a sair thing that, gentlemen, to
ha' to fight the battle o' life alane: no one to
pat ye on th' back, no one to say 'Weel done.'
It hardly gies a man a chance. For gin he
does try and yet fails, men never mind the
tryin', they only mark the failin'.

"I dinna blame ye. There's somethin' bred
in me, it seems, as sets ivery one agin me.
It's the same wi' Wullie and the tykes—they're
doon on him same as men are on me. I suppose we was made so. Sin' I was a lad it's
aye bin the same. From school days I've had
ivery one agin me.

"In ma life I've had three f iends. Ma
mither—and she went; then ma wife"—he
gave a great swallow—"and she's awa'; and I
may say they're the only two human bein's as
ha' lived on God's earth in ma time that iver
tried to bear wi' me;—and Wullie. A man's
mither—a man's wife—a man's dog! it's aften
a' he has in this warld; and the more he prizes
them the more like they are to be took from
him." The little earnest voice shook, and the
dim eyes puckered and filled.

"Sin' I've bin amang ye—twenty-odd years
—can any man here mind speakin' any word

that wasna ill to me?" He paused; there was no reply.

"I'll tell ye. All the time I've lived here I've had one kindly word spoke to me, and that a fortnight gone, and not by a man then —by her ladyship, God bless her!" He glanced up into the gallery. There was no one visible there; but a curtain at one end shook as though it were sobbing.

"Weel, I'm thinkin' we'll be gaein' in a wee while noo, Wullie and me, alane and thegither, as we've aye done. And it's time we went. Ye've had enough o' us, and it's no for me to blame ye. And when I'm gone what'll ye say o' me? 'He was a drunkard.' I am. 'He was a sinner.' I am. 'He was ilka thing he shouldna be.' I am. 'We're glad he's gone.' That's what ye'll say o' me. And it's but ma deserts."

The gentle, condemning voice ceased, and began again.

"That's what I am. Gin things had been differ', aiblins I'd ha' bin differ'. D'ye ken Robbie Burns? That's a man I've read, and ead, and read. D'ye ken why I love him as some o' you do yer Bibles? Because there's a humanity about him. A weak man hissel', aye slippin', slippin', slippin', and tryin' to haud up; sorrowin' ae minute, sinnin' the next; doin' ill deeds and wishin' 'em undone—just a plain human man, a sinner. And that's why I'm thinkin he's tender for us as is like him. *He understood.* It's what he wrote—after ain o' his tumbles, I'm thinkin'—that I was goin' to tell ye:

> ' Then gently scan yer brother man,
>   Still gentler sister woman,
>   Though they may gang a kennin' wrang,
> To step aside is human'—

the doctrine o' Charity. Gie him his chance, says Robbie, though he be a sinner. Mony a mon'd be differ', mony bad'd be gude, gin they had but their chance. Gie 'em their chance, says he; and I'm wi' him. As 'tis, ye see me here—a bad man wi' still a streak o' good in him. Gin I'd had ma chance, aiblins 'twad be—a good man wi' just a spice o' the devil in him. A' the differ' betune what is and what might ha' bin."

CHAPTER XXVIII

THE DEVIL'S BOWL

HE sat down. In the great hall there was silence, save for a tiny sound from the gallery like a sob suppressed.

The squire rose hurriedly and left the room. After him, one by one, trailed the tenants.

At length, two only remained—M'Adam, sitting solitary with a long array of empty chairs on either hand; and, at the far end of the table, Parson Leggy, stern, upright, motionless.

When the last man had left the room the parson rose, and with lips tight-set strode across the silent hall.

"M'Adam," he said rapidly and almost roughly, "I've listened to what you've said, as I think we all have, with a sore heart. You hit hard—but I think you were right. And if I've not done my duty by you as I ought—and I fear I've not—it's now my duty as God's minister to be the first to say I'm sorry." And it was evident from his face what an effort the words cost him.

The little man tilted back his chair, and raised his head.

It was the old M'Adam who looked up.

The thin lips were curled; a grin was crawling across the mocking face; and he wagged his head gently, as he looked at the speaker through the slits of his half-closed eyes.

"Mr. Hurnbert, I believe ye thocht me in earnest, 'deed and I do!" He leaned back in his chair and laughed softly. "Ye swallered it all down like best butter. Dear, dear! to think o' that!" Then, stretching forward: "Mr. Hornbut, I was playin' wi' ye."

The parson's face, as he listened, was ugly to watch. He shot out a hand and grabbed the scoffer by his coat; then dropped it again and turned abruptly away.

As he passed through the door a little sneering voice called after him:

"Mr. Hornbut, I ask ye hoo you, a minister o' the Church of England, can reconcile it to yer conscience to think—though it be but for a minute—that there can be ony good in a man and him no churchgoer? Sir, ye're a heretic —not to say a heathen!" He sniggered to himself, and his hand crept to a half-emptied wine decanter.

.   .   .   .   .

An hour later, James Moore, his business with the squire completed, passed through the hall on his way out. Its only occupant was now M'Adam, and the Master walked straight up to his enemy.

"M'Adam," he said gruffly, holding out a sinewy hand, "I'd like to say——"

The little man knocked aside the token of friendship.

"Na, na. No cant, if ye please, James Moore. That'll aiblins go doon wi' the parsons, but not wi' me. I ken you and you ken me, and all the whitewash i' th' warld 'll no deceive us."

The Master turned away, and his face was hard as the nether millstone. But the little man pursued him.

"I was nigh forgettin'," he said. "I've a surprise for ye, James Moore. But I hear it's yer birthday on Sunday, and I'll keep it till then—he! he!"

"Ye'll see me before Sunday, M'Adam," the other answered. "On Saturday, as I told yo', I'm comin' to see if yo've done yer duty."

"Whether ye come, James Moore, is your business. Whether ye'll iver go, once there, I'll mak' mine. I've warned ye twice noo"—and the little man laughed that harsh, cackling laugh of his.

At the door of the hall the Master met David.

"Noo, lad, yo're comin' along wi' Andrew and me," he said; "Maggie'll niver forgie us if we dinna bring yo' home wi' us."

"Thank you kindly, Mr. Moore," the boy replied. "I've to see squire first; and then yo' may be sure I'll be after you."

The Master faltered a moment.

"David, ha'n yo' spoke to yer father yet?" he asked in low voice. "Yo' should, lad."

The boy made a gesture of dissent.

"I canna," he said petulantly.

"I would, lad," the other advised. "An' yo' don't yo' may be sorry after."

As he turned away he heard the boy's steps, dull and sodden, as he crossed the hall; and then a thin, would-be cordial voice in the emptiness:

"I declar' if 'tisna David! The return o' the Prodeegal—he! he! So ye've seen yer auld dad at last, and the last; the proper place, say ye, for yer father—he! he! Eh, lad, but I'm blithe to see ye. D'ye mind when we was last thegither? Ye was kneelin' on ma chest: 'Your time's come, dad,' says you, and wangs me o'er the face—he! he! I mind it as if 'twas yesterday. Weel, weel, we'll say nae mair about it. Boys will be boys. Sons will be sons. Accidents will happen. And if at first ye don't succeed, why, try, try again—he! he!"

.   .   .   .   .

Dusk was merging into darkness when the Master and Andrew reached the Dalesman's Daughter. It had been long dark when they emerged from the cosy parlor of the inn and plunged out into the night.

As they crossed the Silver Lea and trudged over that familiar ground, where a fortnight since had been fought out the battle of the Cup, the wind fluttered past them in spasmodic gasps.

"There s trouble in the wind," said the Master.

"Ay," answered his laconic son.

All day there had been no breath of air, and the sky dangerously blue. But now a world of black was surging up from the horizon, smothering the star-lit night; and small dark clouds, like puffs of smoke, detaching themselves from the main body, were driving tempestuously forward—the vanguard of the storm.

In the distance was a low tumbling like heavy tumbrils on the floor of heaven. All about, the wind sounded hollow like a mighty scythe on corn. The air was oppressed with a leaden blackness—no glimmer of light on any hand; and as they began the ascent of the Pass they reached out blind hands to feel along the rock-face.

A sea-fret, cool and wetting, fell. A few big rain-drops splashed heavily down. The wind rose with a leap and roared past them up the rocky track. And the water-gates of heaven were flung wide.

Wet and weary, they battled on; thinking sometimes of the cosy parlor behind; sometimes of the home in front; wondering whether Maggie, in flat contradiction of her father's orders, would be up to welcome them; or whether only Owd Bob would come out to meet them.

The wind volleyed past them like salvoes of artillery. The rain stormed at them from

above; spat at them from the rock-face; and
leapt up at them from their feet.

Once they halted for a moment, finding a
miserable shelter in a crevice of the rock.

"It's a Black Killer's night," panted the
Master. "I reck'n he's oot."

"Ay," the boy gasped, "reck'n he is."

Up and up they climbed through the blackness, blind and buffeted. The eternal thunder
of the rain was all about them; the clamor of
the gale above; and far beneath, the roar of
angry waters.

Once, in a lull in the storm, the Master
turned and looked back into the blackness
along the path they had come.

"Did ye hear onythin'?" he roared above
the muffled soughing of the wind.

"Nay!" Andrew shouted back.

"I thowt I heard a step!" the Master cried,
peering down. But nothing could he see.

Then the wind leaped to life again like a
giant from his sleep, drowning all sound with
its hurricane voice; and they turned and bent
to their task again.

Nearing the summit, the Master turned once
more.

"There it was again!" he called; but his
words were swept away on the storm; and they
buckled to the struggle afresh.

Ever and anon the moon gleamed down
through the riot of tossing sky. Then they
could see the wet wall above them, with the

water tumbling down its sheer face; and far
below, in the roaring gutter of the Pass a
brown-stained torrent. Hardly, however, had
they time to glance around when a mass of
cloud would hurry jealously up, and all again
was blackness and noise.

At length, nigh spent, they topped the last
and steepest pitch of the Pass, and emerged
into the Devil's Bowl. There, overcome with
their exertions, they flung themselves on to the
soaking ground to draw breath.

Behind them, the wind rushed with a sullen
roar up the funnel of the Pass. It screamed
above them as though ten million devils were
a-horse; and blurted out on to the wild Marches
beyond.

As they lay there, still panting, the moon
gleamed down in momentary graciousness.
In front, through the lashing rain, they could
discern the hillocks that squat, hag-like, round
the Devil's Bowl; and lying in its bosom, its
white waters, usually so still, ploughed now
into a thousand furrows, the Lone Tarn.

The Master raised his head and craned forward at the ghostly scene. Of a sudden he
reared himself on to his arms, and stayed motionless awhile. Then he dropped as though
dead, forcing down Andrew with an iron hand.

"Lad, did'st see?" he whispered.

"Nay; what was't?" the boy replied, roused
by his father's tone.

"There!"

But as the Master pointed forward, a blur of
cloud intervened and all was dark. Quickly it
passed; and again the lantern of the night
shone down. And Andrew, looking with all
his eyes, saw indeed.

There, in front, by the fretting waters of
the Tarn, packed in a solid phalanx, with every
head turned in the same direction, was a flock
of sheep. They were motionless, all-intent,
staring with horror-bulging eyes. A column
of steam rose from their bodies into the rain-
pierced air. Panting and palpitating, yet they
stood with their backs to the water, as though
determined to sell their lives dearly. Beyond
them, not fifty yards away, crouched a humpbacked boulder, casting a long, misshapen
shadow in the moonlight. And beneath it
were two black objects, one still struggling
feebly.

"The Killer!" gasped the boy, and, all
ablaze with excitement, began forging forward.

"Steady, lad, steady!" urged his father,
dropping a restraining hand on the boy's
shoulder.

Above them a huddle of clouds flung in furious rout across the night, and the moon was
veiled.

"Follow, lad!" ordered the Master, and began to crawl silently forward. As stealthily
Andrew pursued. And over the sodden ground
they crept, one behind the other, like two
night-hawks on some foul errand.

On they crawled, lying prone during the blinks of moon, stealing forward in the dark; till, at length, the swish of the rain on the waters of the Tarn, and the sobbing of the flock in front, warned them they were near.

They skirted the trembling pack, passing so close as to brush against the flanking sheep; and yet unnoticed, for the sheep were soul-absorbed in the tragedy in front. Only, when the moon was in, Andrew could hear them huddling and stamping in the darkness. And again, as it shone out, fearfully they edged closer to watch the bloody play.

Along the Tarn edge the two crept. And still the gracious moon hid their approach, and the drunken wind drowned with its revelry the sound of their coming.

So they stole on, on hands and knees, with hearts aghast and fluttering breath; until, of a sudden, in a lull of wind, they could hear, right before them, the smack and slobber of bloody lips, chewing their bloody meal.

"Say thy prayers, Red Wull. Thy last minute's come!" muttered the Master, rising to his knees. Then, in Andrew's ear: "When I rush, lad, follow!" For he thought, when the moon rose, to jump in on the great dog, and, surprising him as he lay gorged and un-suspicious, to deal him one terrible swashing blow, and end forever the lawless doings of the Tailless Tyke.

The moon flung off its veil of cloud. White

and cold, it stared down into the Devil's Bowl;
on murderer and murdered.

Within a hand's cast of the avengers of
blood humped the black boulder. On the border of its shadow lay a dead sheep; and standing beside the body, his coat all ruffled by the
hand of the storm—Owd Bob—Owd Bob o'
Kenmuir.

Then the light went in, and darkness covered the land.

CHAPTER XXIX

THE DEVIL'S BOWL

It was Owd Bob. There could be no mistaking. In the wide world there was but one Owd Bob o' Kenmuir. The silver moon gleamed down on the dark head and rough gray coat, and lit the white escutcheon on his chest.

And in the darkness James Moore was lying with his face pressed downward that he might not see.

Once he raised himself on his arms; his eyes were shut and face uplifted, like a blind man praying. He passed a weary hand across his brow; his head dropped again; and he moaned and moaned like a man in everlasting pain.

Then the darkness lifted a moment, and he stole a furtive glance, like a murderer's at the gallows-tree, at the scene in front.

It was no dream; clear and cruel in the moonlight the humpbacked boulder; the dead sheep; and that gray figure, beautiful, motionless, damned for all eternity.

The Master turned his face and looked at Andrew, a dumb, pitiful entreaty in his eyes; but in the boy's white, horror-stricken countenance was no comfort. Then his head lolled down again, and the strong man was whimpering.

"He! he! he! 'Scuse ma laffin', Mr. Moore—he! he! he!"

A little man, all wet and shrunk, sat hunching on a mound above them, rocking his shrivelled form to and fro in the agony of his merriment.

"Ye raskil—he! he!   Ye rogue—he! he!" and he shook his fist waggishly at the unconscious gray dog. "I owe ye anither grudge for this—ye've anteecipated me"—and he leant back and shook this way and that in convulsive mirth.

The man below him rose heavily to his feet, and tumbled toward the mocker, his great figure swaying from side to side as though in blind delirium, moaning still as he went. And there was that on his face which no man can mistake. Boy that he was, Andrew knew it.

"Feyther! feyther! do'ee not!" he pleaded, running after his father and laying impotent hands on him.

But the strong man shook him off like a fly, and rolled on, swaying and groaning, with that awful expression plain to see in the moonlight.

In front the little man squatted in the rain, bowed double still; and took no thought to flee.

"Come on, James Moore! Come on!" he laughed, malignant joy in his voice; and something gleamed bright in his right hand,

and was hid again. "I've bin waitin' this a weary while noo. Come on!"

Then had there been done something worse than sheep-murder in the dreadful lonesomeness of the Devil's Bowl upon that night; but of a sudden, there sounded the splash of a man's foot. falling heavily behind; a hand like a falling tree smote the Master on the shoulder; and a voice roared above the noise of the storm:

"Mr. Moore! Look, man! look!"

The Master tried to shake off that detaining grasp; but it pinned him where he was, immovable.

"Look, I tell yo'!" cried that great voice again.

A hand pushed past him and pointed; and sullenly he turned, ignoring the figure at his side, and looked.

The wind had dropped suddenly as it had risen; the little man on the mound had ceased to chuckle; Andrew's sobs were hushed; and in the background the huddled flock edged closer. The world hung balanced on the pin-point of the moment. Every eye was in the one direction.

With dull, uncomprehending gaze James Moore stared as bidden. There was the gray dog naked in the moonlight, heedless still of any witnesses; there the murdered sheep, lying within and without that distorted shade; and there the humpbacked boulder.

He stared into the shadow, and still stared.

Then he started as though struck. The shadow of the boulder had moved!

Motionless, with head shot forward and bulging eyes, he gazed.

Ay, ay, ay; he was sure of it—a huge dim outline as of a lion *couchant*, in the very thickest of the blackness.

At that he was seized with such a palsy of trembling that he must have fallen but for the strong arm about his waist.

Clearer every moment grew that crouching figure; till at length they plainly could discern the line of arching loins, the crest, thick as a stallion's, the massive, wagging head. No mistake this time. There he lay i the deepest black, gigantic, revelling in hi horrid debauch—the Black Killer!

And they watched him at his feast. Now he burrowed into the spongy flesh; now turned to lap the dark pool which glittered in the moonlight at his side like claret in a silver cup. Now lifting his head, he snapped irritably at the rain-drops, and the moon caught his wicked, rolling eye and the red shreds of flesh dripping from his jaw. And again, raising his great muzzle as if about to howl, he let the delicious nectar trickle down his throat and ravish his palate.

So he went on, all unsuspicious, wisely nodding in slow-mouthed gluttony. And in the stillness, between the claps of wind, they could hear the smacking of his lips.

While all the time the gray dog stood before him, motionless, as though carved in stone.

At last, as the murderer rolled his great head from side to side, he saw that still figure. At the sight he leaped back, dismayed. Then with a deep-mouthed roar that shook the waters of the Tarn he was up and across his victim with fangs bared, his coat standing erect in wet, rigid furrows from topknot to tail.

So the two stood, face to face, with perhaps a yard of rain-pierced air between them.

The wind hushed its sighing to listen. The moon stared down, white and dumb. Away at the back the sheep edged closer. While save for the everlasting thunder of the rain, there was utter stillness.

An age, it seemed, they waited so. Then a voice, clear yet low and far away, like a bugle in a distant city, broke the silence.

"Eh, Wullie!" it said.

There was no anger in the tones, only an incomparable reproach; the sound of the cracking of a man's heart.

At the call the great dog leapt round, snarling in hideous passion. He saw the small, familiar figure, clear-cut against the tumbling sky; and for the only time in his life Red Wull was afraid.

His blood-foe was forgotten; the dead sheep was forgotten; everything was sunk in the agony of that moment. He cowered upon the

ground, and a cry like that of a lost soul was
wrung from him; it rose on the still night air
and floated, wailing, away; and the white
waters of the Tarn thrilled in cold pity; out of
the lonely hollow; over the desolate Marches;
into the night.

On the mound above stood his master. The
little man's white hair was bared to the night
wind; the rain trickled down his face; and his
hands were folded behind his back. He stood
there, looking down into the dell below him,
as a man may stand at the tomb of his lately
buried wife. And there was such an expression on his face as I cannot describe.

"Wullie, Wullie, to me!" he cried at length;
and his voice sounded weak and far, like a distant memory.

At that, the huge brute came crawling
toward him on his belly, whimpering as he
came, very pitiful in his distress. He knew
his fate as every sheep-dog knows it. That
troubled him not. His pain, insufferable, was
that this, his friend and father, who had trusted
him, should have found him in his sin.

So he crept up to his master's feet; and
the little man never moved.

"Wullie—ma Wullie!" he said very gently.
"They've aye bin agin me—and noo you! A
man's mither—a man's wife—a man's dog!
they're all I've iver had; and noo ain o' they
three has turned agin me! Indeed I am alone!"

At that the great dog raised himself, and

placing his forepaws on his master's chest tenderly, lest he should hurt him who was already
hurt past healing, stood towering above him;
while the little man laid his two colds hands on
the dog's shoulders.

So they stood, looking at one another, like a
man and his love.

 . . . . .

At M'Adam's word, Owd Bob looked up,
and for the first time saw his master.

He seemed in nowise startled, but trotted
over to him. There was nothing fearful in his
carriage, no haunting blood-guiltness in the
true gray eyes which never told a lie, which
never, dog-like, failed to look you in the face.
Yet his tail was low, and, as he stopped at his
master's feet, he was quivering. For he, too,
knew, and was not unmoved.

For weeks he had tracked the Killer; for
weeks he had followed him as he crossed Kenmuir, bound on his bloody errands; yet always
had lost him on the Marches. Now, at last,
he had run him to ground. Yet his heart went
out to his enemy in his distress.

"I thowt t'had been yo', lad," the Master
whispered, his hand on the dark head at his
knee— "I thowt t'had bin yo'!"

 . . . . .

Rooted to the ground, the three watched the
scene between M'Adam and his Wull.

In the end the Master was whimpering; Andrew crying; and David turned his back.

At length, silent, they moved away.

"Had I—should I go to him?" asked David hoarsely, nodding toward his father.

"Nay, nay, lad," the Master replied. "Yon's not a matter for a mon's friends."

So they marched out of the Devil's Bowl, and left those two alone together.

.   .   .   .   .

A little later, as they trampled along, James Moore heard little pattering, staggering footsteps behind.

He stopped, and the other two went on.

"Man," a voice whispered, and a face, white and pitiful, like a mother's pleading for her child, looked into his—"Man, ye'll no tell them a'? I'd no like 'em to ken 'twas ma Wullie. Think an t'had bin yer ain dog."

"You may trust me!" the other answered thickly.

The little man stretched out a palsied hand.

"Gie us yer hand on't. And G-God bless ye, James Moore!"

So these two shook hands in the moonlight, with none to witness it but the God who made them.

And that is why the mystery of the Black Killer is yet unsolved in the Daleland. Many have surmised; besides those three only one other knows—knows now which of those two he saw upon a summer night was the guilty, which the innocent. And Postie Jim tells no man.

CHAPTER XXX

THE TAILLESS TYKE AT BAY

ON the following morning there was a sheep-auction at the Dalesman's Daughter.

Early as many of the farmers arrived, there was one earlier. Tupper, the first man to enter the sand-floored parlor, found M'Adam before him.

He was sitting a little forward in his chair; his thin hands rested on his knees; and on his face was a gentle, dreamy expression such as no man had ever seen there before. All the harsh wrinkles seemed to have fled in the night; and the sour face, stamped deep with the bitterness of life, was softened now, as if at length at peace.

"When I coom doon this mornin'," said Teddy Bolstock in a whisper, "I found 'im sittin' just so. And he's nor moved nor spoke since."

"Where's th' Terror, then?" asked Tupper, awed somehow into like hushed tones.

"In t' paddock at back," Teddy answered, "marchin' hoop and doon, hoop and doon, for a' the world like a sentry-soger. And so he was when I looked oot o' window when I wake."

Then Londesley entered, and after him, Ned Hoppin, Rob Saunderson, Jim Mason, and others, each with his dog. And each man, as he came in and saw the little lone figure for once without its huge attendant genius, put the same question; while the dogs sniffed about the little man, as though suspecting treachery. And all the time M'Adam sat as though he neither heard nor saw, lost in some sweet, sad dream; so quite, so silent, that more than one thought he slept.

After the first glance, however, the farmers paid him little heed, clustering round the publican at the farther end of the room to hear the latest story of Owd Bob.

It appeared that a week previously, James Moore with a pack of sheep had met the new Grammoch-town butcher at the Dalesmen's Daughter. A bargain concluded, the butcher started with the flock for home. As he had no dog, the Master offered him Th' Owd Un. "And he'll pick me i' th' town to-morrow," said he.

Now the butcher was a stranger in the land. Of course he had heard of Owd Bob o' Kenmuir, yet it never struck him that this handsome gentleman with the quiet, resolute manner, who handled sheep as he had never seen them handled, was that hero—"the best sheepdog in the North."

Certain it is that by the time the flock was penned in the enclosure behind the shop, he coveted the dog—ay, would even offer ten pounds for him!

Forthwith the butcher locked him up in an outhouse—summit of indignity; resolving to make his offer on the morrow.

When the morrow came he found no dog in the outhouse, and, worse, no sheep in the enclosure. A sprung board showed the way of escape of the one, and a displaced hurdle that of the other. And as he was making the discovery, a gray dog and a flock of sheep, travelling along the road toward the Dalesman's Daughter, met the Master.

From the first, Owd Bob had mistrusted the man. The attempt to confine him set the seal on his suspicions. His master's sheep were not for such a rogue; and he worked his own way out and took the sheep along with him.

The story was told to a running chorus of— "Ma word! Good, Owd Un!—Ho! ho! did he thot?"

Of them all, only M'Adam sat strangely silent.

Rob Saunderson, always glad to draw the little man, remarked it.

"And what d'yo' think o' that, Mr. M'Adam, for a wunnerfu' story of a wunnerfu' tyke?" he asked.

"It's a gude tale, a vera gude tale," the little man answered dreamily. "And James Moore didna invent it; he had it from the Christmas number o' the *Flock-keeper* in saxty." (On the following Sunday, old Rob, from sheer curiosity, reached down from his shelf the specified number of the paper. To his amazement he found the little man was right. There was the story almost identically. None the less is it also true of Owd Bob o' Kenmuir.)

"Ay, ay," the little man continued, "and in a day or two James Moore'll ha' anither tale to tell ye—a better tale, ye'll think it—mair laffable. And yet—ay—no—I'll no believe it! I niver loved James Moore, but I think, as Mr. Hornbut aince said, he'd rather die than lie. Owd Bob o' Kenmuir!" he continued in a whisper. "Up till the end I canna shake him aff. Hafflins I think that where I'm gaein' to there'll be gray dogs sneakin' around me in the twilight. And they're aye behind and behind, and I canna, canna——"

Teddy Bolstock interrupted, lifting his hand for silence.

"D'yo' hear thot?—Thunder!"

They listened; and from without came a gurgling, jarring roar, horrible to hear.

"It's comin' nearer!"

"Nay, it's goin' away!"

"No thunder thot!"

"More like the Lea in flood. And yet—Eh, Mr. M'Adam, what is it?"

The little man had moved at last. He was on his feet, staring about him, wild-eyed.

"Where's yer dogs?" he almost screamed.

"Here's ma—— Nay, by thunder! but he's not!" was the astonished cry.

In the interest of the story no man had
noticed that his dog had risen from his side;
no one had noticed a file of shaggy figures
creeping out of the room.

"I tell ye it's the tykes! I tell ye it's the
tykes! They're on ma Wullie—fifty to one
they're on him! My God! My God! And
me not there! Wullie, Wullie!"—in a scream
—"I'm wi' ye!"

At the same moment Bessie Bolstock rushed
in, white-faced.

"Hi! Feyther! Mr. Saunderson! all o' you!
T'tykes fightin' mad!   Hark!"

There was no time for that. Each man
seized his stick and rushed for the door; and
M'Adam led them all.

.   .   .   .   .

A rare thing it was for M'Adam and Red
Wull to be apart.   So rare, that others besides
the men in that little tap-room noticed it.

Saunderson's old Shep walked quietly to the
back door of the house and looked out.

There on the slope below him he saw what
he sought, stalking up and down, gaunt and
grim, like a lion at feeding-time.   And as the
old dog watched, his tail was gently swaying
as though he were well pleased.

He walked back into the tap-room just as
Teddy began his tale.   Twice he made the
round of the room, silent-footed.   From dog
to dog he went, stopping at each as though
urging him on to some great enterprise.   Then

he made for the door again, looking back to see if any followed.

One by one the others rose and trailed out after him: big blue Rasper, Londesley's Lassie, Ned Hoppin's young dog; Grip and Grapple, the publican's bull-terriers; Jim Mason's Gyp, foolish and flirting even now; others there were; and last of all, waddling heavily in the rear, that scarred Amazon, the Venus.

Out of the house they pattered, silent and unseen, with murder in their hearts. At last they had found their enemy alone. And slowly, in a black cloud, like the shadow of death, they dropped down the slope upon him.

And he saw them coming, knew their errand—as who should better than the Terror of the Border?—and was glad. Death it might be, and such an one as he would wish to die— at least distraction from that long-drawn, haunting pain. And he smiled grimly as he looked at the approaching crowd, and saw there was not one there but he had humbled in his time.

He ceased his restless pacing, and awaited them. His great head was high as he scanned them contemptuously, daring them to come on.

And on they came, marching slow and silent like soldiers at a funeral: young and old; bob-tailed and bull; terrier and collie; flocking like vultures to the dead. And the Venus, heavy with years, rolled after them on her bandy legs panting in her hurry lest she should be

late. For had she not the blood of her blood
to avenge?

So they came about him, slow, certain, murderous, opening out to cut him off on every
side. There was no need. He never thought
to move. Long odds 'twould be—crushingly
heavy; yet he loved them for it, and was trembling already with the glory of the coming
fight.

They were up to him now; the sheep-dogs
walking round him on their toes, stiff and
short like cats on coals; their backs a little
humped; heads averted; yet eying him askance.

And he remained stock-still nor looked at
them. His great chin was cocked, and his
muzzle wrinkled in a dreadful grin. As he
stood there, shivering a little, his eyes rolling
back, his breath grating in his throat to set
every bristle on end, he looked a devil indeed.

The Venus ranged alongside him. No pre-
liminary stage for her; she never walked
where she could stand, or stood where she
could lie. But stand she must now, breathing
hard through her nose, never taking her eyes
off that pad she had marked for her own.
Close beside her were crop-eared Grip and
Grapple, looking up at the line above them
where hairy neck and shoulder joined. Behind was big Rasper, and close to him Lassie.
Of the others, each had marked his place, each
taken up his post.

Last of all, old Shep took his stand full in

front of his enemy, their shoulders almost rubbing, head past head.

So the two stood a moment, as though they
were whispering; each diabolical, each rolling
back his eyes to watch the other. While from
the little mob there rose a snarling, bubbling
snore, like some giant wheezing in his sleep.

Then like lightning each struck. Rearing
high, they wrestled with striving paws and the
expression of fiends incarnate. Down they
went, Shep underneath, and the great dog with
a dozen of these wolves of hell upon him.
Rasper, devilish, was riding on his back; the
Venus—well for him!—had struck and missed;
but Grip and Grapple had their hold; and the
others, like leaping demoniacs, were plunging
into the whirlpool vortex of the fight.

And there, where a fortnight before he had
fought and lost the battle of the Cup, Red
Wull now battled for his life.

Long odds! But what cared he? The long-
drawn agony of the night was drowned in that
glorious delirium. The hate of years came
bubbling forth. In that supreme moment he
would avenge his wrongs. And he went in to
fight, revelling like a giant in the red lust of
killing.

Long odds! Never before had he faced such
a galaxy of foes. His one chance lay in quick-
ness: to prevent the swarming crew getting
their hold till at least he had diminished their
numbers.

Then it was a sight to see the great brute,
huge as a bull-calf, strong as a bull, rolling
over and over and up again, quick as a kitten;
leaping here, striking there; shaking himself
free; swinging his quarters; fighting with
feet and body and teeth—every inch of him at
war. More than once he broke right through
the mob; only to turn again and face it. No
flight for him; nor thought of it.

Up and down the slope the dark mass tossed,
like some hulk the sport of the waves. Black
and white, sable and gray, worrying at that
great centrepiece. Up and down, roaming
wide, leaving everywhere a trail of red.

Gyp he had pinned and hurled over his
shoulder. Grip followed; he shook her till
she rattled, then flung her afar; and she fell
with a horrid thud, not to rise. While Grapple, the death to avenge, hung tighter. In a
scarlet, soaking patch of the ground lay Big
Bell's lurcher, doubled up in a dreadful ball.
And Hoppin's young dog, who three hours
before had been the children's tender play-
mate, now fiendish to look on, dragged after
the huddle up the hill. Back the mob rolled
on her. When it was passed, she lay quite
still, grinning; a handful of tawny hair and
flesh in her dead mouth.

So they fought on. And ever and anon a
great figure rose up from the heaving inferno
all around; rearing to his full height, his head
ragged and bleeding, the red foam dripping

from his jaws. Thus he would appear momentarily, like some dark rock amid a raging sea; and down he would go again.

Silent now they fought, dumb and determined. Only you might have heard the rend and rip of tearing flesh; a hoarse gurgle as some dog went down; the panting of dry throats; and now and then a sob from that central figure. For he was fighting for his life. The Terror of the Border was at bay.

All who meant it were on him now. The Venus, blinded with blood, had her hold at last; and never but once in a long life of battles had she let go; Rasper, his breath coming in rattles, had him horribly by the loins; while a dozen other devils with red eyes and wrinkled nostrils clung still.

Long odds! And down he went, smothered beneath the weight of numbers, yet struggled up again. His great head was torn and dripping; his eyes a gleam of rolling red and white; the little tail stern and stiff like the gallant stump of a flagstaff shot away. He was desperate, but indomitable; and he sobbed as he fought doggedly on.

Long odds! It could not last. And down he went at length, silent still—never a cry should they wring from him in his agony the Venus glued to that mangled pad; Rasper beneath him now; three at his throat; two at his ears; a crowd on flanks and body.

The Terror of the Border was down at last!

   •   •   •   •   •

"Wullie, ma Wullie!" screamed M'Adam, bounding down the slope a crook's length in front of the rest. "Wullie! Wullie! to me!"

At the shrill cry the huddle below was convulsed. It heaved and swelled and dragged to and fro, like the sea lashed into life by some dying leviathan.

A gigantic figure, tawny and red, fought its way to the surface. A great tossing head, bloody past recognition, flung out from the ruck. One quick glance he shot from his ragged eyes at the little flying form in front; then with a roar like a waterfall plunged toward it, shaking off the bloody leeches as he went.

"Wullie! Wullie! I'm wi' ye!" cried that little voice, now so near.

Through — through—through! — an incomparable effort and his last. They hung to his throat, they clung to his muzzle, they were round and about him. And down he went again with a sob and a little suffocating cry, shooting up at his master one quick, beseeching glance as the sea of blood closed over him —worrying, smothering, tearing, like foxhounds at the kill.

   •   •   •   •

They left the dead and pulled away the living. And it was no light task, for the pack were mad for blood.

At the bottom of the wet mess of hair and

red and flesh was old Shep, stone-dead.   And
as Saunderson pulled the body out, his face was
working; for no man can lose in a crack the
friend of a dozen years, and remain unmoved.

The Venus lay there, her teeth clenched
still in death; smiling that her vengeance was
achieved. Big Rasper, blue no longer, was
gasping out his life. Two more came crawling out to find a quiet spot where they might
lay them down to die. Before the night had
fallen another had gone to his account.   While
not a dog who fought upon that day but carried the scars of it with him to his grave.

The Terror o' th' Border, terrible in his life,
like Samson, was yet more terrible in his dying.

.   .   .   .   .

Down at the bottom lay that which once had
been Adam M'Adam's Red Wull.

At the sight the little man neither raved nor
swore: it was past that for him. He sat down,
heedless of the soaking ground, and took the
mangled head in his lap very tenderly.

"They've done ye at last, Wullie—they've
done ye at last," he said quietly; unalterably
convinced that the attack had been organized
while he was detained in the tap-room.

On hearing the loved little voice, the dog gave
one weary wag of his tump-tail. And with
that the Tailless Tyke, Adam M'Adam's Red
Wull, the Black Killer, went to his long home.

.   .   .   .   .

One by one the Dalesmen took away their

dead, and the little man was left alone with the body of his last friend.

Dry-eyed he sat there, nursing the dead dog's head; hour after hour—alone—crooning to himself:

> " 'Monie a sair daurk we twa hae wrought,
>   An' wi' the weary warl' fought !
>   An' mony an anxious day I thought
>   We wad be beat.'

An' noo we are, Wullie—noo we are!"

So he went on, repeating the lines over and over again, always with the same sad termination.

"A man's mither—a man's wife—a man's dog! they three are a' little M'Adam iver had to back him! D'ye mind the auld mither, Wullie? And her, 'Niver be down-hearted, Adam; ye've aye got yer mither,' And ae day I had not. And Flora, Wullie (ye remember Flora, Wullie? Na, na; ye'd not) wi' her laffin' daffin' manner, cryin' to one: 'Adam, ye say ye're alane. But ye've me—is that no enough for ony man?' And God kens it was —while it lasted!" He broke down and sobbed a while. "And you, Wullie—and you! the only man friend iver I had!" He sought the dog's bloody paw with his right hand.

> " 'An' here's a hand, my trusty fier,
>   An gie's a hand o' thine;
>   An' we'll tak' a right guid willie-waught,
>   For auld lang syne.' "

.   .   .   .   .

He sat there, muttering, and stroking the

poor head upon his lap, bending over it, like a
mother over a sick child.

"They've done ye at last, lad—done ye sair.
And noo I'm thinkin' they'll no rest content
till I'm gone. And oh, Wullie!"—he bent
down and whispered—"I dreamed sic an aw-
fu' thing—that ma Wullie—but there! 'twas
but a dream."

So he sat on, crooning to the dead dog; and
no man approached him. Only Bessie of the
inn watched the little lone figure from afar.

It was long past noon when at length he
rose, laying the dog's head reverently down,
and tottered away toward that bridge which
once the dead thing on the slope had held
against a thousand.

He crossed it and turned; there was a look
upon his face, half hopeful, half fearful, very
piteous to see.

"Wullie, Wullie, to me!" he cried; only the
accents, formerly so fiery, were now weak as
a dying man's.

A while he waited in vain.

"Are ye no comin', Wullie?" he asked at
length in quavering tones. "Ye've not used
to leave me."

He walked away a pace, then turned again
and whistled that shrill, sharp call, only now it
sounded like a broken echo of itself.

"Come to me, Wullie!" he implored, very
pitifully. "'Tis the first time iver I kent ye
not come and me whistlin'. What ails ye, lad?"

"Dry-eyed he sat there, nursing the dead dog's head."

He recrossed the bridge, walking blindly like a sobbing child; and yet dry-eyed.

Over the dead body he stooped.

"What ails ye, Wullie?" he asked again. "Will you, too, leave me?"

Then Bessie, watching fearfully, saw him bend, sling the great body on his back, and stagger away.

Limp and hideous, the carcase hung down from the little man's shoulders. The huge head, with grim, wide eyes and lolling tongue, jolted and swagged with the motion, seeming to grin a ghastly defiance at the world it had left. And the last Bessie saw of them was that bloody, rolling head, with the puny legs staggering beneath their load, as the two passed out of the world's ken.

.   .   .   .   .

In the Devil's Bowl, next day, they found the pair: Adam M'Adam and his Red Wull, face to face; dead, not divided; each, save for the other, alone. The dog, his saturnine expression glazed and ghastly in the fixedness of death, propped up against that humpbacked boulder beneath which, a while before, the Black Killer had dreed his weird; and, close by, his master lying on his back, his dim dead eyes staring up at the heaven, one hand still clasping a crumpled photograph; the weary body at rest at last, the mocking face—mocking no longer—alight with a whole-souled, transfiguring happiness.

POSTSCRIPT

Adam M'Adam and his Red Wull lie buried together: one just within, the other just without, the consecrated pale.

The only mourners at the funeral were David, James Moore, Maggie, and a gray dog peering through the lych-gate.

During the service a carriage stopped at the churchyard, and a lady with a stately figure and a gentle face stepped out and came across the grass to pay a last tribute to the dead. And Lady Eleanour, as she joined the little group about the grave, seemed to notice a more than usual solemnity in the parson's voice as he intoned: "Earth to earth—ashes to ashes—dust to dust; in sure and certain hope of the Resurrection to eternal life."

.   .   .   .   .

When you wander in the gray hill-country of the North, in the loneliest corner of that lonely land you may chance upon a low farm-house, lying in the shadow of the Muir Pike.

Entering, a tall old man comes out to greet you—the Master of Kenmuir. His shoulders are bent now; the hair that was so dark is frosted; but the blue-gray eyes look you as proudly in the face as of yore.

And while the girl with the glory of yellow hair is preparing food for you—they are hospitable to a fault, these Northerners—you will notice on the mantelpiece, standing solitary, a massive silver cup, dented.

That is the world-known Shepherds' Trophy, won outright, as the old man will tell you, by Owd Bob, last and best of the Gray Dogs of Kenmuir. The last because he is the best; because once, for a long-drawn unit of time, James Moore had thought him to be the worst.

When at length you take your leave, the old man accompanies you to the top of the slope to point you your way.

"Yo' cross the stream; over Langholm How, yonder; past the Bottom; and oop th' hill on far side. Yo'll come on th' house o' top. And happen yo'll meet Th' Owd Un on the road. Good-day to you, sir, good-day."

So you go as he has bidden you; across the stream, skirting the How, over the gulf and up the hill again.

On the way, as the Master has foretold, you come upon an old gray dog, trotting soberly along. Th' Owd Un, indeed, seems to spend the evening of his life going thus between Kenmuir and the Grange. The black muzzle is almost white now; the gait, formerly so smooth and strong, is stiff and slow; venerable, indeed, is he of whom men still talk as the best sheep-dog in the North.

As he passes, he pauses to scan you. The noble head is high, and one foot raised; and you look into two big gray eyes such as you have never seen before—soft, a little dim, and infinitely sad.

That is Owd Bob o' Kenmuir, of whom the tales are many as the flowers on the May. With him dies the last of the immortal line of the Gray Dogs of Kenmuir.

.   .   .   .

You travel on up the hill, something pensive, and knock at the door of the house on the top.

A woman, comely with the inevitable comeliness of motherhood, opens to you. And nestling in her arms is a little boy with golden hair and happy face, like one of Correggio's cherubs.

You ask the child his name. He kicks and crows, and looks up at his mother; and in the end lisps roguishly, as if it was the merriest joke in all this merry world, "Adum Mataddum."

THE END

Popular Copyright Books

At Moderate Prices

Any of the following titles can be bought of your Bookseller
at the price you paid for this volume

Pam . . .	By Bettina von Hutton
Memoirs of Sherlock Holmes .	By A. Conan Doyle
Ben Blair . . .	By Will Lillibridge
The Wheel of Life . .	By Ellen Glasgow
The Throwback .	By Alfred Henry Lewis
At the Mercy of Tiberius .	By Augusta Evans Wilson
A Sword of the Old Frontier .	By Randall Parrish
Lady Betty Across the Water	
	By C. N. & A. M. Williamson
The Lilac Sunbonnet .	By S. R. Crockett
The Adventures of Captain Kettle .	By Cutcliffe Hyne
The Spoilers . . .	By Rex E. Beach
Adventures of Sherlock Holmes .	By A. Conan Doyle
The Trail of the Sword .	By Gilbert Parker
Artemus Ward's Works .	. . .
By Wit of Woman .	By Arthur W. Marchmont
Phra the Phœnician .	By Edwin Lester Arnold

A. L. BURT COMPANY, PUBLISHERS

52-58 Duane Street, New York

Popular Copyright Books

At Moderate Prices

Any of the following titles can be bought of your Book-seller at the price you paid for this volume

THE CONQUEST OF CANAAN	Booth Tarkington
LIN McLEAN	Owen Wister
THE PRINCESS PASSES	C. N. & A. M. Williamson
THE MARATHON MYSTERY	Burton Egbert Stevenson
THE HOLLADAY CASE	Burton Egbert Stevenson
MY FRIEND THE CHAUFFEUR,	C. N. & A. M. Williamson
CARDIGAN	Robert W. Chambers
PARTNERS OF THE TIDE	Joseph C. Lincoln
EXPLOITS OF BRIGADIER GERARD	A. Conan Doyle
THE MAN FROM RED KEG	Eugene Thwing
MYSTERY OF JUNE 13th	Melvin L. Severy
THE SUNSET TRAIL	Alfred Henry Lewis
THE WOMAN IN THE ALCOVE	Anna Katharine Green
THE INDIFFERENCE OF JULIET	Grace S. Richmond
THE MISSOURIAN	Eugene P. Lyle, Jr.

Popular Copyright Books

At Moderate Prices

Any of the following titles can be bought of your Bookselle
at the price you paid for this volume

NANCY STAIR . . Elinor Macartney Lane

MY LADY OF THE NORTH . . Randall Parrish

THE FUGITIVE BLACKSMITH . Charles D. Stewart

VASHTI . . . . Augusta Evans Wilson

FOR LOVE OR CROWN . Arthur W. Marchmont

UP FROM SLAVERY . Booker T. Washington

THE SEATS OF THE MIGHTY . Gilbert Parker

CAP'N ERI . . . . Joseph C. Lincoln

WHEN WILDERNESS WAS KING . Randall Parrish

THE LEAVENWORTH CASE . Anna Katharine Green

MYSTERY TALES . . . Edgar Allan Poe

A COURIER OF FORTUNE . Arthur W. Marchmont

THE QUICKENING . . . Francis Lynde

DOUBLE TROUBLE . . . Herbert Quick

SIR RICHARD CALMADY . . . Lucas Malet

CASTING AWAY OF MRS. LECKS
    AND MRS. ALESHINE . . Frank R. Stockton

A SPECKLED BIRD . . Augusta Evans Wilson

ORDER NO. II . . . Caroline Abbot Stanley

THE BELLE OF BOWLING GREEN . Amelia E. Barr

SARITA THE CARLIST . Arthur W. Marchmont

A. L. BURT CO., Publishers, 52-58 Duane St., New York

Popular Copyright Books

At Moderate Prices

**Any of the following titles can be bought of your Bookseller
at the price you paid for this volume**

THE PRODIGAL SON	Hall Caine
ADVENTURES OF GERARD	A. Conan Doyle
A CAPTAIN IN THE RANKS	George Cary Eggleston
THE DELIVERANCE	Ellen Glasgow
THE BATTLE GROUND	Ellen Glasgow
THE VOICE OF THE PEOPLE	Ellen Glasgow
THE MILLIONAIRE BABY	Anna Katharine Green
THE BRETHREN	H. Rider Haggard
THE BOSS	Alfred Henry Lewis
THE PRESIDENT	Alfred Henry Lewis
BOB, SON OF BATTLE	Alfred Ollivant
NONE BUT THE BRAVE	Hamblen Sears
THE DARROW ENIGMA	Melvin Severy
THE TWO VANREVELS	Booth Tarkington
THE CIRCLE	Catharine Cecil Thurston

Author of "THE MASQUERADERS," "THE GAMBLER."

HURRICANE ISLAND	H. B. Marriott-Watson
THE LONG NIGHT	Stanley J. Weyman
INFELICE	Augusta Evans Wilson
ARMS AND THE WOMAN	Harold MacGrath
THE LANE THAT HAD NO TURNING	Gilbert Parker
THE HEART'S HIGHWAY	Mary E. Wilkins
TALES OF SHERLOCK HOLMES	A. Conan Doyle
ROSE OF THE WORLD	Agnes and Egerton Castle
THAT PRINTER OF UDELL'S	Harold Bell Wright
IN THE NAME OF A WOMAN	Arthur W. Marchmont
THE QUEEN'S ADVOCATE	Arthur W. Marchmont
BY SNARE OF LOVE	Arthur W. Marchmont
WHEN I WAS CZAR	Arthur W. Marchmont

A. L. BURT CO., Publishers, 52-58 Duane St., New York

Good Fiction Worth Reading.

A series of romances containing several of the old favorites in the field of historical fiction, replete with powerful romances of love and diplomacy that excel in thrilling and absorbing interest.

WINDSOR CASTLE. A Historical Romance of the Reign of Henry VIII., Catharine of Aragon and Anne Boleyn. By Wm. Harrison Ainsworth. Cloth, 12mo. with four illustrations by George Cruikshank. Price, $1.00.

"Windsor Castle" is the story of Henry VIII., Catharine, and Anne Boleyn. "Bluff King Hal," although a well-loved monarch, was none too good a one in many ways. Of all his selfishness and unwarrantable acts, none was more discreditable than his divorce from Catharine, and his marriage to the beautiful Anne Boleyn. The King's love was as brief as it was vehement. Jane Seymour, waiting maid on the Queen, attracted him, and Anne Boleyn was forced to the block to make room for her successor. This romance is one of extreme interest to all readers.

HORSESHOE ROBINSON. A tale of the Tory Ascendency in South Carolina in 1780. By John P. Kennedy. Cloth, 12mo. with four illustrations by J. Watson Davis. Price, $1.00.

Among the old favorites in the field of what is known as historical fiction, there are none which appeal to a larger number of Americans than Horseshoe Robinson, and this because it is the only story which depicts with fidelity to the facts the heroic efforts of the colonists in South Carolina to defend their homes against the brutal oppression of the British under such leaders as Cornwallis and Tarleton.

The reader is charmed with the story of love which forms the thread of the tale, and then impressed with the wealth of detail concerning those times. The picture of the manifold sufferings of the people, is never overdrawn, but painted faithfully and honestly by one who spared neither time nor labor in his efforts to present in this charming love story all that price in blood and tears which the Carolinians paid as their share in the winning of the republic.

Take it all in all, "Horseshoe Robinson" is a work which should be found on every book-shelf, not only because it is a most entertaining story, but because of the wealth of valuable information concerning the colonists which it contains. That it has been brought out once more, well illustrated, is something which will give pleasure to thousands who have long desired an opportunity to read the story again, and to the many who have tried vainly in these latter days to procure a copy that they might read it for the first time.

THE PEARL OF ORR'S ISLAND. A story of the Coast of Maine. By Harriet Beecher Stowe. Cloth, 12mo. Illustrated. Price, $1.00.

Written prior to 1862, the "Pearl of Orr's Island" is ever new; a book filled with delicate fancies, such as seemingly array themselves anew each time one reads them. One sees the "sea like an unbroken mirror all around the pine-girt, lonely shores of Orr's Island," and straightway comes "the heavy, hollow moan of the surf on the beach, like the wild angry howl of some savage animal."

Who can read of the beginning of that sweet life, named Mara, which came into this world under the very shadow of the Death angel's wings, without having an intense desire to know how the premature bud blossomed? Again and again one lingers over the descriptions of the character of that baby boy Moses, who came through the tempest, amid the angry billows, pillowed on his dead mother's breast.

There is no more faithful portrayal of New England life than that which Mrs. Stowe gives in "The Pearl of Orr's Island."

For sale by all booksellers, or sent postpaid on receipt of price by the publishers, A. L. BURT COMPANY, 52-58 Duane St., New York.

Good Fiction Worth Reading.

A series of romances containing several of the old favorites in the field of historical fiction, replete with powerful romances of love and diplomacy that excel in thrilling and absorbing interest.

GUY FAWKES. A Romance of the Gunpowder Treason. By Wm. Harrison Ainsworth. Cloth, 12mo. with four illustrations by George Cruikshank. Price, $1.00.

The "Gunpowder Plot" was a modest attempt to blow up Parliament, the King and his Counsellors. James of Scotland, then King of England, was weak-minded and extravagant. He hit upon the efficient scheme of extorting money from the people by imposing taxes on the Catholics. In their natural resentment to this extortion, a handful of bold spirits concluded to overthrow the government. Finally the plotters were arrested, and the King put to torture Guy Fawkes and the other prisoners with royal vigor. A very intense love story runs through the entire romance.

THE SPIRIT OF THE BORDER. A Romance of the Early Settlers in the Ohio Valley. By Zane Grey. Cloth. 12mo. with four illustrations by J. Watson Davis. Price, $1.00.

A book rather out of the ordinary is this "Spirit of the Border." The main thread of the story has to do with the work of the Moravian missionaries in the Ohio Valley. Incidentally the reader is given details of the frontier life of those hardy pioneers who broke the wilderness for the planting of this great nation. Chief among these, as a matter of course, is Lewis Wetzel, one of the most peculiar, and at the same time the most admirable of all the brave men who spent their lives battling with the savage foe, that others might dwell in comparative security.

Details of the establishment and destruction of the Moravian "Village of Peace" are given at some length, and with minute description. The efforts to Christianize the Indians are described as they never have been before, and the author has depicted the characters of the leaders of the several Indian tribes with great care, which of itself will be of interest to the student.

By no means least among the charms of the story are the vivid word-pictures of the thrilling adventures, and the intense paintings of the beauties of nature, as seen in the almost unbroken forests.

It is the spirit of the frontier which is described, and one can by it, perhaps, the better understand why men, and women, too, willingly braved every privation and danger that the westward progress of the star of empire might be the more certain and rapid. A love story, simple and tender, runs through the book.

RICHELIEU. A tale of France in the reign of King Louis XIII. By G. P. R. James. Cloth, 12mo. with four illustrations by J. Watson Davis. Price, $1.00.

In 1829 Mr. James published his first romance, "Richelieu," and was recognized at once as one of the masters of the craft.

In this book he laid the story during those later days of the great cardinal's life, when his power was beginning to wane, but while it was yet sufficiently strong to permit now and then of volcanic outbursts which overwhelmed foes and carried friends to the topmost wave of prosperity. One of the most striking portions of the story is that of Cinq Mar's conspiracy; the method of conducting criminal cases, and the political trickery resorted to by royal favorites, affording a better insight into the statecraft of that day than can be had even by an exhaustive study of history. It is a powerful romance of love and diplomacy, and in point of thrilling and absorbing interest has never been excelled.

Good Fiction Worth Reading.

A series of romances containing several of the old favorites in the field of historical fiction, replete with powerful romances of love and diplomacy that excel in thrilling and absorbing interest.

A COLONIAL FREE-LANCE. A story of American Colonial Times. By Chauncey C. Hotchkiss. Cloth, 12mo. with four illustrations by J. Watson Davis. Price, $1.00.

A book that appeals to Americans as a vivid picture of Revolutionary scenes. The story is a strong one, a thrilling one. It causes the true American to flush with excitement, to devour chapter after chapter, until the eyes smart, and it fairly smokes with patriotism. The love story is a singularly charming idyl.

THE TOWER OF LONDON. A Historical Romance of the Times of Lady Jane Grey and Mary Tudor. By Wm. Harrison Ainsworth. Cloth, 12mo. with four illustrations by George Cruikshank. Price, $1.00.

This romance of the "Tower of London" depicts the Tower as palace, prison and fortress, with many historical associations. The era is the middle of the sixteenth century.

The story is divided into two parts, one dealing with Lady Jane Grey, and the other with Mary Tudor as Queen, introducing other notable characters of the era. Throughout the story holds the interest of the reader in the midst of intrigue and conspiracy, extending considerably over a half a century.

IN DEFIANCE OF THE KING. A Romance of the American Revolution. By Chauncey C. Hotchkiss. Cloth, 12mo. with four illustrations by J. Watson Davis. Price, $1.00.

Mr. Hotchkiss has etched in burning words a story of Yankee bravery, and true love that thrills from beginning to end, with the spirit of the Revolution. The heart beats quickly, and we feel ourselves taking a part in the exciting scenes described. His whole story is so absorbing that you will sit up far into the night to finish it. As a love romance it is charming.

GARTHOWEN. A story of a Welsh Homestead. By Allen Raine. Cloth, 12mo. with four illustrations by J. Watson Davis. Price, $1.00.

"This is a little idyl of humble life and enduring love, laid bare before us, very real and pure, which in its telling shows us some strong points of Welsh character—the pride, the hasty temper, the quick dying out of wrath. . . . We call this a well-written story, interesting alike through its romance and its glimpses into another life than ours. A delightful and clever picture of Welsh village life. The result is excellent."—Detroit Free Press.

MIFANWY. The story of a Welsh Singer. By Allan Raine. Cloth, 12mo. with four illustrations by J. Watson Davis. Price, $1.00.

"This is a love story. simple, tender and pretty as one would care to read. The action throughout is brisk and pleasing; the characters, it is apparent at once, are as true to life as though the author had known them all personally. Simple in all its situations, the story is worked up in that touching and quaint strain which never grows wearisome, no matter how often the lights and shadows of love are introduced. It rings true, and does not tax the imagination."—Boston Herald.

Good Fiction Worth Reading.

A series of romances containing several of the old favorites in the field of historical fiction, replete with powerful romances of love and diplomacy that excel in thrilling and absorbing interest.

DARNLEY. A Romance of the times of Henry VIII. and Cardinal Wolsey. By G. P. R. James. Cloth, 12mo. with four illustrations by J. Watson Davis. Price, $1.00.

In point of publication, "Darnley" is that work by Mr. James which follows "Richelieu," and, if rumor can be credited, it was owing to the advice and insistence of our own Washington Irving that we are indebted primarily for the story, the young author questioning whether he could properly paint the difference in the characters of the two great cardinals. And it is not surprising that James should have hesitated; he had been eminently successful in giving to the world the portrait of Richelieu as a man, and by attempting a similar task with Wolsey as the theme, was much like tempting fortune. Irving insisted that "Darnley" came naturally in sequence, and this opinion being supported by Sir Walter Scott, the author set about the work.

As a historical romance "Darnley" is a book that can be taken up pleasurably again and again, for there is about it that subtle charm which those who are strangers to the works of G. P. R. James have claimed was only to be imparted by Dumas.

If there was nothing more about the work to attract especial attention, the account of the meeting of the kings on the historic "field of the cloth of gold" would entitle the story to the most favorable consideration of every reader.

There is really but little pure romance in this story, for the author has taken care to imagine love passages only between those whom history has credited with having entertained the tender passion one for another, and he succeeds in making such lovers as all the world must love.

CAPTAIN BRAND, OF THE SCHOONER CENTIPEDE. By Lieut. Henry A. Wise, U. S. N. (Harry Gringo). Cloth, 12mo. with four illustrations by J. Watson Davis. Price, $1.00.

The re-publication of this story will please those lovers of sea yarns who delight in so much of the salty flavor of the ocean as can come through the medium of a printed page, for never has a story of the sea and those "who go down in ships" been written by one more familiar with the scenes depicted.

The one book of this gifted author which is best remembered, and which will be read with pleasure for many years to come, is "Captain Brand," who, as the author states on his title page, was a "pirate of eminence in the West Indies." As a sea story pure and simple, "Captain Brand" has never been excelled, and as a story of piratical life, told without the usual embellishments of blood and thunder, it has no equal.

NICK OF THE WOODS. A story of the Early Settlers of Kentucky. By Robert Montgomery Bird. Cloth, 12mo. with four illustrations by J. Watson Davis. Price, $1.00.

This most popular novel and thrilling story of early frontier life in Kentucky was originally published in the year 1837. The novel, long out of print, had in its day a phenomenal sale, for its realistic presentation of Indian and frontier life in the early days of settlement in the South, narrated in the tale with all the art of a practiced writer. A very charming love romance runs through the story. This new and tasteful edition of "Nick of the Woods" will be certain to make many new admirers for this enchanting story from Dr. Bird's clever and versatile pen.

TICONDEROGA : A Story of Early Frontier Life in the Mohawk Valley. By G. P. R. James. Cloth, 12mo. with four page illustrations by J. Watson Davis. Price, $1.00.

The setting of the story is decidedly more picturesque than any ever evolved by Cooper: The frontier of New York State, where dwelt an English gentleman, driven from his native home by grief over the loss of his wife, with a son and daughter. Thither, brought by the exigencies of war, comes an English officer, who is readily recognized as that Lord Howe who met his death at Ticonderoga. As a most natural sequence, even amid the hostile demonstrations of both French and Indians, Lord Howe and the young girl find time to make most deliciously sweet love, and the son of the recluse has already lost his heart to the daughter of a great sachem, a dusky maiden whose warrior-father has surrounded her with all the comforts of a civilized life.

The character of Captain Brooks, who voluntarily decides to sacrifice his own life in order to save the son of the Englishman, is not among the least of the attractions of this story, which holds the attention of the reader even to the last page. The tribal laws and folk lore of the different tribes of Indians known as the "Five Nations," with which the story is interspersed, shows that the author gave no small amount of study to the work in question, and nowhere else is it shown more plainly than by the skilful manner in which he has interwoven with his plot the "blood" law, which demands a life for a life, whether it be that of the murderer or one of his race.

A more charming story of mingled love and adventure has never been written than "Ticonderoga."

ROB OF THE BOWL : A Story of the Early Days of Maryland. By John P. Kennedy. Cloth, 12mo. with four page illustrations by J. Watson Davis. Price, $1.00.

It was while he was a member of Congress from Maryland that the noted statesman wrote this story regarding the early history of his native State, and while some critics are inclined to consider "Horse Shoe Robinson" as the best of his works, it is certain that "Rob of the Bowl" stands at the head of the list as a literary production and an authentic exposition of the manners and customs during Lord Baltimore's rule. The greater portion of the action takes place in St. Mary's—the original capital of the State.

As a series of pictures of early colonial life in Maryland, "Rob of the Bowl" has no equal, and the book, having been written by one who had exceptional facilities for gathering material concerning the individual members of the settlements in and about St. Mary's, is a most valuable addition to the history of the State.

The story is full of splendid action, with a charming love story, and a plot that never loosens the grip of its interest to its last page.

BY BERWEN BANKS. By Allen Raine.

It is a tender and beautiful romance of the idyllic. A charming picture of life in a Welsh seaside village. It is something of a prose-poem, true, tender and graceful.

IN DEFIANCE OF THE KING. A romance of the American Revolution. By Chauncey C, Hotchkiss. Cloth, 12mo. with four illustrations by J. Watson Davis. Price, $1.00.

The story opens in the month of April, 1775, with the provincial troops hurrying to the defense of Lexington and Concord. Mr. Hotchkiss has etched in burning words a story of Yankee bravery and true love that thrills from beginning to end with the spirit of the Revolution. The heart beats quickly, and we feel ourselves taking a part in the exciting scenes described. You lay the book aside with the feeling that you have seen a gloriously true picture of the Revolution. His whole story is so absorbing that you will sit up far into the night to finish it. As a love romance it is charming.

POPULAR LITERATURE FOR THE MASSES,

COMPRISING CHOICE SELECTIONS FROM THE TREASURES OF THE WORLD'S KNOWLEDGE, ISSUED IN A SUBSTANTIAL AND ATTRACTIVE CLOTH BINDING, AT A POPULAR PRICE

BURT'S HOME LIBRARY is a series which includes the standard works of the world's best literature, bound in uniform cloth binding, gilt tops, embracing chiefly selections from writers of the most notable English, American and Foreign Fiction, together with many important works in the domains of History, Biography, Philosophy, Travel, Poetry and the Essays.

A glance at the following annexed list of titles and authors will endorse the claim that the publishers make for it—that it is the most comprehensive, choice, interesting, and by far the most carefully selected series of standard authors for world-wide reading that has been produced by any publishing house in any country, and that at prices so cheap, and in a style so substantial and pleasing, as to win for it millions of readers and the approval and commendation, not only of the book trade throughout the American continent, but of hundreds of thousands of librarians, clergymen, educators and men of letters interested in the dissemination of instructive, entertaining and thoroughly wholesome reading matter for the masses.

[SEE FOLLOWING PAGES]

Abbe Constantin. By Ludovic Halevy.

Abbott. By Sir Walter Scott.

Adam Bede. By George Eliot.

Addison's Essays. Edited by John Richard Green.

Aeneid of Virgil. Translated by John Connington.

Aesop's Fables.

Alexander, the Great, Life of. By John Williams.

Alfred the Great, Life of. By Thomas Hughes.

Alhambra. By Washington Irving.

Alice in Wonderland, and Through the Looking-Glass. By Lewis Carroll

Alice Lorraine. By R. D. Blackmore

All Sorts and Conditions of Men. By Walter Besant.

Alton Locke. By Charles Kingsley.

Amiel's Journal. Translated by Mrs. Humphrey Ward.

Andersen's Fairy Tales.

Anne of Geirstein. By Sir Walter Scott.

Antiquary. By Sir Walter Scott.

Arabian Nights' Entertainments.

Ardath. By Marie Corelli.

Arnold, Benedict, Life of. By George Canning Hill.

Arnold's Poems. By Matthew Arnold.

Around the World in the Yacht Sunbeam. By Mrs. Brassey.

Arundel Motto. By Mary Cecil Hay.

At the Back of the North Wind. By George Macdonald.

Attic Philosopher. By Emile Souvestre.

Auld Licht Idylls. By James M. Barrie.

Aunt Diana. By Rosa N. Carey.

Autobiography of Benjamin Franklin.

Autocrat of the Breakfast Table. By O. W. Holmes.

Averil. By Rosa N. Carey.

Bacon's Essays. By Francis Bacon.

Barbara Heathcote's Trial. By Rosa N. Carey.

Barnaby Rudge. By Charles Dickens.

Barrack Room Ballads. By Rudyard Kipling.

Betrothed. By Sir Walter Scott.

Beulah. By Augusta J. Evans.

Black Beauty. By Anna Sewall.

Black Dwarf. By Sir Walter Scott.

Black Rock. By Ralph Connor.

Black Tulip. By Alexandre Dumas.

Bleak House. By Charles Dickens.

Blithedale Romance. By Nathaniel Hawthorne.

Bondman. By Hall Caine.

Book of Golden Deeds. By Charlotte M. Yonge.

Boone, Daniel, Life of. By Cecil B. Hartley

Bride of Lammermoor. By Sir Walter Scott.

Bride of the Nile. By George Ebers.

Browning's Poems. By Elizabeth Barrett Browning.

Browning's Poems. (selections.) By Robert Browning.

Bryant's Poems. (early.) By William Cullen Bryant.

Burgomaster's Wife. By George Ebers.

Burn's Poems. By Robert Burns.

By Order of the King. By Victor Hugo.

Byron's Poems. By Lord Byron.

Caesar, Julius, Life of. By James Anthony Froude.

Carson, Kit, Life of. By Charles Burdett.

Cary's Poems. By Alice and Phoebe Cary.

Cast Up by the Sea. By Sir Samuel Baker

Charlemagne (Charles the Great), Life of. By Thomas Hodgkin, D. C. L.

Charles Auchester. By E. Berger.

Character. By Samuel Smiles.

Charles O'Malley. By Charles Lever.

Chesterfield's Letters. By Lord Chesterfield.

Chevalier de Maison Rouge. By Alexandre Dumas.

Chicot the Jester. By Alexandre Dumas.

Children of the Abbey. By Regina Maria Roche.

Child's History of England. By Charles Dickens.

Christmas Stories. By Charles Dickens.

Cloister and the Hearth. By Charles Reade.

Coleridge's Poems. By Samuel Taylor Coleridge.

Columbus, Christopher, Life of. By Washington Irving.

Companions of Jehu. By Alexandre Dumas.

Complete Angler. By Walton and Cotton.

Conduct of Life. By Ralph Waldo Emerson.

Confessions of an Opium Eater. By Thomas de Quincey.

Conquest of Granada. By Washington Irving.

Conscript. By Erckmann-Chatrian.

Conspiracy of Pontiac. By Francis Parkman, Jr.

Conspirators. By Alexandre Dumas.

Consuelo. By George Sand.

Cook's Voyages. By Captain James Cook.

Corinne. By Madame de Stael.

Countess de Charney. By Alexandre Dumas.

Countess Gisela. By E. Marlitt.

Countess of Rudolstadt. By GEORGE SAND.

Count Robert of Paris. By SIR WALTER SCOTT.

Country Doctor. By HONORE DE BALZAC.

Courtship of Miles Standish. By H. W. LONGFELLOW.

Cousin Maude. By MARY J. HOLMES.

Cranford. By MRS. GASKELL.

Crockett, David, Life of. AN AUTOBIOGRAPHY.

Cromwell, Oliver, Life of. By EDWIN PAXTON HOOD.

Crown of Wild Olive. By JOHN RUSKIN.

Crusades. By GEO. W. COX, M. A.

Daniel Deronda. By GEORGE ELIOT.

Darkness and Daylight. By MARY J. HOLMES.

Data of Ethics. By HERBERT SPENCER.

Daughter of an Empress, The. By LOUISA MUHLBACH.

David Copperfield. By CHARLES DICKENS.

Days of Bruce. By GRACE AGUILAR.

Deemster, The. By HALL CAINE.

Deerslayer, The. By JAMES FENIMORE COOPER.

Descent of Man. By CHARLES DARWIN.

Discourses of Epictetus. TRANSLATED BY GEORGE LONG.

Divine Comedy. (DANTE.) TRANSLATED BY REV. H. F. CAREY.

Dombey & Son. By CHARLES DICKENS.

Donal Grant. By GEORGE MACDONALD.

Donovan. By EDNA LYALL.

Dora Deane. By MARY J. HOLMES.

Dove in the Eagle's Nest. By CHARLOTTE M. YONGE.

Dream Life. By IK MARVEL.

Dr. Jekyll and Mr. Hyde. By R. L. STEVENSON.

Duty. By SAMUEL SMILES.

Early Days of Christianity. By F. W. FARRAR.

East Lynne. By MRS. HENRY WOOD.

Edith Lyle's Secret. By MARY J. HOLMES.

Education. By HERBERT SPENCER.

Egoist. By GEORGE MEREDITH.

Egyptian Princess. By GEORGE EBERS.

Eight Hundred Leagues on the Amazon. By JULES VERNE.

Eliot's Poems. By GEORGE ELIOT.

Elizabeth and her German Garden.

Elizabeth (Queen of England), Life of. By EDWARD SPENCER BEESLY, M.A.

Elsie Venner. By OLIVER WENDELL HOLMES.

Emerson's Essays. (COMPLETE.) By RALPH WALDO EMERSON.

Emerson's Poems. By RALPH WALDO EMERSON.

English Orphans. By MARY J. HOLMES.

English Traits. By R. W. EMERSON.

Essays in Criticism. (FIRST AND SECOND SERIES.) By MATTHEW ARNOLD.

Essays of Elia. By CHARLES LAMB.

Esther. By ROSA N. CAREY.

Ethelyn's Mistake. By MARY J. HOLMES.

Evangeline. (WITH NOTES.) By H. W. LONGFELLOW.

Evelina. By FRANCES BURNEY.

Fair Maid of Perth. By SIR WALTER SCOTT.

Fairy Land of Science. By ARABELLA B. BUCKLEY.

Faust. (GOETHE.) TRANSLATED BY ANNA SWANWICK.

Felix Holt. By GEORGE ELIOT.

Fifteen Decisive Battles of the World. By E. S. CREASY.

File No. 113. By EMILE GABORIAU.

Firm of Girdlestone. By A. CONAN DOYLE.

First Principles. By HERBERT SPENCER.

First Violin. By JESSIE FOTHERGILL.

For Lilias. By ROSA N. CAREY.

Fortunes of Nigel. By SIR WALTER SCOTT.

Forty-Five Guardsmen. By ALEXANDRE DUMAS.

Foul Play. By CHARLES READE.

Fragments of Science. By JOHN TYNDALL.

Frederick, the Great, Life of. By FRANCIS KUGLER.

Frederick the Great and His Court. By LOUISA MUHLBACH.

French Revolution. By THOMAS CARLYLE.

From the Earth to the Moon. By JULES VERNE.

Garibaldi, General, Life of. By THEODORE DWIGHT.

Gil Blas, Adventures of. By A. R. LE SAGE.

Gold Bug and Other Tales. By EDGAR A. POE.

Gold Eisie. By E. MARLITT.

Golden Treasury. By FRANCIS T. PALGRAVE.

Goldsmith's Poems. By OLIVER GOLDSMITH.

Grandfather's Chair. By NATHANIEL HAWTHORNE.

Grant, Ulysses S., Life of. By J. T. HEADLEY.

Gray's Poems. By THOMAS GRAY.

Great Expectations. By CHARLES DICKENS.

Greek Heroes. Fairy Tales for My Children. By CHARLES KINGSLEY.

Green Mountain Boys, The. By D. P. THOMPSON.

Grimm's Household Tales. By THE BROTHERS GRIMM.

Grimm's Popular Tales. By THE BROTHERS GRIMM.

Gulliver's Travels. By DEAN SWIFT.

Guy Mannering. By SIR WALTER SCOTT.

Hale, Nathan, the Martyr Spy. By CHARLOTTE MOLYNEUX HOLLOWAY.

Handy Andy. By SAMUEL LOVER.

Hans of Iceland. By VICTOR HUGO.

Hannibal, the Carthaginian, Life of. By THOMAS ARNOLD, M. A.

Hardy Norseman, A. By EDNA LYALL.

Harold. By BULWER-LYTTON.

Harry Lorrequer. By CHARLES LEVER.

Heart of Midlothian. By SIR WALTER SCOTT.

Heir of Redclyffe. By CHARLETTE M. YONGE.

Hemans' Poems. By MRS. FELICIA HEMANS.

Henry Esmond. By WM. M. THACKERAY.

Henry, Patrick, Life of. By WILLIAM WIRT.

Her Dearest Foe. By MRS. ALEXANDER.

Hereward. By CHARLES KINGSLEY.

Heriot's Choice. By ROSA N. CAREY.

Heroes and Hero-Worship. By THOMAS CARLYLE.

Hiawatha. (WITH NOTES.) By H. W. LONGFELLOW.

Hidden Hand, The. (COMPLETE.) By MRS. E. D. E. N. SOUTHWORTH.

History of a Crime. By VICTOR HUGO.

History of Civilization in Europe. By M. GUIZOT.

Holmes' Poems. (EARLY) By OLIVER WENDELL HOLMES.

Holy Roman Empire. By JAMES BRYCE.

Homestead on the Hillside. By MARY J. HOLMES.

Hood's Poems. By THOMAS HOOD.

House of the Seven Gables. By NATHANIEL HAWTHORNE.

Hunchback of Notre Dame. By VICTOR HUGO.

Hypatia. By CHARLES KINGSLEY.

Hyperion. By HENRY WADSWORTH LONGFELLOW.

Iceland Fisherman, By PIERRE LOTI.

Idle Thoughts of an Idle Fellow. By JEROME K. JEROME.

Iliad, POPE'S TRANSLATION.

Inez. By AUGUSTA J. EVANS.

Ingelow's Poems. By JEAN INGELOW.

Initials. By THE BARONESS TAUTPHOEUS.

Intellectual Life. By PHILIP G. HAMERTON.

In the Counsellor's House. By E. MARLITT.

In the Golden Days. By EDNA LYALL.

In the Heart of the Storm. By MAXWELL GRAY.

In the Schillingscourt. By E. MARLITT.

Ishmael. (COMPLETE.) By MRS. E. D. E. N. SOUTHWORTH.

It Is Never Too Late to Mend. By CHARLES READE.

Ivanhoe. By SIR WALTER SCOTT.

Jane Eyre. By CHARLOTTE BRONTE.

Jefferson, Thomas, Life of. By SAMUEL M. SCHMUCKER, LL.D.

Joan of Arc, Life of. By JULES MICHELET.

John Halifax, Gentleman. By MISS MULOCK.

Jones, John Paul, Life of. By JAMES OTIS.

Joseph Balsamo. By ALEXANDRE DUMAS.

Josephine, Empress of France, Life of. By FREDERICK A. OBER.

Keats' Poems. By JOHN KEATS.

Kenilworth. By SIR WALTER SCOTT.

Kidnapped. By R. L. STEVENSON.

King Arthur and His Noble Knights. By MARY MACLEOD.

Knickerbocker's History of New York. By WASHINGTON IRVING.

Knight Errant. By EDNA LYALL.

Koran. TRANSLATED BY GEORGE SALE.

Lady of the Lake. (WITH NOTES.) By SIR WALTER SCOTT.

Lady with the Rubies. By E. MARLITT.

Lafayette, Marquis de, Life of. By P. C. HEADLEY.

Lalla Rookh. (WITH NOTES.) By THOMAS MOORE.

Lamplighter. By MARIA S. CUMMINS.

Last Days of Pompeii. By BULWER-LYTTON.

Last of the Barons. By BULWER-LYTTON.

Last of the Mohicans. By JAMES FENIMORE COOPER.

Lay of the Last Minstrel. (WITH NOTES.) By SIR WALTER SCOTT.

Lee, General Robert E., Life of. By G. MERCER ADAM.

Lena Rivers. By MARY J. HOLMES.

Life of Christ. By FREDERICK W. FARRAR.

Life of Jesus. By ERNEST RENAN.

Light of Asia. By SIR EDWIN ARNOLD.

Light That Failed. By RUDYARD KIPLING.

Lincoln, Abraham, Life of. By HENRY KETCHAM.

Lincoln's Speeches. SELECTED AND EDITED BY G. MERCER ADAM.

Literature and Dogma. By MATTHEW ARNOLD.

Little Dorrit. By CHARLES DICKENS.

Little Minister. By JAMES M. BARRIE.

Livingstone, David, Life of. By THOMAS HUGHES.

Longfellow's Poems. (EARLY.) By HENRY W. LONGFELLOW.

Lorna Doone. By R. D. BLACKMORE.

Louise de la Valliere. By ALEXANDRE DUMAS.

Love Me Little, Love Me Long. By CHARLES READE.

Lowell's Poems. (EARLY.) BY JAMES RUSSELL LOWELL.

Lucile. BY OWEN MEREDITH.

Macaria. BY AUGUSTA J. EVANS.

Macaulay's Literary Essays. BY T. B. MACAULAY.

Macaulay's Poems. BY THOMAS BABINGTON MACAULAY.

Madame Therese. BY ERCKMANN-CHATRIAN.

Maggie Miller. BY MARY J. HOLMES.

Magic Skin. BY HONORE DE BALZAC.

Mahomet, Life of. BY WASHINGTON IRVING.

Makers of Florence. BY MRS. OLIPHANT.

Makers of Venice. BY MRS. OLIPHANT.

Man and Wife. BY WILKIE COLLINS.

Man in the Iron Mask. BY ALEXANDRE DUMAS.

Marble Faun. BY NATHANIEL HAWTHORNE.

Marguerite de la Valois. BY ALEXANDRE DUMAS.

Marian Grey. BY MARY J. HOLMES.

Marius, The Epicurian. BY WALTER PATER.

Marmion. (WITH NOTES.) BY SIR WALTER SCOTT.

Marquis of Lossie. BY GEORGE MACDONALD.

Martin Chuzzlewit. BY CHARLES DICKENS.

Mary, Queen of Scots, Life of. BY P. C. HEADLEY.

Mary St. John. BY ROSA N. CAREY.

Master of Ballantrae, The. BY. R. L. STEVENSON.

Masterman Ready. BY CAPTAIN MARRYATT.

Meadow Brook. BY MARY J. HOLMES.

Meditations of Marcus Aurelius. TRANSLATED BY GEORGE LONG.

Memoirs of a Physician. BY ALEXANDRE DUMAS.

Merle's Crusade. BY ROSA N. CAREY.

Micah Clarke. BY A. CONAN DOLYE.

Michael Strogoff. BY JULES VERNE.

Middlemarch. BY GEORGE ELIOT.

Midshipman Easy. BY CAPTAIN MARRYATT

Mildred. BY MARY J. HOLMES.

Millbank. BY MARY J. HOLMES.

Mill on the Floss. BY GEORGE ELIOT.

Milton's Poems. BY JOHN MILTON.

Mine Own People. BY RUDYARD KIPLING

Minister's Wooing, The. BY HARRIET BEECHER STOWE.

Monastery. BY SIR WALTER SCOTT.

Moonstone. BY WILKIE COLLINS.

Moore's Poems. BY THOMAS MOORE

Mosses from an Old Manse. BY NATHANIEL HAWTHORNE.

Murders in the Rue Morgue. BY EDGAR ALLEN POE.

Mysterious Island. BY JULES VERNE.

Napoleon Bonaparte, Life of. BY P. C. HEADLEY.

Napoleon and His Marshals. BY J. T. HEADLEY.

Natural Law in the Spiritual World. BY HENRY DRUMMOND.

Narrative of Arthur Gordon Pym. BY EDGAR ALLAN POE.

Nature, Addresses and Lectures. BY R. W. EMERSON.

Nellie's Memories. BY ROSA N. CAREY.

Nelson, Admiral Horatio, Life of. BY ROBERT SOUTHEY.

Newcomes. BY WILLIAM M. THACKERAY.

Nicholas Nickleby. BY CHAS. DICKENS.

Ninety-Three. BY VICTOR HUGO.

Not Like Other Girls. BY ROSA N. CAREY.

Odyssey. POPE'S TRANSLATION.

Old Curiosity Shop. BY CHARLES DICKENS.

Old Mam'selle's Secret. BY E. MARLITT.

Old Mortality. BY SIR WALTER SCOTT.

Old Myddleton's Money. BY MARY CECIL HAY.

Oliver Twist. BY CHAS. DICKENS.

Only the Governess. BY ROSA N. CAREY.

On the Heights. BY BERTHOLD AUERBACH.

Oregon Trail. BY FRANCIS PARKMAN.

Origin of Species. BY CHARLES DARWIN.

Other Worlds than Ours. BY RICHARD PROCTOR.

Our Bessie. BY ROSA N. CAREY.

Our Mutual Friend. BY CHARLES DICKENS.

Outre-Mer. BY H. W. LONGFELLOW.

Owl's Nest. BY E. MARLITT.

Page of the Duke of Savoy. BY ALEXANDRE DUMAS.

Pair of Blue Eyes. BY THOMAS HARDY.

Pan Michael. BY HENRYK SIENKIEWICZ.

Past and Present. BY THOS. CARLYLE.

Pathfinder. BY JAMES FENIMORE COOPER.

Paul and Virginia. BY B. DE ST. PIERRE.

Pendennis. History of. BY WM. M. THACKERAY.

Penn, William, Life of. BY W. HEPWORTH DIXON.

Pere Goriot. BY HONORE DE BALZAC.

Peter, the Great, Life of. BY JOHN BARROW.

Peveril of the Peak. BY SIR WALTER SCOTT.

Phantom Rickshaw, The. BY RUDYARD KIPLING.

Philip II. of Spain, Life of. BY MARTIN A. S. HUME.

Picciola. BY X. B. SAINTINE.

Surgeon's Daughter. BY SIR WALTER SCOTT.

Swinburne's Poems. BY A. C. SWINBURNE.

Swiss Family Robinson. BY JEAN RUDOLPH WYSS.

Taking the Bastile. BY ALEXANDRE DUMAS.

Tale of Two Cities. BY CHAS. DICKENS.

Tales from Shakespeare. BY CHAS. AND MARY LAMB.

Tales of a Traveller. BY WASHINGTON IRVING.

Talisman. BY SIR WALTER SCOTT.

Tanglewood Tales. BY NATHANIEL HAWTHORNE.

Tempest and Sunshine. BY MARY J. HOLMES.

Ten Nights in a Bar Room. BY T. S. ARTHUR.

Tennyson's Poems. BY ALFRED TENNYSON.

Ten Years Later. BY ALEXANDER DUMAS.

Terrible Temptation. BY CHARLES READE.

Thaddeus of Warsaw. BY JANE PORTER.

Thelma. BY MARIE CORELLI

Thirty Years' War. BY FREDERICK SCHILLER.

Thousand Miles Up the Nile. BY AMELIA B. EDWARDS.

Three Guardsmen. BY ALEXANDRE DUMAS.

Three Men in a Boat. BY JEROME K. JEROME.

Thrift. BY SAMUEL SMILES.

Throne of David. BY REV. J. H. INGRAHAM.

Toilers of the Sea. BY VICTOR HUGO

Tom Brown at Oxford. BY THOMAS HUGHES.

Tom Brown's School Days. BY THOS. HUGHES.

Tom Burke of "Ours." BY CHARLES LEVER.

Tour of the World in Eighty Days. BY JULES VERNE.

Treasure Island. BY ROBERT LOUIS STEVENSON.

Twenty Thousand Leagues Under the Sea. BY JULES VERNE.

Twenty Years After. BY ALEXANDRE DUMAS.

Twice Told Tales. BY NATHANIEL HAWTHORNE

Two Admirals. BY JAMES FENIMORE COOPER.

Two Dianas. BY ALEXANDRE DUMAS.

Two Years Before the Mast. BY R. H. DANA, Jr.

Uarda. BY GEORGE EBERS.

Uncle Max. BY ROSA N. CAREY.

Uncle Tom's Cabin. BY HARRIET BEECHER STOWE.

Under Two Flags. BY "OUIDA."

Utopia. BY SIR THOMAS MORE.

Vanity Fair. BY WM. M. THACKERAY

Vendetta. BY MARIE CORELLI.

Vespucius, Americus, Life and Voyages. BY C. EDWARDS LESTER.

Vicar of Wakefield. BY OLIVER GOLDSMITH.

Vicomte de Bragelonne. BY ALEXANDRE DUMAS.

Views A-Foot. BY BAYARD TAYLOR.

Villette. BY CHARLOTTE BRONTE.

Virginians. BY WM. M. THACKERAY

Walden. BY HENRY D. THOREAU.

Washington, George, Life of. BY JARED SPARKS.

Washington and His Generals. BY J. T. HEADLEY.

Water Babies. BY CHARLES KINGSLEY.

Water Witch. BY JAMES FENIMORE COOPER.

Waverly. BY SIR WALTER SCOTT.

Webster, Daniel, Life of. BY SAMUEL M. SCHMUCKER, LL.D.

Webster's Speeches. (SELECTED.) BY DANIEL WEBSTER.

Wee Wifie. BY ROSA N. CAREY

Westward Ho! BY CHARLES KINGSLEY.

We Two. BY EDNA LYALL.

What's Mine's Mine. BY GEORGE MACDONALD.

When a Man's Single. BY J. M. BARRIE.

White Company. BY A. CONAN DOYLE.

Whites and the Blues. BY ALEXANDRE DUMAS.

Whittier's Poems. (EARLY.) BY JOHN G. WHITTIER.

Wide, Wide World. BY SUSAN WARNER.

William, the Conqueror, Life of. BY EDWARD A. FREEMAN, LL.D.

William, the Silent, Life of. BY FREDERICK HARRISON.

Willy Reilly. BY WILLIAM CARLETON.

Window in Thrums. BY J. M. BARRIE

Wing and Wing. BY JAMES FENIMORE COOPER.

Wolsey, Cardinal, Life of. BY MANDELL CREIGHTON.

Woman in White. BY WILKIE COLLINS.

Won by Waiting. BY EDNA LYALL.

Wonder Book. FOR BOYS AND GIRLS. BY NATHANIEL HAWTHORNE.

Woodstock. BY SIR WALTER SCOTT.

Wooed and Married. BY ROSA N. CAREY.

Wooing O't. BY MRS. ALEXANDER.

Wordsworth's Poems BY WILLIAM WORDSWORTH.

Wormwood. BY MARIE CORELLI

Wreck of the Grosvenor. BY W. CLARK RUSSELL.